BLACK SUN
RED MOON

BLACK SUN
RED MOON
A NOVEL OF JAVA

Rory Marron

SEVENTH CITADEL

Published by Seventh Citadel (www.seventhcitadel.com).
Seventh Citadel, 10 WA4 2XA, Cheshire.

ISBN: 978-0-9576305-2-9 (paperback)
ISBN: 978-0-9576305-0-5 (eBook-Mobi/Kindle)

Cover design from an idea by Rory Marron, developed by John Amy (info@ebookdesigner.co.uk)

Back cover *wayang kulit* photograph © Jim Henry.

The translation of the Imperial Rescript announcing acceptance of the terms offered to Japan at the Potsdam Conference can be found in *Reports of General MacArthur, Japanese Operations in the Southwest Pacific Area. Volume II, Part II.* Washington, DC, 1966.

Maps of Java drawn by L. Maddocks in 1951 for Gale & Polden Ltd. (Attempts have been made to identify the rights-holder, who is invited to contact the publisher.)

Lyrics to 'Ina no Kantaro' © Takao Saeki, 1943. Translation of second verse by Rory Marron.

Come to Java, Official Tourist Office, Weltevreden, 1923.

Wirid references are taken from *The Mystical Teachings of the Eight Saints* by Raden N. Ranggawarsita. Translated from the Javanese by M. Mansur Medeiros. Jawi Kandha/Mij Press/Albert Rusche & Co., Surakarta, 1908.

For my parents;
those eligible for the General Service
Medal, 1945-46 with
clasp for 'South-East Asia';
and
Two Gentlemen of Tokyo,
Who made me welcome.

Names of Characters

Historical fiction often requires reference to actual people and events to give context. Thus the suggestion of someone other than Lord Louis Mountbatten as the head of South-East Asia Command (SEAC) would be odd, so in my story Mountbatten is given (brief) dialogue with a mixture of both historical and fictional characters. In the same way, Sukarno and Dr Mohammed Hatta, key figures in Indonesian history, are not disguised and are given dialogue. My guideline for changing or disguising characters in 'supporting roles' was if there were a danger of taking an historical character beyond a 'reasonable assumption' of dialogue. For example, the characters of Dutch colonial and military officers invented here are creative combinations of dozens of officials whose comments and actions are on record. Other changes were made reluctantly. Official files are full of the names of many men whose service and deeds deserve to be better known. Yet attempts to honour (or vilify) them by using their real names in a work of fiction risk their actions being inaccurately depicted. Most of the names used in this story are therefore disguised.

I also confess to the creation and 'importation' of names that are easier for a native speaker of English to read. In the case of Japanese names, many were chosen randomly from friends and acquaintances. Indonesian names were more problematic, since many Javanese and Sumatrans have only one name, often rather long. Consequently, I invented names. In so doing, unintended syllabic combinations might have occurred. Similarly, relatively few Indian and Dutch names are familiar to, or can be read easily by, the non-native speaker. There were many instances of surname duplication among the 80,000 Dutch and Eurasians interned in camps in Java. For this reason I also used names of Dutch acquaintances, names I read in the KLM Airlines in-flight magazine, and also the Amsterdam and Maastricht telephone directories. I also created combinations of given and family names in memoirs of wartime Java. Fairly late on in the writing I stumbled upon a photograph album of a family by the name of van Damme (a not uncommon Dutch surname) living in Surabaya in the 1930s. I decided, however, not to change the names of my characters because of this coincidence.

500 MILES

500 MILES

INDIAN OCEAN

JAVA SEA

SUNDA STR.

BATAVIA
BUITENZORG
SOEKABOEMI
BANDOENG
AMBARAWA
MAGELANG
SEMARANG
JOGJAKARTA
SURABAYA
MADURA
BALI

THE TOWNS SHOWN ARE THOSE IN WHICH 23 IND DIV OPERATED, EXCEPT FOR JOGJAKARTA, THE INDONESIAN H.Q.

APPROXIMATE CROSS SECTION THROUGH JAVA & BALI

JAVA

12000'

12000'

5

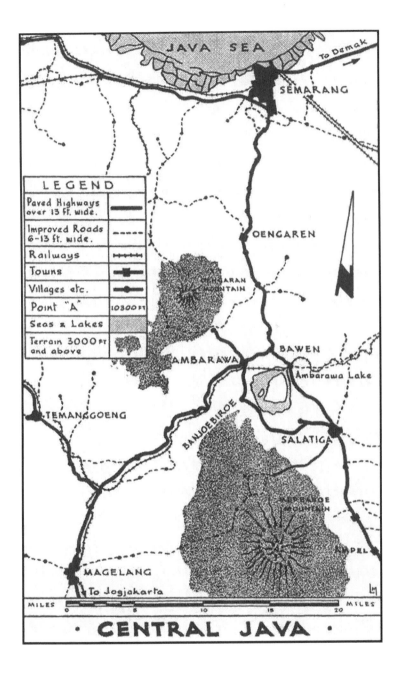

JAVA SEA

To Demak

SEMARANG

LEGEND

Paved Highways over 13 ft. wide.	━━━
Improved Roads 6-13 ft. wide.	-----
Railways	┝┿┿┥
Towns	◀━▶
Villages etc.	●━●
Point "A"	10300 FT
Seas z Lakes	
Terrain 3000 FT and above	

OENGAREN

OENGARAN MOUNTAIN

AMBARAWA

BAWEN

Ambarawa Lake

TEMANGGOENG

BANJOEBIROE

SALATIGA

MERBABOE MOUNTAIN

AMPEL

MAGELANG

To Jogjakarta

MILES   0   5   10   15   20   MILES

· CENTRAL JAVA ·

And I beheld when he had opened the sixth seal,
and, lo, there was a great earthquake;
and the sun became black as sackcloth of hair,
and the moon became as blood...

Revelation 6:12
The Geneva Bible, 1599.

Prologue

A lun MacDonald hated the Chindwin River because he knew that when he came to cross it the Japanese would try to kill him. Sighing, he leant back against the trunk of the large Indian laurel tree that had been supporting him for several minutes. He was tired and dejected. It was four o'clock in the morning but the heat was already building. Soon, though, the monsoon would break and it would get even worse. He would be trudging around knee-deep in mud, risking trench-foot. As if malaria, typhoid and dysentery were not enough, there were poisonous cobras and kraits, ants the size of a sixpence and spiders as large as soup plates.

Ten yards from his position ran the great river. It was the widest he had ever seen but he knew that beyond the Chindwin, deep in Japanese-held territory, was the Irrawaddy, which was even bigger. Everything about Burma seemed big: its vast, murky rivers; dark, towering teak trees and seemingly endless scrub jungle. A few days before, from the crest of the jungle-covered hills now a few miles to his rear, he had glimpsed nothing but a rolling monotony of green that swept onwards as far as some low, ragged hills on the horizon.

Again he scanned the dark canopy of foliage above him, hoping for a sign of the dawn that would signal the end of his penance. All he could see was cloud or the mist that rolled across the surface of the river. In truth, he could not discern where mist ended and cloud began. His ears were filled with the nagging whine of mosquitoes. He jerked his head and blew up sharply over his face to try to keep the tenacious insects from his nose and eyes. Pieces of fine mesh cut from a mosquito net were wrapped around his hat and hands. It was not regulation issue but he didn't care. As far as he was concerned, if the Army could set the rules for the war against the Japanese, he could set his own for his smaller, constant and frustrating war against the insects that thrived in the vast, sub-tropical compost heap that was Burma.

'Bastard mozzies! Bastard Burma!' he hissed.

On his last night 'stag', he had finished his watch with thirty-four bites on his face. That wasn't anywhere near to the record held by his friend, Archie Ferguson. One night a weary Archie had come off stag and had nodded off after going to the latrine. One hundred and three bites and a severe bout of malaria later, 'Archie's Arse' was already legend in the 1st Battalion Seaforth Highlanders.

A distinct but by now familiar splash came from the river. For the first two hours of his watch, every jumping fish had sent him rushing for the cover ready to jerk on the log-line that would alert the next sentry along the Seaforths' defensive perimeter. His Lee-Enfield rifle raised, he had waited tensely for the Japanese patrol he imagined was crossing the river. His nervousness had left him exhausted. Now the splashes barely registered and the line was a few feet away from him, draped over a bush. His rifle stock rested on the ground in front of him, and he held the barrel with both hands. He felt himself falling asleep but the pinch of another insect bite roused him. Wearily he pushed away from the tree and stretched in an attempt to keep awake. He scratched absent-mindedly at a louse on his scalp. Time for another cigarette, he told himself. It would at least help keep the mosquitoes away. He should have had company but the battalion was stretched with many men down with malaria, despite the daily dose of mepacrine that had given his skin a yellow tinge.

Heat, bites, sores, and solitude were not MacDonald's only complaints. Four weeks before he had been one of a hundred men who had gone down with dysentery. For almost a week he hadn't dared move more than a few yards from a latrine. Extra ones had been dug but queues had still been too long and often the Seaforths had no option but to relieve themselves where they stood. Flies had swarmed and feasted as the mess and stench was tramped all over the camp. Before long, infection had claimed the rest of the battalion. Eventually medical officers from Field Hygiene had ordered a new camp set up a mile away and then burnt their uniforms and underwear. After that episode MacDonald had promised himself that when he got home he would never leave Scotland and flushing lavatories again.

Above him he noticed a slight greying above the treetops. Dawn was not far off. At last, he thought, even though it meant the sun would bring the oppressive, sticky heat.

'Not long, now, Mac lad,' he said aloud to himself.

Idly, he glanced down at his boots. Protruding from a lace hole was what looked like a short piece of black string. He bent quickly, catching the leech and squeezing it hard between his finger and thumb trying to burst it.

'Bastard leeches!' He snarled, threw it down and stamped on it. At least he had seen that one, he thought. Instinctively he brushed the backs of his trousers.

If he were lucky he'd get two hours sleep before breakfast. Night stag always left him miserable, he thought. But guarding this place! The top brass had to be joking. As far as he was concerned, if the Japs wanted this godforsaken greenhouse they were welcome to it! After all, the bloody Burmese weren't making the British feel welcome. Apart from the hill tribes, most of them had sided with the Japanese after a quick promise of independence. Ungrateful sods! Absentmindedly he kicked at a twig then farted loudly. His contempt jumped effortlessly to the generals who had ordered the Seaforths to the banks of the Chindwin. Mac had no doubts they were safe, clean and over-fed back in India. 'Wankers!' he spat vehemently.

'Who's that then?'

Mac jumped, bringing his Lee Enfield rifle around. Before he could make half a turn a slim rattan cane forced the barrel downwards. A mouth was at his ear and a hand was pressing lightly on his shoulder.

'Easy there, I'm on your side!' The voice was a good-humoured whisper. Mac stood ashen-faced, staring at a fresh-faced officer.

'Sorry to make you jump like that. I'm Lt Miller, Princess Mary's Own. Relax, the thing is we've got a couple of chaps coming back across the river from a "tiger patrol". We didn't want you taking a pot shot.'

Mac felt giddy. Christ! If it had been a Jap.... Miller stepped away, blending into the bushes.

'It took me a while to find you until I heard and then, well, smelt the beans.' Miller chortled. 'Then you talked to yourself. That really marked your spot. Good job I'm not Johnny Jap!'

'Yes, Sir,' Mac said nervously. He fumbled for his tin of cigarettes wondering if Miller was enjoying his discomfort. Again the shadowy figure admonished him.

'I wouldn't light up just yet. The mist is lifting and there might be snipers about.'

Mac glanced towards the river. A narrow sandbar was now visible in the mass of grey water. He decided the cigarette could wait. He moved nearer to Miller. His mouth was dry.

'Right, Sir, Blimey, I never heard you. I can hardly see a thing!'

'Hmm,' replied Miller preoccupied. He raised an arm and signalled briefly into the bushes over Mac's left shoulder.

Mac glanced quickly behind him but saw no one.

'Should be a doddle,' Miller went on encouragingly. 'But if the Nips open up, give covering fire but not to the left of that sandbar. Remember, you've no foxhole, so change position after each shot. They'll be watching for muzzle flash. Let's hope they haven't rumbled our chaps and try a raid themselves.'

Mac was about to ask what he should do if he did see Japanese when a shrill bird-call sounded from further up the riverbank. Miller gave another quick signal then merged with the bushes.

'Oh shite!' Mac moaned, feeling very alone. Suddenly his hands felt numb and he squeezed his rifle stock to try and increase the blood flow to his fingers. He waited, his stifled breath roaring in his ears.

When the bird-call came again it was much closer, almost directly opposite him on the river. Mac's heart began to race. Miller had said the Japs might try something. What if they knew the signals and the crossing place....

Fifteen yards out into the river the mist was still a dense, grey wall. Mac's eyes began to play tricks on him. Several times he was convinced he saw wading Japanese soldiers only for the shapes to dissolve into swirls. 'Steady now,' he whispered trying to calm himself.

Over to his left he thought he saw something dark amidst the grey, moving very slowly, against the current. Mac raised his rifle to his shoulder praying it was only a water buffalo. Several of the unfortunate beasts had already been shot by nervous Glaswegian sentries.

As the lower mist thinned to wispy fingers he saw it was not an animal but a small rubber boat. Two paddles were dipping noiselessly, leaving barely a ripple. He could not see the paddlers. A gun barrel was protruding over the boat's front but he could not tell if it were a British Lee-Enfield or a Japanese Arisaka.

Gradually the boat drew nearer and he made out two small, hunched figures in dark, soaked shirts. Their heads were still hidden in the mist. Furiously Mac tried to remember the pocket placements on Japanese field dress. His mind was a blank.

Then the men stopped paddling and the boat's momentum stalled as though it were unwilling to leave the clinging protection of the mist. Mac swallowed hard. Wiry brown arms and slender hands held the paddles.

A pang of dread shot through him as he realised he had left the log-line out of reach. He had to warn the others! Then he realised a shot would do just that. Idiot! He told himself to calm down and take his cue from Miller. But what if Miller couldn't see? What if more Japs had already landed downstream and were closing in? His right biceps trembled and he pulled the rifle stock more firmly into his shoulder.

For a few seconds more the boat drifted and then the paddles began dipping once again. As it came closer the Asian features of two men became clear.

Mac mouthed a silent 'Fuck!' Bile rose to the back of his mouth at the thought of a human target. His throat burned as he swallowed. Though he had never seen action he had been well drilled. The wooden stock felt solid against his chest. He eased the safety catch forward. Then slowly and carefully he took the slack out of the trigger. The man's chest filled his front and rear sights. It was an easy, certain shot.

'I'll have you, Tojo!' Mac croaked softly. The smell of gun oil filled his nose. He exhaled and began the final squeeze. Just then the paddler's head dipped and he saw the distinctive 14th Army slouch hat.

Mac flicked his finger away from the trigger, his stomach churning. Jesus, I nearly shot one of ours! Why didn't Miller tell him they were Gurkhas! He lowered his rifle from his trembling shoulders.

Now the boat was moving speedily towards the shelter of the sandbar. The Gurkha in the front was staring directly at Mac's position. As the bird-call sounded again he looked away, then the two men hopped out and waded quickly ashore. In a moment they were hidden by the dense foliage.

Mac inhaled deeply. A clammy, cold sweat soaked his back.

Slight movements in the bushes to his left announced the approach of Miller and the Gurkhas. There were six in all.

'A "milk run", as the RAF boys like to say,' Miller chortled. 'What's your name?'

'MacDonald, Sir.' He looked sheepishly at the Gurkhas. 'Rather them than me.'

Miller smiled and nodded. 'Well done, MacDonald. By the way, Lance-Naik Rai here's worried you've got a touch of malaria. He saw your rifle shaking. You do look a bit pale. Perhaps you should see your Doc?'

Embarrassed, Mac turned to look at the man he had very nearly shot.

Rai was short and wiry, not much over five feet tall. His arms were dotted with leeches yet he seemed oblivious to any discomfort. He grinned at Mac who towered above him. '*Shabash*, Jock!' Bravo!

Mac managed a nod.

Miller spoke quickly to Rai. 'Let's see what you got.'

Rai squatted and Miller did the same. With Mac and the others looking on, Rai, still grinning, delved inside his shirt and brought out a waterproof pouch. He tipped out some frayed and dark-stained pieces of cloth.

Mac realised they were Japanese rank badges and that the stains were blood. He looked at the Gurkha with even more respect. There were also documents. Miller flicked through them, speaking with Rai in Urdu. 'Good show! You can show me their positions later over a brew.'

The Gurkhas straightened and gave Miller textbook salutes that he returned equally smartly. Rai and the others moved off. In seconds they had disappeared.

'He's the best we've got at *shikar*,' Miller said proudly.

Mac frowned. 'Sir?'

'It means "the hunt".'

Behind them the loud swishing of branches, swearing and heavy footfalls announced the approach of Archie Ferguson, who was Mac's relief.

'Mac, where the fuck are you?'

'Password?' Mac challenged half-heartedly.

'Och, yer bugger! I've forgotten the bloody password.'

After the whispers of Miller and the Gurkhas the words sounded blaring. 'Over here,' replied Mac, trying to keep his voice down.

Miller shot him a reproachful look then he, too, was gone.

'Hurry up, Arch. For God's sake keep quiet!' He really needed a cigarette.

Two days later and to his utter dismay, Mac was in midstream on the Chindwin, trying to keep to a steady paddling rhythm with Archie. They were both loaded with kit in a two-man boat and Archie was splashing him with every stroke.

The crossing was going at a snail's pace and, worse, the morning mist was lifting quickly. Visibility was already way too good for Mac's liking. Safety, a sloping, sandy bank, was still a good thirty-five yards away. Any second now, he thought grimly, and the 'woodpeckers'—the Japanese Nambu heavy machine guns—were sure to open up. Caught in the open, he and Archie would be sitting ducks.

In the stillness, a half-stifled cough from behind them sounded like a shot. Mac jumped. Archie swore softly and began paddling faster.

Mac fixed his gaze on his paddle. Time seemed to stand still until suddenly a helping hand was pulling the boat ashore. He rushed up the bank, bent double behind Archie and sank down panting. Back on the river a line of rubber and canvas boats of various sizes was snaking out of the mist.

Mac's platoon was on a joint patrol with the Gurkhas, with Miller as the officer in command. He had been introduced to the Seaforths the night before. Miller's news that a few months previously a British force of three hundred jungle commandos had crossed the Chindwin and moved deep behind enemy lines had surprised, and cheered, them all.

According to Miller, the commandos, called Chindits, had tried to cut the Mandalay railway and disrupt the Japanese lines of communication. It was the first time since the retreat from Burma that any infantry attack had been made on the Japanese. But all was not going well.

'They are in a bit of a spot,' Miller had told them. 'They've had some bad run-ins with the Japs and have been split into small groups. Now they are heading home. Some have already made it but the Japs have got their backs up and have sent their 18th Division after those still on the other side of the river. The 18th was at Singapore....'

Miller had let the last word hang for effect. The quick fall of the 'Fortress City' had been a huge, embarrassing shock to the British.

'These Chindits are in a sorry state and need a bit of help,' Miller had continued. 'They've been short of food and medicines. What's required is a diversion to allow them to cross the river up stream before the net closes. There are enemy observation posts nearby, so the idea is that we give them something to report in this area. At Tonmakeng there are five hundred Japs. We want to keep them distracted.'

That night Mac had hardly slept a wink. But the reality was worse than he had even imagined. Progress through the dense vegetation on the far bank was painfully slow. Razor-sharp leaves and spines swiped them at every step. Steaming heat and ferocious flies adding to their overall misery. They slid repeatedly in piles of elephant dung or tripped on tree roots, exhausting themselves as they pulled each other up. For Mac the bizat bushes were the worst. Tiny white spores that covered their leaves worked down his shirt and boots to rub and itch. Under his collar his neck was red raw.

Eventually Miller led them inland and they hit upon a narrow trail. As the ground became drier and the jungle thinner they made better time. Yet it wasn't long before the twelve Scotsmen were in need of a rest and Miller called the first water stop.

Mac sank down next to Archie. Both of them were soaked in perspiration. They unslung their canvas chaggles and took quick, grateful gulps of the brackish, chlorinated water.

'Jesus,' groaned the older man, 'we've only been going a couple of hours and I'm knackered. It's like wading through a hot bath!'

Mac laughed, his own breathing laboured. 'It's only been forty-five minutes! You'll be a right fit bastard at the end of this ramble, Archie.'

'Quiet back there!' hissed their sergeant, Munro.

A Gurkha carrying a Thompson sub-machine gun trotted past them. Suddenly he turned and gave Mac a grinning thumbs up. It was Rai. Mac returned the gesture. The Gurkha sped off, picking his way easily through the slumped Seaforths. Tucked into the belt on Rai's back Mac saw the heavy, curved *kukri* dagger that the Gurkhas preferred to the bayonet.

'How d'you know him?' Archie asked.

'He's the one I told you about. Scared the shite out o' me!'

'That I can imagine. Did you see him? Fresh as a fucking daisy!'

'Good thing they're on our side, eh?'

'Aye, laddie. That's for sure.'

Two hours and six more brief water stops later they came to a small clearing. Miller gathered them round. His instructions, delivered in the now familiar hushed tones, were matter of fact.

'Absolute silence from here on. There's a Jap post about three hundred yards to the south. There should be no more than four of them, so we're going to give them a surprise. In and out before they know what's hit them.'

Archie and Mac exchanged uneasy glances.

'Prepare your weapons now,' said Miller calmly. 'And fix bayonets.'

To Mac the rasping of rifle bolt-actions and the clicking of ammunition clips sounded raucous. He reached for his bayonet and snapped it into place on his second try. Embarrassed, he looked around. No-one had noticed.

Miller was speaking again. 'Follow and watch the man in front. Ten feet apart. No noise. We'll take positions to the south-west, shoot them up for a couple of minutes then withdraw. Remember, we only need to rattle their cage.'

Despite his nerves, Mac was impressed. Miller came over like an old Tayside gillie at the start of the salmon season.

They moved off as instructed but just minutes later Miller called a sudden halt in another small clearing. Two silent minutes passed, then five. Mac sat back against a fallen log and strained his ears but all he could hear were birds and the occasional chattering of monkeys. His gaze settled on an inch-wide column of ants marching over one of his boots.

A vaguely familiar bird-call made him start. He looked up to see Rai and another Gurkha scurrying back. They whispered urgently with Miller who then waved the platoon in close.

'We're unlucky,' Miller said almost casually. 'A small Chindit group is coming directly for us and there's a Jap patrol right behind them.'

Mac's throat went dry.

'They'll be here any minute,' continued Miller urgently. 'We can't risk hailing them because the Japs are too close. Our chaps are bound to be twitchy, but we daren't backtrack in case they hear us and delay. We're going to have to hide and let the Chindits pass. Then we'll ambush the Japs.'

Miller eyed them confidently. 'I know some of you have not seen action before. Just remember the drill and you'll be fine. If the Chindits suspect something and start shooting, for god's sake don't fire back. Keep down and shout "British! Don't shoot!" That should do the trick.' He glanced at Rai. 'As soon as the last Jap has come past, Naik Rai will toss a couple of grenades. We'll reply with more at the other end to box them in. That's when you open fire. Sweep everything in front of you. Those with Stens, use short bursts. Try to pick your targets but get them all.'

Miller paused and looked at the anxious faces. 'One last thing, finish off any wounded Japs. It's a nasty business but they won't let themselves be taken alive and they'll take you with them if they get half a chance.'

The Seaforths exchanged grim glances. Mac saw that a few had turned pale under their jungle tans. Miller began directing them.

'MacDonald, you partner Rai. You,' he pointed to Archie, 'and Limbau with me. Remember, not a squeak!' Miller turned and headed back down the trail, positioning men off it at intervals.

Across the clearing Rai beckoned to Mac. He began threading through the bushes parallel to the trail. Bent double, Mac followed as best he could.

Soon they were some three feet in from the edge of the trail beside the opening to the clearing. To Mac's right, just visible through the low branches, lay Rai. He was totally still, his ear to the ground.

Mac tried desperately to slow his breath, certain he sounded like a running motor. Stinging sweat ran down his forehead into his eyes. Then he saw Rai's nostrils flare. Seconds later Mac heard slow, laboured footsteps, then panting only yards away. Then he caught a strong whiff of bowel. Oh God, he thought in consternation, someone's farted. It'll give us away!

A pair of badly worn British jungle boots came into view. Their rubber soles had split from the canvas uppers and had been wrapped with a length of tree creeper. Tucked into the boots was a pair of ripped, green trousers. The Chindit's legs, lacerated with leaf cuts and pocked with oozing sores, were little more than skin and bone. Foliage hid the man's upper body.

With alarm, Mac noticed the smell was even stronger now. As the Chindit walked on, Mac saw that his buttocks were exposed. Brown stains ran down the backs of his legs and trousers to his boots. Suddenly Mac understood. The man had dysentery! For the sake of speed he had cut out the seat of his pants. Mac wrinkled his nose in distaste. The Chindit was leaving a pungent trail. If Rai had smelt him at twenty yards so would the Japs….

Mac thought of his own recent experience with dysentery. At the time, he could imagine nothing worse than queuing round the clock with fifty other stricken men, sharing four latrines and struggling to dig more. But now he could: having the shits and the Japs after you as well. The poor bastards!

Five more Chindits trudged by in silence. They were obviously exhausted by sickness and the long march. Two had cut the seat of their trousers like the first. Another lay on a makeshift bamboo stretcher carried by men who themselves were stretcher-cases.

Mac wanted to jump up and help but he knew he could not. Miller was right. The Chindits would shoot at anything that moved. Silently he urged them on. At last their sounds faded but the natural noises of the forest—the bird-calls, the monkey chatter—did not resume.

The Japanese were under two minutes behind them. Mac's first indication was an olive-green, sock-like canvas shoe treading noiselessly on the trail directly in front of him. Above the ankle the leg was wrapped to the knee in green puttees. Mac held his breath, watching the scout pass by, stepping with the patience of a hunter who knows his quarry is near. Seconds later the rest of the Japanese patrol came through in silence. Mac counted eight pairs of puttee-wrapped legs.

Twin booms from Rai's grenades merged into one, shattering the forest stillness.

Mac ducked, his ears ringing. Beside him, Rai was already firing. Vaguely he was aware of shouts and screams as two more blasts sounded and the rest of the platoon opened fire.

A sudden flash of olive-green darted into the bushes to his left. He stayed prone, watching the Japanese slither quickly through the undergrowth in order to get behind them. Mac swung round anticipating the man's direction and readied for a shot. His enemy did not oblige. In the clearing the firing had already become sporadic. Mac scanned left and right frantically in the short, eerie silences. His heart began to pound. He'd lost him!

Shots from a Seaforth to Mac's left resulted in movement. His enemy had been waiting for a target. Quickly Mac re-aimed at a narrow gap in the foliage a few feet from him. As an olive-green cap filled his sights he pulled the trigger. He saw the head jerk up and then drop. Mac watched but the figure lay still.

'Cease firing!' Miller shouted.

Cautiously, Mac moved back out on to the trail. He had to make sure of the Japanese he had shot. Ahead he could see others lying sprawled in the clearing. Miller, Rai, Limbau, Sergeant Munro and Archie, were going through their pockets.

A low moaning stopped Mac in his tracks. Directly in front of him, hidden from the others by a tree stump, was a wounded Japanese. Below the knees his legs were bloody stumps. The man was semi-conscious.

Remembering Miller's instruction about prisoners Mac slowly brought up his rifle. Then the Japanese began to wheeze. Blood frothed in his mouth. Mac lowered his gun. 'Not my job,' he muttered. Instead, he placed the dying man's rifle out of his reach, then worked his way back into the vegetation. He found the body lying face down.

Mac needed to see his enemy's face. This man, he knew, would have killed him without hesitation. He felt strange, not guilty—it was war after all—but somehow unclean. Other men, politicians and generals, had decided that Alun MacDonald would have to kill. This was the result.

He wrestled with this thought as he rolled the corpse over. Flies buzzed above the matted blood that caked the cropped hair. Brown eyes, now dull, stared sightlessly. Mac guessed he was in his early twenties, like himself. A pair of cracked, round-rimmed glasses lay in the undergrowth. For some reason he put them in the man's tunic pocket.

The dull boom sent him diving for cover. Even as he moved he sensed that he was not the target. A short burst of machine-gun fire in the clearing was followed by shouts then silence. Suddenly uneasy, Mac headed back, increasing his pace and ignoring the leaves and branches that slashed his legs and arms. He burst into the clearing and almost ran on to the barrel of Limbau's rifle. He stood awkwardly, realising just how close he had come. Shaking their heads, the other men lowered their weapons. Limbau kept his weapon trained on Mac long enough to make his point.

Mac looked for Archie. He was lying on his back, his face covered in blood. Most of his chest had been blown open.

'Archie!' He stared in disbelief. Beside his friend lay the mangled body of the Japanese Mac had spared.

Miller was looking away sympathetically.

'One of 'em wasn't dead,' Sergeant Munro explained. 'He had a charge wedged in his armpit. When Archie went to search him the bastard let it off.'

Mac felt the cold horror of guilt envelop him. Tears ran down his cheeks as he sank to his knees. 'Oh, Archie I'm sorry! Oh, Jesus Christ, I'm so sorry!' He began to retch.

Magelang, Central Java, March 1944

'Isogi!'—Hurry! *'Isogi!'* The Japanese army captain was in a rage.

Kneeling on the polished teak floor of her well-appointed lounge, Marianne van Dam rushed to comply, snapping shut the suitcase lid. She rose and stepped back to stand with her husband and teenage son and daughter. Two Japanese soldiers pushed the family roughly out of their way.

Anxiously the girl took her mother's hand in hers. 'Mum, what will happen to us?'

'It's all right, Kate,' said Marianne softly and squeezing her hand. 'Just do as they say.'

Other soldiers began rummaging through cupboards and upending drawers. One of them found the drinks cabinet and called to his captain. The bottles were taken outside.

Marianne tensed as she saw her sixteen-year-old son glaring balefully at the soldiers. 'Kees!' Marianne hissed, 'Stop it!' Sullenly the boy obeyed, glancing at his father.

Pym van Dam's face was taut as he watched the hobnailed boots gouge the teak. Marianne slipped her arm inside his. He smiled at her reassuringly.

It had been two years since the Japanese had invaded and conquered the Netherlands East Indies in just nine days. Over the subsequent months most of the Dutch colonists had been interned. On Java, the skills of a few score specialists like irrigation engineer Pym van Dam had still been needed. By agreeing to co-operate with the invaders they had kept their families out of squalid, overcrowded camps.

Pym had worked conscientiously on the vast agricultural estates, maintaining the water supply for the vital rice crops that helped feed millions. He had also trained local staff. That morning he had been told his services were no longer required. He and his family had been given thirty-minutes' notice to pack one suitcase each. Twenty minutes later the Japanese had come.

'*Isogi!*' The captain pointed to the door.

Slowly the van Dams picked up their suitcases. For the last time, Marianne's gaze swept over the furniture, rugs, books and ornaments they were leaving behind. Most distressing to her were the empty photograph frames left askew on the mantelpiece.

Pym led his family out of the room in a dispirited single file. As Kate passed the sideboard her hand darted out and she grabbed a small, red cut-glass tulip.

Outside, a captured Dutch army lorry was waiting for them. In the back, three other family groups sat in grim silence on an assortment of cases and mattresses. Marianne stopped, she had not thought about mattresses. A Japanese soldier shoved her forward. It was too late.

Some yards away stood a Javanese couple and five children. Their few belongings—rattan chairs, pots and pans and rugs—were stacked on a bullock cart. Tethered to the back of the cart was a goat. Pym stared disdainfully at the former assistant who had taken his job and was now taking his home.

Marianne stifled a sob. 'Oh, Pym, our lovely home....'

Her husband put his arm around her shoulders. His voice shook with anger. 'We'll get it back. I promise.'

Nijmegen, The Netherlands, October 1944

In the half-lit cellar, the silence between the barrages from the German 88 mm guns was almost ghostly. Voices were hushed, as if savouring the quiet. Meg Graham felt she could be in a church...or a crypt.

Candles flickered, casting an orange tint on the faces of the tired, tense, young men around her. They also illuminated the specks of falling dust that was coating everything and everyone in the damp, brick-lined basement. Clouds of cigarette smoke hung in the air. She took one last drag on her own then stubbed it out.

'Here you are, Ma'am.'

Meg turned. A soldier in his late teens was offering her an open tin of processed ham and two tack biscuits. He held the tin by its rim, claw-style, in an attempt to keep off some of the dust. Meg accepted it gratefully. She managed to remember his name. 'Thanks, Matt,' she said. 'Say, where are you from?'

'Memphis, Tennessee, Ma'am,' he replied proudly.

'Less of the Ma'am,' she told him smiling. 'Meg will do just fine.'

'Yes, Ma' am,' he replied automatically. He grinned and went back to the portable cooking stove.

Meg had been sheltering in the cellar with the platoon from the 82nd Airborne Regiment for nearly thirty-six hours, sharing K-rations and the odd 'liberated' beer. Operation Market Garden, the joint British-American attempt to seize the German-controlled bridges over the Meuse and Waal rivers at Arnhem, Eindhoven and Nijmegen had stalled. Both sides were exchanging regular artillery bombardments while they regrouped. Each day Meg had watched the patient residents of Nijmegen sweep their roads clean of glass and rubble, leaving neat piles on street corners.

At first the young veterans of the Normandy landings had been polite but a little sceptical of the attractive brunette suddenly in their midst. Yet they were fascinated by the idea of a woman war correspondent and almost as much by the fact that Meg had studied in France and Germany in the mid-1930s.

The paratroopers had been taken aback when they heard that 'their' war was not Meg's first. Blank looks had met her tales of fighting in Spain, China and Finland. Above all, the news that there was another dictator in Spain had left them dismayed and perturbed.

'I'll sure be glad to leave this rat hole,' said one soldier to no-one in particular. 'Maybe have a look round the town.'

Meg saw he was flicking through a copy of the *Blue Guide to Holland and the Rhine*. She had one too. Now that the small town of Nijmegen was the front line she wasn't sure how much of it there would be left to see.

Conversation ceased as a dull, distant boom quickly became a roar and then a shriek. Meg tensed and covered her ears. The shell came down no more than fifty yards away. More dust fell, coating her ham and biscuits. Seconds later the Allied big guns replied in kind.

Twenty minutes later the shelling stopped. During the lull, Matt wandered over and sat down self-consciously beside her. 'Ma'am, I mean Meg. Do you think they'll send us to fight this guy Franco when we've beaten the Krauts?'

Meg hesitated. A part of her had died with the International Brigade in Spain. For a second, the old republican flame flickered in her heart. Annoyed with herself, she doused it immediately in a wave of cynicism. 'No, Matt, I don't think so. Spain's minor league compared with the Nazis. It was ignored in '36 and you can bet it will be ignored in '46. Don't worry, you won't be learning any Spanish!'

Later, feeling a little guilty, Meg set her job aside and talked of other things. She knew how the men liked to hear a woman's voice, particularly an American. It was really such a simple thing and she couldn't begrudge it them when they were so far from home. She gave it her best shot and they sat entranced by her racy descriptions of the pre-war nightlife in Paris and Berlin. Afterwards she was pestered to write the addresses of some of her old haunts.

Eight hours later, the barrage halted and the soldiers received orders to move out. Meg left the basement an honorary member of the platoon and with a hasty promise that one day they would meet in Berlin.

Book One

Chapter One

As usual, gnawing hunger pangs and itching bites woke Kate van Dam long before the return of the women on the night watch who were supposed to rouse her. She lay quietly on the narrow wooden slats that had served as her bed for the last eight months and tried to close her mind to the snoring, coughing and occasional groaning from the other occupants of the crowded hut. The air was sweet with the smell of fresh blood spilled by the feasting bed bugs that infested the woodwork and thin, kapok-stuffed mattresses.

Dawn always seemed the worst time, she thought. It appeared to galvanise the bugs into taking one last bite. Still tired, she lay back and wondered if it were really so, or whether it was only because she was awake and could feel them biting. A sharp nip on her left arm reminded her that it really did not matter either way.

Automatically she brought her right arm over, sliding her hand up from her elbow to her shoulder and brushing at least two of the tiny, tenacious creatures off her. She let her fingers linger, feeling more bone than flesh and she frowned as she imagined herself in another year. In truth, she doubted whether she had got that much time. She was nineteen years old.

Still weary, she pushed herself half-up and felt a bed bug squash under her elbow. She pulled a face, knowing that the pungent, sickly sweet odour would not leave her until it was scrubbed off. Not very long ago the smell would have made her gag but now it was bearable. Perhaps that was an improvement of sorts she thought cynically.

The woven-bamboo screen to her left ballooned towards her as her mother turned over and banged Kate's hip with her knee. Kate winced but fought the urge to push back. Her mother was ill and if she were sleeping at least she was not thinking about food.

Kate glanced upwards. Pinned to the screen was her precious red glass tulip. Its delicate green base had snapped off but now she treasured it all the more. Wistfully she ran her fingertips over the polished surface remembering happier days.

'No, we need it!' The shrill shout came from a few feet away. Kate recognised Annie Klomp's recurrent bad dream. Everyone in the hut knew the scenario: Annie finds her infant son throwing away a half-empty tin of rotten sardines, then she beats him while standing in a kitchen piled high with food.

Now for the crying, thought Kate, glad now that she had to get up. Seconds later the sobbing started.

'There, there, dear. It's only a bad dream,' someone said, trying the routine to calm Annie. But then the complaints started, as usual, even though they all knew Annie would not hear them.

'For God's sake, woman, not again!'

'Noisy cow!'

Soon the shouts woke the toddlers who cried from hunger and sickness every morning.

Kate put her hands to her ears. In the corner of her eye she caught a sudden movement. A small, yellow-green *tikjak*—a gecko—darted halfway down the screen and stopped inches from her face. Its light, leathery underbelly was pulsating in a fast, regular rhythm. *Tikjaks* were all over the camp. They reminded Kate of life before the war when she would watch them cavorting on the ceiling of her bedroom while she lay under a mosquito net in crisp, clean sheets that had been tucked in by her mother. She had felt so comfortable and so safe then. Now it all seemed so distant and unreal that she was beginning to think it had been a dream. But that, she reminded herself sternly, was because she was living a nightmare.

Suddenly the *tikjak* was still. A large, shiny black beetle was heading directly for it. At the last moment the beetle saw the predator and tried to jump aside but it was too slow. In a flash it was held firmly between powerful jaws, its legs working uselessly. Remorselessly the *tikjak* pounded the beetle, smothering it in saliva, until finally it gulped down the crushed mass.

Kate sighed as she realised she was envious of a lizard's full stomach. Behind the screen to her right, her neighbour Mrs Meer, broke wind loudly and then belched. Kate let her head drop, praying yet again for the Allies to come and end her misery. Dear God, she thought, what's taking them so long?

In September 1944 the camp had been thrilled by the reports of the Allied attack on Arnhem, thinking the liberation of the Netherlands would quickly follow and that afterwards Dutch soldiers would liberate Java. Every evening, nervous groups of women gathered, risking beatings and worse in solitary confinement, to listen to the BBC news on hidden radios, hoping to hear the names of hometowns. In the East, said the reports, the Japanese had been stopped in Burma, and the Americans, under MacArthur and Nimitz, were advancing. But more good news had not come and the weeks had dragged into months. They must come soon, she thought. They must!

Cheered a little by the thought of eventual freedom, Kate decided to get up and wash. She was on breakfast duty with eight others. In little over two hours, two thousand women and children would be expecting their breakfast and there would be hell to pay if their tiny portions of rice were not ready.

She gathered her ragged sleeping shirt to her, shuffled down to the edge of the boards and circled her feet trying to find the tops of her *klompen*—sandals made from wood and strips of car tyre inner tube—at the foot of her bed. When she could not, she touched one foot down on the floor. Her toes slid in a gooey mess. Someone had not made it to the latrines in the night. That serves you right, lazy idiot! Kate chided herself. You broke the rules that will keep you alive; your own rules!

Briefly she toyed with the idea of walking barefoot to the wash block but dismissed it because she would risk cutting her foot. No, she would have to wear her klompen to the latrines and then wash it. The danger of infection was too great. Just a few weeks earlier a young girl had trodden on a rusty nail near a latrine pit. The child's mother had washed it as best she could but within two days the foot had swollen to the size of a coconut. Powerless to stop the infection without medicines, the mother and Lucy Santen, the only doctor among them, had watched helplessly as the dark lines of poison had spread up the leg. Eventually the Japanese had accepted their pleas for the girl to go to the nearby hospital but by then it had been too late.

On the day the girl died it had been Kate's turn on burial detail. No formal services were allowed. Because bodies decayed quickly in the heat the Japanese insisted on immediate burial. In the end, a few of the mother's friends had managed to say a quick prayer and sing a hymn out of earshot of the guards. Wood was too precious as cooking fuel, so a large straw basket served as a coffin. Bamboo poles pushed through the front and rear served as handles for Kate and the other bearers. The cemetery was about half-a-mile from the camp. As the basket swayed from side-to-side, a yellowish, foul-smelling liquid had dripped from it, leaving a snail-like trail. The little girl was not buried alone. Kate had made three more journeys that day.

Yawning, she reached for a drawstring bag containing her day clothes and sidled carefully between the rows of sleeping women and children towards the door. Thirty-two people were living in the former classroom. Washbowls, bottles, food bowls and other bits and pieces cluttered the ends of each sleeping space. One or two people sat up, worried in case she pocketed anything.

'Good Morning, Mrs Kepple,' she said to a middle-aged woman who lay watching her like a hawk, cradling a few Red Cross food tins.

'What's so good about it?' The woman scoffed. Her eyes were red with lack of sleep from fear of someone stealing her treasure.

Kate moved on. No-one made any attempt to greet her. Even after eight months in the camp she and her mother were still regarded with suspicion by some. There were many who thought the van Dams had had it easy while they had suffered.

Outside the sky was a light grey but the first faint glow of red was visible above the row of lontar palm trees to the east. She was glad to be out in the fresh air. There was a slight breeze from the north, carrying the faint scent of the sea from Semarang harbour and she paused to savour it. Once the sun came up, the air would be still and heavy until the late evening.

Before the war, Tjandi had been an affluent suburb. When the Japanese decided to intern the Dutch civilians, they had simply cordoned off entire streets using large bamboo fences. Men and women had been separated. In all, the three Tjandi camps were home to nearly eight thousand women and children crammed into houses, shops, schools and other buildings. Kate's father and brother had been sent to a men's camp in Magelang. Every two months they were permitted to exchange postcards.

Kate and her mother had ended up in a former private school for boys. Its main building was an imposing, four-storey structure with twin central towers and wings off either side. When they arrived, all the rooms in the main block had long been claimed, so they had been quartered in one of several classroom huts in the grounds. Sudden deprivation and the shock of new surroundings and new rules had hit them hard. Their time in Tjandi had been thoroughly wretched.

Kate looked around her. Only a few of her neighbours were also up and about. Across the compound three familiar figures emerged from the latrines and started back towards the huts. Kate had known the Harwigs before the invasion. Mr Harwig had worked with her father, and his wife had been a stalwart in the local church choir, as well as secretary of the golf club. Now their two daughters, one fourteen and the other twelve, were half-carrying, half-dragging their barely conscious mother. Their father was already dead. After the Japanese had attacked Pearl Harbor and then, just days later, sunk the British warships *Repulse* and *Prince of Wales* off Malaya, there had been panic. Fears of air-raids led to a local defence corps being formed, and Mr Harwig had been among the first to volunteer. One night, driving home in the black-out after a training exercise, his car collided with a water buffalo. At his funeral, family friends had encouraged his widow and children to go to Australia, but the Indies Government, desperate to maintain morale, had forbidden Dutch residents to leave.

As the Harwigs drew near, Kate tried to keep looking at the girls but her gaze was drawn to their mother's oedema-swollen stomach and the oozing tropical ulcers on her shins. She saw the tell-tale bloodstains and brown streaks on her nightshirt. Kate shuddered. Dysentery literally drained the life out of its victims, especially those already weakened by hunger and malaria. Lotte Harwig was one of many mothers who could not bear to see her children go hungry and had shared her own meagre food ration with them. Warnings from others that her children needed her alive were ignored. Kate had seen dysentery often enough to know the girls would be orphans in less than a week. From the look in their eyes she could tell they knew it, too.

Outside the latrine block Kate washed her foot and sandal beneath a rusting tap. A threadbare but wriggling sock was tied over the end of it to filter out the larger worms. She filled her tin washbowl, took a deep breath and went inside. Quickly she lowered her frayed shorts, trapping them behind her knees as she squatted over the open trench. Since she was eating so little it didn't take long. Using the water from bowl, she washed between her buttocks native style, using her left hand. Then, lungs about to burst, she rushed out into the fresh air. Each day it took her longer to recover. She was getting weaker....

To banish that unwelcome thought, Kate began to anticipate the pleasure of a soak in the school bathhouse. Early morning was her favourite time because it was not crowded and she could use the mandi tubs rather than the outdoor showers that were overlooked by a guard tower. The bathhouse abutted the rear of the main school building. Once the blue-and-white patterned tiles on the walls and floor must have glistened. Now they were dull and streaked with black mould. Kate did not care. It was still one of the cleanest places in the camp. Eight large mandi tubs about six-feet long and three-feet wide were spaced around the room. Most were just half-full of discoloured scum-topped water. At intervals along two walls were rusting pipes, showerheads and controls. They had not worked for as long as Kate had been in the camp and she ignored them. Two women were leaving as she arrived but there was no-one else inside. She was delighted. It had been days since she had enjoyed even five minutes by herself.

Kate undressed quickly and as a matter of routine peered carefully along the open drain channels running around the sides of the baths. She found real treasure, a sliver of soap caught in a crevice. Gleefully she squeezed it on to her own tiny bar of soap. She soaped herself outside the mandi and rinsed by dipping her bowl into the water. After her wash she could not resist the temptation to soak. She eased herself into one of the tubs and lay back with her eyes closed, enjoying the cooling effect, no longer bothered by the hairs, dead flies and dirt suspended in the water. Her thoughts drifted to her old home and her lovely bedroom at the top of the dark, teak staircase. She imagined herself wishing her smiling parents goodnight and then climbing the staircase to her soft, welcoming bed. Then another, much more powerful memory, replayed itself.

Christmas 1941 had been a tense time in Java. Determined to celebrate despite fears of war, Kate's parents had held a large party at their home on Christmas Eve. Among the guests had been Mr and Mrs Muiden and their son Peter, who was a year older than Kate.

Kate had a secret crush on Peter but did not know him well. She had hardly said a word to him all evening when, to her great dismay and embarrassment, her mother had decided it was her bedtime. Her protests had been to no avail and dejectedly she had climbed the stairs. Peter was waiting for her on the landing. Without warning he had pulled her to him and kissed her on the cheek then on the lips. She had been stunned and thrilled. Time had seemed to stand still. Peter continued to kiss her, and then he began stroking her back. His hand had slipped down to the tops of her buttocks. Her heart had raced as his other hand had moved to her front, sliding up over her ribs. His lips had parted on hers and she had felt the moistness of his saliva. She had stood mesmerised, leaning against him. His hand had risen higher and his fingertips were brushing the base of her breast when the loud, deliberate cough had startled them. Peter had jumped away and scurried down the stairs. Stern-faced, her father had said nothing.

Kate often thought of Peter and the feeling his kiss had awakened in her. A sharp, squeaking clang of the changing room door brought her back to the present as three younger, chatting girls appeared. She climbed out of the tub.

Like many of the younger women in the camp Kate dressed native-style in a sarong around her hips and a *kembang*—a long, narrow strip of batik—wrapped around the chest, leaving her shoulders uncovered. Both of her garments were shabby and frayed.

She was slightly late for her kitchen shift and the other cooks were already in the little courtyard rinsing pails of rice, paring half-rotten vegetables, or scraping tiny pieces of beef and pork off almost bare bones. They worked outside because the school's ovens did not work. As a last gesture of defiance the retreating Dutch army had blown up Tjandi's gas mains. The Japanese had seen no reason to restore the supply. Consequently all cooking was done on wood or charcoal fires. Breakfast alone required a small mountain of rice and took almost two hours to prepare.

Chalked on one of the courtyard walls was a faded menu: 'Restaurant Tjandi as featured in Java the Holiday Paradise. Breakfast: Arjana Watercress Gruel, Lunch: Savoury Corn Royale, Dinner: Spiced Porridge à la Tjandi'. The joke had worn as thin as the gruel for the fare had been unchanged for weeks.

A lithe, dark-haired woman chopping some badly discoloured tripe gave Kate a playful wave. 'Good afternoon,

Kate,' Juliette Giroux joked sarcastically. Her French accent was very heavy. 'So glad you could join us today!'

Juliette was twenty-seven and a professional dancer. She had been stranded by the Japanese invasion. Despite her protestations, the *kenpeitai*—Japanese military police—had ignored her Vichy France travel documents and interned her. Once incarcerated, she had accepted her fate stoically and had soon fallen in with the camp routine. Twice a week she helped teach French in the camp school, and her dance classes were very popular. Kate went to them as often as she could.

For the younger women, the well-travelled Juliette was a link to the sophistication of Paris and the glamour of New York. Juliette did her best not to disappoint them. She kept her dark hair short and was never without a wide-brimmed sun hat. As usual, that morning she was wearing two pairs of long earrings, a jewelled black choker and a long pearl necklace. Her necklace was tucked down a skimpy, home-sewn halter-neck top made from a red sports bib scavenged from the school's gym store. Four inches of pearls dangled over her bare, bronzed midriff. A holed sarong, knotted at her hip, reached only to her knees.

Juliette was not alone in wearing jewellery. Most of the women were draped in a mismatched collection of pendants, necklaces and bracelets. Trust, like everything else in the camp, was in very short supply and they all knew that a hungry child could soon turn a loving mother into a desperate thief. There was a ready market for valuables among the guards and Javanese camp administrators.

Kate mouthed a smiling 'Sorry' to Juliette then looked for Mai, the Chinese matriarch who ran the kitchens and who would assign her jobs for the day. As she did so, she saw her friend, Marja Schreurs amidst a cloud of flies, her mouth and nose masked by a handkerchief. On the table in front of Marja were several bloody pigs heads from which she was peeling off strips of cheek. Kate waved and grimaced to her at the same time. Marja merely raised her eyebrows dejectedly.

'Good morning, Miss Kate.'

Kate turned. 'Morning, Mai,' she replied pleasantly.

Mai was middle-aged, bubbly and industrious. Her straw coolie-hat, simple blue cotton trousers and blouse were offset by spectacular jade bangles on each wrist. She spoke almost no Dutch and very little English. Her husband, a former cook for the Netherlands Indies Army, was interned a few miles away.

Before Mai had taken over, families had cooked for themselves on small braziers. Since many of the Dutch women had relied on servants before the war, their efforts had been poor. Firewood had been wasted, food spoiled and badly or wrongly prepared. Worse, it had been unfairly distributed or stolen. Squabbling and fighting had been so frequent that in despair the camp commandant had ordered that all cooking be done communally. Even then, problems had continued with rotas until the day Mai and some of her Chinese and Eurasian friends had marched into the kitchen and evicted all Europeans in what Juliette called the 'coup de cuisine'. Everyone agreed, some grudgingly, that Mai had worked magic. Immediately the food had tasted better and, incredibly, had seemed more varied. No-one dared ask her where she got the extras but most people presumed that her relations outside the camp were smuggling them. After making her point, Mai had accepted a few of the younger women back for 'training'. She ran two kitchens; one for the internees and another for the camp administrators and guards.

Mai pointed to a trestle table set up under an awning in the far corner of the courtyard. A lone Japanese guard stood beside it leaning lazily on his rifle. 'Today, Japan kitchen, please,' she said busily.

Kate beamed at Mai. Cooking for the Japanese brought perks. She went over to the awning and bowed courteously to the guard. *'Ohayo gozaimasu.'*—Good morning, she said politely.

The guard raised his head fractionally then studiously ignored her.

Excitedly Kate stepped up to the laden table. Under a muslin cloth lay thick pieces of fresh pork, fish and vegetables as well as salted radishes, noodles and spiced meats from the local kampong or village. There were also coconuts, bananas and papayas. Her mouth watered and her stomach rumbled loudly. She looked at the guard, knowing that if she were careful she could palm a few vegetable slices and bits of meat for her mother. Kate would eat later, openly, in front of the guards who were always afraid of poisoning and insisted the cooks tasted everything first.

Behind her a door-hinge squeaked. She glanced around to see a tousled-haired youth emerge from a storehouse, rolling an empty oil drum over to the fire. Jans van Basten often helped with the heavier chores like scraping off the burnt rice from the bottoms of the drums. In return, he was allowed to eat the scrapings. He wore shorts, klompen on his feet and no shirt. His underdeveloped muscles strained as he half-filled the drum with buckets of water.

At nearly thirteen, Jans was the oldest male in the camp. The day after his next birthday he would be sent to join his father in a men's camp. Kate knew she would miss the good-looking, cheerful Jans. To her secret embarrassment she often caught herself looking at him. She watched a little jealously as Juliette went over and pinched his biceps. 'You're getting stronger, Jans,' she teased. 'A real man now!' Jans flushed but it was obvious the youth was pleased.

As Juliette hefted a sack of rice under her arm, her scanty top slid to one side, fully exposing one of her breasts. Kate's laugh died in her throat as Juliette made no move to cover up. Instead, Juliette continued to pour the rice into the drum, ignoring Jans, who stared, his face a deep red. Only when the sack was empty did Juliette casually cover herself.

Kate glanced around quickly. Nudity was commonplace in the camp but Juliette's attitude troubled her. She noticed two older women exchanging disapproving looks. Kate busied herself with her work.

A little later Juliette came by. 'Make the most of it,' she joked, 'see you at the class.'

Kate was left unsettled. Not long after she had joined Juliette's dance group her mother had warned her not to socialise with 'the dancer'.

'But why?' Kate had complained in dismay. 'She's such fun and has been everywhere. She learnt the tango in Argentina!'

'Enjoy the dancing but don't become friendly,' her mother had replied sternly. 'She's not a good example.'

It was not until weeks later that Kate discovered the reason for her mother's dislike of Juliette. Kate had been enjoying a late-night soak in the mandi with some of the other girls. With the bathhouse to themselves they had lolled one to a tub. Conversation had turned, as it often did, from fantasy recipes to clothes, and then to boys.

'At school I used to be in love with Pete Muiden,' confessed Anna Veersteeg, lying back in the tub, trying to float. 'I was so jealous of you, Marja!'

Kate reddened and glanced at Marja, who had affected surprise. Marja was a year older than Kate.

'Pete?' Marja shrugged. 'Oh, he was all right, I suppose,' she had said casually, picking at her single long plait of mousy hair. 'Until we came here and the danseuse got her claws into him.'

'You mean Juliette?' Kate said taken aback. 'What happened?'

Marja looked around with exaggerated caution, hamming the conspirator. 'Do you really want to know?'

Anticipating scandal the girls had rushed to gather in or around Marja's tub. She had let their curiosity build. 'Remember that at first the Japs allowed boys to stay here up to sixteen? Well, they say some of the older women went with them. Juliette was one!'

'Eh? Surely not!' Kate exclaimed, her hand over her mouth.

'Yes, it's true!' Anna cut in shrilly. 'I heard Mother talking about it with Mrs Harwig once. Married women were doing it too. They said boys used to wait outside their huts at night!'

Marja was not to be outdone. 'That's not all,' she hissed. 'They say Juliette's still at it with Jans!'

There had been a chorus of indignant gasps as the gossip was devoured. 'No!'—'With Jans?'—'The dirty bitch!'

Rukmini Kuupers was sitting demurely in the tub, arms clasped around her drawn-up shins, her chin on her knees. She had the striking good looks common to the offspring of Europeans and Javanese. Her hazel eyes, honeyed skin and waist-long, raven-dark hair contrasted vividly with the brunettes and blondes around her. 'That must be why the Japs keep sending the older boys away,' she had sighed.

To the distress of the mothers in the camp, the Japanese had lowered the age limit for males first to fifteen, then fourteen and down to thirteen.

Kate, now more embarrassed than ever, had wondered if the rumours were true. After all, she was fond of Jans herself. But for Juliette to actually….

'Oh, how could she!' Lisa Hahn spat the words out.

'I think I know,' Rukmini had whispered.

The others gaped. 'Ruki!'—'What are you saying!'—'Oh, shame!'

Rukmini had blushed. 'No, I mean—I can understand she…' her voice was soft, almost despairing, '…that she doesn't want to be lonely. I don't want to…to die a virgin like Lizzy and Emma. Do you?'

Faces had blanched and heads dropped in stunned dismay at their taboo word. Kate had shivered as she thought of their friends who had died only two weeks apart. For several seconds no-one spoke. Then one by one, avoiding each others' eyes, they had dressed and left separately. But that night and every night since, Kate had asked herself Rukmini's question….

A shout made her jump. 'Miss Kate! Cabbage thick!' Mai was at her shoulder, correcting her grip on the chopping knife. 'Cut thin, thin!'

'Oh, sorry, Mai. I see,' Kate said guiltily.

Mai pulled a face and gestured to a two-foot high woven bamboo screen leaning against the school wall some thirty yards away. 'Mrs Larman make bread. Want pee-pee.'

Kate could see Marja's head and shoulders above the screen. A few feet away a blackened jerry can stood on bricks over a fire tended by another woman. 'Again?' Kate asked lightly.

'Yaah!' Mai shuddered. 'No like bread before. Now never eat bread forever!'

Kate giggled as Marja rose from behind the screen pulling up her shorts. She emerged holding a rusty tin and poured the liquid contents into the jerry can. Bertha Larman waved to Kate then pointed at the tin.

When supplies of yeast had run out even Mai had been unable to obtain the precious ingredient. They had made do with much reduced amounts of flaky, unleavened bread. Months later, a smuggled message from another camp had explained how to produce yeast from urine. Sceptical but desperate, they had boiled and disinfected fresh urine as instructed. Then they had mixed the liquid with dough that, to their delight and astonishment, had risen perfectly with no unpleasant taste. To keep the yeast supply going, Bertha was constantly seeking 'donations'. Still laughing at Mai's horrified expression, Kate went to do her duty.

The next morning was cloudless. Kate was up much earlier than usual. She had done the washing and was taking it to the many lines strung between the backs of the huts and the former sports field that was now divided into small vegetable plots. Most of the residents tried to grow some additional food, as did Kate.

Two months earlier, Marianne van Dam had contracted beriberi and then she had developed tropical ulcers on her legs. She had been in and out of the camp infirmary. Most of the time she was too weak to move from her bed. Dr Santen did not have the medicines to cure her. Every extra scrap of food Kate could find, work or trade went to her mother. For the past week Kate had harvested a tomato daily from her plot. Marianne's condition had improved slightly and Kate was convinced it was due to the fruit.

As she neared her plot she was pleased to see that three small tomatoes had ripened on her spindly plants. A little happier now, she began to peg out the small pile of clothes that represented most of her and her mother's wardrobes. As the line filled it blocked her view of the camp fences. The expanse of clear sky prompted her to hum the 'Blue Danube'.

Familiar voices made her turn. It was Marja and Anna, also carrying washing. Kate had an idea and quickly pegged out a red bib, a pair of her mother's white knickers and, just as the girls reached her, a royal blue blouse.

'Attention!' Kate chortled, saluting the homemade Dutch colours. Marja and Anna saluted as well. Then the three girls burst out laughing. Kate's gaze travelled up to the former guesthouse beyond the fence. A young man was watching her from an open window. He was bare-chested and holding a razor. For a long moment their eyes met and held. Kate caught her breath. His gaze was penetrating. A deep, sensual tingling ran through her. Her lips were forming a shy smile when she realised to her horror that her admirer was Japanese. Shock, guilt and then dread gripped her.

Kate's first thought was to warn her friends who were still joking, unaware of their audience. Her face pale, she was about to speak when two guards entered the garden. Automatically all three girls bowed low, suddenly very afraid. Any display of the Dutch flag was punishable by a beating and solitary confinement. Kate was contrite. It was her fault! They waited, holding their waist-level bows and staring at the earth as the guards walked on chatting and oblivious to the homemade Dutch bunting.

Trembling, Kate braced herself for the shout to the guards. The Jap had seen everything.... How could she have been so stupid! Seconds passed but there was no reprimand. One by one the girls came out of their bows. Kate glanced quickly up at the window. The young man had gone.

She unpegged the blue blouse while Marja and Anna watched the guards.

'Oh, Kate look!' Marja whispered urgently.

Kate turned. One of the Japanese had stepped onto her plot and was picking the three ripe tomatoes. He popped one into his mouth, threw one to his companion and pocketed the other. Then the two guards walked away.

Stunned, Kate walked over to her plants and slumped down on her knees. Anger surged through her. She looked up again at the guesthouse. The young man was back at the window and wearing the short-sleeved khaki shirt and insignia of a Japanese officer. His face was expressionless. Despite knowing the consequences Kate stared at him with brazen disdain. For several seconds he held her gaze then turned away, drawing a curtain. She started to weep.

Chapter Two

The elderly figure standing in the centre of the village square looked frail. His best white shirt was now too large for him and his green silk sarong billowed past his ankles. A mane of unruly grey hair set off his black, pot-shaped *pici* hat as he preached to his respectful audience drawn up in a crescent before him. His name was Maralik and he was the headmaster of the local *pesantren*, the Islamic school.

Maralik's voice had a deep, relentless rhythm that held the villagers as he called upon God to guide and protect the young men graduating that day. Behind him the sun was a low, red ball falling quickly in an orange- and purple-tinged sky. Soon it would drop below the tops of the dense green tree-tops that ringed the village. Dusk would be short. Already the heat was lifting and the bleached, woven palm-leaf roofs of the huts reflected a golden tint. He noticed that his elongated shadow had almost reached the feet of the children clustered in the first row. It was time to finish. He raised his hands, pausing slightly, for emphasis before ending his sermon. 'There is only one God, Allah, and Mohammed is His Messenger.'

Immediately and enthusiastically his attentive audience repeated the profession of faith. With a slow nod of his head, Maralik signalled that the formalities were over. People dispersed quickly and noisily as they moved to chat with family and friends. Many of the men lit *kretek* cigarettes and soon the fragrant scent of cloves swept the square. Women and girls emerged from the doors of the huts carrying steaming, foot-high rice-cones on palm-leaf trays and bowls of meat, fish and vegetables. Giggling, half-naked children came trotting after their mothers or clung to their brightly patterned sarongs.

Excitement was palpable. It had been months since the residents of Sadakan had enjoyed a *slametan*. Today, since boys from two neighbouring villages were also graduating from Maralik's school, three communities had been able to pool their meagre resources for the festival. The young guests of honour were sitting on smoothed log seats next to the headmen of the villages. Unused to fuss, the graduates clowned or fidgeted self-consciously, smiling with embarrassment in reply to shouts of congratulation from relatives and friends. Among them, one youth sat pensively. Lamban's thin, soft features were impassive and he barely acknowledged the shouts of well-wishers. He was relieved when the food appeared because it meant he and the others were no longer the centre of attention.

'I want to eat,' said Karek who was sitting beside him. After the food shortages of the past few months, the smell of the delicacies was mouth-watering. Karek's family lived in the next village. Like Lamban, he had just turned eighteen.

'Be patient!' Lamban growled, annoyed that his friend could be so carefree when he was wrestling with important decisions. 'If you stuff yourself, you'll be sick.'

Chastened, Karek became serious. 'Have you changed your mind?'

Lamban's expression hardened. 'No. I am leaving for Djakarta in a week,' he said determinedly, using the new name the Japanese had given their capital.

Karek looked away in disappointment. Lamban made another try to convince him to go with him. 'Why don't you come too? Things are changing, even Maralik says so. By the grace of God, Indonesia will soon be independent!'

A half-smile escaped Karek and Lamban pressed him. 'Don't you want to be part of it? You can tell your grandchildren how you helped make the country free!'

'But Lamban,' laughed Karek shyly, 'The Japanese have already promised us independence. It's the Jayabaya Prophecy coming true at last! Why can you just wait?'

Jayabaya, a twelfth-century warrior king of Java, had prophesied that the island would be set free from oppressors when a conquering power from the east would expel 'white men' and then leave after the life-span of a maize plant.

Lamban's patience snapped and he gripped his friend's arm tightly. 'That's your mother talking, not you! The Japanese are losing the war. Their promises are worthless!'

'But the Dutch are gone!'

'You're a fool if you think the Dutch won't try to come back. They ran from the Japanese but everyone says they'll sneak back with the Americans. If we let them, we'll be slaves again! We can stop it! We'll be famous. But only if we go to the capital and help Sukarno.'

Sukarno was the leader of the pro-Japanese National Movement for Independence and the most popular of the Javanese nationalist politicians.

Karek had no answer. Lamban waved his arm disdainfully at the scene in the square. 'Look around you! Today we have full stomachs but tomorrow we will be filling up on stale sago again. We can best help by going away. In Djakarta we can be useful. Maralik has taught us to read and write, and we have our training in the Youth Corps. Come with me! If we all join together the Dutch will never defeat us! We'll be heroes!'

Karek's eyes were bright now. He was clearly wavering. 'Will we really be famous? I'd—'

'And while the hero's away who will help his father and brother meet the next rice levy?' Behind them the familiar voice seethed with anger. Lamban looked down, while Karek turned sheepishly. 'You'll be heroes all right,' Karek's mother hissed. 'Just like the dead boys at Kediri!'

Not long before, the Javanese militia in Kediri had mutinied. Rumours had spread that the Japanese had crushed it mercilessly and that many had been killed in reprisals.

Karek's mother set down a leaf-tray laden with roasted fermented yam, sweet and sour fish, roast chicken satay and goat-meat kebabs. Karek could not meet her gaze. As she walked away she shot a cold glance at Lamban.

'Let's eat,' said Karek.

Lamban saw the fire had left Karek's eyes. He knew then he would be travelling alone.

It was several hours later, sitting and watching the traditional *wayang kulit* or shadow-puppet plays, before Lamban finally began to enjoy himself. Adults and children alike cheered and shouted themselves hoarse as the pierced buffalo-hide silhouettes of the gods, ghosts and heroes of the *Ramayana* and *Panji* sagas flickered across the bed sheet-sized screen.

Attracted by the light from palm oil torches, moths and other winged insects settled on the stretched cloth. It was a balmy, windless evening and above them, clove-cigarette smoke formed thick, pungent clouds. Behind the screen, the *dalang* puppeteer worked furiously, reciting from a scroll in ancient Javanese, mimicking different voices and swapping puppets at a frenetic pace. His narration was punctuated with mallet strikes cueing the accompaniment from the gongs, drums, cymbals, flutes and strings of the traditional *gamelan* orchestra.

As the last play began, Lamban was thrilled to recognise it as the tragedy of Diponegoro. The tale of the charismatic Javanese prince who had fought the Dutch only a hundred years earlier was his favourite. It was a popular finale. The audience were swept along in the saga of feud and final, fatal betrayal. Just when the dying prince was about to utter his last line, the *dalang* paused, his mallet raised ready to strike. He let the tension build. His audience were quiet, waiting for Diponegoro's classic, lyrical farewell. Beside him the *gamelan* players, too, were silent and poised. With the strike of the mallet came a modern *ad-lib*, *'Merdeka!'* Freedom! The word voice boomed around the square as the gongs and drums rang out in crescendo. At first the audience were surprised by the startling break with tradition.

Behind the screen there was a flurry of movement before the *merah-putih*, the red-and-white nationalist flag of Indonesia, rose high on a bamboo pole. Suddenly the *dalang's* intention was clear. He began to chant, striking the mallet in time.

'Mer-de-ka!'—'Indo-ne-sia!'

Quickly the audience took up the chant. *'Mer-de-ka!'*

Lamban felt elated and cheered. A few began to sing 'Indonesia Raya'—'Greater Indonesia'—a song banned by the Dutch. Many more joined in.

In the midst of the tumult, Lamban was experiencing an eerie inner calm. Images of the valiant deeds and sacrifices of the *wayang* heroes filled his mind. He felt a new confidence and purpose surge through him. Lamban had glimpsed his destiny.

A day later, just after dusk, Lamban cycled to the narrow wooden bridge at the eastern end of his village. Karek was waiting with his bicycle, a long section of notched bamboo and two canvas bags. It was to be their last foraging expedition.

For some time they rode in silence along quiet lanes listening for Japanese patrols. It would take them about an hour to reach the outskirts of Semarang.

'Which one?' Karek asked excitedly.

'The school at Tjandi,' Lamban smirked. 'They won't expect us again so soon.'

Before long they were in open country and making quick progress on the narrow, raised banks of compacted earth between the neat *sawah*—flooded rice paddy—terraces that stretched for miles.

Lamban glanced skyward. The cloud cover was breaking up and shafts of moonlight were playing over the glass-like surfaces of the terraces. He pulled up. Ahead of them was the Garong river. It was about thirty yards wide at their chosen crossing point.

Carefully they hid the bikes in some bushes and then stripped. They put their clothes into the canvas bags and entered the river. Lamban went first, carrying the bamboo pole. The water reached their necks but it was slow moving and they crossed quickly. As they dressed they could see the lights of north Tjandi a few hundred yards away. To the south, the area around the former school was in darkness.

Lamban and Karek kept low, jogging alongside irrigation ditches for cover until they reached the first houses. Minutes later they were crouching at the foot of the high, woven-bamboo fence around the vegetable plots. From the bags they removed some bamboo pegs, a roll of twine, and a small jar. It took only a few seconds to fit the pegs into the pole to build a makeshift ladder and thread the twine through one end.

Without speaking Lamban stripped again. Karek opened the jar of palm oil and he began smearing him from head to toe.

Karek tapped his shoulder. 'Finished!'

Again Lamban looked up, hoping for more clouds but instead saw it was still clearing. 'I'll be about ten minutes,' he whispered. 'Keep your ears open!'

Karek propped the ladder against the fence.

Lamban climbed quickly, the twine coiled in one hand and one of the bags in the other. At the top he paused briefly then sprang forward. He landed cat-like on all fours, eyes sweeping left then right, his mouth slightly open to sharpen his hearing. Satisfied, he crept back to the fence. 'Now the ladder!' Quickly he stepped back taking up the slack in the rope and began to pull. He felt Karek lift it and seconds later the pole flicked high over the fence. Lamban caught it neatly and placed it along the base of the matting. Against the woven bamboo it was almost undetectable.

He had raided Tjandi Camp III several times, so he was familiar with the layout. Across the vegetable garden lay the first line of unlit huts. To his right was a guard tower, so he circled away from it, crouching and heading for the rear of the nearest hut. He made a mental note to take some peppers on his return.

Shadow at the backs of the huts gave ample cover and he quickly worked his way along. Windows were open and he could hear coughing and snoring. It would have been easy for him to sneak inside but he did not want food on this trip. Yet the first few huts were a disappointment and he was forced to work deeper into the camp.

As he peered around the back of the fifth hut he grunted in satisfaction. Strung between it and the next were rows of full washing lines. He darted among them and began to search. Some large, cumbersome western underwear caught his eye. He was amazed that a woman would wear such things. Next to it hung a frilly cotton blouse about Malini's size. His young sister would be pleased. Seconds later it was in his bag.

Throughout Java there was a shortage of clothing. No-one in Sadakan had a new shirt, *kembang* or sarong since the Japanese invasion. For everyday wear, Malini and the other girls wore sacking or reworked rags. Only the Dutch had extra clothing. In seconds he grabbed two more blouses and a checked bed sheet that would serve as a sarong. Just as he was reaching for another sheet there was a shout.

'Thief!'—'Help! He's taking our clothes!'

Two girls on a veranda were pointing. A commotion began in the huts.

'Swine!'—'Quick, let's get them!'—'Native bastards!'

Lamban ducked back quickly under the rows of washing. Only when he emerged at the edge of the camp's central square did he realise he had gone the wrong way. Cursing his carelessness, he rushed back. As he darted under the last row of sheets he found himself facing several women brandishing brooms and pans. Other women and children crowded the hut entrances and windows. When they saw he was young, naked and alone the women's confidence grew.

'Look! He's starkers!'—'Clara, go inside!'—'Hey, don't chase him away!'

Lamban knew that the guards would be coming to investigate. He let his shoulders slump dejectedly in apparent surrender.

Emboldened the women moved to encircle him, thinning out as they did so. His quick dart forward caught them by surprise. Hands grabbed at him but slipped off his oiled arms and torso. He sped towards the garden losing himself in the shadows. His pursuers were in no condition to give chase and he left them panting and swearing loudly into the night.

Lamban was back at the ladder and over the fence before the guards had even reached the first line of huts.

Guest House Berg, Semarang, April 1945

Beads of perspiration shone on the young man's close-cropped scalp. Below his white cotton headband his neck and shoulders glistened. His thin, sleeveless white vest was soaked at the small of his back and into the top of his thin white cotton loincloth. A ceiling fan whirred in a vain struggle against the heavy afternoon air. In truth he was oblivious to both the temperature and the noise. His angular features were stone-like as he knelt in total concentration at the low table.

The weasel-and badger-hair brush made steady, controlled progress up and down the handmade paper. In its wake, neat columns shimmered a slick black on the white background. Pausing briefly, the writer dipped the brush in a small, ceramic ink bowl before he began his closing paragraph.

> *I ask you to forgive this negligent son for not writing to you for many long months. You have all been in my thoughts each day. I dearly wish I could have helped you with the harvest this year. Please do not worry about me. I am keeping well and have many fine comrades. We are soon to face the enemy once again. Should anything happen to me do not grieve or mourn. If there are no more letters do not be distressed, for you will know I am discharging my duties faithfully. Good-bye.*
> *Your son, Kenichi.*

His hand came to a measured stop in the bottom left-hand corner of the page. Carefully he raised his forearm to disengage the brush cleanly from the paper then placed it gently, point up in a plain bamboo holder. He stared at the drying ink, hands lightly on his knees. His legs ached for he had been kneeling for over an hour. Again he willed himself to ignore the discomfort and re-examine his work. Finally, he exhaled heavily and sat back on his heels, then rolled his head to ease the stiffness in his neck. Around him crumpled sheets of paper lay scattered over the floorboards of his room. He had written the same letter six times but only on this last attempt had he been satisfied with his calligraphy. His gaze flicked to the oiled wrapping cloth that had protected the precious paper and envelopes for nearly three years. There was just one sheet left.

Lieutenant Kenichi Ota of the 16th Imperial Japanese Army had not expected his farewell to take so long to write. It did not concern him that millions of other young men had written the same prescribed phrases justifying their sacrifice. This last letter was all his family would have of him once his body was lost in the battle for Java. No fragment of his bones would rest in the family altar. He was twenty-four years old and a bachelor; no son or daughter would honour him during *O-Bon*, the annual Festival of the Dead.

Ota folded the paper neatly to fit the envelope that was already addressed to his father. He did not seal it because army censors would read it before his family, if they ever received it, for the enemy now controlled the seas and skies beyond Java. He knew he had delayed too long.

At the thought of the final stand his expression hardened. How strange fate had proved! It seemed like only yesterday that he was on the troopship watching the gun flashes from the great naval engagement over the night-time horizon. Their convoy had resumed its southerly course unopposed.

Before them lay the defenceless Indies, the Allied fleet already starting to rust at the bottom of the Java Sea.... Cheers of *Banzai!*—Ten thousand years!—had rolled from ship to ship over the gentle swell. Twenty-five thousand voices greeted the rising sun and saw it anoint the polished steel of their raised bayonets and swords. They had felt invincible—and so they had been. The Indies had fallen to them in nine days!

Now the tables had been turned. The coming Allied invasion meant his certain death. He hoped he would find the *zangyaku-sei*—the brutal, savage spirit—needed to die well and with honour. Yet every night doubts came to taunt him in his fitful sleep.

He sensed where his train of thought was taking him and he desperately tried to fight it but, once again, he failed. For the thousandth time he wondered whether he would die by bomb, bullet or bayonet. Images of the bloodied and maimed dead at Buitenzorg came back to him. He could still smell the cordite.... It had been the only heavy resistance, and his first experience of battle. Just five hundred Australians had held them, fighting tenaciously for two days. Then suddenly they had given up and thrown down their weapons, many reluctantly. He had felt sorry for them because they were good soldiers, shamed by the Dutch General who had ordered their surrender.... A sharp rap on the door made him jump.

'Ota! Ota! *Iru ka?*'—Are you in there?

He recognised the ever-cheerful voice and relaxed. *'Dozo, haite.'*—Please come in, he croaked. His mouth was dry.

Shinichi Nagumo, a fellow lieutenant and also his best friend, entered briskly. Nagumo was short and stocky with an easy, affable nature. They were both from Gunma, a prefecture north-west of Tokyo, where Nagumo's father owned a small sake brewery and Ota's father was a rice farmer.

Behind a pair of black, round-rimmed, military-issue glasses Nagumo's eyes flashed mischievously. His uniform was heavily patched. Harsh sun and monsoon rains had taken their toll on the thin green cotton. It had been two years since they last received new uniforms.

'I've been looking everywhere for you,' he said excitedly, hitching up his sword belt. The curved blade, protected by a leather-wrapped scabbard, was a family heirloom. It was also a little too long for him. Ota found the habitual motion amusing but his friend just shrugged it off, blaming taller ancestors.

Ota knew Nagumo had caught his gloomy expression and would have also guessed its cause. They had known each other far too long. Nagumo's friendship meant a great deal to him. Now, as the end neared, he knew he would need it even more. The two had first met at their university *kendo* club six years earlier but they had been only casual acquaintances. Ota was poorer than most of the other students and had shied away from their epic drinking, gaming and whoring. In contrast, Nagumo's enthusiasm for all three was legendary.

Nagumo whipped off his cap, eased his sword from behind him and dropped heavily onto a chair by the door, carefully keeping his boots on the matt that defined the shoes-on area of the room. He saw the envelope and writing set on the table.

'So you've written the damn thing at last! I did mine months ago.'

Ota did not answer.

Upon graduation, Ota's student deferment of conscription ended. Days later he had received the dreaded 'Red Paper' and instructions to report to the Toyama Military Academy in Tokyo. He discovered Nagumo was in the same intake. Basic training at Toyama had been brutal and harsh for the two provincials who had suffered discrimination and beatings from those who resented the growing numbers of conscripts in the once-elite officer class. Some mornings they had drilled with black eyes and ribs so painful they could hardly bear to stand straight. Not surprisingly the two had soon become firm friends.

The jibing had been silenced in the *kendo* hall. Both Ota and Nagumo were skilled fencers but Ota was exceptionally talented and well trained. There was a long martial arts tradition in his family, and his father had begun teaching him how to handle sword, spear and staff almost as soon as he could walk. The young Ota had proved a natural fencer, and a succession of school, municipal and prefectural *kendo* championships had eventually led to a bursary towards his university fees.

Nagumo was less skilful than Ota but was equally devoted. Though there was little between them in fighting spirit, Ota's technique would usually tell but not without Nagumo's dogged determination forcing Ota to use all his guile. In the tripping and throwing of the last-man-standing mêlées at Toyama, they were invariably the last two competitors. Their prowess led to a new, if grudging, respect at the Academy. The bullying had ceased.

Today, Nagumo was in far too good a mood to let Ota's depression affect him. 'Well now you can forget about it and come and get some exercise before dinner.'

Ota jumped up, embarrassed by his melancholy state. 'Yes, some *kendo* would be good.'

'*Baka!*'—Idiot! Nagumo said rolling his eyes in exasperation. 'I mean the Sakura! I haven't been for days. The girls will have forgotten me!' The Sakura Club was the most expensive of the three brothels for officers in the Central Java Military District.

Ota laughed, his mood lightening. 'Your name perhaps but surely not your tool!'

Nagumo smirked then looked at his watch gleefully. 'Anyway, Saito says they have white women working there again this week!' He paused. 'I expect they'll be a bit pricey.'

Ota frowned, 'How much is it now, anyway?'

Nagumo shot him a vexed look. 'We've stopped saving for retirement, remember? It doesn't matter. Anyway, you can't blame the whores. War's the best time for them to sell "Springtime" after all.'

'Yeah, you're right,' said Ota with an awkward nod. It had been weeks since he had visited the Otowa, another brothel.

Nagumo smiled. 'Good! We've got plenty of time but it'll be quicker to cut through "Little Holland" and catch the tram. Let's go!'

Ota's interest suddenly quickened. Little Holland was their nickname for the adjoining internment camp. He might catch a glimpse of the girl…. 'White women?' he replied, trying to sound casual. 'Are you sure?'

'Of course,' grinned Nagumo. 'Who knows, I might get to plough a blonde furrow before I die!'

Ota laughed and reached for his tunic and trousers, his mind in a pleasant turmoil.

They left the guesthouse and turned right to walk alongside the bamboo perimeter fence of the internment camp until it met the high, brick wall of the old school. Set in the brickwork was a narrow, wrought-iron gate, its original open-work floral design now augmented with barbed wire. A lone guard was squatting at the base of the wall, making the most of a thin band of shade. He was half-asleep and the two officers were upon him before he saw them.

Embarrassed, the guard jumped to attention, grabbing frantically for his rifle. Nagumo stood sternly and stared.

Colour drained from the guard's face. He was clearly expecting the worst.

'Pathetic!' Nagumo shouted haughtily. 'Do you call this doing your duty?' Only Ota caught the hint of teasing.

'*Sumimasen!*'—Please excuse me! '*Sumimasen!*' the guard blabbered in panic.

'I shall report you!' Nagumo bawled. 'Now open the gate!'

The hapless guard rushed to comply.

Once they were inside, Ota grinned. 'How long do you think it will be before he realises you didn't even ask him his name or unit?'

Nagumo guffawed. 'A couple of days at least. He'll be volunteering to wipe his sergeant's arse tonight!'

They walked on casually. When Ota noticed the bowing women and children his good humour left him. A few weeks before he would not have given them a second thought. Yet ever since the incident with the girl they had started to make him feel uncomfortable.

'Unnecessary,' he muttered.

'Eh?' Nagumo queried.

'Oh, er, I was thinking that imprisoning women and children is a waste of time.'

'You're right,' replied Nagumo misunderstanding him completely. 'Those *kenpei* would rather lock people up than help us build defences,' he said derisively. 'The guard units must be bored out of their minds. What a rotten job! Where's the honour in guarding women?'

Ota was looking for the girl. Since he had started taking the shortcut regularly he had seen her just three times. On each occasion she had been in a group. Apart from bowing she had given no hint of recognition whatsoever.

As they reached a small crossroads formed by the junction of four huts Nagumo stopped abruptly. 'Listen,' he said.

Ota heard the yells and the urgent ringing of bicycle bells before a pair of brightly painted pedal carts flashed past them. Each cart carried two boys, one steering with ropes and pedalling furiously, the other leaning out when necessary to balance the cart. Both drivers were screaming for people to make way. The two soldiers watched them until they turned a corner. Angry shouts sounded in the carts' wake.

Ota turned to Nagumo. 'Wow! They've made those!'

'Umm,' said Nagumo cheerfully. 'Maybe we could borrow them and hold a race day! Let's go and have a closer look.'

They followed the bells and shouts and after a quick search discovered the carts parked behind the main school building. Neither of them had ever been in this part of the camp before. The boys were nowhere in sight.

'This must have taken weeks to make,' said Nagumo impressed. 'It even has gears!'

'So has this,' said Ota looking at a low-slung cart equipped with larger wheels at the back than at the front. Two salvaged rattan chairs served as seats.

'Everything's cobbled together from other bicycles,' Nagumo added. 'They even found paint!'

Bursts of suppressed giggling interrupted them. Curious, they walked around the corner of the building to investigate. Jutting out from the wall was a semi-circular, latticed bamboo fence about six feet high. Four boys were standing or kneeling with their faces pressed to the bamboo. Ota and Nagumo approached them quietly. They heard women's voices behind the fence.

One of the boys glanced backwards. He jumped up, alerting the other three. In an instant they were lined up and bowing. Without thinking, Ota went to the fence and peered through. His eyes widened. Several women and girls were showering under a crude arrangement of bamboo piping and a line of pierced buckets. He was about to turn away when he saw the girl. She stood side-on, partly hidden by another woman. He tensed and pressed closer to the fence, willing the girl to move.

Suddenly the woman nearest Ota stepped out from under her shower and the girl started towards him, a ragged towel was draped over her shoulder. Ota caught his breath as she hung up the towel and stood naked before him, bathed in sunshine, less than three feet away. Her girl's arms and shoulders were tanned a deep, rich brown. In contrast, a band across her chest and was alabaster white. She pulled on a cord and water splashed over her. He saw her shiver slightly, her eyes were closed. His heart pounding, he stood mesmerised. Her hands moved to her face, channelling the water between her breasts. His eyes followed the tiny rivulets down over her belly to the second band of pale white skin across her hips and the patch of wispy blonde hair at the top of her thighs. He let the image burn itself in his memory.

From across the enclosure a dark-haired woman called cheerfully. 'Kate! Kate!'

The girl turned. 'Yes?'

'I'll give you a tin of Red Cross corned beef for the rest of your soap.'

'Sorry, Juliette. This is the first real soap I've had in a year! It was a present.'

'Kate, please! A Frenchwoman needs scented soap more than food!'

Ota smiled to himself. Her name was Kate....

'Sugoi na!'—Great! Nagumo muttered under his breath.

Ota shot a horrified glance down to his left. Nagumo's cap was askew and his face was pressed up to the fence.

His face reddening, Ota stepped quickly away, pulling Nagumo with him. The Dutch boys, still bowing, were now turning to look and giggle amongst themselves.

'What's up?' Nagumo was genuinely perplexed.

Ota struggled for words. 'It's—It's wrong to peep!'

'Eh?' Nagumo's jaw dropped. 'What do you mean? It's ages since I've had luck like this!' He looked longingly at the fence as if about to go back. Ota, desperate, moved in front of him.

'You know the Field Service Code. Japanese officers should set an example.'

Nagumo gave him a curious look. 'Well you watched happily for long enough! Any man would if he got the chance. In fact, I wouldn't want to serve with any who didn't!'

Ota tried to change the subject. 'All right. Look, we'll be late. Let's go.' He started to walk away.

Nagumo shared a sly grin with the boys then trotted to catch him up. 'They've the right idea, anyway,' he said casually, enjoying his friend's discomfort.

Ota glanced back and with not a little envy saw the boys were back at the fence. He wondered if Kate were still there....

Nagumo laughed. 'She was a peach wasn't she?'

Ota flushed but did not reply, so Nagumo kept quiet. They were out of the camp before he tried again. 'Ota-*kun*....'

'Yes?'

'Is peeping really against the Field Service Code?'

Ota whirled. 'You arsehole! Can't you drop it!'

Nagumo walked on, his shoulders shaking. Ota could not hold out for long and they were still laughing when they arrived at the Sakura.

The Army and Navy Club, Semarang

'*Kimochi ga ii na!*'—This feels so good! Nagumo said wearily. The water was up to his neck and very hot. Vapour hung in the air.

'Hmm,' replied Ota, not wanting to speak.

They were in a Japanese-style bathhouse in the garden of the Army and Navy Club. Upon their arrival in February 1942 the Japanese officers had found the lounges, dining room and well-stocked bar vacated by their Dutch counterparts much to their liking. Bathing facilities, however, were considered lacking until two homesick officers in an engineering regiment had constructed the bathhouse from bamboos and cypress. Around the walls small stools and buckets were stacked beneath taps for bathers to soap and rinse. Ten men could soak in the large, central square tub. The two engineer officers were long gone, lost to the Burma campaign, but their hot oasis remained.

From one of the club's lounges the words of 'Kantaro of Ina', a popular ballad, drifted out into the garden.

> *Under a brigand's haggard looks*
> *O Moon see my pure heart*
> *Reborn in the Tenyu waters*
> *Reflecting my radiant soul*

Ota settled back and closed his eyes. Except for the chatter of the two Javanese masseuses in the adjoining room, he could easily have been in Japan. His thoughts drifted back to the Sakura. Kiriko, the proprietress, had been having a slow day and had greeted Nagumo like a long-lost son. She was in her fifties, rosy cheeked and every inch the professional Madame. When the war had taken more than two-thirds of her regular customers to Southeast Asia, she had wasted little time in following them. The port city of Semarang had seemed a good location, and the recently 'vacated' Hotel Jansen, the perfect premises. A very grateful military had approved her quick acquisition of the hotel, which she renamed the *Sakurahana Kurabu*, the Cherry-blossom Club.

Ota chuckled as he remembered Nagumo's crestfallen look when Kiriko told him the white women had been moved to the city of Surabaya the day before.

'Nagu-*chan*,' Kiriko had soothed. 'What bad luck! Don't worry, they'll be back in a few weeks, I promise! But why think about them when we have so many beautiful Japanese girls here?' Her eyes sparkled mischievously and she nudged him. 'After all, you can tell them exactly what you want them to do!'

Nagumo had leant forward, lips pinched in mock anger. 'But I've spent hours learning those phrases in Dutch!'

Kiriko had been so amused that she had offered them an extra thirty minutes free of charge. Then, still chuckling, she had shown them through to a large, richly decorated room with a marble floor, ornate plaster work and a magnificent chandelier. Inside were twelve young women. Most were oriental but three were Eurasian and two were Javanese. They sat provocatively in easy chairs along one wall. All except the Javanese wore *yukata*, the light, colourfully patterned Japanese summer robe. Most held small fans which they flicked coquettishly.

Ota and Nagumo had greeted them with bows before sitting down opposite them. As usual, Ota had felt a little awkward but Nagumo seemed to know most of them by name and they him.

'Nagu-*chan*, where have you been? I haven't seen you for weeks!'—'You promised me some stockings!'—'Eh? He promised me stockings, too!'

Nagumo whispered in Ota's ear. 'Let's not waste time. Grab one!'

In the end, chided by his impatient friend, Ota had chosen Yuki. She had very long dark tresses and reminded him vaguely of a girl from his village. As she had led him confidently upstairs, Nagumo had bounded up after him with another girl, shouting that he would see him in an hour.

Yuki took Ota to a room with a large four-poster bed and cream silk sheets. In one practised movement she locked the door, switched on the ceiling fan and began to undress. He was aroused and he had moved to her quickly, pulling her down beside him on the bed. For a few moments he desired her until he saw her flinching. He pulled away from her and undid the sash around her waist, opening the robe. Her breasts, abdomen, inner thighs and pubis were dappled with bruises. His passion cooled abruptly as he wondered which of his fellow officers had beaten her.

Yuki had tried to urge him on but he had stilled her. Then resignedly she had asked him if he wanted a different girl. He had declined. Instead, he had held her loosely, content with running his fingers through her hair and savouring her scent. Hesitantly, he had begun to talk to her about his village and farm, and then about his family.

Intuition had told Yuki that her customer needed to share, so she had feigned interest. At his prompting, she had spoken of her own family in Korea, even telling him her real name, Kyoung-Suk, and that she was sixteen. That far, her story had been the truth. She did not tell him that a year earlier she had been in a group of girls recruited to work in a munitions factory in Japan. Only when their freighter had steamed southeast from Pusan had their 'employment agent' told them they were headed for Java.

Their journey had been a living hell. First they had been robbed and then every night they had been raped by the crew. Army procurers had been waiting for the terrified and now destitute girls at the Semarang docks. Fortunately for Kyoung-Suk, one of Kiriko's pimps had noticed her and outbid them. She had found out later that the other girls had been sent straight to the field brothels in Malaya and Burma, where they were serving thirty or more men a day, while they lasted.

Kiriko had saved her life, then trained her and given her a new identity. For that, at least, she was thankful. Within a few months Kyoung-Suk had saved enough to pay off Kiriko and buy a ticket back to Pusan. But by then the voyage had become too dangerous. Her Navy clients had let slip that American submarines were sinking their ships with impunity. So she had kept working and saving, praying for the war to end and a chance to go home.

'I'm here to help my family,' she had lied, knowing that if she were ever to be her parent's daughter again she would have to take her dark secret to the grave.

Movement disturbed Ota. He half-opened his eyes to see Nagumo climbing out, heading for a massage. 'I hope the Americans don't invade tomorrow,' he grunted, shattering Ota's reverie. 'I can hardly move!'

Two other officers sharing the bath laughed. Ota said nothing as he was reminded yet again that his time was fast running out. He banished the thought by recalling his first sight of the girl he now knew as Kate. He had been shaving when he had heard someone humming a pleasant melody. Curious, he had glanced out to see a pretty, if rather thin, blonde hanging out clothes.

Two more young women had joined her and she had shown them some tomatoes, obviously pleased with them. He saw the girl 'salute' the washing line 'flag'. Her wit and inventiveness had amused rather than angered him. The girls' relaxed laughter had been refreshing. Suddenly she had glanced up. He had stared back, held by her sparkling eyes. Then her face had paled in fear.

Hurt followed by anger had been his initial reactions. How could he have let a scowl from a prisoner rile him? But the blatant theft and something else, a challenge in her look, had left him unsettled. That same night he had resolved, somehow, to make amends.

Nagumo, prostrate under the fast, pummelling hands of the masseuse, let out a deep groan of pleasure.

Ota shifted in the hot water, easing his body but not his mind. With an effort he forced a change in his train of thought. Today had been a very good day. At last he knew her name. And he had seen her naked! He pictured the water running down her body....

'Oi!'

Ota opened his eyes. 'Um? What?'

Nagumo was peering down at him. 'I said, let's have a drink.'

'Oh, right, sorry, I was miles away.'

Chapter Three

Mainly for the sake of her mother, Kate had made light of the theft of her tomatoes, though now she picked the fruits before they were fully ripe. Her distress that day still troubled her but she had accepted Dr Lucy Santen's diagnosis of 'Tjandi shakes', her all-embracing diagnosis for the hundreds of minor neuroses on daily display. Kate was soon back to her routine of garden, then *mandi*, then kitchen.

One morning, a week after the theft, Kate went to tend her plants as usual. Surreptitiously she glanced up at the guesthouse window. As always now, the curtain was closed. She had not seen the young Japanese at the window since that day and assumed he no longer had the room. When she had recognised him walking through the camp she had not dared look at him. During the first few morning roll-calls she had waited a little apprehensively for the summons and punishment for her prank and her defiant stare. And yet for all her anxiety, something told her that he would not report her. There had been something about him....

Kate stopped as she almost trod on a small, knotted sack lying at the edge of her plot. Her first thought was that another early bird gardener had dropped it. Curious, she knelt and untied the knot. Inside were two tins of sardines and a bar of soap. She squealed in delight then caught herself. Nervously she looked round once again, scarcely believing her luck. Who had dropped it, she wondered? A careless smuggler in the night? As casually as she could manage, she buried the tins near one of her plants. She considered what she was doing. Did she feel guilty? Someone had lost a great treasure—but she had found one! That was all that mattered. 'It's mine now,' she said under her breath.

Before she left her plot, she made a point of re-tying and placing the sack exactly where she had found it in case the unlucky smuggler returned. Then, almost skipping with joy, she left the garden and went to the *mandi*. In the evening she returned to unearth one of the tins and found the sack was still there, apparently untouched. The next day it had gone.

Four days later she found another sack, this time deep amongst her plants. At first she supposed that it was the same one but as soon as she lifted it she could tell there was something inside. There were others working in the garden, so Kate knelt while she took a quick peek inside. As well as a tin of fish there were two small bottles, one of vitamin C, the other half-full of sulphonamide anti-infection tablets.

Kate was stunned. Vitamin C was valuable enough but the sulphonamide were worth their weight in gold. Nervously she looked around, certain now that she was intercepting goods meant for someone else. A sudden, chilling thought came to her. What if it were a trap set by the guards? It had been done before….

Punishment for smuggling was a shaved head, a public beating and a week in the cells. Kate shivered at the thought of it but even as she weighed the risk she was pocketing the bottles and burying the tin of fish. She left the garden quickly. For the rest of the day and night she was on edge, waiting for the sudden inspection by the guards. It did not happen. Gradually she allowed herself to relax.

A few days later another sack appeared. And so it went on. Her mystery benefactor regularly left tins of fish or meat and fruit. Every three weeks there would be sulphonamide or vitamin C and a small bar of soap.

Extra food and medicines brought quick results. Within days, her mother's condition had markedly improved. Kate herself also felt stronger and fitter. Over the weeks her hair regained its lustre, her nails stopped splitting and her gums stopped bleeding. More dramatic proof came when she had her first period for three months.

Slowly Kate dared to dream that she might survive Tjandi. She did not question her good fortune. For a while she convinced herself that one of her father's former employees had followed them to Semarang and was sneaking food into the camp. But the tins carried Japanese labels and this fact troubled her. She came to the uncomfortable but inescapable conclusion that the gifts were left by a camp guard, one of the Javanese administrators or one of the hated military police, the *kenpeitai*. Only they could come and go as they wished. Though she tried to put it out of her mind one night it was apparent that her mother's curiosity was returning along with her strength.

'But who's it from, Kate?' Marianne asked quietly.

Kate hesitated. 'Oh, one of Dad's workers.'

'Who?'

'I don't know....' Kate replied, truthfully.

'You must have some idea,' Marianne persisted.

'No. Whoever it is sneaks in at night'.

Marianne looked imploringly at her daughter, her eyes brimming with tears. 'Promise me, Kate. Tell me you're not doing what Inge did....'

Inge Witsen was the wife of a Dutch airman. In the chaos of the invasion her husband had escaped to Australia but had left his new bride. A delicate, fastidious woman, Inge had been unwilling to face the camp's deprivations. When one of the guards had offered her extra food in exchange for sexual favours, she had accepted. In late 1944, Inge had given birth to a healthy Dutch-Japanese baby boy. Ostracised by many, Inge remained unrepentant and eventually went to live with the guard. 'They are quick to judge me, Kate,' Inge had once said to her. 'But they are also quick to die. I will not be buried here as a reward for following their rules!'

As the food shortages worsened and sickness and the number of deaths began to rise, other women had accepted similar proposals. Kate had sworn that she would never let Inge's fate befall her. Yet now she knew her own life and that of her mother depended on the extra supplies. She was trapped and would not, could not, give them up. Sooner or later she would have to pay the price.

Marianne was staring at her, waiting.

'No, Mother,' Kate said trying but failing to meet her mother's gaze. 'I'd never do that.'

Increasingly, Kate found herself watching the Japanese for a sign of recognition. Often she was rebuked or slapped for her arrogance in daring to look them in the eye.

The women of Tjandi had given the guards nicknames such as 'Sloppy', 'Specs Jap', 'Flatfoot' and 'Dopey'. 'Small Whacker' or 'Big Whacker' were two who were particularly violent. The one who helped himself to their vegetables was 'Johnny Tomato'. Collectively they were referred to as 'Japs', 'Nips' or 'the Bastards'.

Once Kate had felt forced to take a serious interest in the guards, she had been surprised at the physical differences among them. Not all were Japanese; some were Korean or Formosan Chinese. Most were short but not all. She had been amazed at the range in their facial features and skin tones. From observation and experience she knew they were not all brutes, especially when they were alone. One or two had even been known to turn a blind eye and let the women eat from the crops while working in the fields. Nearly all of the guards seemed to like small children. But when a child misbehaved, they almost always punished the mother, usually with a beating.

Try as she might, Kate could not understand these men who treated them so callously and with such contempt. The thought of having to give herself to one of them depressed her more each day. Jokes about the guards rang hollow and she listened uncomfortably to bitter gossip and insults about women kept by Japanese. Inge's defiant words continued to haunt her.

Gradually, Kate became obsessed by the need to discover the identity of her benefactor. A solution came to her while she was burying the food tins; she would hide in the vegetable garden and see who it was. For three days she was on tenterhooks. Then, finally, the night came. After lights out at eight o'clock she joined the steady streams of people heading for the latrines. On her way back she slipped unobserved behind the hut and ran quickly to the vegetable garden. She settled down behind a tall patch of peppers opposite her plot to wait. She prayed she wouldn't see any snakes or rats. The sky was clear and she decided to pass the time and ignore the mosquitoes by naming the constellations. But her mind played tricks on her. All she could visualise were the faces of the guards and *kenpei*.

Kate had compiled a list of her 'preferred suitors'. Her first choice was a guard in his mid-thirties who was often on duty by the main gate. She thought of him as her 'older man'. He was well groomed and always had time for the toddlers. Kate liked that and thought he had kind eyes, a little like those of the young officer.... She cast a glance at the window of the guesthouse. There was no light visible.

'Kate van Dam,' she said aloud, 'if the nuns at school could see you now!' With an effort she moved on to 'Number Two'. He was a much younger guard, perhaps no more than twenty, who regularly supervised the preparation of food in the Japanese kitchen. He always looked bored but he was never violent.

There were eight more men on the list but Kate had to admit that there was not much going for numbers three to ten. Then there was her other list. All those on it frightened her, for it was a list of the most brutal and callous. One truly scared her. That was Shirai, the *kenpei* major who always seemed to take great pleasure in the punishment beatings. She had often noticed him staring at her and other girls when he carried out the snap searches for hidden radios and 'spies'. There were also rumours he visited women in the punishment cells.

A soft scuffling sound made her duck and tense but it was only guards on their rounds in their rubber-soled boots. They passed the entrance every hour but never ventured into the garden. Kate began to nod off.

Just before dawn a soft rustling roused her. Kate's hair stood on end. At last, she thought, it's him! She held her breath as a shadowy form darted from plot to plot. When the figure finally stepped from the bushes and turned towards her, Kate was stunned. It was Anna! In dismay she watched her friend stealing half-grown green beans and red peppers. Anna left as quietly as she had come.

Upset now, Kate waited. By sunrise insect bites were all that were keeping her awake. Birds were singing and cicadas were chirping. It was time to go back to the hut. Tired, disappointed and stiff, she started to get up.

A moving curtain at the guesthouse stilled her. It was the young officer. Kate was happy somehow in knowing he was still there. She stayed hidden as the window opened and he climbed out on to a small balcony. He wore only a white loincloth and began some push ups and stretches.

For some time Kate watched him a little wistfully. She was about to leave when he stopped exercising and reached inside his room. When he turned back he was holding a sack! Kate's heart skipped a beat. Hardly daring to breathe she watched him hold it over the balcony, gauging its weight as it swung, then let go. The sack landed with a soft thud in the middle of her plot.

Kate was almost giddy with relief, her pulse racing. She could only stare open mouthed. After a few more cursory stretches the officer climbed back into his room and closed the curtain almost to. It occurred to Kate that it was timed for just before her usual visit to the garden. He had probably watched her take the food and bury it every time!

For a moment she tried telling herself that since the officer had nothing to do with the camp he could expect nothing from her but she knew her reasoning was faulty. She reminded herself guiltily that she would be his sex slave not his lover. This thought sobered her until she remembered the weeks of worry and sleepless nights over the men it could have been. She suppressed a shudder. No, she decided calmly, she was very fortunate... But what now?

She walked to her plot wondering what to do. On a whim she looked deliberately at the window then bowed formally. Then, without looking back, she buried the tins and left the garden.

Up in his room Ota was reeling. Kate's appearance had left him stunned. Elation and embarrassment surged through him in equal measure. In the end he had done nothing and peeped as she hid the food. How long had she known?

He began pacing around his room. 'I must be out of my mind,' he said aloud. Now the secret was shared the danger to them both was doubled. If Kate were ever caught with the food he had no doubts the *kenpei* would quickly force her to talk. That meant certain execution for him but what of her?

Gradually he calmed down. He had considered the consequences weeks before. It doesn't matter, he thought. One way or another his own life was forfeit. He accepted that as a matter of course but he found it ironic that in trying to help Kate he was also endangering her.

Why am I being so reckless? Because of a few tomatoes and a pretty girl's tears? In frustration he kicked out at a chair. *'Kuso!'*—Shit!

His expression softened as he imagined another desperate, crying girl. Would the gods heed his prayers, he wondered, and move an American soldier to do the same for Haruko when the battle for Japan was over? He would never know.

Lucy Santen noticed the steady improvement in Kate's health and often asked her to help with the night rounds in the infirmary. The twelve beds and forty mattresses were usually the last stop for the sick before the cemetery. Circumstances had forced Lucy to extend the ward so that it took up the entire top floor of one wing of the old school building.

It was unpleasant and tiring work but Kate made the best of it. The only perk for her and the other helpers was being able to sleep on the brick parapet between the school's towers. It was cooler than down in the huts, much cleaner and almost insect free.

Juliette was the other regular. As they scrubbed floors and washed sheets they spent the time speaking in French and English, correcting each other along the way. Talking about the camp was not allowed. Instead, they fantasised about shops and restaurants in Paris, Amsterdam, London and

New York. They became very close friends, sharing confidences and some of Kate's extra food. The one thing Kate kept from Juliette was the source of the bounty.

'*Je suis fatiguée*,' Juliette sighed as she lugged her mattress on to the parapet. 'I keep thinking I can't get any more tired but I do.'

Kate did not reply straight away. She was pensive, sitting and looking at the thick blanket of grey clouds. Two more young children had died that day. Her gift of medicines had made no difference.

'When I'm up here,' Kate said gazing up at the sky. 'I know I'm higher than the fence. Higher even than the guards in the watchtowers. I feel free of them. Do you think that's silly?'

'Not at all,' Juliette answered with a yawn. 'We all need to escape somehow.'

There was a brief break in the cloud cover. Kate watched the moonlight playing on the smooth, neat roof-tiles of the school and nearby houses.

'Oh, it's so humid,' sighed Juliette, pulling her slip over her head and standing naked. 'There! Tonight I sleep like a mistress on the Rîve Gauche!'

Kate giggled. 'Juliette! The guards might see you and get ideas! Have you no shame?'

Juliette gave a shrug and sat down beside Kate. 'Shame? About my body? *Non*.' She looked at Kate mischievously. 'I'll tell you a secret. When I was a poor student in Paris I helped pay for my tuition and rent by dancing at parties. I mean private parties for men. I danced the "Seven Veils". Do you know what I mean?'

Kate's mouth opened in surprise. 'Striptease!'

'Certainly not! Juliette huffed, pretending to be affronted. 'I was an *artiste*, I "interpreted" ancient dances!'

'Oh, I didn't mean…,' Kate floundered.

Juliette tittered, rocking back holding her knees with her hands. 'Oh Kate, you're so innocent! I started posing for painters when I was fourteen. But painters never have money, only passion. Those dinner parties paid very well and I met some wonderful and generous lovers!'

Kate, still a little uncomfortable with Juliette's carnal candour, reddened slightly. Her gaze went to the floor. 'Juliette…' she said hesitantly. 'When you were my age, had—had you already…?'

'Oh, la la!' Juliette laughed again but not at Kate. 'I was sixteen. He was forty. A painter of course! We were lovers for two years then he moved to a Pacific island, thinking he was another Gauguin. I stayed in Paris. You never forget the first! Even now the smell of oil paint affects me!'

They both laughed. Then Juliette looked pityingly at Kate. 'I feel so sorry for you little Kate. So young and pretty and stuck in here. Has there been anyone? A boy at school? A Javanese prince perhaps?'

Kate blushed a little and lowered her head. 'No, never….'

'Oh, my poor Kate,' whispered Juliette. She reached out and stroked Kate's cheek tenderly. 'All we can do here is dream.'

Kate tried to change the subject. 'What do you dream of?'

'Food, then love of course!'

They both laughed again. Then Juliette looked at Kate questioningly.

'And you, quiet, secret Kate. What is your dream?'

Kate blushed a much deeper red.

'Aha!' Juliette smiled. 'Love then food! Tell me quickly, who do you dream of?'

Kate tensed, embarrassed under Juliette's scrutiny. Her need to confide in someone was suddenly very strong. 'I— He's a soldier. I never see his face,' She did not want to lie but knew she had to. What will Juliette say, she agonised, if I confess to her that the face is Japanese?

'Oh, I understand your dream!' Juliette declared warmly. 'You want a knight in shining armour to ride up to the castle and save you from the evil Japanese dragon!'

'Yes, that must be it,' Kate whispered, forcing a smile. During the day, Kate could almost convince herself that the Japanese officer was her enemy as well as her gaoler, and that she was taking from him without obligation. But at night her thoughts were different. In the moments before sleep she could not hate him.

Juliette sighed and leaned towards her. '*Bonne nuit, ma petite.*'

Kate lifted her cheek for the kiss. Instead, she felt Juliette's moist, open lips brush her own. Before she could react, Juliette rolled away to curl up on her own mattress.

Kate lay down, unsettled, looking at Juliette's perspiration-dotted back and telling herself that the kiss was an accident. No-one had kissed her that way before, not even Pete Muiden. It was, she thought, the way a man would kiss....

She looked at Juliette again but saw from the easy rise and fall of her shoulders that she was already asleep. Kate stared up at the stars but she found no peace. A cool, moist trace of the kiss remained on her lips. Guiltily she slid her tongue to it, willing the sensation to return. She closed her eyes, picturing herself with him in a place far away where there was no war.

Chapter Four

L amban awoke just before dawn, eager to start his most important day. He slipped quietly out of the house and took the dusty track towards the main road that ran about a mile away from the village. It was almost light when he reached the road, so he waited cautiously listening for vehicles. At that time of the morning a patrol was unlikely but the Japanese were getting increasingly nervous about spies and he did not want to have to explain his movements to the *kenpei.*

The road was clear so he darted across and was soon on the narrow trail to Taruna's home and workshop. It was still gloomy in the forest but he made good time. He had taken the trail several times a week for over ten years, often before and after classes at the *pesantren.* Today he would bid Taruna farewell.

For Lamban's father, entrusting his rebellious, temperamental young son into another's care had been a last resort. He had held little hope in life for such a restless, obstinate boy, so he had gambled. Taruna was an enigma, part-Javanese, part-Sumatran with more than a sprinkling of Chinese blood. Respected yet feared, many believed him to inhabit the twilight world of spirits and demons. For Taruna was a *djago*—master—of *pentjak-silat* combat. He was also a famous *empu*—a swordsmith—whose blades were among the most sought after in Java. When Taruna had accepted Lamban as a student his father had been hugely relieved, if sceptical. Yet from that first day the boy had been more afraid of those piercing eyes and sharp tongue than any thrashing from Maralik at the *pesantren*. Now the boy had become a man and he respected no-one more than Taruna.

Lamban settled into a steady, ground-covering run. After a few minutes he was surprised to hear the clash of bamboo staves and shouts. He lengthened his stride, wondering how he could be late on this special day! Yet as the last bend came into view he sensed something was not right. Mere instinct was enough. In mid-step he dropped and rolled into the thick vegetation beside the trail.

He lay still, then slowly eased himself up to scan the trail ahead. When he saw nothing unusual he closed his eyes, straining his ears. Everything seemed calm. Stealthily he crept forward, pausing every few yards, peering ahead. A tiny movement on a tree branch caught his eye. A second twitch revealed it as a human foot. He glanced upwards and saw a large fishing net strung over the trail. Trying not to laugh, he relaxed and let his breath out slowly. His fellow students had so nearly caught him! I'll let them wait, he thought. Then the thought struck him that this might be part of the *talmat*, the martial test that he was to take that day.

A few seconds later his patience was rewarded when a face bobbed up from behind some hibiscus bushes. Another one! Lamban thought, pleased with himself. Quickly he foraged two lengths of thin creeper and a piece of rotten root. Then he began to steal behind his ambushers. When he reached the one in the tree, he tossed the root back down the trail. As it caught in branches and rustled leaves, he looped the creeper over the twitching foot, tying it lightly.

The second ambusher was lying prone, under a bush. At his side was a bamboo stave. Deftly, Lamban slid another piece of creeper around his ankles and fastened it to a thick, exposed root. As he backed away, Lamban slid the stave out of reach. Smirking he crept back, then cupped his hands to his mouth. Angry grunts of a male wild boar shattered the forest silence.

Reaction was instantaneous. Leaf monkeys and gibbons screeched and squawking birds took to the wing. As the figure in the tree tried to scramble higher Lamban gave a sharp tug on the creeper. A youth was left dangling and wailing. Further away there was a howl of pain as a second youth jumped up and then tripped. Jubilant, Lamban moved forward to see who had tried to best him. A second later his body stiffened in a numbing, dizzying paralysis. He fell.

When Lamban regained consciousness he was lying in semi-darkness on a reed-mat floor. An earthenware water jar was close to his face. It was vaguely familiar, as were the sounds of the class practising outside. His head was fuzzy. As he tried to move a stab of pain ran down his back. He groaned sharply. A flash of sunlight made him squint as the door swung open. Through the glare he recognised a pair of legs and heavily calloused feet.

'Fool!' The man scolded. 'You celebrated too soon. What have I spent ten years drumming into you?'

Despite the reprimand there was warmth in the voice. Lamban tried to move but could not. Taruna noticed his discomfort and squatted behind him. Hard, bony fingers sank deep into Lamban's neck probing for nerve points. In an instant the fuzziness and stiffness vanished allowing Lamban to roll on to his knees and touch his forehead to the floor in a respectful greeting.

'Good morning, Master. I—'

'Could have been dead,' quipped Taruna sharply. 'Run through some *djuru* to loosen up.' *Djuru* were the martial practise sequences or forms. 'I hit you a little harder than I

86

intended. Drink some water but eat nothing for the rest of the day.'

'Yes, Master.'

As he was leaving Taruna turned and pointed to the darkest corner of the hut. 'There is something else. There are three ingots over there. Pick up each one and drop it on the hearth. Choose the one which calls to you. Place it outside.' He closed the door behind him and semi-darkness returned. Outside Lamban heard the other students began drilling again.

Lamban took a long drink from the jar and padded gingerly across the hut. His excitement soared when he saw the ingots that would become sacred *keris* daggers. Tradition required that the recipient of a blade chose the steel by the sound it made when struck. Lamban could hardly believe his good fortune. Taruna was going to make him a *keris*!

He sat cross-legged and stared at the ingots. All three were a very similar dark, grey-black. He lifted and felt the surface of each but was unable to feel any difference in weight or texture. For a moment he was tempted to examine them in more light but then dismissed the notion guiltily. His Master would know.

Unsure of what to do, he picked up an ingot quickly and then let it fall. There was a sharp clang. He did it twice more but to his dismay the other two blocks sounded much the same. Telling himself he was rushing, he took some deep breaths. He closed his eyes and took hold of the first ingot again, holding it at arm's length. He dropped it. Again it sounded dull. The second was almost the same. Anxiously he picked up the third. After a slight hesitation he let it drop. It landed end down on the centre of the hearth stone. A clean, metallic tone enveloped him, resonating deep within his chest.

Outside he examined his choice. Sunlight was reflecting off thousands of tiny bright flecks in the metal. Lamban placed it down by the hut entrance hut and began his solitary practice session.

By late morning he was on edge. When the other students paused for a sparse meal of rice and fruit, he excused himself saying he could not watch them eat. In truth he could not bear their chit-chat. He wandered over to Taruna's main living hut which stood on thick, wooden pillars about four feet off the ground. Much of Lamban's early *harimau*—'tiger' or ground-level—training had taken place under this hut. Here he had learned balance control and how to step, slide and spin in the low stances. How he had hated it. For months his skull had ached and his shoulders had been rubbed raw from the constant banging and scraping against the teak boards above. He had despaired of ever being able to match the smooth movements of the other boys, yet his desire to improve had never faltered. Just as one technique had become familiar Taruna would introduce another. Perpetual challenge was blended with progress imperceptible to the student but not to the master. Now, some ten years later and almost fully grown, he could move under the hut almost as easily as boys half his size.

On a whim, he ducked under once again to practise several forms, his hair just brushing the floor planks. Satisfied, he sat by one of the pillars for a rest. Memories of his early training returned. At first he had done nothing except dig Taruna's latrine pits, milk and water his goats and pull up clump after clump of elephant grass to help build up his weak thigh muscles. He still ran errands for his teacher. It occurred to him that he had never discussed his leaving with his master. Yet already another student had gathered the fruit for the midday meal, and the pots and pans in Taruna's hut had been washed and stacked. For a moment he felt a little sad about being replaced so smoothly until he reminded himself how long he had been waiting for this day.

Around noon, after the arrival of some senior students who would be Lamban's sparring partners, the *talmat* began. Taruna started slowly, testing him on single punches, kicks and rolls. This was followed by sequences with one, and then two opponents. When Taruna signalled for the advanced forms at full speed and power all levity ceased.

Lamban felt the adrenalin surge, knowing that this was no crowd-pleasing display for a local festival. It was *buah*, the lethal, hidden essence of *pentjak-silat*. At Taruna's command fists, elbows, knees and feet flew at Lamban in a blur. He moved quickly and economically to block, spin, dodge and weave, never allowing more than one opponent to face him at a time. His kicks, jabs and throws blended seamlessly. In seconds the four students lay sprawled at his feet. Taruna, his expression deadpan, pointed solemnly to the racks of practice-weapons. 'Now the staffs.'

For more than an hour Lamban demonstrated staff, short trident, dagger, spear and other weapons forms against single, then multiple opponents. Finally, in mid-afternoon, Taruna asked the others to leave.

Lamban was drenched in perspiration, his breathing heavy but controlled. His performance so far had been flawless but his nervousness returned as Taruna began stretching and flexing. He sensed the enormous gulf in their skills. Suddenly there was no doubt in Lamban's mind that he would lose his next contest.

Taruna signalled he was ready; his face was expressionless. Lamban felt the cobra-like eyes fix upon him. Master gave student the traditional salute to an opponent, palms pressed together then rolling his right hand in a fist brushing his left palm. It was a prayer for peace yet also a display of the steel required for battle.

Lamban saluted in the same manner and waited. To his surprise the onslaught never came. Instead, Taruna began slowly, as he might have done with a novice. The *talmat* evolved into a priceless lesson in Lamban's own weaknesses. Each time Taruna struck home or left him helpless, he repeated the attack until Lamban saw and learned from his mistake.

The sun was setting when Taruna selected two straight *klewang* swords from a different weapons rack. Each blade was about three-feet long, with a crescent-shaped tip and slightly narrower at the hilt than at the point. They were razor sharp.

Taruna handed one to Lamban and came on guard. Lamban's pulse began to surge. He had never performed the *buah* form using a live blade with a partner. At full speed, the slightest error would leave one of them maimed or dead.

Taruna circled, then launched a whirling attack. Even though he knew the pattern by heart Lamban had never had to perform it so quickly. They darted forward and back, spinning and leaping as they slashed, thrust and parried. Again and again he felt the draft from Taruna's blade on his face and heard the deadly swoosh of steel inches from his head and neck. Suddenly Taruna was still, facing him, his sword in the final guard position. Amazed, Lamban saw that he, too, was in perfect position. The *talmat* was over. He had no conscious recollection of the sequence. His movements, drilled to become second nature, had been unthinking, mirroring his master.

Taruna let him recover for a few seconds. 'You did not disappoint me, Lamban, as I expected. Now we must bathe before the ceremony. Come.'

Lamban was experiencing such an intense inner calm that the words reached him like a distant, muted shout. He watched Taruna pick up a bag and then push through some bushes. Lamban followed and found himself at the top of a steep, overgrown track. After a few minutes he heard sound of rushing water.

At the base of a narrow gully, half-hidden by a lush growth of orange rhododendrons and trees wrapped in strangler figs stood an almost circular pool. One wall was sheer exposed rock from which water spouted in a graceful arc several feet above their heads. Lamban was amazed. Taruna was kneeling at the side of the pool filling small bottles. He gestured to Lamban to bathe.

Lamban slipped off his sodden clothes and waded into the thigh-deep water. It came from the depths of the earth and was icy cold. He braced as the waterfall struck him like a thousand needles, pounding his body. Refreshed and calmed, he stepped out of the pool.

Taruna stood and undressed. Lamban had never seen him naked before. Though he was very thin, tight bands of muscle covered his small frame. Across his back was a patchwork of scar tissue. Lamban had heard the tale that in his youth Taruna had been imprisoned for rebellion.

As the water cascaded over him, Taruna closed his eyes and began to recite the *inat*, the act of contrition of the faithful. '*Nawaitu raf'al hadast shaghirata...Allah akbar.*'—I shall wash away my venial and mortal sins for the sake of the Creator. God is most great!

For a few moments Taruna stood in contemplation, then climbed out. 'Now we will enter the cave,' he said softly. He emptied the bag. It contained a clean, plain white sarong and headscarf for them both. Lamban bent to gather up their dirty clothes but Taruna bade him not to touch them. Then they set off back up the path.

Years before, Lamban and the other children had often dared each other to enter the Cave of Dreams. Rumours of ghosts and monsters had always sent them fleeing in terror. Even now he was apprehensive over what might occur inside.

The cave mouth was a low, jagged slit barely wide enough for a man. Taruna squeezed through. Lamban followed and found himself bent double in a narrow, dark tunnel. Immediately he smelt the faint aroma of sandalwood. His fingers reached out and he realised the limestone walls had been chipped smooth. Gingerly he went forward, feeling a cold, cobbled mass of cave pearls under his feet. As children they had believed they were treading on the tail of a sleeping *naga*, the sacred, giant river serpent. None of them had ever gone further.

After a few feet the tunnel turned sharply and Lamban found he could stand. Ahead an orange glow was flickering on the walls. Another sharp turn, this time to the left, led him into a roughly rectangular cavern about twenty feet square. In the centre Taruna was tending a freshly lit fire.

Shielding his eyes from the glare of the flames, Lamban looked around him. Many centuries before the walls had been hewn smooth, firstly by ice, then by water, and lastly by man. Stone and bronze statues of Vishnu, Kali, Shiva, Garuda and the Buddha were dotted around the cave, as were huge clam shells and spectacular conches. Freshly dug ferns and banyan sprigs had been placed in the four corners. As his vision adjusted, he saw that the walls were covered in images from Hindu scriptures, the life of the Buddha and Koranic verses in Arabic. Higher up were coloured handprints and ancient depictions of mousedeer, stick-like human figures and what looked like a rhinoceros. Lamban felt the eyes of all the gods of all the ages upon him. He shivered.

Taruna sat cross-legged on a mat of woven reeds. Beside him was Lamban's ingot His eyes were closed and he was chanting verses in a language unfamiliar to Lamban. Behind him was a low mound of layered white cloth. Over these were strewn the slender, pearl white petals of the *wijaya kusuma*, the holy coronation flower.

Fascinated, yet ill at ease, Lamban watched his Taruna take pinches of powder and crystals from some tin bowls and ground them in an earthenware mortar.

Taruna raised the dish, smelt the concoction and added a small silver coin to the mixture. Using tongs he placed the dish on a stand in the centre of the fire. In seconds the flames turned from orange to a cold, wispy green. A pungent scent of incense permeated the cave.

Taruna beckoned him to sit on the cloths, then leant forward and hung a small, intricately woven ring of edelweiss over Lamban's left ear. He paused, closed his eyes and then began the invocation of the *Wirid*, the teachings that fused animist, orthodox and mystical tenets into the vast spiritual pantheon that was the *Ke-Jawan*. 'As the Holy One whispered in the left ear of Sayidina Ali, open your mind to the True Divine Revelations of the *Hidayat Jati.*'

The air was heavy. Suddenly Lamban was short of breath and perspiring heavily. He began to feel dizzy.

Taruna was speaking in a low, hypnotic monotone. *'Surengpati…'*—Unafraid of death….

Lamban was having difficulty concentrating. Taruna sounded distant. Through half-closed eyes he watched him pick up a small glass vial and anoint him with drops of oil on his chest and arms. A thick floral scent filled his nose and throat. He tried to speak but could not.

In slow, deliberate movements Taruna raised burning incense first to Lamban's left ear, then to his nose and finally to his chest, pausing each time to recite. 'Fire, earth, wind and water. *Keris manjing waranga.*' A sheathed keris is as the soul within the body.

Carefully he placed a necklace of intertwined strands of betel palm and banana leaves around Lamban's neck. *'Margasupana…'*—Open to the spirits….

Lamban could barely hear Taruna. His eyelids became heavy....

Only embers remained of the fire when Lamban awoke. For a few moments he had no recollection of where he was or the purification ritual. Light from a small serpent-shaped oil lamp guided him to the tunnel and, still groggy, he crawled to the cave mouth. Darkness had fallen but the full moon bathed the forest in a soft, silver light. Revived by the fresh air Lamban hurried back along the trail. Soon he heard the clanging of a hammer on metal. Taruna was already at work.

The open-sided forge cast a red glow far across the clearing. When Taruna saw him he pointed to a set of foot-operated bellows. Lamban had never dared enter the workshop before. Despite a steady breeze he felt the sticky heat engulf him. He looked around. A massive slab of teak serving as a work surface ran across the floor. Several anvils were set into it at intervals. Around them were scattered hammers and chisels of different shapes and sizes. Along one wall, half-finished daggers, swords and machetes lay in small piles. A steady stream of cold water poured from a bamboo pipe into a trough in which floated a single, white coronation bloom.

Taruna came over to him and took hold of his right arm, straightening it out to measure by tying knots in a length of green silk. '*Pasikutan...*'—Elbow to finger. Then he pinned the silk to the bench so that it was taut.

Lamban understood. His *keris* would be exactly this length. A custom measurement ensured the blade would be true to his heart alone. He sat over the bellows and started pumping. Within seconds he was perspiring.

After several minutes Taruna spoke without taking his eyes from the glowing coals. 'You chose very unusual elements for your blade. Most of the iron and nickel is from a meteorite I found years ago. It is *tosan isi,* a magic metal. A gift from heaven!'

Lamban lost count of the number of times the ingot was heated, split, folded, twisted and measured. In spite of his exhilaration, he began to tire. In contrast, the staccato rhythm of Taruna's hammering never faltered. In time the metal took a wavy shape symbolising the *naga* serpent It was a potent symbol of life. Lamban kept pumping.

'Last time,' Taruna grunted as yet again he returned the blade to the fire, this time for several minutes. When he withdrew it he held it upwards. Against the velvet black of the tropical night sky the glowing steel of the *keris* pulsed like a blood-red moon. Taruna's face was tense, all his concentration on the subtle changes in the metal's colour as its temperature fell. Suddenly he quenched the steel in the trough, immersing it completely. There was an angry, snake-like hiss.

When Taruna pulled the blade from the water it was a dark, dull grey. He looked at it with satisfaction and handed it casually to Lamban. Even without a handle the *keris* had a marvellous balance.

'It has nine *luq*,' explained Taruna, referring to the number of waves. 'That was to ensure *panimbal*—tranquillity—the symbol of heaven. That, at least, I could control. But its *pamir* is in the hands of God.'

Pamir, the surface pattern, would become visible only after polishing, after which the blade's special powers would be released. Lamban knew the legends. Some *keris* brought prosperity while others could warn the wearer of danger. Equally, some could be cursed.

Taruna took back the blade and squatted at the bench to use first the chisels, and then the sharpening and polishing stones. Lamban sat beside him in silence. It was late afternoon, after the rays of sunlight penetrated the forge, when they paused for water. Only then did the passage of time seem to register with the swordsmith. Neither of them had eaten for over twenty-four hours.

Taruna stood, rolling his head and stretching his shoulders and back. His joints cracked like snapping dry twigs. He laughed. 'I'm getting old.' From a cupboard he brought out a glass jar fastened with a large rubber stopper. It contained a yellowish liquid with a crystalline sediment. He pointed to a large enamel bowl in one corner of the forge. 'Bring the blade and that bowl. Make sure it is clean and dry, then bring four limes.'

Grateful for the chance to move, Lamban sprang up to wash the dish. When he returned with the limes Taruna had already prepared a cushion, a collection of bottles and a bowl of water. 'Watch,' he said taking the fruits from Lamban. 'The juice will bring up the nickel and reveal some of the *pamir*.'

Taruna took the *keris* and cut the limes in half. The blade sliced them effortlessly. Quickly he rubbed the exposed fruit halves over the metal, covering the blade in juice which collected in the bowl. Flecks of silver began to shine in the otherwise dull metal. All eight lime halves were used before he was content. Much of the blade now shone brightly.

Next Taruna scooped up a handful of dust, letting it fall slowly off his palm. It swirled in a small cloud towards a goat and kid tethered on one side of the clearing. Tut-tutting to himself, Taruna led the animals away. When he returned to his cushion he saw Lamban's puzzled expression and pointed to the jar.

'This is *alrahgar*, an acid containing arsenic. It's poisonous, so keep behind me, up wind. But be ready, the breeze is playful today. If the gas reaches you, close your eyes. Do not breathe in.'

'Yes, Master,' Lamban replied nervously.

Taruna placed the *keris* back in the dish of lime juice and shook the jar. Keeping it at arm's length, he pulled out the stopper and let the acid trickle over the blade. Immediately it began to froth, and a dense yellow cloud billowed upwards before it was caught by the breeze and carried away. Vigorously Taruna began to rub in the acid with a cloth.

'What—!' Lamban gasped in amazement. The exposed iron in the blade was turning a deep black.

Taruna continued his painstaking work, adding drops of rose and jasmine essence to the bowl of water before rinsing a last time. The delicate scents banished the sulphurous odour of the arsenic.

Lamban stared at the *keris* in sheer wonder. A pattern of broad, horizontal silver bands ran down the blade. At last the *pamir* was revealed.

Yet Taruna seemed perturbed. 'I was afraid of this,' he sighed.

'Master?' Lamban asked quietly.

'It is *buntel mayit*—the Death Shroud—only the strongest and truest of warriors can control such a powerful blade. It is an omen. Make of it what you will.'

As he offered the blade the smith's expression was grave. Lamban was not listening. Awed, he gripped the *keris* hilt reverently, letting the sunlight play over the dazzling *pamir*. It was the most beautiful thing he had ever seen.

Imperial Japanese Navy Liaison Office, Djakarta

Commander Tashiro gave a sharp double, then single rap on the polished teak double-doors. It was a simple signal but it reminded his superior, Rear-Admiral Ishida, that a Japanese army officer was about to enter. Even though his visitor was expected, Ishida instinctively checked once more that there was nothing on view that could be of interest to the rival service. He heard Tashiro speaking.

'*Shitsurei shimasu.*'—Please excuse me.

Ishida knew that Tashiro would be bowing before, with imperceptible delay, placing his hands on the gilded handles, straightening—again the formality covering the deliberate slowing tactic—and pulling them towards him with a flourish. Yet even now, Tashiro's arms, spread wide across the entrance, effectively blocked any forward movement.

Ishida's gaze settled on a top-secret signal he had just sent Naval Headquarters in Tokyo. It was an embarrassingly short list of the warships available for the defence of Java. He pursed his lips and covered it with a report on rice inventories on Bali. He was certain that Army Intelligence knew of the parlous state of the Japanese Navy, just as the Navy was equally aware of the Army's reduced capability. For the previous twenty years, however, neither he nor any officer he had served under had ever volunteered information to the Army. He was not about to start now. Like most Japanese naval officers, Ishida blamed the expansion-obsessed Army for Japan's dire military situation. Time after time the Army had rejected the more cautious policies of the Navy. Now, thanks to them, Japan's fate was sealed.

'Admiral Ishida, Major-General Yamagami is here.' Tashiro was standing just inside the room, the guest still caught in the web of etiquette at the threshold. I must congratulate Tashiro, Ishida thought, I could have composed a *haiku* by the time Yamagami was finally in the room!

In the doorway, the straight-backed, stocky Yamagami was looking politely but inquisitively at Ishida. His tailored uniform was spotless, as was the white, open-necked shirt that emphasised the rows of campaign ribbons across his chest. Like Ishida he favoured knee-high boots. He held his long, curved sword by its leather scabbard in his right hand, point forward and edge down. It was a traditional samurai courtesy indicating no ill intent.

Yamagami entered the room briskly. If he was irritated by
Tashiro's exaggerated formality, or if he had even noticed, he
was not letting it show. Ishida eased his lanky frame up from
his seat to greet his visitor formally. Yamagami had become
Gunseikan—Chief of Staff—of 16th Army a year before but
they had first met in early 1942, just after the conquest of the
Netherlands Indies. Ishida squirmed inside as he remembered
bragging to Yamagami that the Pacific Ocean was now a
'Japanese lake'. Soon afterwards had come the disastrous naval
battle at Midway, and then last October, the shambles at
Leyte Gulf.

'General, you are most welcome! It has been some time
since I had the pleasure of talking with you privately.' Ishida's
voice bore no indication of the nervousness he felt. After the
invasion, the Japanese Army had been given control of Java
and Sumatra; and the Navy all former Dutch territory east of
Bali. On Java itself the Navy's presence was confined to the
yard at Surabaya on the east coast and a liaison office in the
capital. Relations with the Army had not been smooth.

Yamagami bowed stiffly. Ishida deliberately returned the
bow much lower than etiquette demanded, emphasising the
respect he was giving his visitor. That at least, Ishida thought,
should arouse the old fox's curiosity! He felt his stomach
flutter. Yamagami was no fool. He also greatly outranked
Ishida and was a most politically astute career officer. Ishida
was sure that had the war gone differently the General would
have risen to join the military government in Tokyo. For now,
though, he was the most influential man in Java. Without his
assistance, or at least tacit approval, Ishida's plan would fail.

'Indeed Admiral,' replied Yamagami with an easy formality.
'I only wish the circumstances were as pleasant as previously.
At that time, I recall, we of the Yamato race were winning
victories beyond compare.'

With a huge effort Ishida kept his features impassive, though he was seething at the veiled insult, certain that the General had said 'Yamato' quite deliberately. The name of the ancient kingdom was often coined as a poetical reference to Japan, so it was not odd in itself. Except that *Yamato* also happened to be the name of the battleship in which Admiral Kurita had fled from Leyte Gulf, after his flagship had been sunk. Yamagami was insinuating that the Navy was responsible for Japan's present difficulties. Ishida fumed, his features impassive. Damn those arrogant army fools! He was sorely tempted to offer Yamagami his choice of Indian, Burmese or Japanese tea. Since the invasion of India had failed and their troops were now in humiliating retreat across Burma, it would have made his point perfectly. Instead, he let the barb pass, reminding himself that he could not afford to waste his opportunity.

'Yes, alas times have changed.' He gestured towards a pair of colonial-style teak and rattan-weave chairs. 'Please sit down. May I offer you some iced Java tea?'

'No thank you, I am pressed for time.'

With a clipped bow, Tashiro left, closing the doors with a soft click. Yamagami took off his cap and tossed it on to low table between them. His close-cropped hair around his bald pate was shot through with grey. Until recently, Ishida remembered, it had been far darker. To his surprise, his visitor lounged, his booted right calf resting on his left knee and his sword propped against his right thigh.

Ishida had decided long before to come straight to the point. It was a dangerous approach because he would be leaving himself open to a charge of defeatism. But he had gone over the scenario a hundred times and decided it was the only way to appear sincere.

'General, I know you are very busy, so I must speak frankly.' His mouth was dry. 'Please excuse my rudeness but I wish to give you my thoughts on the future of this country.' He wondered if he had put too much emphasis on the last word.

'Indeed? I am listening.'

Ishida cleared his throat. 'Japan has freed the peoples of Malaya, Burma, the Philippines, Indo-China and Indonesia from the yoke of colonialism. How can we ever forget the warmth of the welcomes for our soldiers and sailors after the Western Powers were swept away? "All Asia Under One Roof" was our dream!' His voice fell to a whisper. 'We were so close. Alas, now our dream is…fading.'

Yamagami's face was a mask.

Ishida watched him raise a hand and begin to stroke his chin. He pressed on. 'Freedom, however, is treasured by those who receive it. I am sure you, like me, desire to see this legacy survive Japan's coming…departure.' He saw the first unease register in Yamagami's eyes but ignored it, very glad now that he had rehearsed his lines. 'For all we know, the enemy might invade Malaya, Sumatra or Java tomorrow. Already the 16th Army is preparing for last stands in the mountains near Cianjur and Wonosobo.' Ishida watched for a reaction. Yes, we are reading your signals! But Yamagami did not even blink and Ishida pressed on, admiring his self-control.

'We both know that Japan is on her knees. Our merchant shipping losses are catastrophic. No oil or raw materials reaches our factories, so there are no spare parts for tanks, artillery or ships! The Navy faces other problems. Our diesel stocks are close to zero. We have little aviation fuel, which means no air cover, so our few serviceable ships cannot operate far from port.'

Ishida pressed on. 'Here, General, in confidence, we can admit privately that we can do little to help our homeland other than ensure that the Allies pay the maximum price for the Indies. I believe the Indonesians would sacrifice millions to retain their freedom. In this, our cause can become their cause. For this reason, I urge you to use the sixty-five thousand men in the Java militia in the coming campaign. By doing so we can gain valuable time for Japan. But in return, of course, we must do our utmost for the *nation* of Indonesia.'

Yamagami sat up, his eyes hawk like. 'Do you have information that the Centre is ready to grant independence to Indonesia?' By 'Centre' Yamagami meant the military government in Tokyo.

'Un—unfortunately no,' Ishida stammered, slightly unnerved by Yamagami's direct question. 'At least not yet. I simply wish to help our Indonesian friends defend themselves. I fear the Centre does not appreciate the urgency of the situation. In years to come Japan will need allies in Asia. We can lay the foundations of those relationships now.' His chest tightened as he waited to be berated.

Yamagami's face gave nothing away but his fingers were flicking idly at the red and gold silk tassel hanging from the pommel of his sword. When he spoke it was with tired exasperation. 'As you well know, only a few months ago some of our closest Indonesian "friends" rebelled at Kediri and killed a number of our men. We trained the militia. We trusted them. To my great dismay they have betrayed that trust. I am aware that our Government has not yet made good certain promises but that is hardly the responsibility of the Army...or the Navy.'

Ishida gave a conciliatory nod and raised his fingers to smooth his thin moustache.

Yamagami let some of his irritation show. 'More immediate problems require our attention. An enemy invasion for one. Food and clothing are scarce. My men are on reduced rations! If the Indonesians blame us for their troubles and consequently we are no longer popular or, if we cared to know, even welcome here, that does not concern me. It should certainly not concern you. Our sole duty is to Japan.'

Ishida was not surprised by the stock answer. After all, no General was about to admit to a Vice Admiral that they were going to lose the war. He wondered just how much credence Yamagami gave to information coming from Tokyo. The Centre was riven with factions. As MacArthur and Nimitz advanced on Japan, so the heads rolled and the idiocy increased! His own command was still receiving orders to deploy ships that had been laid up for lack of spares or battle damage for months. He held Yamagami's gaze and committed himself in a rush.

'The rebels were just a few ungrateful hotheads and they were severely punished. True, there have been problems and incidents but the vast majority of the Indonesians will rally to us. I have three suggestions that I respectfully ask you to consider. The first is that General Nagano should request the Centre to announce Indonesia's immediate independence.' Nagano was the senior military commander on Java but he was no politician, which was why Ishida needed Yamagami.

'Second, all spare arms and ammunition captured from the Dutch should be handed over to the militia. Third, the more co-operative nationalist leaders such as Sukarno and Hatta should broadcast on the radio, encouraging the people to join us in our stand.'

Yamagami sat in silence, truly stunned by Ishida's audacity in even thinking of such a direct proposal. What arrogance, he thought. Never mind the admission that the Navy was reading their communications which was bad enough! As for the militia, army policy was to disarm them quietly over the next few weeks and isolate the nationalist leaders in case of further rebellion. Did the Navy know that too?

A little unnerved by Yamagami's silence, Ishida shrugged his shoulders to lessen the tension. 'Only suggestions,' he said waving his hand. 'I simply wish to contribute in some way to the defence of Java and thus of Japan.'

Yamagami looked at his watch. 'I shall certainly consider what you have said.' I may also mention it to the authorities he thought acidly. 'I agree we should overlook nothing that might help us in our war operations. Having said that, the military and political implications are considerable.'

Ishida nodded cautiously. Yamagami continued. 'As you know, agreed policy foresees eventual independence for Java only. Sumatra and Malaya are nowhere near as advanced and are to become provinces of Japan. Your proposal—I mean your suggestion—would require Imperial approval and now...well, such procedures take time.'

Yamagami stood up. The meeting was over. 'You must excuse me. As you know, I am in a hurry to reach Semarang.'

'My apologies, I have delayed you long enough,' said Ishida.

He rose, ringing for Tashiro as he did so. 'Please convey my regards to your staff.'

'Very interesting to hear your ideas, Ishida. Until next time.' Yamagami bowed casually and turned on his heels. The doors opened as he approached them, allowing him to continue without breaking his stride.

Pleased with himself and more than a little relieved, Ishida returned to the elegant antique desk and ran his hand over the polished wood. Rendered in exquisite veneer in the top was the crest of the old Dutch East India Company. He pushed the chair back to stretch his legs and looked around the huge, ornately decorated room. It was almost as big as his house in Japan. Until the invasion it had been the office of the British Consul. Portraits of the former consuls still hung on two walls. Ishida's staff had wanted to take them down but he liked the room immensely and had insisted that his predecessors remained in place to bear silent witness to Japan's triumph.

Over the fireplace, a framed photograph of Emperor Hirohito looked incongruous in the large space that had been occupied by a gilt-framed oil painting of King George VI. Not for the first time Ishida wondered how his own portrait would look on these same walls in a hundred years. He laughed aloud at his own vanity. There was a single knock on the door. Tashiro entered.

'Your horse is saddled, Admiral, and your escort is waiting.'

'How am I for "ammunition"?'

Tashiro arched an eyebrow. 'Enough for a *small* army, Sir.'

'Good,' he replied happily, walking to the open French windows to check the sky. It was unnecessary in the predictable climate of Java but the sailor's habit was ingrained.

A few minutes later he was taking the salute of his four-man escort. In reality he thought it unnecessary and paid them scant attention as he trotted through the open gates. Instead, he guided his horse towards a small group of scruffy, barefoot boys aged nine or ten holding wooden rifles. As he approached, one of them called out in Japanese. *'Sasage tsutsu!'*—Present arms! They saluted and came to a fidgety attention. Ishida returned the salute with mock gravity, then reached into the saddlebags for the small twists of paper. At the sight of the sweets the boys rushed forward, shouting and laughing.

Amused by the instant, total collapse of military discipline, Ishida urged his mount on in a walk. Behind him the boys fell in noisily and out of step. The Marine lieutenant in charge of his escort drew up next to Ishida and looked back scornfully at the boys.

'Excuse me Admiral, but you should not encourage them. It is demeaning to your position.'

'Is that so? Ishida frowned. 'Would you rather see unhappy, surly children, Lieutenant? Isn't it better that these boys remember us fondly? We are nurturing seeds here. The harvest will come later.'

Mumbling an apology the Lieutenant dropped back in line. Ishida sighed, sad that so many officers—Army and Navy alike—were so hostile to the Indonesians when he liked their easy-going ways and was fond of their company.

At the entrance to the park he gave instructions for his escort to follow at a walk. Then he spurred his horse into a brisk canter, relishing the solitude. He was an expert horseman and he rode aggressively, enjoying the motion and strength of the animal which was soon lathered in sweat.

Ishida was too good a rider to abuse his mount in such heat so he slowed carefully and then urged it gently up a small hill. It was a favourite spot where he often went to think. From the crest he had a sweeping view of the city below and out beyond the harbour at Tandjong Priok. Small, brightly coloured fishing boats and ferries criss-crossed the water. At anchor and dominating the bay was a minelayer, the *Wakataka*.

Ishida dismounted and led his horse to shade under some tamarind trees. From the hill the ship looked imposing enough—which was precisely why it was there—yet it had barely enough fuel for four days at sea. Two months ago *Wakataka* had limped in for repairs at Surabaya, its bow buckled by an enemy mine. Now it was twenty feet shorter.

He thought back to his conversation with Yamagami, wondering if the General had any idea of his real aim. In truth, he was not concerned about the forthcoming defence of Java, or even the inevitable battle for Japan. Months before he had decided that military defeat, though unpalatable, was inescapable. But he saw future political and economic victories that could still be won. In fifty or sixty years Japan would be strong once again. She would need friends in Asia; friendships she could make now.... If only those in Tokyo could see the opportunities!

Of course the British, French and Dutch would try to turn back the clock but the Burmese, Malays, Vietnamese and Indonesians would resist the return of their white masters. That much was obvious. Maeda was dedicating what time he had left to the Indonesians, whatever the personal consequences, even if it meant a short-term disadvantage to his own blinkered Government.

What mattered was that the Indonesians had to be able to resist the returning Dutch. Every available weapon had to be given to the militia. Not, as he had proposed to Yamagami, so that they could make a foolhardy stand with the Japanese but for a war of independence. He doubted the Americans would seek a fight with the Indonesians. The Dutch would be on their own and sooner or later they would give up. Then Indonesia would be free and Japan's great sacrifice in this part of Asia, at least, would not have been in vain.

A clatter of approaching hooves disturbed him. He took a last look at the view then climbed nimbly back on to his horse to re-join his escort.

Chapter Five

The Mitchell B-25 bomber was trailing a thick plume of black smoke and quickly losing height. Behind it, two Mitsubishi Zero fighters continued to harry it with short, staccato machine-gun bursts.

Nagumo looked up, shielding his eyes from the sun with his cap. 'It's all over. Why don't they save their ammo?'

Ota did not reply as the stricken plane pitched forward and began a wide spin. He saw a tiny speck tumble from it. Seconds later a parachute billowed like a huge white chrysanthemum in the azure sky. It was dropping very fast.

'He left it too late,' said Ota stating the obvious.

'Hmm. He might get caught in the bamboo grove over there,' replied Nagumo a little doubtfully.

They watched the B-25, now a fireball, plunge into a rice paddy four hundred yards from them. There was a small explosion and thick black smoke drifted up towards the parachutist who hung limply in his harness. He came down hard in another paddy, his chute smothering him. Men from Ota's platoon converged on him at the run.

When Ota and Nagumo reached the scene, their men were still searching frantically under the chute, delving into the murky, knee-deep crop.

'Found him!' A soldier heaved, bringing the body to the surface and dragging it to the earthen embankment. Ota thought the airman was dead until the soldier turned him over and slapped him on the back. He began to wheeze and cough weakly.

'Lift him up!' said Ota. The man moaned and collapsed as he was raised. Both his legs were broken. Ota saw at least one bullet wound in his abdomen. 'Cut bamboo for splints and stretcher handles,' Ota ordered pointing to the grove. 'You two, take off your tunics. Give him some water.'

He watched his men bring lengths of bamboo and slide them inside the buttoned jacket sleeves to make an improvised stretcher. 'Clean his face.' Ota was curious to see his enemy.

A soldier tipped a canteen over the airman's mud-encrusted head to reveal cropped fair hair. His eyes opened slightly and Ota saw they were blue. He guessed they were about the same age. Again the man passed out.

'I'll take my platoon to see if there's anything left of the crew.' Nagumo said gruffly. As he turned he noticed a black Packard saloon pulling up at the edge of the fields. A half-track with *kenpeitai*—military police corps—markings was close behind it. 'You should have left him in the mud,' he said quietly to Ota, eyeing the approaching MPs.

Two minutes later Captain Shirai had reached them. His tone was gleeful. *'Mo hitori kikusaku teki da!'*—Here's another enemy scheduled for Hell! He turned to Ota. 'Ah, Lt Ota isn't it? My rival for the *kendo* championship! You've done well!'

Ota saluted and wished the officer a good afternoon. Shirai made no attempt to reply. He was staring exultantly at the captive.

Now Ota understood what Nagumo had meant. Shirai's intention was clear. The airman had been already been sentenced to death. Ota hid his disquiet.

Shirai looked at him challengingly. 'Perhaps you would like to test the sharpness of your sword, Lieutenant?' His eyes were glinting, almost toying.

Ota forced a thin smile. 'He's dying. His comrades will provide ample opportunity soon enough.'

'Yes, and they'll all pay like this one,' Shirai said almost to himself. 'We'll take him now. Really, the stretcher was quite unnecessary.'

Ota remembered the Australian troops at Buitenzorg. Suddenly he heard himself speaking. 'He was just doing his duty—'

Shirai looked at him with disdain. 'We are not on the field at Sekigahara.' The great battle in 1600 had been the last great clash of samurai armies. 'He's a foreign dog,' Shirai continued scathingly, 'and will die like one!'

Shirai barked an order and two of his men came forward. They hauled the airman off the stretcher and dragged him away. Ota watched them sling their groaning prisoner over the tailgate of the half-track like a sack of rice. He reminded himself never to be taken alive.

Kate closed her eyes as she tried to shut her mind to the sweltering heat, thankful that she had grabbed her straw bonnet on the way to the sudden roll call. They had been lined up for over an hour when the camp commandant, flanked by more officers than usual, finally appeared. *Kenpei* and camp guards took up a position every twenty yards around them. Long bayonets were fixed to their rifles.

Kate was one row back. The waiting had taken a heavy toll. Two women in the front row had fainted and lay where they fell. She had heard others collapse behind her but she was afraid to look because the guards were in a savage mood. One woman who had tried to tend to the two at the front had been clubbed back into place with a rifle butt. In the corner of her eye Kate could see she was now swaying groggily.

A corpulent sergeant stepped forward to call them to attention with a bellow that was almost a scream. *'Kiotsuke!'* The camp commandant's route took him close to the front row and he and his minions stepped over the prone women with hardly a break in their stride.

Despite their exhaustion, the women forced themselves to straighten. Kate could see the Japanese were unusually tense. Something—smuggling or perhaps the latest war news—had infuriated them. The previous night the BBC had reported large bombing raids on Tokyo around the Imperial Palace. Maybe, thought Kate glumly, the Japs were going to take it out on them once again. Allied victories in the Pacific brought both pleasure and pain. Successes were always secretly cheered but they resulted in cuts in their rations or electricity, sometimes both, for days on end. Their only consolation was the knowledge that the Japanese were taking a beating.

A tremor of unease ran through the women when they recognised Shirai. Since the chief *kenpei* torturer only appeared to dish out punishments, Kate was sure that someone must have been caught. She hoped desperately that it wasn't one of her friends.

'Rei!' Obediently, the women and children bowed low.

The commandant, on tenterhooks in the presence of the *kenpei*, saluted. Eagerly, Shirai sprang on to the dais and surveyed his audience with unveiled contempt. He let fly with a tirade then signalled to the camp interpreter, a haughty, middle-aged Javanese woman who was also the commandant's secretary. 'White imperialists continue their futile aggression. They do not see that their power is broken and that they will never rule in Asia again. Instead, they now use indiscriminate methods to wage war.' Her voice was equally strident. Kate had little doubt her hostility was genuine. 'We will not accept such attacks passively. Since they are your forces you are therefore all guilty.'

Across the compound the cellblock door opened and two camp guards led out two girls by ropes tied around their necks. They had been stripped to their camp-made bras and knickers and their heads shaved. Their wrists and shoulders were lashed to bamboo poles.

A third prisoner, a barely conscious white man also bound to a pole, was dragged out by two *kenpei*. His clothing was ripped and blood-stained. When he drew near and she saw his injuries, Kate's stomach turned. His short hair was matted with dried blood and dirt. She wasn't sure if either of his eyes was open because his face was so badly swollen. Bruises and bloodstains covered his torso and arms. His breathing came in quick, laboured hisses through jagged, bloody stumps that were all that remained of his teeth. She could not tell his age.

Shirai paused again for the interpreter as he indicated the two cowering girls. 'Last night these two were caught smuggling. It is a crime against the war effort. They, and you, know the penalty. If any of you look away their punishment will be doubled!'

Kate sighed when she finally recognised the girls from Juliette's dance classes. They were sisters aged fifteen and seventeen. At Shirai's signal the guards raised thin, whippy canes. The girls began to sob.

Shirai led the count. '*Ichi, ni, san.*'—One, two, three.

Screams echoed and merged over the courtyard as the guards thrashed the girls powerfully and methodically across their backs and fronts.

'*Yon, go, roku,*' continued Shirai.

Kate counted too, silently, watching the strikes leave a checker of thin, bloody lines.

Wailing, the girls dropped to their knees, squirming to evade the blows but the leverage from the poles enabled the guards to flip them around effortlessly. Piece by piece the girls' underwear fell away as the threadbare cottons were slashed.

Kate stopped counting at ten.

Shirai did not. *'Ju-ichi, ju-ni...'*

Finally, at fifteen, it ended. *'Yame!'*—Stop.

The guards stepped away leaving the girls whimpering in the dirt. Flies began to settle on the open, bloody welts. Kate pitied them but she knew they were strong enough to recover. She was more concerned about the man. Kate held her breath as Shirai began haranguing them again.

'Before you is an Australian flyer who attacked Surabaya harbour. It was a hopeless gesture and a doomed mission! Now, my former colonial ladies, I thought you should see for yourselves the fate of Japan's enemies.'

The interpreter paused as Shirai snapped out another command. The unconscious Australian was dragged forward.

Shirai jumped from the dais and positioned himself to one side of the airman. In a slow, deliberate arc he drew his sword. The women began muttering.

'Dear God!'—'Oh, please no!'—'The rotten bastard!'

Shirai seemed oblivious to the reaction. Carefully he lowered the blade to the back of the airman's neck, gauging the cut. Kate saw a glazed, distant look in Shirai's eyes. Amongst the rows of women, hands reached silently for hands. Mothers gathered their children to them to shield their eyes then closed their own.

A prayer began as a whisper and was taken up. '...hallowed be Thy name....'

Kate mouthed the words but could barely speak them. She felt a chill grip her as she saw the sword rise slowly above Shirai's head. It seemed to hang in the air, glinting in the sunlight. The airman was still unconscious and she was glad for that small mercy. As the blade flashed downwards she closed her eyes and tensed. There was an oddly familiar clink followed by a dull thud. It was the sound of the kitchen, of a cleaver chopping bone.

'Oh, God!'—'The poor boy!'—'Jesus Christ!'—'Murderer!'

Kate forced herself to look. Shirai stood as if frozen, his arms extended and his sword held just below the severed neck. Arterial blood sprayed over the blade, pooling and frothing on the packed earth. The head had rolled to lie face down near Shirai's feet. Thick blood oozed from it, staining the dusty ground.

Kate felt faint. To her left a woman vomited, causing Kate to gag. She fought it, determined to keep her eyes on Shirai. His eyes were still glazed and his nostrils flared. Without looking, he sheathed the sword in one quick, fluid motion, then turned and strode toward the camp gate.

General Yamagami had enjoyed the short flight from Djakarta to Semarang's Kalibanteng airfield. He was looking forward to the company of soldiers rather than, as he saw it, bureaucrats dressed as soldiers. As the twin-engine Mitsubishi Ki-57 army transport touched down and bumped across the cracked tarmac he saw half-a-dozen bombers and fighter-trainers laid out in a dispersed pattern in case of air raids. Dotted along the airfield's perimeter were the burnt-out shells of Dutch aircraft destroyed during the invasion. He frowned, wondering how much longer he would be able to fly to inspect his men. Once the Allies had a base on Sumatra or Lombok, no Japanese aircraft would be safe from their fast Hellcats and Thunderbolts.

Yamagami pushed the thoughts of the enemy advance to the back of his mind and stepped down on to the tarmac.

Major Kudo and the senior officers of the Central Java Command Area were lined up a few yards away.

'Welcome, General,' said Kudo warmly as he bowed. He had served under Yamagami as a captain in the China campaigns of the 1930s.

'Ah, Kudo, it's good to see an old comrade!' Yamagami said laughing. He clapped the much younger man on the shoulder. 'I know I needn't bother inspecting your men. You're always on top of things,' he said loudly. Then in a whisper to Kudo alone, 'I needed a break from the pen-pushers!'

Kudo led him to greet the other officers. 'Your timing is perfect, General,' he said warmly. 'Coincidentally, this afternoon is the second annual Central Java *Kendo* Championship. We should have plenty of time for you to inspect the defences and enjoy a few of the bouts.'

'Really? I shall look forward to it. What a pleasant surprise!' Both men knew it was nothing of the sort. The General's fondness for *kendo* was no secret and he had planned his itinerary very carefully. 'By the way,' he added casually, 'I hope you've scheduled me an hour at that wonderful bathhouse!'

'How could I forget that, General!' Kudo grinned. 'After all, it's one of Semarang's greatest attractions. Almost as good as the Lotus Pools at Quin Lo.'

Yamagami clapped Kudo's arm. 'Ah, you still remember! What a place!' He looked slyly at the tense, well-groomed aide beside him. 'Of course, I was much younger then!' He looked at Kudo. 'I heard Mao's rabble controls that area now. Do you suppose....'

'I'm sure business is booming!' Kudo quipped. 'Please, General, this way.'

As they walked to the cars, Kudo glanced at the carved wooden plaque over the entrance to the airfield offices.

Originally it had read 'Royal Netherlands Indies Air Force, Semarang' above the outline of an aircraft in Dutch livery. In the aftermath of the Japanese victory, the 'Royal Netherlands' had been crossed out and 'Imperial Nippon' daubed over it crudely in red paint. A wooden model of a Zero fighter had been nailed above the Dutch aircraft but, unnoticed, it had slipped and now hung as though falling.

Yamagami also glanced the sign.

'It was amusing in 1942,' Kudo said quietly, annoyed by the slip-up. His guest said nothing.

Yamagami's inspection tour lasted two hours. By four o'clock, when he arrived at the barracks, the *kendo* competition was underway. His party were shown to an open-sided tent that gave protection from the burning sun but not the heat and the dust which, in spite of repeated dousing from watering cans, rose in small clouds in the open arena. Several hundred noisy and enthusiastic soldiers sat on tiered bench seating that was open to the elements.

Kudo soon observed that the General's aide looked particularly uncomfortable. He was dabbing regularly at his forehead. In contrast, Yamagami was genuinely enjoying himself, untroubled by the red dust speckling his uniform and the heat. There was only a faint sheen of perspiration at his temples. To his aide's dismay he also had barely touched the glass of the iced tea placed beside him. His aide's glass stood empty.

Throughout the day officers from neighbouring units had been visibly anxious to please Yamagami. Kudo had not been concerned. None of the others had fought the Russians and Chinese, who had nearly killed them both on a number of occasions, or experienced the extreme heat and cold of China.

Yamagami was glancing quickly down a list of competitors. Suddenly he looked up. 'Ota Kenichi? Is he by any chance the same Ota who won the University Championships in '41?'

'That's him, General,' said Kudo. 'You have a good memory.'

'I was there as a guest! He's such a skilful fencer and so fast!'

'Today, he's the second seed,' replied Kudo. 'Last year's champion, *kenpei* Captain Shirai, is the first.'

'Really?' Yamagami raised his eyebrows. 'He beat Ota last year?'

'No. Ota was on manoeuvres.'

They settled down to watch the remainder of the competition. The seeding was proving accurate as both Ota and Shirai progressed. Ota qualified for the final with a quick despatch of a *kenpei* lieutenant. So far he had not conceded a point in four bouts. Across the arena the scoreboard showed only one other fencer with a clean sheet. It was Shirai. Ota waited, sitting under an awning for competitors, as Nagumo prepared to take on Shirai in the other semi-final.

Nagumo had also done well, taking only three hits in five bouts. The year before he had lost easily to Shirai, so Ota was pessimistic about his friend's chances. Earlier in the afternoon Ota had seen Shirai quickly despatch two average fencers. Their later bouts had always coincided, so Ota had only managed to catch glimpses of his technique.

Around the arena spectators quietened in anticipation. All eyes were on the two men bowing to each other and the referee. Army *kendo* did without the traditional garb of thick jackets and very wide, ankle-length pleated trousers. Instead, the competitors wore standard PT kit of calf-length cotton shorts and a thin, short-sleeved shirt. Only the target areas—head, chest and wrists—were given protection. Their padded, grilled helmets were close-fitting, resembling a baseball catcher's mask. A narrow, reinforced leather flap hung down to deflect thrusts to the throat. The chest armour was a lacquered bamboo breast-plate fastened behind the back. Thick gauntlets covered their hands, wrists and forearms. In place of a sword was a four-foot length of tightly bound, thin bamboo slats called a *shinai*. Competitors were distinguished by a simple red or white ribbon attached to the rear ties of the breast-plate. For this fight Nagumo wore white, Shirai red. At each corner of the competition area sat a judge who would raise red or white flags if they saw a point land.

'*Hajime!*'—Begin! Nagumo and Shirai began to circle each other warily.

To his surprise, Ota saw Nagumo lifting his *shinai* to take a high guard, one favoured by Ota, rather than his preferred middle defence. Ota soon realised what his friend was doing. Damn it, he thought angrily, he's showing me how Shirai defends. He's throwing his own chance away! The clashing of bamboo echoed over the arena.

Nagumo was soon in trouble. He parried three quick attacks but then tried an ambitious counter. He was a fraction too slow. 'Wrist!' Shirai shouted in triumph. Two red flags from the judges acknowledged the point. The referee brought the fencers back to the centre for the restart.

Ota watched carefully, noting Shirai's rhythm, balance and posture, watching for any tell-tale twitches or pauses that preceded an attack. Nagumo was defending well but he was forced into giving up ground and was warned for stepping out of the area. A few seconds later, again inches from the boundary, Nagumo countered Shirai's attack with a fast cut to the head. At the last second Shirai dodged and the blow landed, not scoring, on his shoulder. Immediately Shirai caught Nagumo with another whip-like crack to the right wrist. Red flags shot upwards. The bout was over.

Nagumo bowed to Shirai and walked backwards to the edge of the arena where he gave a final bow to the judges.. He was panting heavily as sat down next to Ota. He pulled off his gloves while Ota undid his mask.

'You didn't have to do that,' Ota hissed quietly.

Nagumo, his face flushed, was unrepentant. 'I know. But the sod was going to beat me anyway. I wanted you to see his counter to the wrist. It's fast!'

'I saw it all right!' Ota said, kneeling and reaching for his own mask. Nagumo moved behind him to help tie it. He also added the white ribbon that identified his corner. As the surface was swept for the final, Ota pulled on his gloves. The judges also changed, handing over their flags with crisp bows. Ota and Shirai were called forward.

'Hey, do your best!' Nagumo called out encouragingly.

Ota rose and bowed to Shirai who stood on the opposite side of the arena. He was conscious only of his own breathing and the aggressive look from Shirai behind the grille of his mask. Ota, his face set, stared back confidently.

The two fencers came together for the traditional salute. Slowly they extended their bamboo swords, towards their opponent. Letting the tips cross, they lowered into a straight-backed squat, then rose, sword tips still crossed—still within hitting distance—their eyes fixed on each other.

'*Hajime!*'

Neither Shirai nor Ota moved for several seconds. They stood poised and tense. Then Shirai jumped neatly backwards and launched a running attack to Ota's head. Ota parried high, deflecting the sword to his right, then stepped forward with a horizontal slash to Shirai's exposed right side. Shirai anticipated and blocked by bringing his sword almost vertical in front of him. Their weapons slid against each other, then locked at the guards, glove against glove. Their faces were only a foot apart. They glared at each other unblinking.

Ota felt Shirai's breath on his face and could see the perspiration on his cheeks. Suddenly Shirai jerked his arms back and slammed his sword hilt at Ota's fingers at the same time sweeping his front leg forward in an attempted trip. It was an old trick and Ota caught the hilt cleanly on his, nimbly stepping over Shirai's leg. They jostled, pushing then and shoving, sensing the other's movement, each wary of a throw or grab.

'Zaaah!' Shirai bellowed and heaved, spattering Ota with spittle. Ota absorbed the shove smoothly but was forced to give some ground. He felt the greater strength in Shirai's arms and backed away again. Shirai's eye's shone as he sensed Ota give and he pushed again. Between them the crossed hilts began to rise. Whoever broke away first would also be vulnerable to a fast counter. Both men continued to push. Suddenly Ota jumped backwards. Shirai reacted a split second later. Both went for the head strike and the swords thudded down onto the padded masks.

'*Men!*' Head!—'*Men!*' Two shouts merged as each claimed the point.

Their movements had been lightning fast. Ota knew he had been the quicker and looked expectantly for the two white flags, certain the point was his. Two whites were up but, incredibly, two reds as well. Ota looked to the referee who hesitated then crossed his two flags together in front of him making the signal for simultaneous hits. No points scored! Ota was incredulous.

Shirai darted forward catching Ota with a snapped flick on his lower right arm. 'Wrist!' Shirai claimed loudly.

Ota was stunned because the referee had yet to signal a proper restart. Once again the same two judges raised red flags. Open-mouthed, Ota turned to the referee to see him also raise a red flag. Only then did Ota notice the judges flagging red wore black *kenpei* chevrons. He grunted in frustration. Shirai had a half-point lead.

At the restart, Shirai attacked with a fast wrist, head and trunk sequence but Ota was ready. He dodged the first two and as Shirai slashed for his open right chest, he took a half-step back to parry vertically by crossing his wrists, squatting low and pulling his sword close to his body. It was a classical battlefield defence. The bamboo weapons slapped together.

Ota's unusual block caught Shirai by surprise, leaving him stretched and slightly off balance with his arms extended uselessly. Ota took his opportunity and deftly stepped to the side to cut neatly for Shirai's wrist. The thwack of the hit on his opponent's glove was clearly audible. White flags shot up. The half-point was Ota's. Shirai bowed.

The referee brought them together for the last time. 'Begin!' Shirai attacked furiously with torso and head combinations. Ota was parrying neatly but backing away. He knew he was close to the edge of the area.

'Halt!' The referee pointed to a red flag raised by one of the *kenpei* judges who indicated he had stepped out of the area. Ota knew he had not done so but accepted the warning with a bow. If it happened again he would lose the bout.

Shirai sensed his advantage and came at him once again, lunging with a straight thrust at his throat. Ota stepped back, then aside. He cut quickly for Shirai's right side, forcing him to dart backwards and snatch his sword back in a low-angled block outside his body line. Now Shirai's left side was exposed. Ota whipped his sword up for a reverse trunk attack, a cut from high right to lower left. It was a rarely used technique because of the feudal-era legacy when a second, shorter blade was worn at the left side. For such an attack to be effective it would have to cut through the second blade and any armour beneath. For it to score it required immense force and perfect form. In reality, it was a desperate, last resort.

Ota cut high to the right and his legs flexed visibly as he strained to gain the extra power. Shirai pulled back neatly into a mid-range guard as Ota launched himself. Shirai's parry would not stop the hit but it would impede it enough to deny Ota any hope of a point. Worse, Ota's head would be exposed to a certain winning counter. Yet even as Shirai braced, he saw Ota's wrists roll, flicking the sword over his lateral parry to a new target. A whip-like crack carried around the arena as Ota's sword slapped Shirai's head. Ota's swept forward, past his opponent. 'Heeaad!' His shout was triumphant.

Awed gasps from the spectators were followed by thunderous applause. Ota knew he had won, biased judges or not. He turned to see two white flags already high followed, a little hesitantly, by two more. The referee then raised his own white flag confirming Ota's victory. Behind his mask Shirai's eyes blazed but his bows to Ota, the referee and the judges were courteous and crisp. Both men left the arena to a round of further applause.

Nagumo was elated and barely able to contain himself. 'Brilliant! You did it! But why didn't you take a high guard?'

'That's what he expected,' Ota gasped. He sank down on to his knees and Nagumo began untying his mask.

Nagumo laughed. 'That's what *they* expected you mean,' he whispered. 'I don't think all the judges were neutral!'

'I would never have guessed,' Ota smirked. Nagumo handed him some water and he gulped it down.

'Well, well,' Nagumo said quietly. 'Look who's with Shirai's group. It's Kato from Ordnance. He practised with us sometimes. The sneak never let on he was in with the *kenpei*. And the things I said!'

Ota looked at the sullen group of policemen who were keeping their distance from a clearly displeased Shirai.

'Hey,' Nagumo suddenly asked. 'Why did you pull the reverse cut? You had him!'

'Yeah,' Ota heaved, 'but there was no way the judges would have given me the point. They could rule all sorts: too weak, bad form, questionable sportsmanship....'

'Shirai would do it. That wrist point of his was a joke!'

'I was counting on that.'

Nagumo's jaw dropped. 'You mean you set him up?'

'Well,' Ota said nonchalantly, 'I just hinted at the move. He did the rest.'

Nagumo guffawed. 'Tonight, "Musashi-*sensei*", the drinks and the girls are on me!' Miyamoto Musashi was the most famous swordsman in Japanese history. 'I'll see you at six. Hey, you better look sharp, the General's getting ready to present you with the trophy!'

By early evening, General Yamagami was in a relaxed, jovial mood. He was also slightly drunk, as was Kudo. They were sitting on the veranda of Kudo's requisitioned house. Three empty porcelain sake flasks lay horizontally on the small, low table between them. A half-empty fourth was buried to its neck in a silver ice bucket.

Kudo, as host, was waiting patiently for his guest to say what was really on his mind. Yamagami's inspection of radio communications, gun emplacements, ammunition stocks and tank traps had been very thorough as Kudo had expected. It had also been a rather elaborate front to watch a *kendo* tournament. The General had appeared well satisfied with what he had seen. That, on top of the excitement of the kendo, a bath, a massage and then a sumptuous early dinner at the Officers' Club had made for an unusually full but satisfying and pleasant day for them both.

The deep, melodious voice of a *muezzin* calling the faithful to the day's fifth and final prayers hung in the air. Yamagami sank back in his chair with his eyes closed, listening until the last echo of the call had faded. 'That must be one of my favourite sounds of Java,' he sighed. 'Such a restful yet haunting quality. Sometimes I think it's a pity that Islam is forever closed to we Japanese.' For several seconds he was silent as he mused on his casual heresy. When he spoke again his voice sounded flat, almost tired. His eyes flicked open and fixed on Kudo. 'Exclude all militia formations from your defence plans. Don't trust them.'

There! Kudo thought at last. After four flasks Yamagami had finally unburdened himself. He emptied his tiny sake cup and Kudo refilled it immediately.

Kudo raised his eyebrows. 'All ten battalions?'

'Our spies tell us that mass desertions are planned for immediately after the American invasion.'

Kudo frowned. 'After?'

'Yes, it seems the nationalists intend for us and the Yankees to fight it out and then pick up the pieces.'

Kudo nodded. 'It's understandable. They must be assuming the Americans can't commit unlimited men to Java. It's what I am hoping for.'

'Yes,' agreed Yamagami. 'At least not until...Japan falls.' The two soldiers stared at the floor rather than each other, uncomfortable with the thought of defeat.

Yamagami cleared his throat. 'I have advised Tokyo that we cannot hold Java for long. I also urged them to evacuate the Sixteenth to China where we could combine with our Kwantung forces. They are self-sufficient and could continue fighting even if Japan was...occupied. Officially my idea was rejected for "strategic reasons". In fact, we don't have any troop ships left.'

Kudo pursed his lips. 'So we're in another tight corner!'

'Yes, my friend, and this time we stand alone. Anyway, I'm ordering the militia disarmed. Tactfully, of course, but they'll certainly be unhappy.' He placed his palms flat on his thighs and made a barely perceptible bow. 'I think I'll call it a night.' When he stood up he rocked a little. 'I'll leave this way,' he said indicating to the path that led around the side of the house. For the first time Kudo noticed the deep lines around the older man's eyes.

Kudo rang a bell and there was a brisk, soft padding of footsteps as a woman appeared carrying Yamagami's tunic, sword and boots. She bowed formally, almost horizontally. A red bougainvillaea flower appeared to float in her lustrous coiled hair. Her pale cream shoulder-covering *kebaya* bodice glittered with silver floral motifs and a line of moonstone buttons accentuated the swell of her breasts.

'General,' said Kudo cheerfully. 'Let me introduce Lena-san.' Kudo read Yamagami's envious look and continued quickly. 'This was her home. Her husband served in the Dutch Navy. He was killed in the Battle of the Java Sea. She is now my housekeeper.'

Yamagami stood mesmerised. 'Here's another of my favourite things about Java! I'd forgotten the advantages of lower rank. Alas Generals have far too high a profile!'

Lena looked up and smiled, revealing porcelain white teeth behind sensual, full lips. Both men laughed but only Kudo knew the hollowness of the look and the simmering pride it disguised.

Yamagami finished dressing. 'Kudo, one more thing,' he said half turning. His tone was serious again. 'Whatever happens, don't count on the Navy. Ishida's a slippery one. Sometimes I think he and his boss Shimizu are more interested in Indonesia's future than Japan's!'

Kudo wondered at the implications. Vice-Admiral Tadakatsu Shimizu, the senior Japanese Navy commander in the Indies, was based at Surabaya. 'There are only a few companies of marines at Surabaya, General,' Kudo replied nonchalantly.

Yamagami shrugged. 'Yes, you're right. What can they do?' He bowed formally. 'Thank you. Kudo. Quite like old times. We will declare Djakarta, Bandung and Buitenzorg open cities. I don't want to see those attractive buildings destroyed.' He paused. 'At the end, if you have no objection, I'll try and reach your unit....'

Kudo bowed equally formally. 'We would be honoured, General,' he said with total sincerity.

Yamagami turned and, unbidden, Lena sped daintily down the path to see him to his car.

Kudo watched, admiring her poise and style. Then he walked back into the house, pausing to finish the last of the sake as he went upstairs. He threw off his shirt and trousers and lay on the carved teak four-poster bed, enjoying the light breeze and moonlight coming through the open French windows that led to the balcony. He dozed, waking every few minutes in a pattern ingrained from years at the front line.

From the heady bougainvillaea scent he knew Lena was close by. He pretended to be asleep because otherwise she would insist on fetching him ice water from the kitchen. He sensed her move away and he half-opened an eye. She was sitting, bathed in moonlight, combing her waist- long hair. He watched the tresses rise and fall and was reminded of waves lapping up a night-time shore. Her thin-strapped nightdress was gossamer light and when she stood the moonbeams undressed her. She stood staring at the stars for several seconds before turning suddenly and arranging the thin mattress on the floor at the foot of his bed. Then she lay down out of sight.

Kudo felt the familiar ache in his loins. He remembered the first time he had seen her. It was two days after the Dutch capitulation. The single road along the coast had been strewn with cars, luggage and possessions abandoned in panic by Europeans trying to reach long-departed or long-sunk evacuation ships. Chaos reigned in the cities and towns. Looting had been rife and Semarang was no exception. Searching from house to house for Allied soldiers, his battalion had come upon dozens of murdered white men, women and children.

At their approach to one elegant gateway they heard a shot. Kudo led a platoon up a neat curving driveway to find a well-dressed young woman, trembling but defiant, at the front door. She was keeping a gang of looters at bay with a large calibre revolver, holding it with both hands. Two bodies lay on the ground. One was an elderly European, the other a Javanese.

The looters were jeering at her and creeping nearer. One of them charged. The woman fired and the looter dropped heavily on the steps, dead. Another edged nearer and she pulled the trigger again. A sharp, hollow click from the empty chamber was greeted with a roar of triumph as the gang surged forward. She dropped the gun and flung herself back against the door, her hand darting inside her blouse and drawing a small, curved knife which she pressed hard against her neck.

Her determined look stopped the looters again. Kudo, still unseen and still some twenty yards away, had been full of admiration. His pistol was trained on the gang. One of them lifted his sarong and gestured lewdly as he stepped forward. He spun and fell with a bullet in his head. Panic ensued as the looters tried to flee. Six more were shot before the rest flung themselves to their knees begging for mercy.

Kudo's eyes had not left the woman. He had bowed politely and then moved quickly up on to the veranda. She was quivering and her fierce gaze almost looked through him. The blade was still at her throat, her knuckles white around the haft. A thin trickle of blood was running down her neck, staining the collar of her blouse. 'Madame, excuse me,' he had said to her softly in English, 'I am the law here. You are safe now. But I must search this house.'

Slowly he had reached for her hand, gently easing the knife away from her neck. Her eyes flashed at him, suddenly calm. Then she had run sobbing to the dead European.

By the time Kudo had come out of the house the woman and the body of the European had disappeared. Kudo had been disappointed. Two days later, when offered a requisitioned private residence for his own use he had chosen the same house. When he arrived, a suitcases was on the steps. The woman was waiting inside. Through an interpreter he learnt her name was Lena, that she was twenty-four and recently widowed. Her father-in-law had been murdered by the looters. Kudo had given her the choice of a camp or to stay on as his housekeeper. Lena had stayed, gradually relaxing in his presence. He altered nothing inside the house except to ask her to remove the now banned photographs of the Dutch Queen, Wilhelmina. Lena had picked up basic Japanese quickly and when he entertained his officers at home she was always the perfect hostess.

One night, some five months after he had saved her from the mob, he had drunk too much and tried to kiss her. In an instant the knife was again at her throat, her meaning very clear. The next morning he had apologised.

For over two years she had cooked, cleaned, sewn and waited on him without complaint. Every night she slept at the foot of his bed like a dutiful Javanese servant. And every night he fell asleep wondering if she did it to punish him, or whether she even cared about the occasional trace of the Sakura girls' perfumes on his clothes.

Tjandi Camp III

Ota was taking the short cut through 'Little Holland' to meet Nagumo. Still elated from his tournament win, he was almost upon Kate before he saw her. She was alone and bowing but smiling hesitantly. *'Domo arigato.'*—Thank you very much, she said quietly.

Ota flushed. Instinctively he began to bow back, a smile forming. He froze as Shirai and two junior *kenpei* suddenly rounded a corner. In panic his face twisted into a ferocious scowl. The back of his hand flashed out catching Kate hard across the face.

'Aaah!' She reeled away clutching her stinging cheek.

Ota's stomach twisted with guilt. But he knew that if Shirai ever suspected that he was interested in her, she would be brutalised without hesitation. He pictured the *kenpei* finding some of the rations he had given her. It would all have been for nothing! He carried on with his cruel but vital charade. *'Tadashi rei no benkyo shite!'*—Learn to bow properly! He bellowed, genuinely angry with himself for being caught off guard and certain that the *kenpei* had noticed something.

Kate saw Shirai and dropped to her knees bowing repeatedly, her face ashen. *'Gomenasai!'*—I'm very sorry! Her shoulders shook in genuine terror.

Ota spun to greet Shirai with a sharp salute. Shirai stopped, glancing down casually at Kate. He did not return the salute. 'Well, Ota, at least you know how to treat these scum! Or is it something else?' Shirai stared inquisitively at Kate, then at Ota.

Ota tensed. He could think of nothing to say.

'Thought you'd try a little white meat? She's pretty enough, isn't she?' Shirai stared at Kate grinning slyly. He made to move away, then paused, his eyes icy. 'There will be a re-match, Lieutenant. Of that be certain.' With a nod to his minions to follow he strode off without a backward glance.

Ota sighed with relief. Kate was still on her knees, her forehead on the ground trembling. He desperately wanted her to look up so she would see the remorse in his eyes. But she did not move. Nearby two middle-aged women who had witnessed the encounter were watching Ota furtively. Embarrassed and contrite, he whirled and stomped away. The women rushed to Kate.

'It's all right now, dear,' said one. 'You know how touchy they are,' the other tut-tutted. 'What on earth did you say to him?'

Kate ignored them and stared after Ota's as he crossed the compound heading for the main gate. Tears were streaming down her face.

'Well, don't worry,' said one of the women looking around carefully. 'It won't be long now before they get some of their own medicine. They say MacArthur's reached Borneo!'

'Oh, wonderful!,' the other exclaimed happily. 'The swine won't be laughing then!'

Ota went straight to the bar of the Officers' Club. When Nagumo arrived he sensed his friend's foul mood immediately. For the first time in a year Ota got very drunk. He awoke with a terrible hangover on a *futon* in Nagumo's billet. Later that morning he was instructed to take his platoon to relieve a detachment at Ambarawa, some twenty-five miles inland. The order was effective immediately.

Chapter Six

The evening was humid and without a breeze, so Ishida had received his two visitors and their interpreter on the veranda. Both men were in their early forties. They came as plaintiffs but the contrast between the two, one a Javanese the other a Sumatran, could not have been starker.

Sukarno, the Javanese, was tall, solidly built and dressed in a neat, short-sleeved white silk shirt and blue tie. Dr Hatta, the Sumatran was short, round-faced and wore a rumpled cotton suit. Where the former was outspoken and impatient, the latter was restrained and deliberate. While Sukarno had become the voice of Indonesian nationalism, Hatta was the brains behind the movement.

Both were frequent visitors to Ishida's home and they spoke freely, as equals, and almost as friends. Yet tonight Ishida was irritated. First, because Sukarno had been repeating himself for nearly thirty minutes, and second because, in deference to Hatta's devout religious beliefs, he was forgoing his usual evening drink.

Sukarno leant forward with his hands clasped in an appeal to Ishida. He was clearly a very worried man.

'But you must have heard something? Surely you can give us an approximate schedule? It's been so long!' The interpreter, an effacing, slightly built Japanese youth of about seventeen who had grown up on Java, sat between and behind the Indonesians. His interpretation was almost simultaneous but devoid of the emotion of the original.

Ishida's despair and embarrassment were genuine. Months earlier the Japanese Government had announced it would consider the conditions necessary for Indonesian independence. Ecstatic, the nationalist leaders had appointed a constitutional committee and started tabling issues for discussion. Yet Ishida had suspected it had been merely a feeble attempt by Japan to embarrass the Dutch. He had been proved right. Army administrators controlling Java had let the committee meet just twice.

'Our support outside the cities is weak,' added Sukarno dejectedly. 'We still have no organisational base in rural Java. The Islamic associations are virtually unopposed. Rice seizures and the labour call-ups do our campaign no good at all. Many go hungry. People criticise the National Party openly.'

Ishida could not help but feel a cynical amusement at Sukarno's sudden concern for his party's standing. For three years the man had willingly broadcast and toured the Indies, urging full co-operation with Tokyo's policies and urging his people to support Japan's war effort. The Japanese had chosen him and in so doing they had taken a minor activist and made him the voice of Indonesia! And now that the Japanese sun was setting, he was afraid of becoming tainted. Such ingratitude, thought Ishida. How selfish, but then how predictable!

Hatta cleared his throat and adjusted his simple, round-framed glasses before speaking. Ishida knew him well enough to know he was also tiring of Sukarno's bleating.

'It is true, Admiral, that Japanese policies are causing friction in the countryside,' Hatta began. 'Naturally our representatives get short shrift from starving farmers. But we also face other difficulties. We are well-educated, well-travelled townsmen. In truth we have little in common with ignorant, superstitious villagers on the bottom rung of a feudal ladder. Their idea of progress has little to do with *The Rights of Man* or *Das Kapital* but much to do with promises of full stomachs.'

'As you well know, I have no influence on Army policy regarding labour programmes or rice levies,' Ishida replied regretfully. 'My capacity is limited to liaison and certain educational initiatives. I regret I cannot do more.'

All three knew Ishida's comment was an understatement. To the Army's consternation, one of his 'initiatives' had been the *Asrama Merdeka*, the Independence Study Centre. There, to the fury of the excluded *kenpeitai*, the Navy had sponsored open debates on Indonesia's political future. Even vociferous opponents of the Japanese like Sjahrir and Jarisha had been invited to lecture.

'No-one doubts your enthusiasm for our cause,' Hatta interjected politely. 'But unless we get approval for party offices throughout the country our influence with the masses will never be great. Also, we need permission to travel to the other islands and hold meetings.'

Ishida opened his palms in a gesture of helplessness. 'Both those things are solely in the remit of the Army. Unless they are instructed by Tokyo nothing will change. Alas, our Government is now preoccupied with other things. Please, consider our situation.'

Sukarno hands balled into fists. 'Japan must grant us independence soon. You are losing the war. Time is running out!'

Hatta sat back, his fingers interlaced on his lap looking every inch the lawyer he was. His tone, once again, was conciliatory yet precise. 'What my colleague means is that it is vital we face the Allies as a *legal* sovereign state, recognised as such by another, major sovereign state, namely Japan, *before* the Dutch attempt to return. If not, the Dutch will be able to deny us representation in the new United Nations. Then our chance will have been lost.'

Ishida was greatly impressed, yet again, by Hatta. Such a brilliant mind, he thought. He had never met anyone so dedicated or purposeful. It was easy to understand how much of a problem Hatta had been for the Dutch. Twenty years earlier, when Hatta was living in Amsterdam, he had been charged with sedition, but the young lawyer had won his case in the courts. When he had returned to the Indies he was arrested again, this time under repressive colonial laws that allowed no trial, and exiled to a disease-ridden island wilderness. He had been there for fifteen years until the Japanese had freed him in 1942.

It was strange, Ishida considered, how the Dutch exiled their opponents but then, after Pearl Harbor, how they had panicked and rushed them back to Batavia to conjure up a place in a future Dutch commonwealth for Java. Clearly it was an act of desperation. Why else would they have invited Hatta and Sukarno to flee with them to Australia! But Hatta had long known the Dutch Empire was built on sand. In just nine days the Japanese *tsunami* had swept it all away.

'Admiral, anything you can do in these difficult times to help us make our case will be greatly appreciated,' Hatta added. 'But for now, I think we have said enough.' He stood up to leave. To Ishida's relief Sukarno glumly followed suit.

'I understand completely,' agreed Ishida. He rose and shook hands with his guests. 'You have shown great patience. Keep petitioning the Army and let us hope it will not be too long before your efforts are rewarded.'

When he was alone Ishida silently cursed his lack of influence. He had realised long ago that Hatta saw him simply as a useful pawn but it did not bother him. Hatta had understood, even written, that a Pacific war was necessary before Indonesian independence could occur. He had bided his time, waiting for the Dutch to be ejected. Now he was just waiting again, this time for the Japanese to pack up and go. Then he would pick up the pieces and fashion a country.

Ishida had to admire the man's strategy. How the *kenpei* loathed him! Sad though, he mused, that he needs an arrogant lightweight like Sukarno. But if not Sukarno then who else would bring the Javanese to the party? It's a pity that Hatta's from Sumatra. He's too intellectual, just like Sjahrir and Jarisha, also Sumatrans. But the Javanese won't stand for a non-Javanese leader and the Sumatrans distrust the Javanese. So much for tolerance and national unity! But what does it matter? Even if Japan does grant independence they'll soon be squabbling among themselves and the Dutch will simply stroll back to power, playing one island off against another.

He stretched, easing his neck, then paused dejectedly. Sukarno was right about one thing at least. Time is running out! What are they doing in Tokyo?

Impatiently he rang for a servant. In seconds an elderly, effacing man trotted out on to the veranda and bowed.

'Sake!' Ishida snapped, his evening thoroughly ruined. The servant whirled and rushed to obey.

Tegal, central Java coast

Lamban stopped at the roadside stall and unslung his backpack. He sat on a bench under a palm-leaf awning while he rummaged for a half-rupiah coin to buy a coconut and star fruits.

It was the sixth day of his journey west. On the fourth he had woken to find his bicycle had been stolen. He had carried on, walking in the early mornings and late afternoons, and resting during the hottest part of the day. At night, he had respectfully claimed the hospitality for the traveller required by Islam and had slept comfortably in the clean but Spartan hut each hamlet or village kept for that purpose. In normal times he could have expected a meal as well, but only the first three had a meagre amount of food to spare. Fortunately, he had a small bag of rice with him. Now the bag was almost empty and he was still several days' walk from the capital. Nowhere could he buy rice or bread.

Along the coast the roads had been surprisingly busy. Few questions had been asked of him. Most of the travellers were half-starved farmers and plantation workers from the interior who had given up on the land and were heading for the larger coastal towns and cities to try and find work or alms. Many were young or middle-aged men. Only rarely did Lamban see a man accompanied by a wife and children. At night around camp fires there was little talk of home. Many had abandoned their families.

People quickly became suspicious of him when he asked about Sukarno or even where he could get rice, thinking him either a Japanese spy or a black-marketer. Only the day before, he had seen the hanging, mutilated corpse of a Chinese merchant. The man's arms had been hacked off and the word 'usurer' cut into his chest.

'I can't make a living anymore,' grumbled the tiny, wizened woman serving him. 'No one has money for coconuts and fruit these days. They go on hikes to pick their own. Nothing but bad news and misery. It wasn't like this when the Dutch were here.'

Lamban sighed. It was not the first time he had heard people speak favourably of the Dutch, so he was no longer surprised by such sentiments. His own experiences and the deprivation he had seen on the road had left him chastened. Yet despite that, he could not let the statement pass unchallenged. 'That will change soon,' he replied with forced confidence. 'Once we have won our independence we will be free to—'

'Starve to death!' quipped the crone. 'Tell me, my would-be Diponegoro, while you are winning our freedom who will be planting the rice and wheat?'

'Well, I—' he stammered, caught off guard.

Enjoying his confusion she prattled on. 'I've seen many rebellions in my time: Bantam, Solok, Kediri. I lost a son to one. They all ended the same way. Executions, prison and higher taxes! You young fools know nothing!'

'But if we don't try—' They were interrupted by revving from a tired engine. Lamban glanced down the road. An old, rusting lorry was approaching. A large, rectangular green flag fluttered above the passenger window.

'*Masjumi,*' whispered the woman, her expression now bright in the expectation of a sale. The *Masjumi* was the largest Islamic association in Java. For many Javanese its word was law. But not Lamban. To him it was too subservient to the Japanese. Unconcerned, he returned to the awning to rest his legs and eat his coconut.

The lorry lurched to a stop, its brakes squeaking. From the irregular rattle of the motor and the smell of the exhaust, Lamban guessed it was running on alcohol. Its solid rubber tyres were badly perished. Faded letters on the lower part of the door read 'East Indies Tea Estates'.

Two slim, thin-faced men in their mid-twenties jumped out of the cab. They wore the dark headscarves and green-check sarongs favoured by the devout and white, short-sleeved shirts. Lamban would have paid them no further attention except that as one of them retied his headscarf a lock of hair dropped well below his ear. Swiftly he pushed it back under the scarf, glancing warily at Lamban as he did so.

They bought two coconuts and joined Lamban under the awning. The one with the long hair was half-turned away from him but the other chose to watch him keenly.

'*Salam aliyah kum,*' said the man using the formal Arabic greeting to a stranger.

'*Aliyah kum salam,*' Lamban replied equally politely.

The man's eyes were bright and restless. He kept looking repeatedly back down the narrow, dusty road. 'Have you travelled far?' He continued in Javanese.

'From the east, near Semarang,' volunteered Lamban.

'And where are you heading?'

'Djakarta.'

His eyes widened. 'On foot? That's a long way!'

'My bicycle was stolen.'

'Disgraceful! And people call themselves Muslims!'

'Perhaps it was a Communist?'

His inquisitor was not put off. 'Let's hope so. Do you have relations in Djakarta?'

'No,' replied Lamban. He had no desire to talk, so he decided to be slightly rude. 'If possible I intend to work for Sukarno.' Sukarno was not noted for his piety or for his good relations with the *Masjumi*. For an instant Lamban thought he saw a flash of genuine amusement in the other's eyes. He rose to leave.

'A noble cause,' replied the man. 'I wish you a safe journey. May God watch over you.'

'And over you too,' replied Lamban automatically.

A short time later the lorry passed him on the narrow road. Except for two wooden crates the flatbed was empty. Plenty of room there for a tired traveller, thought Lamban. But the lorry did not stop and it swept round a tight bend. Seconds later he heard the harsh squeal of breaks followed by angry shouts.

Lamban quickened his pace, moving instinctively into the cover of the bushes at the roadside. He peered round the bend. A rope was strung across the road. Four men, the two *Masjumi* and two others, one holding a pistol, were standing by the lorry's cab. Two more men were prising open the crates. Lamban slipped off his pack and crept closer until he was level with the cab.

A triumphant shout from the flatbed sent one *Masjumi* dashing for the undergrowth. By the cab, a powerfully built man, spun quickly, flicking out his arm. With a gasp the runner went sprawling at the edge of the road. He lay motionless a little more than five feet from Lamban, His headscarf had slipped off and long hair hid his face. A knife was buried deep between his shoulder blades.

The killer moved to retrieve his weapon, Lamban watched the other *Masjumi*. He had moved around slightly, keeping the other bandit in view. Something told Lamban he would make a move when the other man was farthest away. He gauged the distance to the gunman and from him to the flatbed.

When the killer reached his victim he placed his foot casually on the man's back for purchase then bent to reach for the hilt. Lamban sprang forward. As the killer's head jerked up in surprise Lamban's shin slammed against his throat, crushing his windpipe. His eyes bulged and he went down in near silence, clutching frantically at his throat, his legs thrashing. Lamban was already rushing for the gunman.

Distracted, the bandit with the gun turned. Instantly the *Masjumi* grabbed for the weapon and the two men began to struggle. The bandit shouted. Two seconds later Lamban was chopping at his elbow, numbing his arm. The pistol fell to the ground. Lamban gave a low snap kick and felt the bandit's knee-cap dislocate. With a howl the crippled man toppled. The *Masjumi* snatched up the gun.

One bandit jumped down from the flatbed with a half-drawn machete at his waist. Lamban's instep slammed upwards into his groin, bending him double. Grunting, the bandit slashed wildly with the machete. Lamban sensed rather than felt his keris in his hand as he closed and thrust. His assailant crashed against him, then slumped to the ground dead, his aorta severed.

Even as the man fell, Lamban was reaching for the machete, ready to face the fourth bandit. But he had jumped down on other side of the lorry. Lamban could hear someone plunging through thick vegetation. He let him go.

'Ampun!'—Mercy! *'Ampun!'*

Lamban turned. The *Masjumi* was kneeling, holding the pistol to the injured bandit's temple.

'Allah akbah!'—God is great! The *Masjumi's* voice was solemn. There was a muffled report and the bandit was still. The man glanced indifferently at the body and then at Lamban. His expression was cold and quite calm. 'Is that one dead?'

Lamban nodded.

'Your timing was perfect! Thank you, my friend!'

'Are we friends?' Lamban asked staring at the pistol.

The man smiled thinly, then looked deliberately at the machete in Lamban's hand. 'At least we are not enemies. We should go,' he said confidently, stuffing the pistol into the top of his sarong. 'First, let's hide the bodies. We must also take poor Wodjana with us,' he added glancing at his late companion.

For some reason Lamban was not surprised that the *Masjumi* did not want to report the attack. He did not complain. The idea of talking with the *kenpei* or even the local police did not appeal to him either. He dropped the machete.

The *Masjumi* bent to take hold of the man's ankles and waited for Lamban to take the man's wrists. 'Communists!' he spat dismissively. Then he looked up at Lamban and laughed. 'Perhaps they were the ones who stole your bicycle?'

It took them only seconds to dump the bodies in the vegetation beside the road. Then they wrapped the dead *Masjumi* in a tarpaulin and put it on to the flatbed. The *Masjumi* began to collect the wads of religious pamphlets that had been emptied from the crates. Lamban did the same. As he went to replace them the man moved quickly to block his way, taking the pamphlets from him but not before Lamban had seen the automatic pistols in the crate. He said nothing. Five minutes later they were driving west.

'My name is Sarel.'

'I am Lamban.'

'Are you a student?'

'No. Just a traveller. And you?'

'*Masjumi!* Isn't it obvious?'

Lamban turned and looked at Sarel. 'You are dressed as *Masjumi*,' he said calmly.

Sarel grinned but did not reply.

'What did the bandits—I mean the Communists—want?' Lamban asked blandly.

'Oh, they wanted me dead.'

'Why?'

Sarel turned to look deliberately at Lamban. 'Because once I was one of them.' A second later his easy affability returned. 'Please be patient, my friend, everything will be explained soon. You have my word.'

Kalisari Village

Sarel spoke rarely during their journey, so Lamban had plenty of time to think back on the fight. He had taken life for the first time. What surprised him was how little it bothered him. In one sense, since robbery and murder were abhorrent to his faith, his actions had been no more than his religious duty to aid the innocent. He had not hesitated to draw his *keris* and kill. Taruna had trained him well.

By the time they reached Kalisari the sun had set.

'Nearly there!' Sarel announced as he braked and swung off the main road and on to a narrow but unpaved track. After a few hundred feet three men armed with staves barred their path. Sarel flashed the headlights and they moved aside. Two minutes later they were among the village huts.

Kalisari was much larger than Sadakan, Lamban's home, but there were few villagers in sight. As Sarel pulled up outside a large hut several young men emerged. Sarel told Lamban to stay in the cab and got out. As he whispered and gestured, the men crowded round him, glancing keenly at Lamban. Then they began to unload the boxes and the body.

After a few minutes Sarel returned. 'Bring your things,' he said. 'You are safe here. But please, for now ask no questions.'

Lamban followed him. The boxes and body were nowhere in sight.

Sarel clapped him on the back. 'You must be hungry! We have enough food here. Tonight your hut will be guarded. Please do not be offended. Tomorrow we will talk.'

Lamban was shown into a small, windowless hut. After a few minutes a youth brought him a small portion of roast chicken and rice. The youth did not speak to him. Lamban ate with gusto then lay down to sleep.

Familiar, early-morning sounds of village life woke Lamban just before dawn. Soon there was a knock on his door and a different youth invited him to bathe. He was led down a steep track to a river. A rock cascade formed several pools accessible by stepping stones from the bank. The residents of Kalisari used the lower ones for laundry, the deeper top ones for bathing. When he returned to his hut a breakfast of coconut milk, banana and cassava was waiting.

He was told to wait. Later there was another knock on the door and Sarel entered. 'Good morning. I hope you spent a comfortable night.'

'Very,' replied Lamban.

'Good. I must leave for a short time. When I return we will talk. Please feel free to move around.' He closed the door abruptly and Lamban heard him give instructions that he was to be watched discreetly throughout the day.

Lamban enjoyed an easy day wandering around the village. Dusk had fallen before he saw Sarel again. 'Tonight you will meet some people who feel very much as you do,' Sarel said cheerfully. 'I will be there soon.' He left a young boy to guide Lamban to the much larger hut where they were to have dinner.

A teenage girl in her best but threadbare *kebaya* and sarong greeted Lamban politely and invited him inside. Eight young men were sitting quietly on the floor around a mat laden with rice cones, fruits, grilled fish and chicken. Each of them had at least shoulder-length hair. They eyed him cautiously but with a certain respect.

The girl brought Lamban a finger bowl and showed him to his place. Then she served him a piece of fish and some rice. Lamban's stomach was growling but he noticed none of the others had started, so he waited. After a while the youths began talking among themselves.

Sarel joined them a few minutes later. Now bareheaded, thick, loose coils of hair hung past his shoulders. He sat and raised his hands for silence. 'Lamban, it is time for me to keep my promise. You should know with whom you share the funeral feast.' He looked around him, deliberately holding the gaze of each of the youths in turn. 'As you have already guessed we are not *Masjumi*. We call ourselves the *Banteng Hitam*—Black Buffalos. We have dedicated ourselves to securing independence, first for Java and then for our Muslim brothers in the rest of Indonesia. This village is just one of our bases.' Satisfied, he sat back affably, his palms open. 'Eat! Eat!'

Still the others did not reach for their food.

Sarel sighed, 'We must look forward' he said sombrely. 'Yesterday we lost Wodjana. I, too, came close to death. Tomorrow it could be anyone of us. Have you forgotten our pledge so soon? No mourning until we can mourn as free Indonesians! We cannot fight for independence if we are weak with hunger. Now eat I say!'

Slowly, the youths reached for the food. As they did so, Sarel began to recount at length how Lamban had saved his life.

Gradually the others livened up except for one who sat in glum silence. When Sarel described the fighting they looked at Lamban with undisguised admiration.

'Pentjak silat!' said one excitedly, 'No-one round here knows it anymore. The Dutch banned it years ago.'

Another cut in, 'And the selfish Chinese won't show us their way of fighting.'

Lamban said nothing. He thought of Taruna who had shared with him the deadly *kuntao*.

'Indeed, you are fortunate to have been taught the *silat* of old,' Sarel enthused. All we know are the festival dance routines! Of course the Japanese taught those of us in the militia some unarmed combat but it is nothing compared to your skills. You all should have seen him! We are very lucky to have found you, Lamban.'

'I am obliged to you,' said the glum youth suddenly. Lamban turned to look at the young man. His eyes were tearful. 'I am Kurja. Wodjana was my brother. Thank you for avenging his murder.'

'I'm sorry I could not prevent his death,' said Lamban softly. The young man got up and left them.

'Give him time,' Sarel said with a shrug. He turned to Lamban looking at him earnestly. 'So you want to work for Sukarno and the National Party. That's very worthy but why waste your time giving out leaflets and collecting alms for Djakarta's poor? Don't you want to do more?'

'I want to help us to became free in any way I can,' said Lamban proudly. Sarel became thoughtful as he heaped rice on to his own plate and then Lamban's. 'Many people say they want freedom. It means different things to people in Java. Some, like our aristocracy and the upper-class *priyaji* bureaucrats, want freedom from the Japanese, naturally enough. But they also want the Dutch to return.'

'Why?' Sarel continued confidently, 'because they, too, like their Dutch-given privileges and position over us! And let's not forget that the Communists want the freedom to make us all godless Marxists!'

Expressions on the faces of the Buffalos hardened at the mention of their chief rivals for the affections of young Javanese.

Sarel's contemptuous tone grew louder. 'As they do so, a select few, while expressing sincere regret, will become rich and powerful.'

Heads were nodding rapidly in agreement.

'And let's not forget the Chinese! All they want is the freedom to get rich at our expense. Even as our people go hungry, they still put their profits first!'

Lamban thought of the lynched Chinese shopkeeper he had seen a few days before.

Sarel was warming to his theme. 'Politicians like Sukarno-*tuan* and Dr Hatta talk of grand ideas like freedom of speech and freedom of assembly, of rights to this and that and about elections. Yet *they* still co-operate with the Japs! Isn't it strange how our leaders oppose the West with one hand but cling to Western ideas with the other? It's all they know! Dr Hatta is a most pious, dedicated man, of that I am sure. Yet they expect to lead us! Why? Because they are wealthy and because they speak Dutch, so they can "negotiate" with our masters! Isn't that rather arrogant?'

He paused for effect, then carried on. 'Now Dr Sjahrir, true, will have no truck with the Japs and I respect him for it. But he and Dr Jarisha want a parliamentary democracy!' Sarel laughed scornfully. 'What use are the debates and referendums of democracy for millions of half-starving peasants and illiterate shanty dwellers?'

Sarel's eyes settled on Lamban. 'Take Sukarno. He is a wonderful orator who can hold a crowd in the palm of his hand. And a true Javanese. His vision of a free, united Indonesia is a powerful one. But he, too, knows only western methods. The temporary political alliances he favours will only make him weaker in the long run.'

Lamban shifted on his cushion and reached for some rice. He knew nothing of political alliances but felt the need to say something. 'What about the *Masjumi*?'

Sarel looked pleased. 'A good question. It is true they are our Muslim brothers but, like the aristocracy and the religious associations their eyes are fogged. They have become dependent on obligation and patronage. They want only a symbolic change at the top and nowhere else. If not, they might have to prove anew that they are worthy recipients of the peasants' respect and, of course, their donations. That prospect scares them.'

He sat back, raising his arms for emphasis. 'In truth, Lamban, none of them has anything *new* to offer. Who else is left? Only we *pemuda*—the youth—can go forward without the trappings of the past.'

Lamban found himself nodding with the others. He had seen too much pining for the old days.

'The world is changing,' Sarel continued. 'The Japs lied to us. They would never have given us our freedom even if they had won. Soon they will be defeated. Sukarno and Hatta know it. But still they keep asking the Japs to approve this committee or that association. You've heard Sukarno on the radio. Why does he keep asking us to meet ever-higher rice levies when people are dropping dead in the street from hunger? Why does he ask us to send our young men to work for the Japanese in Burma and Malaya, even though he knows they are treated like beasts of burden and are dying like flies? Why does he encourage our young women to nurse the brave, wounded Japanese, knowing they will end up in Jap brothels? The answer, Lamban, is because he thinks that by doing so he can remain a leader. But how can the Japs help him after they have lost the war?'

'No!' Sarel's expression was one of despair. 'Things are happening, Lamban. For three years we have waited, our lives stalled. I was a law student in Bandung. Wodjana was my classmate. The Japs closed our institute. I returned home with no qualification, no job. My wedding had to be cancelled because I had no future. There are thousands like me. But we did not give up. We set up study groups to circulate ideas and news. Our numbers grew. When the Japs formed the *Angatan Pemuda*—the Indonesian Youth Movement—it was a perfect cover for us. There is an IYM co-ordinator in almost every large village!'

'All the time our elders encouraged us to think and question. They thought they could use *hormat* to control us but they miscalculated.' *Hormat* was the traditional respect offered to an older or socially superior person. Sarel rocked back on his hips. 'It works between ignorant peasants and aristocracy but not when debating independence, suffrage and tithes. Let me give you an example. A month ago the Japanese organised a national IYM conference in Bandung. I was there with two hundred others. Two resolutions were carried unanimously. The first was a demand for immediate independence for Java. The second was a declaration: *Merdeka atu mati!*—Freedom or Death!'

A ripple of excitement ran through the youths. Galvanised by the phrase, they raised clenched fists and chanted. '*Merdeka atu mati!*'

Sarel's enthusiasm was infectious and his audience was hanging on to his every word. 'Two weeks ago, five thousand high-school students held a public rally in Ikada Square in Djakarta. They also demanded immediate independence and pledged to carry on the struggle against any oppressor! With one voice they swore the "Freedom or Death" blood oath then slashed their hands. It's true. The square is still stained red! Afterwards, a delegation demanded to see Sukarno. He told them, "The future of Indonesia lies in the hands of our youth." I swear those were his very words!'

A beaming, near ecstatic smile lit up Sarel's face. 'Just a week later Sukarno and Hatta invited our representatives to join the new National Indonesia Independence Party. Can you imagine our elation, Lamban? At long last, our leaders could see and value the strength of the *pemuda*, the youth of Indonesia.'

His expression darkened. 'For three days we stood and debated with Sukarno and Hatta in person! We called on them to end the negotiations, the endless delays and the fawning to the Japs. They listened, smiling, then dismissed us as impetuous and naive!'

Sarel shrugged. 'They still do not *see* us, Lamban. Neither do they see that Japan is finished nor that all their procedures and committees are pointless. Our fight will be with the Dutch and *anyone* who helps them. There must be no negotiation, no bargaining, no more meetings. In this we *pemuda*, we who have nothing with which to bargain and so nothing to lose but our lives, must take the lead. With God's help we will succeed!'

A chorus of approving shouts greeted the end of the speech. 'Yes! It's the only way!'—'We will push the Dutch back into the sea!'—'God is with the righteous!'

Sarel let them be then motioned for quiet. 'Lamban, soon the Dutch will return and the fighting will commence. It is a matter of a few months, no more. Everyone in this room has pledged his life for our country. Also, we have taken an oath not to lie with women or cut our hair until Indonesia is free. Why? Slaves only breed more slaves. Our hair serves as our badge. We did not hide our oath from the *kenpei*. As it grows longer, so it is more difficult to disguise and so more dangerous for us not to act.'

'No-one here doubts your bravery, Lamban. We know you love your country and that you are our true Muslim brother. It is more than enough for us. We invite you to join us and become a Black Buffalo. What is your answer?'

Lamban looked at the expectant faces. He felt excited, certain now that his meeting with Sarel had been God's will. But he also remembered the swift execution of the Communist. He was under no illusion as to Sarel's nature. Already he knew too much about the group to be allowed to live should he refuse. But he did not want to refuse. He stood up.

With great formality Sarel handed him a copy of the Koran.

Lamban spoke without hesitation. 'I swear on this holy book that I will give my life for the independence of Indonesia. Until my country is truly free, I will not lie with a woman or cut my hair. *Allah akbah!*'

Around Lamban the Black Buffalos began the Freedom chant.

'Merdeka!'—*'Merdeka!'*—*'Merdeka!'*

Chapter Seven

Tjandi Camp III

For a few days Kate tried to convince herself that the stoppage of the extra food was an understandable precaution on the part of the Japanese lieutenant. After a second week, she wondered whether he was punishing her. His slap had hurt but the instant she had seen Shirai she understood that she had risked far worse for her indiscretion.

Her small reserve of food and medicines was soon exhausted. Cramping, sickly hunger pangs soon returned with a vengeance, and they seemed worse than she ever remembered them. She had started to feel weaker and her mother's condition also regressed.

By the end of the third week, Kate was starting to despair. Frequently she risked a beating and solitary confinement by smuggling her mother bits of food from the Japanese kitchen. But it was never enough. Somehow she knew she had to see the lieutenant and beg for his help, whatever the consequences.

Kate spent long, lonely vigils watching the guesthouse. Finally, one morning nearly three weeks after the incident in the camp, her heart sank when she saw a different male face at the window. She left the garden close to tears.

Raised voices were coming from her hut. Kate groaned when she recognised the haughty tones of Julia Stam. 'But Lady Teresa is the Governor-General's wife!'

Julia was a tall, slim, slightly stooped woman of about fifty-five who stalwartly maintained the colonial tradition of fawning. She lived in the main school building where Teresa van Gaal and a small group of Java's former well-to-do held court. They had been among the first arrivals in Tjandi and had laid claim to far more than their fair share of living space. Less deferential inmates referred to them scathingly as the 'Bridge Club'.

In the early days, Lady Teresa, her teenage daughter Elizabeth, Julia Stam and the other members of the Bridge Club had loftily assumed that they were exempt from gardening, cooking and latrine duties. Their assumption had been short-lived and had ended with several being given black eyes by their social inferiors. Despite that painful humbling, they would occasionally try to reassert their lost status.

Kate could see Julia was struggling to maintain her poise. 'All we ask is that Lady Teresa and Lizzy be allowed a few minutes' privacy while they bathe.'

Julia's was arguing with the feisty Gretchen Herfkens. Gretchen had run a bar—and, rumour had it, a brothel—on the Semarang waterfront. Before the war, Julia would have crossed the street to avoid her. Now she was sharing the same latrines.

Gretchen was fuming. 'Privacy! You got to be kidding! The Japs in the watchtowers can see us showering and peeing for Christ sake! Why don't you ask them if milady's shit smells any different from mine!'

'How dare you be so disrespectful!' Julia hissed.

'Disrespectful to who?' Gretchen raged. 'Pompous fools who lied to us and then let the Japs walk all over us!'

Livid, Julia drew herself up to her full height. 'When you insult Lady Teresa you insult her Majesty Queen Wilhelmina!'

'Julia, have you forgotten that the great and the good wouldn't let us leave Java? That it's their fault we're stuck here?'

Julia was not listening. 'I should have expected this from rubbish like you!'

Gretchen flared. 'Rubbish am I! You arrogant bitch! For three years you've been trying to lord it over us. Two thousand half-starving women and children. People dying every day and all you can worry about is who's eligible for your bloody club and what's happened to your silverware!'

'You cheap—'

Tenko! Tenko! Two guards and a civilian administrator, a Javanese woman called Salina, strode into the hut announcing a roll-call. Their argument forgotten, the women bowed immediately to the guards and to Salina, who enjoyed her work.

'Hurry!' Salina demanded sharply in Dutch. 'Over sixteen and under thirty-five-year-old whites and half-castes only.' She turned quickly and marched out to the next hut.

Perplexed, the women moved to obey. Fifteen minutes later almost six hundred women were lined up. Kate stood next to Rukmini. Unexpectedly it was Shirai who strode up to the podium. Salina, a male civilian administrator and Shirai's interpreter stood nearby.

'I have an official announcement…,' Shirai began casually. His interpreter's delivery was quick and crisp. 'As of today, all women separated from their husbands for more than twelve months are hereby declared legally divorced under Japanese law.'

Gasps of astonishment ran through the assembled women.

'Shizuka ni shite!'— Be quiet!

Instantly they were silent, their eyes lowered.

Shirai held up a strip of red cloth. 'Also, from today all women aged between sixteen and thirty-five are to wear these

armbands. You will line up and collect one now. That is all.'
Shirai strode away.

Salina and the other administrator set up a trestle table and
opened cardboard boxes full of armbands. One by one the
women were called forward. Kate gave in her name and was
ticked off the list. Then she was handed an armband. A single
Japanese character had been stencilled on it in white ink. As
Kate walked away she turned and saw Rukmini speaking
respectfully to Salina who replied sharply in Javanese.

'What did you say to her?' Kate asked her quietly.

Rukmini looked troubled. 'I asked what this meant.'

'And?'

'She said it means "Adult" or something like that.'

'But what's it for?' Kate pressed.

Her friend shrugged. 'She said we'd find out soon enough.'

Rukmini's question was answered just before midday when
printed leaflets advertising work as waitresses, dance partners,
musicians and singers at officers' clubs in Central and East
Java were distributed through the camp. Jobs were open to
single women over sixteen and under thirty-five. Benefits
included off-camp housing, three full meals a day, soaps,
cosmetics and clothing. Volunteers would be collected the
next day. The ad was signed 'H. Guttmann'.

That night the divorce order and the leaflet were the only
topics of conversation. Many of the married women were
openly distraught. There were regular rumours that Javanese
women were being provided to the men in their camps. For
many, the order served as confirmation.

'They can't do it!' sobbed one. 'We've been married
nineteen years!'

Agnes Kuyt held out her arms. 'If my husband saw me like
this, a bag of bones, he'd want a divorce all right.'

Another scoffed. 'You really think he'll look any better?'

'It's fine by me,' said Margaret Martens sternly.

There were several sympathetic glances. Margaret's husband was a senior officer in the Netherlands Indies Air Force. Two days before the surrender he had flown to Australia, taking his Javanese mistress with him.

For a time the hut fell silent as each woman wrestled with private thoughts and fears. Finally Gretchen cleared her throat and looked at Kate and some of the younger women. 'Well then, "young" ladies, how many of you are going to volunteer?'

Irene Jansen, a missionary's wife, scowled. 'It's for one thing only,' she said scathingly. 'Prostitution!' She spat the word out.

'Obviously,' said Gretchen impatiently. 'But it's a way out of here and to a full stomach.'

'You said it,' snorted one of the younger mothers, 'full with a bastard Jap baby!'

'I'm not letting my girls go,' declared another, older inmate.

'I'd rather die!' said a brunette in her twenties.

Gretchen turned to her unimpressed. 'If you stay here that's a certainty,' she snapped. The woman began to cry.

Kate looked slowly around the room. Anna and Marja shook their heads quickly. Only Rukmini would not meet her gaze.

Later, Kate went to the infirmary. Her mother had already heard the news. She was pale and very weak. 'Promise me you won't do this, Kate,' she pleaded.

'Mama, we both need food and you need medicine. You know that.'

'Oh God! Kate, please, no!'

At roll-call the next afternoon, Kate stood next to Juliette. Both were wearing the red armbands. Neither spoke to the other. Salina was checking the register but Shirai and half-a-dozen *kenpei* were standing nearby, watching with interest. An open-backed Isuzu lorry was parked at one side of the compound.

After a few minutes a dark blue Packard saloon swept through the camp gate and stopped near the Isuzu. To some consternation, a plump, well-dressed white woman got out and mounted the podium. She addressed them in a confident, heavily German-accented Dutch. 'Good afternoon, ladies, my name is Helga Guttmann. I am an employment agent. There are job vacancies at clubs patronised by Japanese officers. In remuneration you will get three good meals a day, your own bedroom, hot baths, clean sheets and new clothes. All the comforts of home!' She paused, searching out and smiling maternally at some of the prettier girls. 'Also, you will be able to send food parcels to your families here in the camp. Are there any questions?'

The women stood silently, eyes darting left and right.

'No?' Guttmann continued smiling. 'Good. All those who are interested, please come forward and wait by the truck.'

Kate's stomach twisted and she took a deep breath. With her gaze fixed firmly on the ground she took a step forward. As she moved, she heard Marja's voice. 'Kate, come back!' She did not stop.

Along the rows, other pleas rang out. 'Melanie, no!'—'Ruki!'—'Sophie, please don't!'

As Kate pushed through the front row she glanced up and saw Shirai staring at her intently. Despite the heat she suddenly felt cold. She lowered her gaze until she was safely screened by the lorry. There were footsteps behind her and she turned dreading who it might be. With relief she saw it was Juliette. They hugged each other. Rukmini was following close behind.

Juliette tried to joke. 'Food then love!' Kate was feeling queasy and could not reply.

Sixteen had volunteered. They stood in silence, avoiding each others' eyes.

Helga Guttmann ushered them quickly into the lorry. Kate found herself by the tailgate, next to Juliette, and facing a relaxed and overweight Japanese guard.

Gradually the women lost some of their reticence and they even managed a weak cheer as they went through the camp gate. A few minutes later they pulled over behind Guttmann's car to wait while a small convoy unloaded men and equipment outside a barracks.

Kate gave a sudden start. Standing in the road and brushing dust from his uniform was the young officer. He turned to look at the lorry. When he saw Kate his eyes widened in surprise and dismay. She gave him a regretful half-smile then looked down as the lorry pulled away. At the first turn she glanced back and saw him staring after her. Her knuckles were white as she gripped the tailgate.

Djatingaleh Barracks, Semarang

Ota found Nagumo in the mess hall. His friend greeted him warmly. *'O-kaeri!'*—Welcome back!

'Thanks,' said Ota.

'How were the hot spring baths up there?' Nagumo asked between noisy slurps of his noodles. 'I was so envious!'

'Um? Oh, very pleasant,' Ota said distractedly, his train of thought far away. He looked around almost furtively. 'I need to talk to you about something.'

'Eh?' Nagumo looked a little surprised as Ota led him to a corner table out of earshot of the other diners. 'Aren't you hungry?' Nagumo asked him. 'These aren't bad at all,' he said, slurping again.

'I'll eat later,' said Ota quickly, his voice low. 'This morning I saw some of the women leaving Little Holland. One of the guards told me they've accepted jobs at the brothels. I need to know when and where they are going to start.'

Nagumo grinned. 'I don't think it will be a secret for long!'

'No, you misunderstand,' Ota said impatiently. 'I want to get there first.'

'Don't we all!' Nagumo guffawed, spilling his soup.

'No, not that! I want to find one of them before—Look, will you help me?'

Nagumo stopped eating and ran his tongue over his teeth. He looked at Ota sternly. 'Let me guess. It's "shower girl" isn't it?'

Ota reddened. 'Yes.' Embarrassed, he looked away.

Nagumo looked at him in exasperation. 'I knew it. You're daft! Why didn't you set her up in a house in town like Omura and Ishii did with their women?'

Ota sighed. 'I can't explain now. Can you find out from the clubs if they have any Dutch girls starting?'

Nagumo shrugged. 'New girls usually start on a Saturday night. It brings in business for the whole week. It's "word of arse" as you might say,' he added with a smirk. 'Anyway, what are you going to do if you find her?'

'I want to talk with her. If necessary, I'll pay.'

Nagumo scratched the stubble on his chin, frowning. 'Talk? She's young, pretty, probably a virgin.'

Ota looked at him askance. 'I don't see what—'

'It means it'll be a very expensive chat,' Nagumo explained in friendly exasperation. 'And there might be competition.'

Ota's face fell. 'Oh, I hadn't thought of that.' Then he shrugged. 'It doesn't matter. As you keep saying, we aren't saving for retirement.'

Nagumo lifted his bowl and drained it noisily. 'Well, as I remember she's skinny, so maybe you'll get a discount! What's her name?'

'Kate,' said Ota quietly, saying her name aloud for the first time.

The Guttmann House, Semarang

Nearly thirty minutes after leaving Tjandi, Kate and the others arrived at an imposing, three-storied mansion on a former colonial estate. A second vehicle carrying volunteers from two other camps arrived a few minutes later. Waiting for the new arrivals in a courtyard at the rear of the house were several bubbly Javanese girls who insisted they strip on the spot. They then escorted them to spotlessly clean *mandi* rooms, a seemingly inexhaustible supply of soaps, shampoos and soft, clean towels. Within a few minutes the house was echoing with feminine laughter and squeals of delight. Small plumes of smoke rose from the courtyard as their camp clothes were burned.

Helga Guttmann was true to her word. Each day the women received fresh food and copious vitamin pills. Meals were small but frequent. Helga explained that this was to remove the temptation to gorge. When they were not eating or bathing, they rested under mosquito nets and fans on clean sheets and feather pillows. On the third day they were also examined thoroughly, and intimately, by a Javanese woman doctor.

Kate shared a twin room with Juliette. Neither had realised how exhausted camp life had left them. They both gave in willingly to the pampered, lazy routine of the house, sleeping for hours on end, their days merging into nights. Yet they could never quite forget that soon they would be called upon to pay for their comforts. And so, in the quiet moments before sleep they would discuss the inevitable.

'Oh, Juliette! I could never do that!' Kate was curled up on her bed in a pair of pink silk pyjamas. Her hand was over her mouth and she was blushing furiously.

Juliette was sitting cross-legged in a short nightdress on her own bed across from Kate, her extended thumb held up for the demonstration. 'Now I've told you, aren't you a little bit curious?'

'No! Well...not with someone I didn't love. I just couldn't. Not for money.'

'Umm, I see,' Juliette said nonchalantly. Then she got up and jumped on to Kate's bed, pulling her up on to her hands and knees. 'Then there's this one. *Comme les chiens!*'

'Another one?' Kate craned her neck as Juliette positioned herself behind her, placed her hands on her shoulders and then began to bounce playfully against her raised buttocks. For a moment Kate was open-mouthed but then she started giggling. Seconds later they both collapsed on the bed, convulsed with laughter.

Juliette went back to her bed, pretending to be vexed. She opened a jar of moisturising cream and began rubbing it on to her legs. 'Kate, you're a bad student! I'm not going to show you any more!'

'I'm sorry, Juliette,' Kate said giggling. 'Sometimes you are so funny!'

'Well, I'm doing my best,' Juliette sighed. 'You know I haven't got the...the equipment.'

More laughter exhausted them. They drifted into another short, dreamless sleep.

On the sixth day, five hairdressers worked all morning cutting and styling their hair. As a tonic, it was almost as good as food. In the afternoon there were manicures and pedicures. Afterwards a smiling Helga led the bewildered but willing group to an upstairs landing, where she opened doors to two large rooms. Each was crammed with rails of dresses, skirts, blouses, underwear and shoes. Many still carried their pre-invasion boutique price tags.

Helga clasped her hands like a schoolmistress pleased with her class. 'Tonight, ladies, we are dressing for dinner. Enjoy yourselves!' Her charges needed no prompting. Shrieking with unsuppressed delight they descended on the looted clothes.

That night Helga confessed she found the transformation astonishing. 'Ladies,' she said sincerely. 'You look beautiful!' They sat basking in her praise until Helga pulled a sad face. 'Unfortunately, in three days you will be leaving us.'

Her audience quietened immediately but she ignored their worried looks. 'From Friday you will have your own lovely rooms here in Semarang, Magelang or in Surabaya. In a few minutes you will meet a potential employer.'

Her audience shifted nervously. Helga carried on. 'You will start work in a few days. It is really very simple. You are to be dance partners and companions, "hostesses" as the Japanese call it. Let us be quite clear about things. Certainly the Japanese officers will ask you to go to bed with them. If you accept, you can make money. With it you can purchase food and medicines for your families. If you refuse an invitation when you are 'available', I regret you will be sent back to your camp. Now, has anyone changed their mind?' She looked about her slowly, confident that few would want to return to the hunger, squalor and disease. No one spoke.

After dinner they rose and stood in an embarrassed, fidgeting line as the first of the employers was introduced. A jovial, middle-aged Japanese woman wearing a cream kimono embroidered with designs of purple peonies greeted them warmly. *'Kiriko desu-wa, hajimemashite.'*— I'm Kiriko. Pleased to meet you. She bowed.

The women returned it. Kate had never felt so self-conscious of her appearance.

Kiriko walked down the line once fairly quickly, then began to walk back again, much more slowly.

Kate felt her knees go weak. The events of the last few days had seemed almost a dream but now she knew it was very real. Oh, God! I'm for sale, she thought cringing. She held her breath as Kiriko stopped in front of Juliette, looking at her appreciatively up and down. Kiriko tapped Juliette's arm lightly with her fan and nodded to Helga. Then she moved on.

Kate felt a stab of panic at the thought of being separated from her friend. Then Kiriko turned back and considered Kate again. Helga whispered something in Kiriko's ear and her eyebrows lifted slightly, She peered at Kate and then gave her arm a tap. Kate felt relief sweep through her. Juliette's hand squeezed hers.

Kiriko chose five women then left. Kate, Juliette and the three others were asked to move into another room. Two of them, both blondes, were from another camp and Kate did not know them. Rukmini was the fifth. She came over to hug her sniffling. 'Are you scared, Kate?'

'We're alive, Ruki,' replied Kate, trying her best to sound strong. 'That's all that matters.'

Djatingaleh, Semarang

Ota spent several tense days until Nagumo finally told him he had news of Kate. 'I had to spend a small fortune,' he teased.

Ota shot him an impatient look.

'All right, I'll tell you!' Nagumo grinned. 'Kiriko says she has five new girls starting on Saturday night. Four are white and one is a half.'

'And the Akebono?'

'Six starting on Saturday. But you needn't bother, she's at the Sakura.'

'Are you sure?' Ota pressed him.

'Yes. I popped in last night and I asked Kiriko about new girls. She described them to me to whet my appetite. Anyway I saw her name and description in Kiriko's book.'

'You're sure?'

Nagumo looked pained. 'Yes! "K-a-t-e". Just as you wrote down. Age 19, blonde, 150 centimetres, volunteer from Tjandi Camp III.'

Ota relaxed and let out a slow breath. 'Nineteen.... Sorry. And thank you. Where is she now?'

'At the Swiss pimp's place in the hills. Tomorrow she goes to the Sakura. By the way, Kiriko complained the prices she paid were extortionate, so take all your cash.'

On the Saturday evening Ota and Nagumo were at the Sakura by five forty-five. Ota was very nervous, pacing back and forth. Nagumo sat smoking, thoroughly enjoying his friend's discomfort. 'You remind me of a high-school boy on his first visit to a Yoshiwara whorehouse! Relax will you!'

Just before six o'clock, two other young officers from a different regiment arrived. They greeted Nagumo but kept to themselves. Ota kept staring at them and at the door of the Sakura. Finally in frustration he sat down next to his companion. 'Shit! Do you think they know about the new girls?'

Nagumo's eyes rolled. 'Probably. After all, we are outside a brothel! But I don't think you need to worry about them.'

'Why?' Ota asked eagerly.

'They're queer!'

'Eh?' Ota's eyes widened then closed in despair as he saw Nagumo's smirk. 'You sod!'

Contrite, Nagumo held up his hand. 'All right. They're regulars here and at the Otowa. Twice a week, so they haven't got much spare cash and won't want to blow it on an overpriced, one-off screw. They're only here early because they'll be playing *mah-jong* later.'

Ota looked exasperatedly at Nagumo, then stared at the two officers, desperately hoping he was right.

At six precisely the Sakura's doors opened and two smiling and bowing Japanese women wearing bright, floral kimono ushered them into the opulent reception. Nagumo led Ota to some buttoned-leather Chesterfield settees and ordered beers. Moments later Kiriko appeared and greeted them. '*Irasshaimase!* Ah, Nagu-*chan*! *Domo!* You're very early. Don't tell me you're here for one of my new girls?'

Ota made to speak but Nagumo was quicker.

'Oh, no. They'll be too expensive for us,' he sighed heavily, his regret only partly false.

'Nonsense!' Kiriko chirped. 'You can at least have a look, then tell me what you think.'

As she spoke a dark panelled door opened and Ota saw a blonde girl in a red, knee-length silk dress, stockings and delicate evening shoes bringing their beer on a tray. She was half way to their table before he realised it was Kate. He stared open-mouthed.

Kate approached bashfully, head down. When she saw Ota her eyes bulged and she began to blush furiously.

Kiriko detected Ota's interest in the blink of an eye. 'Oh, this is Kate-chan,' she said casually. 'Isn't she lovely? Nagu-*chan*, see how your friend has embarrassed her by staring like that!' Kiriko's eyes sparkled, sensing this was money in the bank.

Kate put the tray down, bowed with her palms pressed to her thighs, and then poured the two glasses of beer as she had been trained, holding the bottle in both hands. Ota and

Nagumo held the bases of their glasses, tipping them slightly to make it easier for her to pour. Kate's hands were shaking so much she kept hitting the neck of the bottle against the glasses. Kiriko struggled to hide her irritation at her lack of grace. Kate bowed again, then left. Ota stared after her.

Nagumo, admitting defeat, let out a long breath. 'I think Lieutenant Ota quite likes her.'

'Ha! I can see that!' Kiriko fluttered her fan to hide her avaricious grin. 'Such a sweet little thing. And only a thousand yen!'

It was three months' pay. Ota's eyes widened.

Nagumo gasped. 'A thousand yen for a fleshless, clumsy amateur like that! How about six-fifty?'

'Na-gu-mo-*san*!' Kiriko's snapped her fan shut testily. 'Not only is she a lovely young woman but she is a virgin. Naturally there is a premium and—'

The door bell rang. Four *kenpei* entered, one of whom was Shirai. Ota's mouth went dry. His eyes signalled a warning to Nagumo.

Kiriko saw Ota's look, glanced at the newcomers and smoothly pressed home her new advantage. '—and, perhaps, interest elsewhere?'

Ota swallowed hard. 'All right, one thousand!'

'There, now!' Kiriko cooed, fanning herself again. 'Here's a man who appreciates quality.' She beckoned to one of her staff and whispered instructions. The girl bowed and scurried away.

Kiriko rose. 'I'm sure you'll find a delightful partner, too, Nagu-*chan*. Please take your time with your drinks and go through when you are ready.' She indicated a pair of large polished teak doors at one end of the lounge. She left them.

Ota was halfway to the doors before Kiriko had finished her bow of welcome to Shirai's group.

Nagumo caught him up. 'Take it easy!'

Ota hardly heard him. As he reached the doors he realised his heart was pounding. He knocked far too loudly. It was opened by a Javanese girl in a turquoise *kebaya* and sarong, and a white bougainvillaea flower in her hair.

Ota barely noticed her. He entered hurriedly looking for Kate. She was standing in a corner among a small group of Europeans. Their eyes met briefly before her gaze went to the floor.

Nagumo came in cheerfully, greeting those girls he knew. Yuki looked expectantly at Ota but he ignored her and walked over to Kate. She was still looking down. He bowed and held out his hand. 'Please, Miss Kate,' he said as gently as he could, still afraid she would refuse him.

Kate looked at him weakly. For several seconds she did not move then she glanced anxiously at Juliette. Then, slowly, Kate took Ota's hand.

'*Omedeto!*'—Congratulations! 'At last…' Nagumo muttered sarcastically, his eyes already drawn to Juliette.

As she had been schooled, Kate led Ota silently out of the room. She did not look at him. He noticed her shoulders were trembling. In silence they went up two flights and halfway along a hallway.

He heard her take a deep, nervous breath as she opened a door and bowed for him to go first, again her hands flat on her thighs. Once inside she moved quickly away from him. He gave her a reassuring smile and went to open the shutters.

When he turned round she had already slipped off her shoes and was undoing the buttons at the back of her dress. Startled, he lifted his hand to stop her. She looked at him nervously. He tried to put her at ease. 'I don't want you to do that.' His slow, but fluent American-accented English caught her by surprise.

'What—What do you want?' she whispered.

He shrugged. 'For you to go back to Tjandi.'

'I can't do that, not now.' Her face was pale. 'I owe you a lot, Lieutenant. May I know your name.'

He bowed, grateful for the shield of formality. 'My name is Kenichi Ota. I am very pleased to meet you, Kate.'

She bowed back. 'My name is Kate van Dam. Thank you for so many things, Lt Ota.'

'Here you can call me Kenichi…or Ken,' he added quickly. It was what his family called him.

For a few seconds Kate seemed undecided but then she gathered herself and looked him in the eye. 'I'm glad it's you tonight, Ken.' Her hands rose to her shoulders, slipping off the dress. It fell around her ankles and she stood before him in a white lace brassiere and knickers. She saw him force himself to look away.

Ota sat down heavily on the end of the bed, looking fixedly at the wall. 'Kate, please understand. You do not have to do this. If I say you changed your mind and refused me they will send you back to the camp. Nothing will happen to you.'

She shook her head emphatically. 'I will die there,' she said coldly.

He turned to her. 'No you won't. I promise I will give you food and medicines like before. I was sent away unexpectedly. Trust me, please!' He saw she was wavering and pointed at her dress. Shyly she pulled it back up.

'Please sit down,' he said gesturing for her to sit on the bed. She hesitated then complied.

Before he could speak she turned swiftly to face him. 'Why did you leave the food? Why choose me?' The words came out angrily, almost as a challenge. She regretted them instantly.

'I—I'm not sure,' he said uncomfortably, unprepared for her question. 'I see no reason to imprison women. Japan is…I have a sister, she is….' He looked away in frustration. 'I'm sorry, I can't explain. I don't know the words.'

Kate's expression softened. Keen to make amends, she changed the subject. 'What is your sister's name?'

Much of the tension left his face. 'Haruko.'

'It's a pretty name. What does it mean?'

'Spring child.'

'That's lovely. How old is she?'

He thought for a moment. 'Oh, she'll be eighteen now. I haven't seen her for nearly four years.'

Kate did not let him dwell on thoughts of home. 'Well, I didn't expect you to speak English.'

He laughed diffidently. 'I only speak a little. An American missionary lived in my village for a few years. I have not spoken English for a long time.'

She frowned. 'A missionary? Are you a Christian?'

'No,' he replied quickly. 'But my mother was baptised,' he added softly.

Kate raised her eyebrows. 'I didn't know there were any Christian Japanese.'

'Oh, there are tens of thousands,' he said relaxing at last. 'Most of them live in a city called Nagasaki. There are many old Dutch houses there.'

She looked at him for a few seconds. 'You are very kind and patient, Ken,' she said quietly.

Her words threw him and for a long time they were silent. When he looked at her again she was fighting back tears. He sat helplessly as they splashed over her tightly crossed arms. From his pocket he took a white handkerchief and laid it on her arm.

She gripped it and began to sob. 'I don't want to be a whore! I tried to be brave, like Juliette. I really tried but I can't....'

Unsure of what to do, Ota gently put his arm around her. She collapsed against his shoulder, unbalancing him. He fell back on the bed with her nestled against him. He was aware only of a feeling of contentment. Gradually her sobs subsided into sniffles. He closed his eyes, surrendering to his own nervous exhaustion.

'O-sore!'—That's it! *'O-sore!'* Nagumo crooned, repeating the folk-dance chorus. As he sang, he raised an open fan in one hand above his head, turned his body one hundred and eighty degrees, then stamped his bare feet. He finished by striking a dramatic, hands-raised pose but wobbled, and narrowly avoided tripping over one of the small tables he had moved to make a space.

Juliette, red-faced with laughter, was gamely trying to follow his lead. 'Oh, *merde!*' she giggled, 'I've gone wrong again!'

They were both wearing white- and indigo-checked *nemaki* sleeping robes. Juliette had long since given up on the fan and wore it tucked into her cotton belt. Neither of them was in total control of their movements. A half-empty bottle of *anuck* palm spirit lay on the rumpled silk bedclothes. Next to it lay an English-Japanese dictionary that Nagumo had borrowed from Kiriko.

For the hundredth time that night Nagumo attempted to guess what Juliette had said. *'Kantan na...* It's a simple dance performed by farmers. It's not difficult!' he teased in Japanese.

Juliette understood his tone. 'Oh, you're just making it up,' she pouted.

Nagumo ignored her and started another verse about harvesting the rice crop. Juliette tried the steps again and this time kept up with him, surprising them both.

'I did it!' She laughed delightedly.

Nagumo applauded. 'Hmm, *yokatta!*'—Well done! Laughing, he continued in Japanese. 'But your clothes aren't quite right. Back home the women don't cover their tits when they're working in the fields!' He reached over and yanked open the left side of Juliette's robe, exposing her breast and shoulder.

'That's better!' He spoke with such obvious satisfaction that no translation was needed.

Smiling, Juliette shook her left arm completely out of the wide sleeve as Nagumo came to an unsteady stop. He glanced down at his front. The tip of his penis was jutting out from his robe. '*Ora!*—Hey! He exclaimed, '*Aka Fuji da!*'—Red Fuji!

Juliette was taking a swig from the bottle and burst out laughing, spraying her drink down her front. '*Oui! C'est un petit Fuji-yama!*' Her knees went and she collapsed in a fit of helpless giggles on the bed.

Nagumo grinned, delighted that she had got the pun. Juliette lay sprawled, her legs slightly spread with one knee raised. He was staring between her thighs.

She met his gaze coquettishly, letting her knee fall open. 'You like what you see, I think, my little Japanese bastard?'

Nagumo grunted. 'That's enough dancing anyway,' he announced brusquely, dropping the fan on to the floor.

When Ota awoke there was a pillow under his head. He sat up and looked at his watch. He had dozed for ten minutes. Kate was standing at a cabinet pouring two glasses of iced water. She had changed into a cream silk robe.

She caught his movement in an ornate oval wall mirror and turned. There was no trace of her tears. 'I'm sorry I cried for so long,' she said softly.

'The time doesn't matter,' he said casually. Without thinking he added, 'I bought you for the night.'

She blushed. He tried to apologise. 'Sorry, I wanted—I meant to say that you can relax.'

Her shoulders shrugged and she pursed her lips. 'I am relaxed now. Thanks to you.'

He looked at her carefully. It was still not the right time to ask but he desperately needed to know. 'Will you go back?' He deliberately avoided mentioning the camp.

She nodded quickly. 'Yes. But I will owe Kiriko-*san*.'

'No, I won't ask for my money back. She won't complain.'

Kate walked towards him and leant with one knee on the bed to hand him the glass of water. Her robe was clinging and his gaze dropped to the outline of her breasts under the thin cloth. She saw his look and sat down on the edge of the bed.

'You bought me,' she said deliberately. It was a statement not an accusation.

'Yes.' He was embarrassed again. 'I just wanted to speak with you, to convince you to go back.'

'How much did you pay?'

He laughed dismissively. 'It doesn't matter.'

'It does to me!' There was an edge to her voice and he knew that she was serious.

'One thousand yen.'

Her surprise was genuine. 'That's a small fortune!'

'I thought so too,' he replied quietly, dropping his guard.

She knew then that the sum had stretched him. A sudden, mischievous thought struck her. 'How much was the Frenchwoman standing next to me? She had short dark hair.'

He shrugged. 'I didn't ask. Perhaps five hundred.'

'Oh, but why so much more for me?'

'Virgins are always expensive,' he said casually. 'Tomorrow you would have been much cheaper.'

For a moment Kate sat nonplussed, her lips parted but soundless. A tide of crimson surged over her face and on to her neck and chest. She rose hurriedly, trying to cover her embarrassment by refilling her glass.

He watched her colour deepen in the mirror and could not help laughing. 'I'm sorry. You did ask me,' he said making no attempt to hide the amusement in his voice.

She turned around, her face still crimson. 'Yes, I did, didn't I! I wasn't expecting you to be so...so well informed!' Sheepishly she went back to the bed and sat much closer. 'Kenichi, what else do you know about me?'

'Only that you are nineteen.'

'How old are you?'

'Twenty-four.'

She looked at the tiredness and the lines on his face. If he had said thirty-four she would have believed him. War does that, she thought to herself. Suddenly she needed to know more about him. 'When is your birthday?'

'February 4th.'

She clapped her hands in surprise. 'Oh, an Aquarian!'

'Aq— what?'

'It's your star sign, in the Zodiac. Aquarius is the Water-Carrier. In the camp we spend hours casting horoscopes.'

'Oh, I see. Then you are a tiger, I mean a tigress!'

'I beg your pardon?,' she said frowning.

He laughed. 'In Japan we say your birth year makes your character. There is a circle—sorry, a cycle—of twelve animals. You were born in 1926, the Year of the Tiger.'

'And what are you?' Kate asked warmly.

'A rooster.'

'Rooster? Oh, I know, a cock!'

Suddenly she blushed and began to giggle, remembering Juliette's lessons in English sexual slang. She was in a brothel with a cock...

He looked at her in confusion. 'Uh? I'm sorry—'

'Don't worry.' Gently she patted his hand. 'Cock, a cockerel, is another name for rooster.' She did a quick calculation. 'Oh, so it's rooster again this year?'

'Yes, that's right. It's supposed to be an important year for me.' He shrugged and looked away, his eyes distant.

She forced a smile, trying to lift him. 'A tigress! Well, I'll take it as a compliment. But I thought this was 2605? That's what I have to put on my postcards to my father.'

It had been meant lightly but she saw his look darken. 'That's only for the Japanese,' he muttered glumly. 'It's the 2605th year since the first emperor.' In seconds the easy mood between them had vanished.

She became serious again. 'Kenichi, how can you be so certain I won't die in the camp?'

'Because you won't be in it for much longer. Soon the Americans will come and then you will be free.'

Cheered by that thought, she replied automatically. 'And you?'

He stared at the floor. 'It does not matter about me,' he said quietly.

His words chilled her and she watched as his thoughts took him away from her again.

'You know you can't beat them,' she said fumbling for a way to break his silence.

'I know,' he said softly. 'Everyone knows…inside.'

'Then why fight? What's the point?' Suddenly she wanted him angry.

He tried to calm her by placing his hand on her arm. 'Because the harder I fight the longer it will take them to reach Japan. My family is there. I must help them.'

'By dying uselessly?' Her voice was becoming shrill.

'Kate-*san*, please, I'm a soldier. There is no other way with honour. I—'

'What noble rubbish!' She snapped back. 'I see people die every day. My friends. It's awful! I'm dying slowly. And it's your fault!'

Ota was taken aback. 'I have no choice!'

In a rage Kate rose up on her knees on the bed. 'You don't really believe that! No matter what you do, Japan's going to lose. You don't care about me. When you see me selling myself for food you just see Haruko doing the same. But you can't help her and you know it!'

He grabbed her shoulders hard, bruising her. 'Stop!' He shouted. Then he saw her tears and felt her trembling. He pulled her to him.

She wailed softly into his chest. 'I don't want to die! I don't want anyone else to die!'

They fell back on the bed and he landed half on her, his thigh between hers. She clung to him, her breath coming quick and warm on his neck. He felt himself against her but he did not, could not, pull away.

Kate lay still, amazed at the heat where their bodies touched. Her heart began to race as she yielded to her desire. This was not the romance she had once dreamed of but it was enough, now, for her to know that with this man—a man who cared for her—she could escape filth, hunger and death for a few hours. It was all she had....

At first he mistook her stillness for reproach. He stared at her body. Her robe had parted and one of her nipples had slipped from the cup of her brassiere but she made no move to cover herself. Instead, she looked at him softly. Slowly his fingers went to her hair and then to her face. Her hands held his arms tightly. Only when his lips brushed hers did she briefly let go so she could lock her arms round his neck.

He cradled her gently as they kissed, not wanting to startle her. His hands moved on her and she gasped and tensed as his flattened his palm rubbed her nipple. Impatiently he ran his mouth over her neck and on to her chest, pulling her brassiere aside to kiss her breast. He took the firm, pink tip tightly between his lips. She moaned and pushed against him, her fingers entwined in his hair, holding him to her.

Reluctantly he broke from her embrace to struggle out of his uniform, throwing his tunic aside and kicking out of his trousers. She sat up to look at his lean body. His chest and thighs glistened with perspiration. Her gaze settled on the bulge under the white loincloth. A second later he was naked, his penis erect and twitching. Kate stared, mesmerised.

He returned to the bed, quickly freeing her arms from her robe and removing her brassiere. She lay back, waiting, her arms across her breasts, then gulped in surprise as he jerked her knickers down and off over her feet. Instinctively her hands moved to cover her crotch but she stopped herself and, self consciously, dropped them at her sides, letting him look at her. She watched his face intently. For a moment he stared, savouring her body, before he lowered himself back down, hard and hot against her body.

They kissed deeply in a tangle of restless arms and legs. His mouth went to her belly and she closed her eyes in anticipation as his mouth slid over her pubis then found the wet heat. She moaned. Their bodies were sticky with perspiration as he slid smoothly back over her and settled between her thighs. He kissed her softly as he eased himself into her. Her eyes were closed and he saw she was biting her lip. He willed himself to go slowly, desperate not to hurt her, yet feeling an overwhelming desire to bury himself within her.

Kate was aware only of an intense, building tension. She braced involuntarily beneath him but the burning, tearing pressure was unrelenting. Her breath was hot and rasping on his neck. Short, tiny moans escaped her.

Suddenly her flesh ceased to resist and he was enveloped in a luxurious softness. She was arching against him, matching his frenzied rhythm until the wave that swept them along finally released them, leaving them spent and basking in a velvet heat.

They passed the night either loving or recovering. Ota dozed but Kate was determined to stay awake. She snuggled against him, not wanting to miss a moment of the night. Though her body was bruised and ached, she felt wonderfully charged and used. She was amazed at the pleasure he had given or taken. He stirred in his sleep and she stroked then kissed his forehead.

All too soon the sky began to lighten and a pang of sadness gripped her. When the first birdsong woke him, she watched him stretch and yawn, fascinated by the lines of his body. He reached for her again and they made love urgently again for a last time.

Afterwards she slipped into her robe and cut them some fruit for breakfast while he bathed. He ate and then dressed in silence, steeling himself for the parting. She stood staring out of the window while he lay back on the bed and lit a cigarette. Over the lush mountains the golden-red sunrise was spectacular. She felt herself acutely aware of the light, almost within it as the first warm beams touched her.

He came to stand behind her, his hands lightly on her shoulders. When he spoke it was in a whisper. 'I can get food to you from the day after tomorrow and then every few days until we deploy to face the Americans. When we leave, go to them as quickly as possible.'

'Yes, I will,' she said quietly.

'Kate-san, I will never forget you,' he said huskily.

She closed her eyes, fighting the tears as he turned her to face him. He was smiling, doing his best, his eyes bright. 'Soon you will be safe. I promise.' His arms went around her and they kissed. She pressed against him, her lips rising to meet his. Suddenly he broke away and left her, closing the door behind him without looking back.

Kate sank down on the edge of the bed noticing the bloodied sheets for the first time. She reached for his pillow and hugged it to her face, her tears obliterating the last traces of his warmth.

Nagumo was waiting for Ota on a sofa along the landing. He was drinking green tea. He jumped up. 'About time!' he said exasperatedly. 'I knew I shouldn't have come here last night. Four hundred and fifty yen even with a discount! I must have been mad. But she was French!'

As usual, Nagumo's good humour did the trick. Ota was smiling even before he started down the flight of stairs.

Nagumo turned to him expectantly. 'So tell me. Was she worth a thousand yen?'

Ota grinned happily. 'She's going back to the camp today.'

'Eh? Well I hope you at least had a shower together!'

'That's enough!'

As they walked down the staircase, a door opened on the landing above and they glimpsed a striking Eurasian girl in a sheer white silk nightdress. She had dark, waist-length hair and was bowing Japanese style, bidding farewell to her unseen customer.

When they were out of earshot, Nagumo let out a groan. 'How did I miss her?'

Ota laughed. 'Have you forgotten so soon? Last night you were in Paris!'

'Hmm,' Nagumo grunted. 'I think I'll have to take out a loan!'

'Let's get some breakfast,' said Ota happily.

Chapter Eight

Kalisari Village, Central Java

Lamban made the most of the chance to rest and relax. Sarel was often absent from the village for days at a time, usually attending youth conferences or anti-white imperialism rallies organised by the Japanese. On each trip he took with him a different member of the group but never Lamban. Though the Black Buffalos were friendly he sensed they were still wary of him. It seemed that they had been ordered not to talk freely about their plans. He was not really surprised or even concerned about Sarel's caution. Spies and informers were everywhere. Those barriers, he knew, would break down in time. Instead, he devoted himself to the politics of revolution.

To help him, Sarel had selected some booklets and pamphlets. Generally, Lamban found them heavy going but he persevered. During the long, after-dinner discussions about capitalism, imperialism and communism, land ownership or the role of Islam in a future Indonesian state, he rarely had the confidence to speak. Though he did not admit it, Marxism-Leninism, the proceedings and resolutions of the First and Second International all left him cold, as did assessments of Gandhi's non-violent campaigns against British rule in India. Lamban much preferred the simple, uncomplicated calls for independence in the flyers produced by the youth organisations. It was only when he discovered in Sarel's library a cheaply duplicated translation of *On Guerrilla Warfare* by the Chinese revolutionary Mao that Lamban recognised his calling. If he could not be a revolutionary politician he could serve the revolution on the battlefield, or as Mao described it, as one of the million fleas that would drive the large, powerful, imperial dog mad enough to leap into a raging torrent and certain death.

Lamban also began instructing the group in *pentjak silat*. It had been Sarel's suggestion and proved a popular diversion in the lull before the back-breaking work of the harvest. His classes were popular and his fighting skills soon accorded him considerable respect.

Yet as time went on Lamban became frustrated. Upon each return from a trip, Sarel seemed more vibrant and charged. He would report enthusiastically and then quote his favourite extracts from the latest nationalist pamphlets, boxes of which arrived from Djakarta and Bandung at the local station each week for distribution at soccer matches and festivals, as well as at mosques and schools.

One afternoon at the end of the first week in August, Sarel gathered them round. His expression was grave. 'Reports about the Atomic bomb are true,' he told them. 'With this weapon the Americans are unstoppable. The Soviet Union is expected to attack Japan at any moment. It means it's only a matter of time for the Japanese now.' He paused, letting the news sink in.

Yarek, the most studious of them, raised his hand. 'Now that Churchill has lost the British election, both Britain and The Netherlands have socialist governments. This should help our cause.'

Sarel looked sceptical. 'It's true socialism and colonialism are not compatible but it does not really seem to trouble the British or the Dutch. The 'Holland Calling' broadcasts still promise death for Sukarno, Hatta and others!'

'Yes, perhaps we are too idealistic,' Yarek sighed. 'Ideals do not win independence, people do.'

'That's right,' Lamban added, 'and strategy.'

'Don't forget guns and ammunition,' said another.

'Good strategy includes obtaining guns and ammunition,' Lamban added casually.

Sarel, impressed, looked carefully at Lamban.

'What happened at the National Youth Congress?' Yarek asked eagerly.

Sarel grinned. 'Ah! There were two-hundred delegates from all over Java! Everyone spoke with a single heart and a single voice! Isa from Bandung made a brilliant speech savaging the Fatherland Party. He called it repressive and full of timid collaborators! He's absolutely right!' Sarel became serious. 'Also, we've just heard that Sukarno and Hatta have been in Saigon to see Field-Marshal Terauchi, the Japanese Southern Area Commander. He's scrapped the People's Movement and officially announced an Indonesian Independence Committee!'

'That's wonderful news!' Yarek exclaimed, his face alight.

'It will be,' Sarel agreed with a nod, 'but only if it delivers independence. More delay is the last thing we need. It's still just another committee. Also this one is Japanese-controlled. I've seen the list of members. All of them are older and mainstream. Only a handful come from the Islamic organisations and,' he paused eyeing them, 'there are no *pemuda* at all!'

They were indignant. 'No!'—'They dare not ignore us now!'—'We are the future of Indonesia!'

Sarel watched, savouring their fury. As it subsided, Lamban spoke. 'But Sukarno has said time and again that the younger generation must have a voice.'

'Yes,' Sarel shot back. 'But only as long as the voice says what he wants to hear! There's been open argument and distrust between us and the leadership. Remember Isa's speech? There's something else. All those nominated for the Independence Committee have reputations from *before* the war. Isa said it looks more like a committee designed for negotiation not revolution. This is very worrying. Tomorrow I am going to Djakarta to consult.'

Suddenly they were tense and silent, waiting to hear who would accompany him on this most important of missions. Sarel looked at Lamban. 'We will leave at dawn.'

Djatingaleh, Semarang, 15th August 1945

Clad in *kendo* armour, Ota and Nagumo were on a former grass tennis court practising bayonet combat with elongated, rifle-shaped staffs when a young private came trotting up excitedly to interrupt them.

'Excuse me, Sirs,' he gasped breathlessly as he saluted. 'The Major's orders. The battalion is to assemble for a ten o'clock radio broadcast by His Imperial Majesty!'

Ota and Nagumo exchanged glances. Ota looked at his watch. It was nine-fifteen. 'Understood,' he said calmly.

'Sirs!' The soldier saluted and sped off, the long stock of his Arisaka rifle banging against the back of his thigh with every step.

Nagumo let out a long sigh. 'So, it's time. The Yanks will soon be here. But at least the Emperor is to honour us before we die.'

Ota felt the knot back in his stomach. 'Come on, there's not much time.'

The two men got changed quietly and walked briskly towards the compound in silence. They paused by the barracks gate and, almost as a reflex action, straightened their uniforms and belts. Ota noticed a streak of mud on one of his boots. He would have to clean them before the parade but he decided he would first check in at the Officers' Mess.

The sentry gave them a formal salute as they entered the barracks. Men were milling around the parade square awaiting the full complement of their platoons prior to forming ranks. They all knew the reason for the parade and their mood was subdued.

Two technicians were busily stringing a cable to a large, bell-shaped metal speaker fastened to a veranda pillar. Nagumo noticed some of his platoon across the square and left Ota to see to them. Ota carried on to the Mess.

As he entered, he saw several of his superiors, including Kudo, standing around the large map table at the far end of the room. Two other officers, one a lieutenant and the other a captain, stood to one side, talking quietly. Ota saw the black *kenpeitai* chevrons and realised the captain was Shirai. Ota switched his attention back to Kudo, who was giving a briefing.

'We cannot defend Semarang, obviously, so we'll fall back from the port hinterland towards Ambarawa, fighting a delaying action until we reach our prepared positions in the mountains above Magelang.'

Ota was halfway to the table when Shirai's voice stopped him in his tracks. 'Lieutenant, you are about to be addressed by His Imperial Majesty and you are wearing dirty boots.' Although the tone was casual, it cut across the room. Conversation at the table died. Heads turned except for Kudo who still stared at the map.

Blood drained from Ota's face. Being incorrectly dressed on parade was a serious offence. He was about to stammer an apology when Kudo spoke. 'Ota, this meeting is for officers with the rank of captain and above. No doubt you have only just heard that His Majesty will speak to us. I suggest that you first see to yourself and then to your men. Some of them may also have dust on their boots.'

Ota was still trying to think of something to say when he saw Captain Seguchi, who was standing behind Kudo, cast a slow and deliberate look towards the door.

'Ye— Yes, Sir. At once!' Ota saluted Kudo and Shirai, then turned and left the Mess in a cold sweat. Nagumo was about to mount the steps. Ota lifted his hand to stop him going inside.

'We have visitors. *Kenpeitai.*'

Nagumo pulled a face. 'They're getting jumpy these days,' he whispered. 'Don't give them any excuse!'

'Too late. I'm in their book for insulting the Emperor.'

Nagumo gaped. 'What!'

'Don't worry, the Major got me off the hook. I think....'

Inside, Kudo waved his hand dismissively after Ota. 'Captain Shirai, I'm sorry you had to trouble yourself with such sloppiness. But as you see, everyone is rushing to prepare for the broadcast and what will follow.'

'Does that excuse an officer in the Kudo Butai being improperly attired, particularly when addressed by His Imperial Majesty?' There was the barest hint of challenge in Shirai's voice.

Inwardly Kudo was irritated by Shirai's pettiness but he was furious with Ota for providing Shirai with an opportunity to embarrass him in his own Mess. But Kudo knew he was on dangerous ground. A report citing poor discipline would mean an inquiry at the very least. His reputation would count for a lot but disciplinary overreactions were rampant in the face of Allied gains. Like most career soldiers, Kudo had nothing but disdain for the *kenpeitai* but he had to be careful. A *kenpei* officer could arrest anyone up to three-ranks his senior. Kudo was within Shirai's range. An official charge of allowing one of his officers to insult the Throne, however flimsy, would see him in the cells in minutes, and Ota with him.

'Captain,' Kudo replied calmly, 'I can assure you that any of my officers and men found to be improperly attired will be punished. But as all my officers and men *will* be correctly attired by the time of the parade our discussion is surely academic. So please, Captain, sit down and have some more tea. No doubt we will not be enjoying these pleasant surroundings for much longer.'

For two full two seconds the men's eyes locked. Then Shirai gave a polite, clipped bow. 'Your confidence in your junior officers is most encouraging, Major. Thank you, but I do not think this is a time for tea. We shall wait outside.' Shirai strode out of the room with his lieutenant at his heels. Tension remained in the room.

Kudo read the concern in the faces of his officers and shrugged. 'We could do without such distractions at this time. Seguchi, go and make sure that Ota is as spotless as a guardsman at the Imperial Palace!'

They laughed and their mood lightened. Kudo made some more comments on their defence plans for a few minutes then straightened his collar. 'It is nearly time, Gentlemen,' he said formally. 'Let us go outside.'

One by one they filed out behind Kudo and took their places in the square. Kudo stood on the veranda and surveyed his men. Their lines were sharp, their equipment polished and their faces expectant. Kudo allowed himself a brief moment of satisfaction over the thought that Shirai would have found nothing amiss on his surreptitious inspection.

The ranks were drawn up facing east, the direction of the Emperor in Tokyo. Kudo glanced up at the flagpole. The Rising Sun flag was hanging limply. He checked his watch again and stepped down to the front of his men. His commands rang out in the stillness. 'Attention! Bow!'

Behind him the five hundred men of the Kudo Butai bent to seventy degrees as if joined at the hip. Kudo held the bow far longer than usual.

'*Yame!*'

It was nine fifty-nine. In Tokyo it would be two hours later. Undulating whistles and hissing came through the speakers before the sombre strains of the anthem 'Kimigayo' filled the parade ground. When the music stopped, men stood up straighter, anticipation on their perspiration-streaked faces. None of them had ever heard the Emperor speak. The 'Voice of the Crane' was just one of many Imperial mysteries.

Kudo prepared himself, certain that His Imperial Majesty would refer to Java and Sumatra and declare *Sonno foi!*—Revere the Emperor! Drive out the Barbarians! How his men would cheer….

After a few, crackling-filled seconds a hesitant voice began…

> *Watakushi-tachi no... Our most loyal subjects... Following considerable reflection on the conditions in the world and within our Empire at this present time, We have chosen to seek a solution...*

Poor reception and the oscillating signal made listening difficult, but it was the flowery, formal language of the Imperial Court that caused Kudo the most difficulty. One thing was clear, this was not a battle cry.

> *...an unexpected course of action...instruct our diplomats to open negotiations with the United States, Great Britain, China and the Soviet Union...*

Kudo's mouth half-opened in shock. He could barely believe what he was hearing.

> *Although everyone has done their utmost to secure victory—our soldiers and sailors, our civil servants and our one hundred million devoted citizens—the going of the war has continued to progress to Japan's great disadvantage both within the Empire and beyond...*

Finally the full implication of the announcement rocked Kudo to his core.

> *What is more, our enemies now posses a new weapon of incalculable destructive power that threatens the lives of millions. A decision to continue our valiant fight would result in the Japanese nation being obliterated from the face of the earth.... In grave recognition of this prospect we shall instead embark on a journey of peace for all those generations to follow by 'enduring the unendurable and suffering what is insufferable...'*

Gradually the voice faded, leaving only the crackling from the speakers. Again the anthem was played, but this time there was no straightening in the ranks. No-one was listening.

Kudo was incredulous. Japan had surrendered! Or had it? His Majesty had not actually said 'surrender'? He had said, 'accept provisions' and 'pave the way to a grand peace'. Wasn't that the same thing? It was so vague.... And the new bomb! What on earth was it? A few days earlier, Radio Tokyo had mentioned explosions in Hiroshima and Nagasaki where 'all living things had been seared to death by the tremendous heat. The Emperor had said 'obliteration'... Kudo felt a chill run through him. What had happened to his beloved homeland? He thought of his wife and children in Tokyo and prayed that they were safe.

Shuffling and sobbing behind him brought him back to the present. He looked at his men. They were still at attention but many were tearful. Some had bowed their heads. Others were in shock, their expressions blank and confused.

Kudo tried to think. It had been a simple enough defensive plan: fight to the death, taking as many of the enemy with them as they could. Now there would be no last stand. The war was over and he was still alive! What then for him, an officer in a beaten army? Surely honour called for his own death to atone for this terrible failure? To his surprise, he dismissed the thought immediately. The Americans would occupy Japan! His family needed him alive…. His expression began to soften as he realised he might take his men home after all.

Ota's mind was spinning. Defeat had been expected, eventually, but his fellow officers had always avoided the subject. Instead, they had talked about 'sacrifice' and 'death' but never surrender! Their Field Code specifically forbade surrender. *Japan* would never surrender! Now they were all shamed. But they were alive….

His private, most innermost hopes and fears had always been protected and hidden by a maze of subconscious mental walls. The sudden gift of life from what had been certain death left those walls shattered. Sadness and guilt surged through him, followed by immense, near-euphoric relief. His private nightmare, a haunting image of his father, mother and sister charging with bamboo spears against American machine guns, was now nothing more than a bad dream. With life came hopes. Now he might see his family again, even find a wife. In his mind he saw green eyes and blonde hair….

He peered along the ranks looking for Nagumo. Ota watched him scratch his cheek absentmindedly. Then Nagumo, too, snapped out of his shock. Guiltily, he looked around to see if anyone had noticed his lapse. His eyes met Ota's.

A crash of splintering wood and the clang of twisting metal silenced the muttering. Heads turned. The radio speaker, now dented, was rolling on the ground, tethered by its cable. Up on the veranda Shirai was glowering. He held the remains of a chair.

'It's not true!' Shirai screamed. 'It's an American trick. That was not our Emperor. Japan will never surrender!'

Kudo faced him. 'I believe you are mistaken, Captain. I suggest you return to the Mess.'

Shirai glared. 'You, of all people, Kudo! You believe these lies?'

'I obey His Majesty's orders.'

'Fool!' Shirai screamed, almost hysterical. 'The Yankees will shoot you where you stand, all of you. And in Japan they will take their pleasure with your wives, daughters and sisters before they kill them as well!'

Murmuring began among the ranks, and men shifted uneasily.

Shirai raised his hands in a frantic appeal. 'Surrender is treason! It is the Army's duty to protect the national essence. True faithfulness to the throne demands it, even if it means temporary disobedience to the Emperor! Can you live with the shame of watching your families suffer under the enemy?'

All eyes went to Kudo. Just as he was wondering how to silence Shirai, a figure broke ranks. It was the *kenpei* lieutenant. He was walking dejectedly, head down, toward the flagpole. Shirai saw him, too.

'Matsuba! Come here!'

The *kenpei* made no acknowledgement. He stopped beside the pole and looked up briefly at the flag. Then he dropped weakly to his knees. Too late, Kudo realised his intention. 'Don't—'

Matsuba drew his pistol, put it against his temple and pulled the trigger. He slumped forward, legs twitching in death spasms.

Shirai stared at the dead man then, without a word, turned and strode to his car. Tyres screeching, he sped out of the compound.

In the ranks men were talking loudly. Kudo knew he needed to restore his authority and quash any rash urges among his own officers.

As Kudo stepped back up on to the veranda, Sergeant-Major Tazaki called the men to attention. In an instant the lines were sharp and silent but many of the faces were questioning. Kudo wasted no time. 'Well, men, it appears that the war is over. You must, as I do, feel shocked and confused. Whatever has happened, I remind you that you are still soldiers in the Sixteenth Army. You have not been defeated in battle. Our future is now uncertain but we are loyal soldiers of the Emperor and we will obey the imperial command.'

Even as he was speaking, Kudo was puzzling over the fate of the Emperor. Clearly the broadcast was a recording and could have been made *days* before. What if the Emperor had already committed suicide? Where did that leave his armies? Kudo realised that if he had had trouble understanding the speech then so would most of his men.

'Obviously, His Imperial Majesty has not ordered his armies to surrender so that they can commit mass suicide. Since the Emperor has denied it for himself, it is denied to us all.' Kudo searched for something positive. 'Tonight, everyone is to write to his family so that they can plan for your eventual return home.'

At the mention of home and family, faces brightened. With relief, Kudo could see he was settling them but he also wondered if he were raising false hopes. 'There will be a parade at 0700 tomorrow when I will give you more information. Your letters will be collected then. In the meantime all regular duties and patrols will continue as normal but the preparation of defences shall cease.' He was about to dismiss them when he remembered General Yamagami's warning. 'Also, you are not to mention or discuss the end of the war with anyone other than members of our unit. Unfortunately, the local Javanese must now be considered potentially hostile. That is all. Dismissed.'

Before him the ranks broke up. Some men sat alone, others stood talking in small clusters. Kudo went into his office to await instructions from Saigon and Singapore. He sat down heavily at his desk and pulled out an unopened bottle of Bols gin from a bottom drawer. Three years earlier, the former Dutch commander had left it behind in his rush to leave. Kudo had been saving it for a special occasion. He broke the seal, poured himself a long drink and sat back. A proverb came in to his mind: 'After the battle, tighten your helmet cords!' It had been coined by the great seventeenth-century *shogun*, Tokugawa Ieyasu. Kudo raised his glass to the official photograph of the Emperor on his office wall. 'To tight helmet cords!' he said sombrely, draining his glass.

Kroja, Central Java

Lamban was awake very early. He had never travelled by train before and he was looking forward to seeing Djakarta for the first time. The group gathered to see them off, regarding Lamban with open but good-natured envy.

At Kroja station Japanese soldiers were checking travel papers but Sarel produced travel passes issued by the Navy Liaison Office and they were waved through. Sarel then bought two return tickets. The train was late. Sarel sat contemplating the ripped and faded 1942 timetable on the wall facing them. 'Look at that,' he said after a while. 'At least the Dutch could run a train service. There used to be seven expresses a day each way. Now there's one slow train—if we're lucky!'

Their train, six carriages pulled by a straining, dilapidated locomotive eventually arrived over two hours late. At least sixty people were waiting by then and Sarel just managed to find a seat. Lamban chose to stand by a window. In a few moments the corridors were jammed tight with passengers and he lost sight of Sarel. As the train moved off, Lamban found himself smiling. He marvelled not only at the scenery but also at the railway itself, the Dutch railway.

'Remember, Lamban,' Sarel had told him while they waited, 'it was built by the Dutch to take the wealth of Java, our wealth, to the ports and then on to Holland. This railway helped destroy our way of life. It tied us down with Western hours and minutes and brought the Dutch overseer with his whip; and Dutch soldiers to put down revolt. Our sultans' palaces, once sacred sites of pilgrimage, are now minor stations on the way to those ports.'

Sarel had then given him a sudden, quizzical look. 'Should we therefore hate and reject this Dutch machine?'

Lamban's confusion amused Sarel. 'Perhaps. But it also brought the Dutch doctors who circumcised you with a sterile scalpel instead of some doddering priest with a rusty knife! It has brought Dutch engineers with knowledge of irrigation; and rice and wheat when there was famine. Now it helps us distribute our pamphlets and attend rallies. It's working—very inefficiently, I admit—but it's working, finally, for Indonesians without the Dutch. That's what matters!'

He thought about Sarel's words as the train ran through wide valleys, inside long, neat brick-lined tunnels or crossed gorges and canals on graceful stone and ironwork bridges. He thought of the knowledge—the Dutch knowledge—behind such construction.

For the first time, too, he looked upon his country and saw it desolate. Stacked rice terraces appeared to wrap themselves around the steep volcanic slopes, framing mile after mile of abandoned plantation. Acre upon acre of stunted tea, coffee and cocoa plants that had been chopped down then left un-watered to sprout feeble, spindly shoots. Decades of cultivation were now in ruins, and forest jungle, once relegated to the peaks, was already reclaiming much of the fertile higher slopes. Only the rubber, cinchona and sesame, deemed essential for the war effort by the Japanese, were still tended.

Once again the train slowed almost to a crawl then screeched to yet a another stop. Supplies of coal had run out long ago, so the locomotive was burning wood. Countless stops were needed to take on fuel.

Some six hours after they left Kroja they reached Bandung with minutes to spare to catch the last train for Djakarta. Two men were waiting for Sarel. They handed him a wrapped parcel. Lamban managed to find two seats and watched as the three conversed animatedly on the platform until the train began to pull away. Sarel had to jump aboard.

Lamban was in a rickety but crammed third-class compartment. Outside dozens clung precariously to the footboards or sat on the roof for a free ride. When Sarel finally reached him he was visibly excited. He gripped Lamban's arm and put his mouth to his ear. 'There is news! Did you notice the big tower on the way into the town? 'That was the radio station mast. Some of our people who work there told me Hirohito has announced Japan's surrender!'

Lamban stared at him. 'Then we've run out of time!'

'Let's just say the time for discussion has finished,' Sarel replied resolutely. 'Keep it to yourself, for now.' He released Lamban's arm. 'Now I have things to prepare.' With that he returned to his papers in silence, his face set.

Lamban sat restlessly for a while then gave up his seat and pushed through to find a window.

From Bandung the tracks turned north through more mountains before descending to the coastal plain where they ran parallel with the coast. After five hours they reached Tjikampek, a main junction and their progress quickened. As they neared the capital, Lamban noticed large, newly settled *kampong*s, already slums, clustered around each station. Furtive, hungry-looking men, women and children begged at every stop.

As they crossed the bridge over the Tjileungsir river, Sarel made his way to Lamban. It was almost dusk. Another large *kampong* stretched ribbon-like beside the tracks. Sarel pointed at the makeshift shelters and small fires. 'This is Bekassi. Three years ago its population was eight thousand. Now it's fifteen and growing every day. There's no work and little food here. See over there, that high wall?'

Lamban peered at a high, red-painted wooden palisade two hundred yards from the rail tracks. 'The Chinese quarter,' said Sarel casually. 'The Chinks control the rice trade from here to Krawang. They have food but they won't share. Just look at this place, these people. Filthy! Soon there will be trouble.' Sarel had spoken as if it were fact. Lamban said nothing. He had heard the same tone after Sarel had killed the bandit.

Thirty minutes later the train arrived in Djakarta. Much of the city was in darkness but the Central Station, a cavernous, tiled building, with a glass roof and intricate wrought-iron columns and supports, was teeming with travellers and beggars. Javanese police checked their papers and again they were let through. No Japanese troops or *kenpei* were to be seen.

Once outside, Sarel led Lamban quickly to a line of two-seater bicycle-rickshaws called *becaks*. They climbed into the front one and the driver, who sat behind the cross-seat, began pedalling. Sarel gave the driver their destination. 'To Weltevreden, 31 Menteng. Please hurry.'

Lamban recognised the address of the headquarters of the National Youth Movement. His excitement began to soar.

Bodjong, Semarang

Kudo read through the short letter to his wife a second time then folded it and placed it in the envelope. His tunic, shirt and pistol belt hung over the back of his chair. He was in his vest because he had wanted to write home not as a defeated soldier but as a husband and father. After all the years it had not been easy. He leant back in his seat behind the dark, polished teak desk in the study and rubbed his red, tired eyes. The bottle of Bols from his office stood half-empty in front of him.

Following the Emperor's broadcast, Kudo and his staff had kicked their heels for seven hours for confirmation and new orders. It had seemed like seven years. Finally, at ten thirty, a message had come from Singapore informing them simply to expect a signal the next morning. Kudo decided that Fifth Army HQ had no idea at all what was going on in Tokyo. He had dismissed his officers and had returned home, going straight to the study.

He looked around the formally decorated yet comfortable room, knowing that he was there for the last time. Tomorrow he would leave the house...and Lena. His eyes settled on a photograph of her husband. Kudo sighed. He had never been master here. A dead man's house. At least, he thought, he would be free of the ghosts. And in Japan he would no longer be under Lena's spell. He wondered if she had heard the news. Rumours about the surrender were rife.

Wearily he sat up and took a deep breath, then eased his neck. He poured himself another gin and began to rummage through the desk drawers, pulling out his belongings. Among them was a small leather pouch containing brushes and gun oil. He placed it on to the desk, then reached behind him for his pistol.

The door opened and he saw Lena entering with a tray. Her hibiscus-patterned blue silk robe seemed to float behind her. She paused, clearly surprised by his slightly dishevelled appearance, then padded towards him. 'I thought you would like some iced tea and mango,' she said casually.

From her tone he sensed immediately that she knew Japan was defeated. He grunted and looked away, only to hear her gasp, followed by a crash as glassware shattered. He spun round.

The tray was on the floor. Lena stood transfixed, her face pale. She was staring at the desk.

Perplexed, Kudo followed her gaze and saw the bottle, the letter and then the pistol. He read her thoughts. His laugh was hollow and sarcastic.

'No!' Lena screamed. She lunged wildly at the pistol, sweeping it off the desk. Then she flung herself against him, pinning him in his seat and sobbing against his chest. 'Don't do it! Please, don't you die, too!'

Kudo sat stunned. Tentatively he reached to stroke her hair. Lena did not resist him.

Chapter Nine

The momentous mid-August morning began much as any other. Kate had overslept and she rushed down from the infirmary to the kitchens. She found her fellow cooks waiting and chatting in front of the small storerooms.

'They're still locked,' Anna told her. 'Mai has gone to find out how long for this time.'

Kate sighed. Locked storerooms meant a punishment of a day or longer without food. Even so, she was glad she was back in Tjandi. Her departure from the Sakura had been regretted rather than opposed. Kiriko had even given her fifty yen and some soaps and shampoos that were worth a small fortune as barter in the camp. After Kate had signed a short letter of resignation she had only a few minutes to find Juliette to tell her she was leaving. Kate made her promise to return to the camp as soon as the Americans invaded. When she went out to the car that was to take her back, she found Rukmini inside holding similar gifts from Kiriko.

'Kate! You too!' Rukmini had smiled shyly, hugging her. 'Oh, I'm so glad!'

Yet there was a new awkwardness between them and they had travelled back in silence. Since their return, they had never talked of the Sakura. Ota had told her to say she had changed her mind at the last minute. Rukmini had told the same lie. Although there had been comment their quick return stalled the gossips, and the questions soon turned to envious enquiries about the food, clothes and facilities at the Guttmann House. Juliette and the others who had not returned were discussed with undisguised contempt.

Kate was surprised by how quickly she got back into the camp routine. For four weeks Ota had kept his promise to supply the extra food. Something else made life bearable. When she collected the sacks she would look up at his window. More often than not he would show himself briefly.

'Everybody gone!' Mai returned, panting. She waddled quickly across the compound waving excitedly. 'No Jap! Nobody!'

Kate looked up at the nearest watchtower and saw it was unmanned. She squinted at the far tower. Again, there was no sign of a sentry. They looked at each other questioningly, suppressed excitement growing. Unbidden they started to walk silently towards the camp entrance. When they saw the deserted guardhouse Kate's pulse began to race.

They halted in a nervous huddle a few feet from the gate. Kate moved forward gingerly and raised her hand to one of the thick bamboo crosspieces. Her heart was in her mouth as she pushed. It was unlocked! She heaved and watched incredulously as the gate swung open. Ahead of her stretched the main road into Semarang. There were no Japanese in sight, only a few farmers heading for their fields.

Kate's hands went to her mouth. Tears filled her eyes. Next to her someone sobbed. Suddenly they were all shouting at once.

'Oh, God it's over!'—'I don't believe it!'—'We're free!'— 'The Americans have come at last!'

Kate hugged Mai and Anna, then laughing and crying she sped off to tell her mother.

Like wildfire the good news spread. In minutes the assembly area was teeming with joyously excited women and children. People were embracing tearfully and noisily. Many held hands in little groups to say prayers or sing hymns. Kate rushed among them looking for her friends. She hugged Marja and Rukmini, and even Julia Stam. Her elation was now tinged with regret over what her freedom meant for Ota but she could not help herself.

Around her groups broke out into spontaneous choruses of the 'Wilhelmina', the Dutch national anthem. For some it was too much and they wept uncontrollably. Others cheered and waved pieces of orange clothing, the banned colour of the Dutch royal house. Renditions of 'God Save the King' and the 'La Marseillaise' blended as British and French internees burst into song.

At the sudden, chilling boom of the gong there was instant silence as two thousand apprehensive faces looked to the podium. Hundreds snapped to a conditioned, fearful attention. When Jenny Hagen, the camp leader, stepped up there were gasps of relief and then cheers. Grinning, Jenny beckoned them to her. 'We have wonderful news!'

They surged forward expectantly. Jenny did not disappoint them. 'The BBC says that Japan surrendered yesterday. The war is over!' A momentary silence was followed by roaring cheers.

Kate felt giddy. There would be no fighting! Ota would not die. Her chest felt tight. She sat down to catch her breath.

Jenny was struggling to make herself heard and was waving for quiet. 'Please! Please listen! Of course we can celebrate but a Holland Calling broadcast advised us not to gloat or antagonise the Japs in any way...or to leave the camp.'

Her audience looked at her quizzically. Many were dumbfounded. There were groans of dismay.

'It makes sense,' Jenny pleaded. 'The atomic bombs have completely destroyed some cities in Japan. We don't know how the Japs here will react, so please, no loud singing and dancing.'

One shout carried above the others. 'Where are the Americans?'

Jenny shrugged. 'As far as we know the Americans have not invaded. I'm sure they will come soon. Until then, we must wait and conserve our food rations as before.'

Disappointment and resentment was tangible. 'We need food!'—'What about my husband?'—'They can't make us stay here!'—'I must find my family!'

Jenny tried to shout above the chorus of disapproval. 'Please, try and be patient just for a few days!'

More angry shouting drowned Jenny's pleas until a Japanese army lorry entered the camp at speed. In another uneasy silence the women watched it circle them and then stop. For several seconds there was no movement. Finally the cab doors opened and two expressionless Japanese guards emerged. Ignoring their audience, they dropped the tailgate to reveal a stack of Red Cross food parcels. The women of Tjandi cheered.

Djakarta

Rear-Admiral Ishida was slumped in his chair, flicking through a sheaf of papers. His open shirt was creased and he was unshaven. Empty sake bottles were lined up on the desk amidst piles of documents. Wafts of smoke entered the office through the open French windows where Tashiro, looking equally unkempt, was patiently feeding paper into a large brazier on the patio.

Ishida dropped the file on top of a pile at his feet and picked up another. Like many, it was stamped 'Secret'. Ishida opened it and smiled thinly. It was a Naval Intelligence report on a *kenpei* plan to assassinate Dr Hatta and then fake his death as a road accident. Ishida had intervened just in time to prevent it. Fortunately for Hatta, he had visited Tokyo soon afterwards and had been decorated personally by the Emperor. The award had scared off the *kenpei*, though they had continued to watch Hatta very carefully.

Ishida placed the file on the 'safe' pile, the one that would not be destroyed before the Americans arrived. There was, he thought, no reason why Hatta should not be grateful to him in the future. Another wave of depression hit him. What future! He had, after all, been prepared for Japan's defeat for many months. It was the manner of it that bothered him now. Unconditional surrender! That possibility had never occurred to him. It was unbelievable!

The brief warning he had received in code from his superior, Admiral Shimizu, had not lessened the almost physical shock he had felt on hearing the broadcast. His entire staff had squeezed into the small radio room to listen. Many had been left pale and tearful. And Hiroshima and Nagasaki, what of them? Obliterated! His aunt's family had lived in Nagasaki.... How could he ever face his own for allowing that to happen? Once again his eyes went to the holstered Nambu automatic pistol on his desk. 'Duty first, *Admiral*,' he muttered to himself.

The telephone rang and he answered immediately. 'Ishida... Very well. In thirty minutes will be fine. I'll need you to interpret.' He cradled the receiver and looked at Tashiro who was watching from the patio. 'That was Nishioka at the Research Office. Sukarno and Hatta are with him. They are coming here.' Ishida stood up and stretched, then saw his reflection in the ornate mirror behind his desk. 'Let's clean ourselves up.'

When his three visitors arrived at Nassau Boulevard, Ishida was shaved and in a clean shirt and pressed uniform. Tashiro, also now smartly dressed, showed them into a small lounge away from the chaotic office. Hatta and Sukarno sprang out of their seats as Ishida entered. Exhaustion and anxiety were etched in both their faces.

Sukarno, tie-less, his tailored suit showing stains and creases for once, spoke in a loud, breathless rush. 'Admiral, the news, is it true?' As he began, Nishioka, the interpreter, moved to stand just behind Ishida, so that Sukarno and Ishida maintained eye-contact, something that Ishida always insisted upon. The interpretation was almost simultaneous. 'General Yamagami wouldn't—actually no-one—would see us at Army Headquarters! There are all sorts of rumours. The BBC....'

'Admiral,' Hatta interrupted sharply, 'we heard there was a broadcast by the Emperor. Please, tell us what he said. Has Japan surrendered?'

Despite his reserve, Ishida swallowed audibly and half-bowed. 'Gentlemen, it appears that the war is over. His Imperial Highness spoke of ending hostilities. I fear that Japan has failed Indonesia. I cannot be certain because we have had no official report. We are waiting for confirmation from Tokyo.'

'Confirmation!' Hatta's shout startled Ishida. The Sumatran was staring at him with an expression of wide-eyed incredulity. It was the first time Ishida ever heard him raise his voice. The moment passed. Hatta and Sukarno exchanged looks of alarm. Sighing, Hatta sat down and let his head drop into his hands. Sukarno also sat slowly in silence, his face pale.

After a few moments Hatta regained his composure. 'I can't believe it has happened now, just days away from our declaration of independence.'

Sukarno's dejection was total. 'I have never felt so useless! Japan promised us independence. Three years you have been here. We helped you, obeyed you! And for what?'

Ishida stood in silence, his face dead-pan. Inside he cringed with bitter regret and shame.

'It doesn't matter,' Hatta said suddenly, his voice taut with emotion. He stood up quickly. 'Admiral, you must excuse us. We have much to discuss.' In silence the two nationalists filed out of the room.

When the door had closed, Nishioka looked imploringly at Ishida. 'Admiral, is there nothing we can do?'

Ishida frowned. 'Be patient. It depends now on who moves quickest, the Dutch or the Indonesians.'

Weltevreden, Djakarta

It was late evening when the *becak* tricycle turned into the entrance of the imposing building at 31 Menteng. At one side of the drive the red and white Indonesian flag flew from a pole. The *becak* stopped in front of a large veranda supported by a row of four thick white stone pillars. High above the lintel, Lamban made out 'Hotel Schomper' set out neatly in relief in the whitewashed stone work. Below it, neatly but simply painted on a wooden board was 'Asrama New Generation'.

Sarel paid the driver extra to wait then led Lamban up the wide steps and into the elegant and spacious reception lounge of the former hotel. Small groups of young men and a few women stood engaged in noisy, animated conversation.

'Everyone knows the war's over!' Sarel shouted to him with a grin.

They moved quickly down one of the building's two wings towards the sound of applause and shouting. As they got nearer, the crowding increased and they were soon having to elbow their way through.

Eventually they entered what had been the hotel's banquet room. It was crammed; every chair was taken and people were sitting on tables. Around the sides of the room people stood four deep. Ceiling fans were struggling to cope with the thick clouds of cigarette smoke. Several raucous discussions were going on simultaneously and crude, anti-Japanese and anti-Dutch slogans were being bantered across the room. The mood of the students was excited and expectant.

Sarel exchanged casual waves with several others as he and Lamban threaded their way to stand halfway along one wall. Sarel pointed out people to Lamban. 'The one in the red shirt is Isa,' he said warmly. 'That's Surubo speaking now. He's the general-secretary. We get on, even though he's a headstrong Marxist. The thin one next to him is Kabuno, another Marxist. Somehow both of them work for the Japanese propaganda office!'

The thick set and animated Surubo was working his audience into a rage. 'All along our leaders have been too cautious. They prefer to compromise and submit rather than demanding what is ours by right!'

Loud cheers drowned his voice. He raised his hands for silence. 'We will not kow-tow to the Japanese any more than we would to the Dutch. We must be ready to fight!' He sat down to chants of *'Merdeka!'*.

Kabuno jumped up on to a table. He was tall with narrow features and piercing, dark eyes bright with emotion. The crowd clearly wanted more of the same and he did not disappoint. 'My fellow Indonesians!' Kabuno bellowed. A roar of approval rippled round the room. 'There is no Indonesian state. Why? Because of our own weakness and fear! We must *take* our freedom. Seize our own independence!'

Again the chanting began. 'In-do-ne-sia!'—*'Merdeka!'*

Just as the chorus began to falter, Sarel moved forward purposefully, hand raised, chanting 'Free Djakarta! Free Djakarta!' The new cry gathered volume. When he reached the centre he was embraced by the other student leaders.

Quickly Sarel climbed up next to Kabuno and began to pump the air with his fists, changing the chant to 'Freedom or Death!' It was quickly taken up, becoming more strident, the rhythm pounding. Soon the enraged students and *pemuda* were little more than a mob in waiting. Sarel drew a knife and held it high over his head. 'Free Djakarta now!' he roared. Dozens of almost berserk youths spilled out of the room heading for the streets.

Sarel jumped down from the table and worked his way back to Lamban. 'This is good,' his voice was hoarse. 'Look at them! Ready to die!'

Lamban could see Sarel was right.

'Come on, let's go!' Sarel was already pushing his way through the mêlée, still encouraging people to take action. Once outside the emotion left him immediately, as though he had taken off a mask. 'We'll go and see Wadana at the *Asrama Merdeka*. The Navy might have information about the Americans' arrival,' he said calmly.

Lamban had seen Sarel play the *dalang*, the puppet master, before. Around them gangs of rowdy students were heading menacingly towards the city centre. Many carried staves or stones.

Their *becak* was still waiting. 'To 80 Kebon Sirih,' Sarel said to the driver, settling back contentedly. 'Lamban, we arrived at just the right time. Some of them might even challenge the Japanese tonight.'

Once again Lamban recognised the calculating tone. He gave Sarel a quizzical look. 'But they stand no chance against armed soldiers. Why encourage them?'

Sarel looked at him patiently. 'Angry students are one thing; dead ones—nationalist, socialist, communist—are martyrs. And every revolution needs its martyrs!'

Parapatan, Djakarta

Just before dawn the slow-moving convoy of three large cars, driving without lights, turned quietly off the Kramat Boulevard and drew up outside 56 Parapatan Timur. Four men stepped up to the veranda, forced the door and darted inside. Other men armed with pistols and swords took positions at the front and rear cars.

Lights flashed on in the house and then went out. Minutes later, a man and a woman clutching a sleeping baby were led down the path and ushered into the middle car, a Mercedes saloon. Its single other passenger watched nervously as he moved over to make room for the family on the rear bench-seat.

The cars pulled away. In the Mercedes, Sukarno put his arm around his wife's shoulders to comfort her. He glanced worriedly at Hatta. Neither spoke as they sped west out of the city.

Kebon Sirih, Djakarta

In sharp contrast to 31 Menteng, the mood at the *Asrama Merdeka* was gloomy. The half-dozen students there were sitting in miserable silence.

For several minutes, Sarel had sat huddled in muted conversation with Wadana, a dour-looking, thin youth with wiry, unkempt hair, who worked for the Navy Liaison Office as a translator. From where Lamban sat, Wadana's part in the conversation consisted solely of shaking his head.

After a while Wadana got up dejectedly and left the room. Sarel, looking pensive, moved over to sit with Lamban. 'It's all true. Wadana heard it himself. It's unconditional surrender. The Allies ordered the Japs to maintain law and order until they come.'

Lamban leant forward. 'When will that be?'

'No-one has any idea. There's more bad news.'

'The Dutch?'

'No, but bad enough.' Sarel paused. 'It looks as though the British are coming to Java, not the Americans.'

'Does it make a difference?'

'Anti-colonial Yanks would have been better. The British want to hold on to their empire, so do the Dutch. After the fighting in Europe the British and the Dutch are very close allies. We must assume the British will be pro-Dutch.'

'But that's disastrous…' Lamban suggested.

Sarel shrugged. 'As God wills….'

Late next morning Wadana and another student woke them noisily, their eyes wide with excitement. 'Surubo plans to seize the Radio Station tonight!'

Lamban glanced at Sarel and saw the glint of satisfaction.

'It's true! The other student could hardly contain himself. 'They're going to broadcast a declaration of independence at midnight!'

Sarel snorted. 'Surubo and a few students? Meaningless!'

The student shook his head. 'No! Sukarno will make the announcement.'

'Sukarno?' Sarel asked quizzically.

'Yes!' Wadana gushed. 'A *pemuda* delegation went to see Sukarno and Hatta to demand a declaration! Now Kabuno has taken them to write it! We must be ready to fight!'

'Wait!' Sarel demanded, fixing him with an icy stare. 'What do you mean by "taken", and where?'

Wadana's enthusiasm wilted. 'They—they were taken out of the city early this morning,' he muttered weakly. 'It was for their own safety....'

'What?' Sarel threw up his hands. 'You mean they've been abducted!'

Wadana stared at the floor. The others looked on in astonishment.

'Surubo's a moron!' Sarel started pacing about the room. 'Doesn't he know he's putting Sukarno's life in danger? And Hatta's too? May God help us all! An independence declaration will bring tens of thousands of people on to the streets. It'll be chaos! You can bet the *kenpei* already know about the broadcast and will try to arrest him at the radio station. If Surubo and Kabuno resist, Sukarno could end up dead! Don't you understand? Nothing must happen to Sukarno. Nothing!'

Wadana was ashen. 'But we had to do something!'

'Surubo's mad!' wailed one of the students. 'The Japs will mow them down if they attack the Radio Station!'

They were all watching Sarel. He stopped pacing suddenly. 'The Japanese *Army* will shoot,' he said calmly. 'But what about the Japanese *Navy?*'

Wadana looked puzzled. 'Why should the Navy help us now?'

Sarel pursed his lips. 'They founded this *asrama*. Admiral Ishida's sympathetic to our cause. Also, Sukarno and Hatta are his friends, he won't want them dead or in a *kenpei* cell. If they were under the Navy's protection, they'd be safe from the students and the Army couldn't arrest them.'

'Then what shall we do?' Wadana asked uneasily.

Sarel's eyes flashed. 'Tell the Navy interpreter, Nishioka, what's happened. They'll need to get someone with authority to Sukarno and Hatta as soon as possible. Where's Kabuno holding them?'

Wadana hesitated. 'I promised not to—'

'Where?' Sarel glared menacingly.

'Rengasdenglok,' mumbled Wadana. 'At the militia HQ.'

Admiral Ishida's Residence, Nassau Boulevard, Djakarta

'Well?' Ishida looked up from his desk, glancing impatiently at his watch. It was nearly five in the evening. His frustration was beginning to show.

Nishioka was in the doorway. 'Nothing yet, Admiral. I expect to hear very soon.'

Ishida's initial fear was that Sukarno and Hatta had been seized by the army at the request of the Allies. He had telephoned the *kenpeitai* HQ who told him they had not heard that the two Indonesian leaders were missing but that they would start a search. Ishida had not been convinced until Wadana arrived later with more details.

'It's taking too long,' Ishida said half to himself. He was appalled by the prospect of mass demonstration and the bloodbath that would ensue. 'Rengasdenglok is only thirty miles away.' He stood up. 'I'm going to see Yamagami. If the *kenpei* find out about the Radio Station they will deploy in force. I must prevent it.'

The phone rang in the outer office. Both men tensed. Tashiro spoke briefly then put the call through. Ishida grabbed the phone from its cradle.

'Ishida!' He relaxed a little as he listened, nodding at Nishioka. 'Good. Bring them here as soon as you can. Give the details to Nishioka.' Ishida handed over the phone and waited as Nishioka conversed for several minutes in Javanese.

Nishioka hung up, relief showing on his face. 'Kabuno told Sukarno and Hatta there had been a *coup d'état* and they were being taken out of Djakarta for their own protection. When they were asked to write and sign a declaration of independence they called Kabuno's bluff and refused. It wasn't long before the students started arguing among themselves. That's when our messenger arrived with your offer. He had a hard time persuading them, even with your guarantee of immunity. They'll be here in an hour. I've promised Kabuno there will be a declaration by noon tomorrow or he can shoot me!'

Ishida gave a hollow laugh. 'They'll have their declaration but Yamagami might well end up shooting me—and you!' The phone rang again in the outer office.

'Admiral,' Tashiro called through the doorway. 'That was the duty officer at *kenpei* HQ. They have no news of the Indonesian leaders but they have arrested a group of armed students near the Radio Station.'

'Hell! Any shooting?'

'No, just a few broken bones.'

'Good. I'll try and help them later. Warn the kitchen staff we're going to have visitors. It will be a long night!' He stood up, buttoning his tunic. 'I still need to talk with Yamagami. If the army would only agree to turn a blind eye. Just for a few hours.'

Ishida's offer of a meeting room for the Independence Preparation Committee had been gratefully received. Word had spread quickly. Throughout the evening Committee members had been arriving from their homes or hotels in Djakarta.

Not all had come alone. Tashiro had been watching from a window. 'Admiral,' he had warned, 'I think the Committee members must be under surveillance.' Ishida had looked out down the long drive to see a group of loitering men. '*Kenpei* lackeys looking to earn their last few yen,' he said dismissively.

A moment later, a maroon Packard 120 convertible flying Ishida's personal pennant swept into the drive, hood up to hide its passengers. He greeted Sukarno and Hatta with genuine concern but thought they looked none the worse for their ordeal. After offering them the use of the guest *mandi* rooms to wash and shave, he sent Sukarno's wife and baby home in the Packard. It was six thirty. At the end of the drive he noticed the number of informants had reduced. Probably on their way to report, he thought. Time for him to talk with Yamagami!

As he turned away, a flash of headlights announced more visitors. This *pemuda* delegation was arriving. Ishida could not hide his amusement when a surly Kabuno and four other youths refused to sit with the Committee. Instead, they were shown to a separate lounge already stocked with refreshments by the ever-efficient Tashiro.

Ishida picked up the phone. An echo on the line made him wonder who else was listening. 'General Yamagami? Ishida here. Good evening. It is late, I know, but as I am sure you are aware—'

'I know Sukarno and Hatta are at your house,' Yamagami interrupted.

Ishida was impressed but remained composed. 'That's correct. They wish to meet with you to discuss—'

'Listen to me, Ishida,' Yamagami thundered, 'I know what you're up to. It's too late. I've just had formal notification from General Itagaki in Singapore that the terms of surrender require the army to maintain the *status quo* in all occupied territories. Specifically, all political activity is to be frozen as at August fifteenth.'

'But General, this is not just politics—' Ishida grimaced as Yamagami cut him off again.

'Hear me out! Now that *I* have been informed, *I* am *personally* responsible for any infraction. Therefore, it is out of the question for *me* to talk about Indonesian political aspirations with *anyone.*' Yamagami paused then continued in a conciliatory tone. 'I accept, however, that the *Army* needs to be briefed about the abduction, so I suggest you see Major-General Honda in General Affairs as soon as you can.'

Yamagami's meaning finally registered with Ishida. Silently he cursed his slowness.

'I quite understand, General. Excuse me.' Ishida slammed the phone down and twisted to face Tashiro. 'Quick, get another car! I'm taking Sukarno and Hatta into the city.'

The walls of Major-General Kazuo Honda's office, which had once belonged to the Chairman of the Royal Indies Bank, were lined with white marble. In contrast, the furniture was dark leather and polished teak. Art-Deco clocks, glassware and bronze figurines decorated the room.

Honda, his shaven-head glistening with perspiration, sat stiffly behind a long table flanked by four of his officers and an interpreter. Across from them were Sukarno, back in neat collar and tie, and Hatta in his trademark crumpled jacket. Ishida sat over to one side on a luxurious padded Chesterfield that would let him observe Honda.

Sukarno and Hatta knew Honda well enough, so the formal pleasantries had been completed very quickly.

'My commiserations, Gentlemen, on your defeat.' Hatta stressed the last word and much of the haughtiness left the four men facing him. 'First, General Honda, I wonder if you can tell me when British forces will arrive in Java?'

Honda looked at his minions for confirmation. They remained impassive. 'We have no information at all,' Honda said quietly.

'I see,' Hatta said exasperatedly. 'Well then, have the Allies made any comment about an independent Indonesian Government?'

Surprise showed on Honda's face. Again he turned to his officers. They mumbled among themselves briefly then Honda looked back at Hatta. 'There has been no comment. Since Indonesia is not independent there is no Indonesian Government...'

Hatta leaned forward, changing tack. He did not mince his words.

'General, we need to be frank. We request a full explanation of the Japanese position regarding the independence of Indonesia. In particular, we are asking for confirmation that independence will go ahead as planned.'

Honda made to speak but Hatta stalled him with a raised finger. 'If not, will the Japanese Government permit an immediate declaration of independence, backdated to August 11, the date Marshall Terauchi gave formal approval?' Hatta put his hands together and waited.

Ishida heard Honda swallow.

Honda's face was a mask and his lips bloodless as he replied. 'Any move to declare independence is unacceptable to the Allies. Japanese military authorities have been given responsibility for maintaining the *status quo*. If we allow the Independence Preparation Committee to continue we would be liable to severe penalties. The Committee was set up by the Japanese, as such it falls under the terms of the surrender agreement. We cannot allow....'

Ishida listened carefully, intrigued, by the prepared speech. A secretary was taking detailed minutes of the meeting. Honda was merely going through the motions. He was leading—or hoping to be led—to something. Hatta would see it too, he thought, even through an interpreter.

Hatta did not disappoint. 'But if something were to happen outside the Committee?'

Honda shifted in his seat, suddenly much happier. 'Outside?'

Hatta leant forward again. 'Yes, for example, what if there were civilian disturbances.'

Honda shrugged, staring at Hatta. 'Well, I suppose....'

Finally Sukarno saw the ruse too. 'What if an independence declaration was made outside Japanese control? Would that be acceptable political process?'

'Absolutely not,' replied Honda. He looked at the colonel sitting to his left and then firmly at the secretary who stopped writing. 'Of course, if it were done without our knowledge we probably could not prevent it.'

Ishida took a deep breath. There it was! Tacit agreement that the army would not intervene. All they wanted was an alibi.

Hatta and Sukarno looked at each other, then over to Ishida. It was more than enough.

Ishida's study was choked with cigarette smoke. Sukarno, Hatta, Nishioka and a man called Matoba from the Army Propaganda Office sat with Ishida around a small table. Ishida was presiding as Chairman.

Bleary-eyed, Hatta stretched. 'Is there any word of Dr Sjahrir and Dr Jarisha? Really, they should be here.'

Sukarno's irritation was clear. 'We cannot delay. Now, are we agreed on "administrative"?'

There were tired nods around the table. The single paragraph had taken them nearly two hours to compose. Each time they presented a draft to the religious, civic and *pemuda* representatives waiting in the adjoining room the *pemuda* objected that it was too tame and made changes. Ishida was striving to avoid the use of any language implying a formal transfer of sovereignty. At the same time, he was desperate to prevent violence against the Japanese.

'Once again then, please,' said Ishida. Sukarno began to read. 'The Indonesian people hereby declare their independence. The existing administrative organs must be seized by the people from the foreigners.'

Ishida grunted in disapproval. 'Wait! Not "seized from foreigners". It's crude. I understand the *pemuda* enthusiasm, but phrases like that will only provoke the Army. It may have surrendered but it is still proud. Don't risk insulting them.'

Hatta concurred. 'How about something like "transfer of power"? That's vague enough.'

'That's better,' agreed Sukarno. 'The *pemuda* will just have to accept it.'

There were more weary nods around the table and Sukarno laboriously crossed out the changes and began to write again on a fresh sheet of Ishida's writing paper. Sukarno began reading again. 'We, the People of Indonesia hereby....'

When he finished speaking there was silence for several seconds.

'At last,' sighed Hatta standing with relief.

The others also rose, looking tired but elated at the same time. As Ishida shook hands with Sukarno and Hatta it occurred to him that he had probably donated the paper for his own death warrant. He bowed. 'Congratulations, Gentlemen!'

'Now we are on our own,' Hatta said to him quietly. 'We had better go through and get the others' signatures.'

Ishida looked at his watch and sat down. It was four-thirty in the morning. It was not long before they heard the howls of dissatisfaction. The exchanges were loud enough for Nishioka to provide a commentary. 'The text is too tame. It has no revolutionary spirit! The *pemuda* will not sign with the "*kenpei* nominees" on the Independence Committee because the

Committee is a Japanese creation.... Now the Committee will not sign with the *pemuda*.... Sukarno and Hatta are refusing to change a word.' Finally, Nishioka was smiling. 'The vote has been carried!'

Ishida closed his eyes.

Ten minutes later, as the Indonesians were leaving, Nishioka showed him the paper. It bore only two signatures, Sukarno's and Hatta's.

At noon that same day, Sukarno stood outside his home at Parapatan with Hatta by his side and addressed a small crowd. His speech was brief. 'We, the people of Indonesia, hereby declare the independence of Indonesia. Matters concerning the transfer of power and other things will be executed by careful means and in the shortest possible time.'

As Sukarno spoke, the *merah-putih*—the red and white—flag was raised and the group sang 'Indonesia Raya' as their anthem for the first time.

Word spread by word of mouth, telephone and telegraph. At seven o'clock that evening, Radio Bandung's hourly broadcasts of the declaration in Javanese and English were fed through to the short-wave transmitter and out into a largely indifferent world.

Book Two

Chapter Ten

Admiral Lord Louis Mountbatten, Supreme Allied Commander South-East Asia, was pensive as he sat listening to his political advisor, Esler Dening, summarise the latest in a long and growing list of instructions and urgent requests from London. Mountbatten was not unhappy about this but he did not like being pushed.

Dening cleared his throat in an attempt to reclaim his superior's attention. 'Well, Admiral, the highest priority is to get troops into Hong Kong. The Navy are rushing a couple of destroyers there from Australia to fly the flag but General Chiang's forces are a bit too close for comfort. We want our troops there a.s.a.p. Up to now, Chiang has agreed to us taking the Jap surrender but London is understandably nervous. They suggest, and I quote, we "divert troops previously earmarked for Operation Zipper, the now cancelled invasion of Malaya", unquote.'

Mountbatten was in no mood for instructions and his irritation showed. 'You would think that by now Whitehall might credit me with knowing something about Zipper! Perhaps I should remind them it was an invasion scheduled for three months' time and for which we now have few troops and no transports. For God's sake, doesn't anyone in London have any idea of how thinly spread we are?'

Dening shifted uncomfortably. After thirty years in the Foreign and Colonial Office he didn't like to hear his Ministry criticised. Yet he had to agree. London's wish list was changing and growing by the day. He tried to sound sympathetic. 'I think from this point on we must concentrate on Malaya, Hong Kong and Singapore. Everything else must take its turn. We need to impress the Malays that we have the men and equipment to do the job. Lord knows, in 1942 we had neither! It's important, too, that the Japanese see our current strength before they are repatriated.'

Mountbatten shifted in his chair and stretched out his long legs under the desk. Once again he ran through his 'priorities'. It was a long list: disarming and confining close to three-quarters-of-a-million enemy soldiers, then screening them for war crimes; providing food and medical care for a so far unknown number of Allied prisoners of war; planning for the repatriation of a quarter-of-a-million British and Indian troops; and trying to maintain law and order in the tinder kegs that were Burma and Malaya. As if that was not enough, several million people in the region faced starvation unless he sent them food he did not have on ships he did not have. Virtually overnight he had effectively changed from a military commander with a single, clearly defined mission to defeat the Japanese army to a glorified administrator who had to consider the political implications of his every move. As it was, he was lucky if he got six hours of sleep as he tried to keep up with the signals. Peacetime was certainly harder than war!

His reply was measured. 'I am not going to send troops to Hong Kong, Singapore or anywhere else for that matter until we know that the surrender order is being obeyed. You've heard the stories of the suicide squads. In Malaya and Sumatra the Japs are still undefeated. And they could carry on in China for years!'

Mountbatten sat back and closed his eyes. Everything had changed since the A-Bomb. He had been told about it only on 29th July. Sworn to absolute secrecy, he spent ten days planning troop movements that he suspected might never be needed. He had hated to deceive his officers but the Americans had been insistent. When, finally, on 8th August, confirmation of the Hiroshima bombing had been heard on Japanese civilian radio he had called an immediate meeting of his officers and led a discussion on the implications of the new, ultimate weapon. They, like him, had been astounded. Japan had surrendered a week later, four days after a second bomb had been dropped on Nagasaki. Among his officers the consensus was that the bombs had shortened the war by at least two years.

Dening took a deep breath. He did not like being the bearer of bad news but it was time to deliver General MacArthur's latest order. 'Admiral,' he ventured quietly. 'Your area of responsibility has been increased.'

'What! Again? Where?' Mountbatten was incensed.

Dening kept his eyes down on his file as he read. 'General MacArthur has assigned the entire Netherlands East Indies east of Sumatra from his command to SEAC. You are now in charge of an additional 300,000 square miles of enemy-occupied territory and approximately 70 million people on the islands of Java, Madura, Lombok, Borneo and several hundred others.'

'London has approved this?' Mountbatten's face was flushed.

'Yes,' Dening replied softly, in awe of the fury building before him.

Mountbatten stood up shouting. 'Where's MacArthur now? We'll see about this!'

Dening tried to keep his voice calm. 'He's in Manila, preparing the formal surrender document before he flies to Tokyo.'

Mountbatten checked and then sank back slowly into his chair. A genuine laugh escaped him. 'And I thought I had problems!'

Dening was relieved. His boss was now his usual composed self. They would have a productive morning after all.

'Quite an empire,' ventured Dening.

'Not as big as MacArthur's,' Mountbatten smiled cynically. 'He'll see to that!'

Dening produced a map of the Netherlands East Indies from under his arm and spread it out on the desk in front of Mountbatten. Unusually for a SEAC map it was not annotated. Even the largest islands of Java and Sumatra were unmarked. Mountbatten looked up quizzically. Again Dening felt uncomfortable, embarrassed by the lack of preparedness, even though they could not have expected this eventuality.

'We have no information on the current situation in the Netherlands East Indies,' he said apologetically. 'I have asked London to liaise with the Dutch Embassy, the Dutch Government in The Hague, and the Netherlands Indies Civilian Administration in Australia to let us have copies of all their latest intelligence reports.'

'They'll have to do a lot better than that,' Mountbatten grunted. 'A lot better.'

Berlin, Germany, early August 1945

Meg Graham was picking her way along rubble-strewn and cratered streets. Berlin was like one enormous builder's yard. Devastation was total. Every wall was holed, every pane of glass shattered. Scarcely a brick had escaped a hit from a bullet or shrapnel. Around her the dark, shattered ruins reminded her of rows of enormous decaying teeth. She paused briefly to jot down the allusion for her next article.

Despite the warm day and cloudless sky, she was in sturdy, scuffed boots and her Press Corps uniform jacket because she did not want to be mistaken for a German civilian. After she turned on to what remained of the once-imposing Kufurstendam she headed for the fire-blackened shell of the Brandenburg Palace. Allied servicemen were everywhere and the atmosphere, for them, was festive, even though it was already over two months since the German capitulation. Some were pocketing bits of masonry for souvenirs. Others were posing for photographs amidst the ruins of the Third Reich.

Ignored by the soldiers, elderly women were queuing quietly at makeshift stalls for watery soup and stale bread, while old men and boys scratched in the ruins for firewood. Younger women and girls stood bartering for food and clothing. They had only one thing to trade and were not ignored. Meg saw their thin, drawn faces and empty smiles chasing likely clients. She felt no pity. Instead, she pictured the same faces cheering and waving swastika flags as their menfolk had marched and promising them a thousand, glorious years.

'You reap what you sow,' she said to herself without emotion.

Meg was restive. In truth, the notion of peace still troubled her and secretly she was afraid she was becoming bored. Newspapers and magazines in the United States were insatiable for stories about Berlin. But always the same stories. 'Our boys standing on the ruins of fascism,' as her editor in New York liked to put it. Those stories were still selling papers and Meg was meeting some soldiers for that very reason but her angle would be that little bit different.

She was seeing some of the paratroopers she had met in Nijmegen. At the time, the suggestion to meet in Berlin had seemed merely a hasty, parting throwaway. In fact, the platoon had not forgotten and now, ten months later, she was delighted to be keeping the promise. Yet with every step she was steeling herself to ask, as she knew she had to, how many of them had been lost on the painfully slow four-hundred mile trek to Berlin.

Sudden shouts made her jump. 'There she is!'—'Meg, over here!'

Meg saw a group of waving and smiling GIs. Two of them were arm-in-arm with German girls. She waved back.

'Hey, guys! How ya doin'?'

They swarmed round her, grabbing her hand or hugging her like a long-lost friend. Their bright faces were already losing the stress-lines of war. Boys again, she thought happily. Death no longer walked with them. They were all speaking at once.

'We didn't think you'd make it.'—'I read all your stuff. My Mom sends me the magazine every week!'

They did not notice that she could not remember their names. To hide her embarrassment she turned quickly to greet others behind her and stumbled on some loose bricks. Several pairs of arms steadied her.

'Can you join us for dinner?'—'When are you going home?'

Here I am, she thought, with these guys again and still surrounded by rubble! Then she remembered it was German rubble and she was not sorry about it, or for that matter, Japanese rubble. With Japan's surrender a week earlier the world was at last at peace, or so she had thought. That morning she had received a three-word telegram from her editor. It read, 'Fighting in Java!'

Looking around, she made her decision. This story on the 82nd would be her last from Germany. If she were quick, she could still catch the last of the war against Japan. With the decision came a faint rush of adrenalin.

'Sorry guys, 'I won't be going home just yet.' Suddenly Meg was no longer bored.

Imperial Japanese Army HQ, Djakarta

General Yamagami did not get up to greet his guest. 'Well, Ishida, you got what you wanted. I must say you've got some nerve, coming round here after the trouble you've caused.' The General paused to sip his tea, eyeing his visitor in quiet exasperation.

Ishida tried to be affable. 'In a few years, General, you will be an Indonesian hero. You are, after all, the man who made their independence possible.'

'Don't patronise me, Ishida!' Yamagami snapped. 'As I see it, you played me for a fool. You've also written a warrant for my execution. Ha! Two days after I'm ordered to maintain the *status quo* what happens? The Republic of Indonesia is declared! Have you any idea how that looks to the Allies?'

'With respect, General, I don't think it matters. They do not know the situation here. If the Dutch try to reassert control by force, then the Indonesians will resist. There will be another war. I am not sure that the Allies can dare allow that to happen. They have made too much talk of freedom and 'self-determination' to suddenly ditch those ideals in the first few weeks of peace.'

Yamagami raised his eyebrows. 'We'll know soon enough!'

'That's the reason I'm here, General,' Ishida said, nodding. 'Java is the key to the Indies—to Indonesia. Even if the Dutch take back the outer islands, which they probably will because the Republic can't defend them, without Java the rest is not viable as a colony. If they don't have Java they won't hold the other islands....'

'What do you want?' Yamagami asked cautiously.

Ishida hesitated, pursing his lips before he answered. 'The Indonesians need weapons and ammunition. You disarmed most of the militia. If they are not rearmed the Dutch will walk back into power. There is confusion all over Java. If you were to abandon the armouries to the militia they—'

'Don't say any more!' Yamagami said holding up a hand, his temper fraying. 'After I have just told you that the Allies are screaming at me over the independence declaration, you seriously expect me to disobey a specific order not to let weapons fall into the hands of Indonesians! You must really want to see me dancing at the end of a rope!'

Ishida felt the anger but kept calm. 'Of course not, General. My point is that the militia is an established organisation. The Allies do not know that they were recently disarmed—'

'Let me tell you something,' Yamagami interrupted. 'If you had consulted the Army or even waited before accepting the surrender we could have let the Independence Committee meet as planned on the 18th August and make their declaration on the 19th as planned. Japan could have recognised the Republic within the *status quo*.' Yamagami's eyes bore into Ishida's. 'Tokyo had agreed to terms, not to cease administering the Empire. Your actions obliged us to accept here in Djakarta terms offered to Tokyo! My forces stood down only on 22nd August. In those lost days we could have done a lot more for the Indonesians!'

Ishida was nonplussed. 'I hadn't considered—'

'Obviously not!' Yamagami snapped back. 'Now you have a Republic without recognition and arguably unlawful because our surrendered administration was not in a legal position to grant independence. That's it! The Republic of Indonesia is on its own. From now on I must carry out Allied orders to the letter.'

Ishida gave up and accepted Yamagami's decision with a bow of his head. 'You can still make a difference here, General,' he said with a trace of bitterness in his voice. 'Is there no attraction in seeing the Allies forced to continue fighting in Asia even as their "atomic peace" has just been imposed?'

Yamagami straightened his arms to push himself back in his chair. Though the bombings of Hiroshima and Nagasaki angered him, he knew revenge was no longer an option. 'And what if the Allies accuse the Emperor of complicity in all this? Have you given any thought to that possibility and what it could mean for the future of the monarchy?'

Ishida looked sharply at Yamagami. 'I believe that the Emperor is…irrelevant.'

Yamagami's eyes narrowed. 'At least the *Army* is still loyal…. Good-bye, Admiral. Do not come here again.'

Djatingaleh Barracks, Semarang

Ota looked at his meagre *hinomaru bento* or 'sun-flag lunch'— a half-bowl of rice topped with a single red, salted plum—and sighed. For three weeks since the surrender the garrison had been reduced to a rice lunch and an equally small rice and dried fish or vegetable dinner.

'I'm fed up with this,' he said to Nagumo.

'Yeah,' replied Nagumo. 'What I'd give for some seared bonito!'

Ota groaned. 'Oh, don't mention proper food!'

'On that subject,' Nagumo said with exaggerated formality, 'later on, Private Second Class Kondo is going after something for the pot later on. Want to come along?'

'With Kondo?' Ota said warily. 'I thought he was on a charge for running a still?'

'Two charges, actually. The Adjutant can't do anything until the court martial documents come back from Singapore.'

'He'll have a long wait!'

'Yes, Major Kudo thinks so too, so he let Kondo and everyone else out on parole.'

'After what, exactly?' Ota asked. 'There's not even a three-legged dog left round here!'

'Guess?' Nagumo grinned. 'He's going after a crocodile!'

Ota's jaw dropped. 'The gods have mercy! Not even the Chinese eat those—or do they?'

'Well, Kondo's going to try it, and so am I. He says they're supposed taste a bit like chicken.'

Ota pulled a face. 'What's he using for bait? An officer he has a grudge against?'

'A three-legged dog!'

Ota grimaced.

'Not to worry,' laughed Nagumo. 'Kondo says crocs aren't fussy.'

'That's good to know,' said Ota. It could be risky.'

Nagumo shrugged. 'Of course it will! But we'll have meat. Are you in or not. I'm not giving you any of my share!'

'All right,' Ota replied uneasily. 'I'm in.'

Three hours later Nagumo, Ota, Kondo and Private Yano, Kondo's regular side-kick and co-defendant, were making for the river in a half-track. It was a still, hot afternoon. Yano was at the wheel with Nagumo next to him, while Ota and Kondo sat on the bench seats in the back.

Kondo was a burly, unkempt man with a four-day stubble and a hangover. At his feet was a stained, putrid-smelling sack which contained the bait. Even closed it was attracting a swarm of flies. Before being conscripted Kondo had worked at

Tokyo's massive Tsukiji wholesale fish market. His short temper, limited but highly colourful vocabulary and an antipathy for authority meant that after five years of service he still held the lowest rank in the army. Kondo had spent most of those years either in the battalion's kitchen or the stockade. His *yakuza* connections meant his punishments were never severe. None of the officers or NCOs wanted their relatives in Japan to suffer a visit from the mafia.

Kondo took a swig from his canteen then offered it to Ota. 'Would you like to try this? It's still a bit young.'

Ota smelt the raw palm wine on Kondo's breath and declined. Kondo shrugged then, as an afterthought, poured a healthy measure over the sack to mask the rank odour. For the rest of the journey he sang snippets of folk songs out of tune.

They parked in a culvert. Kondo jumped down heavily with his rifle in one hand and the sack in the other and lumbered towards a clump of reeds. He took the cloud of flies with him. Behind, trotted the lanky Yano, carrying a coil of rope and another rifle.

'The good thing about crocs is that they aren't shy, Nagumo-san,' Kondo called back casually over his shoulder, showing no respect for rank.

'Yes,' Ota added quietly to Nagumo, 'the drunken hunter's favourite prey!'

Ota and Nagumo caught up with the other two at the riverbank then immediately backed away as Kondo untied the sack and tipped out the dead dog. Its almost hairless body was covered in a mass of wriggling white maggots. Flies descended upon the carcass in seconds.

Kondo nonchalantly lifted the dog's hind legs and tied one end of the rope tightly around the animal's haunches. He stood up with the bait swinging against his boot. 'Shouldn't take long,' he quipped, chuckling at the expressions of disgust on the faces of his audience. He gave the other end of the rope to Yano to tie off. 'You bloody well watch like a hawk in case anything comes near me!'

'I think I remembered to load the rifle,' Yano said, his face deadpan.

'I'm not fucking joking, you know!' Kondo bawled as he walked unsteadily into the water, sinking ankle-deep in mud with each step. He began swinging the carcass, gaining momentum for the throw.

Ota and Nagumo realised a fraction too late what would happen. They were showered in maggots.

'Ugh!' Nagumo muttered. 'I never did like fishing.'

Ota held his breath, brushing himself down.

Kondo released the rope and the bait plopped noisily in the middle of the river. Mere seconds later something stirred in the reeds on the far bank and a six-foot crocodile slid quickly into the water.

'Shit!' Kondo spat. 'We want a bigger fucker than that!' He began to pull on the rope.

Suddenly it jerked in his hands and he toppled headfirst into the water with a great splash. Yano charged in after him, pointing his rifle wildly at the swirling water.

Kondo was scrambling to his feet. 'Don't point it at me, idiot!' he shouted.

'Look!' Nagumo yelled.

In the middle of the river the water was churning where another, much bigger, crocodile was at the surface, rolling and gulping down the bait.

Kondo beamed. 'Waa! Great, it's at least ten feet!'

Yano started to haul in the rope. 'Not yet, not yet!' Kondo shouted. 'Give him time to get it down!'

They watched the water quieten, then the rope went taut. 'Now!' Kondo roared. 'Heave!'

The four men dug in their heels and strained. Out in the river the crocodile rolled and thrashed but yard by yard they drew it nearer.

Ota's muscles ached and the rope burnt the palms of his hands.

'It's getting tired!' Kondo shouted. 'Pull! Pull!'

Miraculously the fight seemed to go out of the beast and they hauled in quickly until the reptile was just ten yards from the bank.

'Keep the tension!' Kondo urged them as he readied his rifle.

The huge, gnarled head was high out of the water, its mouth open, showing rows of jagged teeth. Ota could see the fraying rope wrapped around its upper jaw and disappearing down its massive throat. The crocodile slid half-up the bank, straining against the rope and panting aggressively. Its jaws gaped and the hunters caught a pungent whiff of rotten flesh on its breath.

'Shoot the bastard!' Yano grunted through clenched teeth.

Kondo fired three times before it was still. He ran forward and put two more shots into the skull at point-blank range then sat astride its neck and plunged a bayonet deep into one of the eye sockets. Finally satisfied the animal was dead, he sat back triumphantly, his arms raised. *'Yatta zo!'*—We did it!

Exhausted, the others slumped down, still wary of the huge creature. They watched Kondo re-tie the rope firmly around the huge jaws then fling the free end over a sturdy tree branch. 'We'll use the half-track as a winch,' he said confidently. 'Yano-*kun*, bring it over.'

In a few minutes the crocodile was suspended over the branch with half of its tail still on the ground.

'Now for the messy part,' Kondo informed them. He began to take off his clothes.

Ota and Nagumo looked at each other then, reluctantly, followed suit. When they were all naked Yano handed each of them a freshly sharpened cleaver.

They stood in a ring around the hanging crocodile and watched Kondo slice off a six-inch strip of gnarled, leathery skin and fat that was nearly half-an-inch thick. 'Start at the top and work down,' he instructed. The others started to copy him, but the skin was so tough they could manage only much smaller lengths.

Before long, they were caked in blood and bits of fat and skin. Clouds of flies and mosquitoes swirled around them. Then more crocodiles, attracted by the smell of blood, began to creep up the bank towards them. Twice they had to shoot.

'You know,' Ota said trying to clear his throat, 'I read in *King* once that crocodiles stopped evolving over a million years ago.'

'Well,' replied Nagumo, 'this sod certainly smells a million years old!'

Kondo grunted in amusement then casually sliced open the beast's stomach. A flood of intestines, bile, half-digested flesh and bone and the mangled carcass of the dog splattered around their feet. A cloying, stomach-churning stench filled their throats and nostrils. Ota had never smelt anything so vile in his life.

Yano's eyes bulged, then his cheeks. Arms raised, he shook his head in frantic apology then vomited spectacularly, setting off Nagumo and Ota in turn. The three of them sank on all fours retching in the blood- and bile-soaked mud. Kondo looked on, laughing uproariously then launched into another folk song as he returned to work.

It was another hour before the crocodile was skinned and butchered. By the end, even Kondo was showing signs of fatigue. Tired and filthy, they drove, still naked, for over a mile along the river bank to wash in a safer spot.

That night Kondo prepared grilled crocodile steaks with rice and vegetables. He even had soy sauce and sake. The meat was chewy but a very welcome change. 'Just like chicken,' he declared with genuine satisfaction. 'Next time we should try for a younger one!'

Ota, Nagumo and Yano eyed each other in silence then reached for more.

Singapore, Malaya, mid-September 1945

Meg was on the terrace of the Raffles Hotel enjoying a gin and tonic in the recently renamed 'Shackle Club'. She was sharing a table with a tall, tanned US Navy quartermaster, who was drinking beer. It was late afternoon and the air was clinging.

At the neighbouring tables, groups of thin and wan women were intent on making the best of the bar's happy hour. They were also casting frequent, malevolent glances at a party of shirtless Japanese repairing the road in front of the hotel. Two very bored-looking Sikh infantrymen were guarding the prisoners.

Meg had met some Indian troops in Europe and had warmed to their determined yet polite manner. She had never understood why they were fighting so far from home. It was the Japanese, though, that fascinated her. They were her first sighting of the recent enemy. She watched as they swung pick-axes and ferried stones and sand. To her surprise, she saw they appeared to be quite willing workers.

Across the table the sailor's dark eyes followed her gaze. He raised his glass. 'Here's to peace on earth and full employment,' he said sarcastically.

She lifted her glass to his while nodding towards the Japanese. 'They're keeping them busy.'

'Why not? The Japs build good roads. We could use 'em in Texas!'

Meg laughed but was distracted again by the cold looks the Japanese drew from the women on the terrace.

'So what,' the sailor asked trying to keep her attention, 'does a war correspondent do in peacetime, anyway?'

'Find another war, I suppose,' Meg replied, far more enthusiastically than she had intended.

'Is there a war in Java?'

'My editor says so.'

'And you want to go?'

'Yeah.'

He grunted and stood up. 'Lady, good luck. I'm looking for the quiet type.' He left without looking back. Meg barely noticed and went back to her guidebook.

> *Java the Wonderland! Have you not yet visited Java? If not, do so now! Java, the peerless gem in that magnificent Empire of Insulinde which winds about the equator like a garland of emeralds, is the ideal tropical island.*

She had left Berlin for London three weeks previously. With the end of the war, there was no longer a formal requirement for press accreditation from South-East Asia Command but she applied for it anyway. In any case, the only flights into Singapore were on Royal Air Force aircraft, and she thought it would make her life easier with the document-obsessed British.

Eleven buttock-numbing days in converted bombers and transport aircraft had taken her via southern France, Malta, Alexandria and Aden. Twice she lost her seat at the last minute to British officers claiming priority. One, out of habit, had chided her with 'There's a war on, Madame.' In reply she had pointed out that the war had ended and then loudly accused him of queue-jumping. Red-faced, the officer had still taken her place.

As the weather got warmer, she found herself relaxing. After the dusty, grey misery of Berlin and food-rationed London, the novelty of plentiful fresh food was a blissful distraction. She made the most of the trip with bits of sightseeing, eating at restaurants and, for the first time in years, shopping, mainly for cottons and silks. From Aden she had flown to Bombay, Colombo and finally on to Singapore where she had run into a wall of bureaucratic confusion and obfuscation. The British were clearly not interested in helping her reach Java.

Singapore was awash with colour, noise and, she soon noticed, smiles. The Malays and Chinese seemed to have shrugged off the war in just a few weeks. Markets were thriving and shops were well-stocked and busy. Children played in the streets and entertainment went on until the early hours. Swept up by it all, she had a stab at an article but abandoned it when she realised her editor would not want to read about happy Malays. Instead, she went looking for a guidebook and maps of Java. That had turned into a quest in itself because the British had apparently bought up everything they could find. Finally, at the fifth second-hand bookshop, she struck gold with a 1923 edition of *Come to Java*, which contained a fold-out colour map of the island.

Two days later, Meg was at the harbour. A helpful hotel clerk had mentioned to her that a ferry service between Singapore and Batavia was restarting. She decided it was worth a try and arrived at dawn. Java was over five hundred nautical miles to the south. According to her guidebook, the journey would take around forty hours.

The dockside was teeming with sailors, soldiers, labourers and refugees. Freighters of all shapes and sizes, many still in camouflage paint, crammed against the wharfs. Lines of coolies snaked from each vessel. Eventually she found the embarkation point written for her by the hotel clerk. At least twenty other people were waiting for the ferry, all were impoverished-looking labourers, who she discovered were Javanese.

Hours went by but the Javanese remained convinced the ferry was coming. Meg was close to giving up when, just after noon, a battered, rusting steamer chugged its way to the quayside. A tattered Dutch flag hung limply at the stern of the *Melchior Treub*. She smiled as she recognised the name from her guidebook.

With shouts and laughter the waiting Javanese swarmed aboard. Meg picked up her two small bags and started up the gangplank. A youth wearing a dirty white shirt, khaki shorts and sailor's cap that was too-large for him intercepted her with a sharp shout.

'Bukan tonlok!'

Meg looked at him and shrugged. 'What's your problem, fellah?' She took another step forward.

The youth held up his hand. *'Bukan tonlok!'*

'What? Goddamn it!' She began to thumb through the English-Malay phrases in her guidebook.

A male, Dutch-accented voice made her turn. 'Excuse me, Madame, he thinks you are Dutch.' The man was a slim, Asian in a tropical suit and a worn panama hat.

'Oh, I see. So what?'

His eyes were inquisitive, almost playful. 'The crewman "regrets" that no Dutch are allowed on board.'

'Then can you tell him I'm an American journalist.'

His surprise showed. Quickly he explained to the youth. At the word 'American' the young seaman visibly relaxed and shouted to a man watching them from the wheelhouse. There was a brief discussion among the Javanese.

'If you don't mind,' the man in the panama said politely, 'the Captain does not read English and has asked me to examine your papers.'

Meg handed over her passport, press card and her British accreditation. The man flicked through the documents, translating aloud for the benefit of the youth. He looked at her quizzically. 'Miss Graham, would you mind telling me how you knew this ship was sailing today, and from this berth?'

Meg shrugged, 'I've been trying to get to Java for a few days. Mr Darusman, a clerk at my hotel, told me about the ferry.'

'Ah, Darusman! I see,' he said suddenly relaxed. He handed back her papers. 'Thank you, Miss Graham.'

The crewman, now all smiles, stepped aside. From the wheelhouse the captain grinned and raised his peaked cap.

'I must thank you, Mr?' Meg asked, offering her hand.

The man took it and doffed his hat to reveal carefully combed thick, dark hair. 'Dr Saltan Jarisha at your service.'

Without the hat he looked much younger. Things were not turning out so badly, Meg thought to herself. A handsome, mysterious stranger, on a tropical cruise....

Jarisha looked at her admiringly. 'I must admit that I never expected the company of a lady on this voyage.'

Meg shrugged. 'Well, there are a few of us around.'

'I meant that Java is not safe.'

'That's why I'm here.'

Another crewman appeared, picked up her bags then waited by a stairwell.

'I hope we can talk later,' Meg said.

'I shall be delighted,' Jarisha replied, doffing his hat yet again.

Below, the ship smelt of damp and oil. A small, wire-cased safety bulb emitted a dull, off-white light in the long corridor. When the crewman opened a door to a cabin the shaft of daylight from the porthole was almost blinding.

Her cabin, or what was left of it, was stifling and humid. Apart from the built-in wooden bed frame, the room was bare. There was no mattress. Fixtures and fittings had been stripped. Large patches of rotten carpet were worn through to the brown-painted steel floor beneath. She opened a narrow door to discover a mouldy *en-suite* bathroom and several of the biggest cockroaches she had ever seen. There was no toilet seat and the pan was heavily stained. She grimaced and tried the flush. Nothing happened. With a sigh she closed the door.

For a minute she struggled with the porthole but the catches were encrusted with rust. Frustrated and a little dejected, she sat on the bed. On a whim she decided to cheer herself up by changing from her khaki tunic and trousers into a white cotton skirt and sleeveless blouse. By the time she had finished, she was perspiring. She looked wistfully at the bare wires in the ceiling where there once had been a fan. Then she remembered the advertisement in her guidebook and searched for it again. She read it aloud, in the light from the porthole. 'Royal Packet Navigation Company vessel, *Melchior Treub*. A fast, modern twin-screw steamer. Electric lights and luxurious accommodation. Surgeon carried.'

She sighed, feeling sad for the ship. 'Well, at least there is a doctor on board…' she said to herself. Then, unable to bear the heat any longer, she reached for a light jacket and went back on deck.

Chapter Eleven

The *Melchior Treub* had already cast off and was nosing its way through the cluster of barges, small freighters and tugs on its way to the main channel. Meg could see nothing but massive, grey steel hulls looming above them. She abandoned her hope for a view of the city.

In the wheelhouse, the captain was struggling with a chart of the harbour and shouting repeatedly at the lookout in the bows for signs of a passage through the steel maze. After a few minutes, she decided that he looked a little too nervous even for the difficult task at hand. With growing unease she began to consider the possibility that the *Melchior Treub* might not be the straightforward ferry she had assumed. After all, the ship had docked for little more than thirty minutes. Meg had bought no ticket, seen no port officials or paperwork of any kind. Only she had presented travel documents. Also, there had been no advertisement about the sailing. It was more than a little odd.

She spent several minutes taking a casual turn around the deck, picking her way through a pile of engine parts, tools and rice sacks. One item of cargo, several long, narrow wooden crates stacked neatly behind the funnel, stood out. The crates were partially covered by a ragged tarpaulin. On the lower boxes she could see stencilled Chinese characters. Instinctively she knew what was inside. Eight years earlier she had seen similar-looking cargo on fishing boats off the Spanish coast. Yet she knew she had to make sure, so she found a jemmy among the tools, pulled back the tarpaulin and prised open the top box. The unmistakable smell of gun oil reached her even before she saw the rifles inside.

Meg groaned. 'Here we go again!'

A crewman trotted by and stopped to look at her. Startled, Meg stepped back nervously. The young man merely pointed at the crates and grinned cheerfully. 'Jap guns good!' He then sped off towards the bow, pausing to shout up at the wheelhouse. The Captain leant out, looked at her sheepishly, and then went back to his charts.

Meg was reassured by the Captain's demeanour and she relaxed. It dawned on her then that she had been allowed on board as cover. She hammered down the lid, replaced the tarpaulin and found a seat in the shade.

Thirty minutes later the *Melchior Treub* had left the inner harbour and was heading beyond the giant breakwater. Waiting freighters were strung out to the horizon, and dozens of water taxis and vendor boats were doing a roaring trade plying between them and the quayside. Meg noticed the visible concern of Captain and crew as the ship' course carried it directly towards a row of anchored warships. Then she noticed Dr Jarisha leaning against the wheelhouse and decided it was time to find out if he was in on the gun-running.

Jarisha greeted her courteously, doffing his hat again. 'Miss Graham. It's much more pleasant on deck isn't it? You might be interested to know that Dr Melchior Treub, the gentleman after whom this ship is named, was a former director of the famous botanical gardens at Buitenzorg. Dr Treub—'

'Dr Jarisha,' she interrupted politely but firmly, 'wasn't it risky to dock at Singapore with a cargo of Japanese guns?'

Jarisha raised his eyebrows. 'Yes, but it was a calculated risk. With so many ships coming and going, who has the time or—what's the word, inclination?—to look hard at a mere ferry?'

'The guns were already on board, Doctor. And the stop was very brief. Maybe the trip to Singapore was a detour to pick up something else, perhaps a special passenger?'

'Indeed,' he said nonchalantly, 'perhaps a relative of the Captain's...or even a war correspondent?'

Meg gambled. 'Or a revolutionary on a secret mission?'

Jarisha's eyes shone and he laughed warmly. 'Hah! You're very astute, Miss Graham. Let me assure you that you are in no danger from us. I allowed you on this ship because your occupation and nationality might help our cause. But I clearly underestimated you and for that I apologise unreservedly.'

There was suddenly much less of an accent in Jarisha's English. Meg found herself liking him and repaid the compliment.

'I think I underestimated you, too, Doctor. My apologies.'

She proffered her hand and noted the firmness in Jarisha's clasp. She wondered who and what he was. 'Do you know Mr Darusman at the hotel?'

'Actually I do. We have broadly similar interests,' Jarisha answered casually. He gestured at the scene around them, genuinely awed. 'Have you ever seen so many ships? Such resources. Astounding!'

'Actually, I have. At Normandy.'

Impressed once again, Jarisha drew back slightly. 'You covered the invasion?'

'I got there a couple of days after the landings. The US Navy wouldn't let me near a destroyer, so I posed as a nurse and stowed away on a British hospital ship. There was a floating city off the Normandy coast.'

Jarisha did not reply. Instead, he was looking hard at her. He nodded as if confirming a diagnosis. 'One day, I hope to read your account.'

Meg decided to press her advantage. 'What's the story with the guns?'

Jarisha shrugged. 'Oh, I'm not involved with those. They are from a Japanese armoury in Sumatra. Conveniently, the old ferry service ran from Sumatra to Singapore then on to Java. It was a perfect cover for—'

Frantic shouts from the wheelhouse interrupted them. Binoculars in hand the Captain was gesturing at the warships ahead. Meg waited for Jarisha to interpret. He seemed both concerned and amused.

'If you don't mind, the Captain requests that you to go to the bow and make yourself "visible". There's a Dutch frigate moored ahead and it might present a problem. He'd like you to distract the Dutch crew. If they are suspicious about this ship and have a launch they may try to board us, or radio another ship to intercept us in the Straits.'

Meg went forward wondering why she was helping. Her policy was to be neutral but, she reasoned, she first had to reach Java. Being escorted back to Singapore by the Dutch Navy did not appeal to her at all.

She gave the Captain a vexed glance. There was a pleading look in his eyes. She laughed and took off her sun hat, tied her jacket around her waist, unfastened the top two buttons of her blouse and leant over the bow rail, enjoying the sea breeze in her hair and on her shoulders.

The line of warships lay about half-a-mile away. The narrow channel was taking the *Melchior Treub* very close to them. She saw there were very few men on deck. Most of the crews would either be having lunch or avoiding the midday sun. Meg wondered then whether the Captain's timing was deliberate.

It was not long before the steamer was noticed, and then Meg. Sailors began waving and shouting to her. She drew herself up and waved back, savouring the thought that she was probably the first white woman many of them had seen in months. 'Sorry I'm no Mae West, fellahs,' she shouted unheard into the wind. Whistles and shouts from the men carried back to her. There was, she thought, obvious method in the Captain's madness.

By the fourth warship she was beginning to enjoy her role. The fifth, a frigate, flew the Dutch flag. They would pass it by a mere fifty yards. Suddenly the *Melchior Treub* seemed very small and fragile.

Meg imagined one of the warships' gun turrets turning on them and felt the adrenalin rush. She laughed and placed her right foot on a lower rail to show some leg and let her hips sway provocatively with the rise and fall of the ship. Meg saw the frigate's name, *Tromp*, on a banner hanging over the side. Her face beaming, she blew kisses enthusiastically at half-a-dozen Dutch sailors who almost fell over the side, waving and shouting back at her.

'Ahoy!' she yelled, smiling and waving.

Only then did she see the submarine. Sleek and grey-black, it was nestled against the frigate, riding high in the water and rocking gently. Two bulbous torpedo tubes at its sharp prow made it resemble a giant predator. On its conning tower a white silhouette of a shark shone in the sunlight. Beneath it was a name, *Tijgerhaai*.

'Tigershark,' Meg muttered aloud, seeing the closeness to the word in German. Suddenly she felt much less confident about the Captain's bluff. There was no sign of life on the submarine but she was greatly relieved when there was no challenge. She put on her jacket and went back to Jarisha. 'I think it worked. I didn't see anybody rushing to a radio.'

Jarisha was clearly delighted, as were Captain and crew. 'Your performance was superb. Well done!'

Meg glanced up at the wheelhouse. 'Tell the Captain he's a first-class pirate.'

'He'll be horrified. He's a servant of the revolution!'

She changed the mood. 'What are our chances, Doctor?'

'Good, provided we don't hit a mine! The Captain says there are not yet many Dutch ships in the area. We have seen two in port today, so that's two fewer to chance upon us at sea—unless they come after us!'

Beneath them the ship checked and its roll suddenly became more pronounced as they entered the deeper waters of the Singapore Strait. She looked back solemnly at the armada and wondered what would become of it now that the war was over. Then she remembered the crates of guns. On Java another war was about to begin....

Singapore-Ceylon Air Corridor, late September 1945

Wrapped in greatcoats and blankets, the eight passengers RAF C-47 Dakota were making the best of the noise and uncomfortable canvas and steel seats by trying to nap, read or contemplate. The aircraft was an hour from Ceylon but conversation was discouraged by the loud, constant drone from the twin engines.

Until three days previously, the windowless C-47 had been an air ambulance. In its hasty conversion to an air-taxi, two stretchers, one blood-stained, had been left bolted to the exposed internal fuselage ribs.

Four of the men and the two women passengers were British, and on the second leg of their return to England. They were taking the overcrowding and inconveniences imposed on them in their stride. The other two men were not. Since leaving Brisbane in Australia, they had made no attempt to mingle at any of the refuelling stops. Instead, they had remained aloof. One of them, was tall, overweight and in his late sixties. He wore a Dutch uniform and admiral's stripes. The other, much younger, was dressed in an expensively tailored tan uniform. His full beard was almost as disconcerting to the British as the gold-stamped 'CvZ' monogram on his attaché case. British reserve was further increased by the mysterious 'NICA' insignia on his uniform, which remained unexplained. In truth, 'Netherlands Indies Civil Administration' would have meant little to his fellow passengers anyway.

There was another, more obvious, difference between the two sets of passengers. The British were all in high spirits; still riding the wave of euphoria generated by the Japanese surrender. Consequently, they found the makeshift seating bearable and the minimal attention afforded them by the flight crew irrelevant. On the other hand, His Excellency Dr Charles Van Zanten, Acting Governor-General of the Dutch East Indies and his companion, Admiral Jurgen Hurwitz of the Royal Netherlands Navy, were rather glum. Hurwitz, though, had managed to fall asleep. Van Zanten could not, for he had much on his mind.

One of the crew appeared from behind a wall of crates and made his way around the passengers with a lid-less, deep-sided biscuit tin in one hand while he steadied himself with the other.

'Cuppa, Sir?' The airman mouthed, rather than spoke the words, not even attempting to battle the noise.

Van Zanten's lips curled in undisguised distaste at the sight of the milky brew in the chipped enamel mug. He could not tell if it were coffee or tea. Spilled liquid sloshed around the base of the tin. He took a mug because he was cold and it at least looked hot. It was too hot and he splashed his trousers. By the time he looked up to ask for a cloth the crewman had already turned away and was oblivious to his call and wave.

Van Zanten sighed, then swore. *'Stront!'*—Shit! No one heard him.

Although it was out of character, the expletive made him feel a little better and he toyed for a second with the idea of saying it again. Then he scowled, annoyed at his loss of composure. The spill was a further if minor mishap in what had been a disastrous two weeks. Idly he glanced over at his companion. Hurwitz dozed fitfully.

Van Zanten's head was throbbing after three days of constant engine noise. He was exhausted and craved sleep. Above all, he needed time to think about the disaster that had befallen him. Time he did not have. Simply put, Charles Van Zanten had managed to let control of the Netherlands East Indies slip from his fingers. Now, he had to try and to get it back. All he had so far were vague promises….

During the war, the Allied governments had, in public at least, committed themselves to the return of all colonial territories captured by Japan. In fact, Van Zanten knew the Dutch were powerless to assert any claim on their former territory. They had neither troops nor ships in Southeast Asia. This weakness was making the Dutch Government in The Hague very nervous. There was a great deal at stake. The Netherlands' East Indies territory made the Dutch empire the third largest in the world, and the Dutch had every intention that it would remain so. Planning and preparation to achieve that goal had been both intense and very expensive.

In mid-May that year, Van Zanten had been able to return to the Netherlands, via the United States, for the first time in six years. Germany had surrendered only days before. His rushed visit lasted less than a week, during which he had assured his new Government that all was going well with plans for the return to the Indies. The pressure on him, from official and unofficial quarters was considerable. At one Foreign Ministry dinner he had been button-holed by Johann Heysel, a senior director of Royal Dutch Shell, the Netherlands' largest company. Clutching a large glass of rye whisky, the jovial oilman had led him aside, then tried to grill him for information. Van Zanten had been polite but evasive. Heysel had quickly become blunt.

'I should not have to remind you, *Acting* Governor-General, of what the Indies means for the Netherlands. Forget—if you can—your title, your palace and your servants. Java alone can provide us with coffee, tea, lumber and rubber worth billions of guilders a year. Oil from Borneo an equal amount. Look around you. What do you see here? A bloody wasteland! The Nazis took everything. Fuel, plant and machinery, ships, locomotives. Holland is an empty shell. If we are ever to recover our economic strength and influence then we must have the Indies back soon! Even then it will take years to repair the damage to the infrastructure.' Heysel emptied his glass and immediately took another from a waiter who was hovering with a tray of replacements.

Van Zanten, ever cautious, had reeled off a stock reply. 'The Allies are committed to returning our territory. There are agreements that—'

'Don't try to palm me off with that rubbish!' Heysel interrupted. 'Remember, my company funds this Government! You're to be the Government's man out there. If you fail the Government, you fail us. The consequences for your own future should be obvious.'

Van Zanten had begun to wonder whether the encounter was the coincidence it first seemed, for Heysel had not finished. 'Agreements are nothing more than promises.

Promises are often broken. Times are changing, and empires are fast going out of fashion.'

Once again, Van Zanten chose to be diplomatic. 'But the British have signed—'

'What have they signed?' Heysel snarled, losing his patience. 'A worthless, three-page "Understanding" between London and The Hague. Open your eyes! The British have already agreed independence for India and Ceylon. Once the war's over, Malaya and Burma will surely follow. Look at the wider picture. You've been stuck in Australia for too long, worrying about a few troop movements and supplies. Haven't you read the Atlantic Charter? It's hardly pro-Empire!'

This time Van Zanten's surprise had been genuine. 'You're not suggesting that the Charter applies to Asiatics! Our natives won't be ready for independence for another century.'

'That may be,' Heysel had said lowering his voice, 'but Royal Dutch takes great pains to know what is going on in Washington. It is, of course, only prudent when our competitors have such enormous resources. You perhaps don't know it but the American newspapers are suddenly demanding self-determination for the peoples of Southeast Asia. Why now? The answer is simple. The Americans want access to those markets, and so they want the Southeast Asians to "self-determine" that trading with them and not Europe is to their advantage.'

Heysel knocked back his drink and beckoned for yet another. Van Zanten was now convinced the conversation was far from accidental. Heysel had looked around them and then drawn closer.

'Have you any idea of the size of Royal Dutch's investment in the Indies? In many ways the Indies *are* Royal Dutch. We do not want competition. What the Americans say officially and do unofficially are quite different. Look at Indo-China. They are spouting on about the gallant Vichy

French forces but they won't help them. Our sources say most of their supply drops are deliberately going to the Vietnamese nationalists. Paris is very worried. So are we.'

His warning delivered, Heysel had muttered an excuse and left. Van Zanten, convinced that he was far ahead of the other players in the game of empire, had quickly dismissed the oilman's concerns.

The Dakota lurched suddenly and he grabbed at the seat next to him. Hurwitz barely stirred. Van Zanten leaned back in his seat and allowed himself a blast of self-pity. He *had* been so far ahead! For two years he had played Mountbatten's Command against MacArthur's, fuelling rivalry, carefully withholding information on the Indies and deflecting any plans that might have given either a base in the islands.

It had been clear to Van Zanten that the United States was to be a key, new player in the game. His only advantage was that the Americans themselves had not quite realised the fact. He had thought he had time. America could not police all of Southeast Asia even it wanted to. First they had to invade and conquer Japan. That should have taken them another eighteen months. The equipment and manpower required would be immense—an operation bigger than the D-Day Normandy landings—and against hostile civilians as well.

Holland's public relations campaign in the United States had been very slick. President Roosevelt, ever conscious of his Dutch origins, had been swayed by the lobbying. At one photo-call with Queen Wilhelmina, the gushing Roosevelt had publicly assured the Dutch monarch that they would regain the Indies. Of course, this had been said in the dark days of the war when words had been cheap—the oilman had been right about that—but they had been recorded and filed away for future use.

In London, the British, with eyes on their own weakened empire, had given similar pledges. Van Zanten did not trust them. He suspected that if the British got a toe-hold in the Indies they would try to gain access to the islands' vast natural resources for their own companies. At least, that was the unofficial Dutch line in Washington and it had got them some sympathy. Over in London, their representatives lobbied against American presence in the Indies equally effectively.

Their strategy had been working well. Van Zanten and his NICA staff had canvassed support in Washington, New York, Chicago and Los Angeles, hinting at trading opportunities in the Indies as 'just' recompense for American war aid. He had found a ready audience of businessmen who naturally did not wish to see those opportunities shared with other nations. Various pro-Dutch articles had appeared in American newspapers, placed by The Netherlands' new friends in Washington.

It was a risky course of action but it was the only way he could keep the American stay short and the British out. It was a good plan and the Americans had fallen for it. Almost all of the East Indies had been assigned to the Americans. Only Sumatra was earmarked for British occupation, and MacArthur had been keeping Mountbatten on a very tight leash by denying him equipment and ships for troop movements beyond Burma. In any case, the British should have been busy for months with a new campaign in Malaya.

Van Zanten had calculated that by the time the British were in a position to invade Sumatra, the Dutch would have been well established in Java and the other islands and about to wave a tearful farewell to the Americans as they headed off to invade Japan. With a legal Dutch administration up and running in the rest of the Indies, the British would be presented with a *fait accompli* and have no option but to hand over control of Sumatra sooner rather than later.

He had been so sure of his plan that occasionally he had allowed himself to consider just how grateful his country would be for his services. A peerage was a certainty, and with it estates in Java and money for houses in the Netherlands.... All had been going so smoothly. For the last few months he and his staff had been in relaxed, even buoyant mood as the Americans had swept the Japanese from the Philippines. Allied assaults had been scheduled on Saigon and Singapore. Java was third in line. All he had to do was wait. It would have worked...if not for the A-bombs!

Japan's surrender had shattered Van Zanten's world. The moment was etched in his memory. He had been at his desk in Brisbane when the sound of car horns in the street outside had distracted him. A beaming Australian secretary had come bursting into his office, shouting 'Turn on the radio. The war's over! Japan's surrendered!' Van Zanten had felt a sudden, sinking feeling in his stomach. His carefully laid plans were in ruins. The contrast between the cheering Australians and the sombre Dutch officials had said it all. His staff knew as well as he that they were not ready. It was nine months too soon.

That night, while Brisbane celebrated wildly, he had railed against the Americans in a drunken rage, cursing their scientists and their secrecy. The Dutch were allies and they had not been told! The British *must* have known about the bomb and they had kept it secret too! Next morning the bitter facts remained: Japan was defeated, Dutch troops were still in the Netherlands and the United States was the *de-facto* ruler of Southeast Asia and the Pacific.

Beside him, Hurwitz finally woke. 'How much longer?' he shouted against the engines.

Van Zanten bit back his irritation and shrugged. As Hurwitz shut his eyes again Van Zanten eyed his travelling companion with contempt. He found him an arrogant bore. What rubbish they had concocted about this man, he thought. 'Hero of the Java Sea!' 'The Dutch Churchill!' My God, we must have been desperate! He knew for a fact that Hurwitz spent the Battle of the Java Sea ashore in Batavia. The man had probably never seen a shell fired in anger since 1918! Now he had been appointed his senior military commander....

Soon after the first blow to Van Zanten's plans had come the second. MacArthur, busy preparing for the occupation of Japan, had ignored Dutch protests and assigned the entire Netherlands Indies to Mountbatten's Command. The British would occupy the Indies after all! Then, just as he had assumed things could not possibly get any worse he read the Reuters news report that Sukarno and Hatta had declared the independent Republic of Indonesia.

For three weeks he had been kept waiting for a flight to Ceylon. Now he had to go cap-in-hand to Mountbatten. It was checkmate to the British.

Alor Gajah, Malaya, late September 1945

For the first time in five years Alun MacDonald was polishing his boots willingly. He glanced around the open-sided, eight-man tent then looked at Stan Nesbit who was oiling his Lee Enfield rifle on the next bed. The entire battalion was caught up in the excitement of the day.

'Hey, Nessy,' called Mac. 'Look at that then! You really can see my handsome face in these boots.'

Nesbit laughed. 'You'll see the RSM's face in them soon enough, Mac. He'll think he's dreaming. If we'd looked this good in Glasgow we'd have made guard duty at Bucky Palace!'

Mac shook his head, smiling. 'Sod that! This is the only one that counts for me. I've waited five years for it. We all have.'

Nesbit was grinning. 'The buggers will want a few more parades out of us before they say "Cheerio", Mac.'

'That may be, but the war's over. Today the Japs surrender to us. To us, mate! This is the one I'll want to remember, not some daft square bashing in the rain so some English general can look good.'

Mac sensed a sudden quiet. He glanced at Nesbit and saw him peering very closely at his rifle. Other heads were down and curiously silent. That meant only one thing and he braced himself for the tirade from Regimental Sergeant-Major Cox. He jumped up and turned around. The bearded, stocky Cox stood resplendent in his medals with his favourite ash swagger stick under his left arm.

'MacDonald, your views on parades, spit and polish and senior officers are well known to all and sundry, so that's enough of that.'

'Yes, RSM. Sorry.'

'Good grief! Are those your boots?'

'Yes, RSM,' Mac's voice was pained.

'Well now, you see what you can do when you put your mind to it. I may even have you doing mine until you're demobbed and the army loses your obvious talents.'

Mac's face fell but he sensed he was safe. The rest of the platoon laughed. Cox, caught up in the general mood, allowed himself a smirk.

'Now lads,' Cox added more earnestly, 'Mac here's right about one thing. Today is special and I want you at your best out there. When those Japs march in and see you I want them bloody well dazzled. Remember, we've all suffered for this day and lost a lot of muckers along the way. Get cracking!'

'Stand at...ease!' Cox's voice boomed and five hundred pairs of shining boots stamped down in unison on the hard, bare earth. The sound echoed around the small soccer stadium. It was mid-morning and very humid. The sun was burning. Even the short march from the barracks had left the men with dark sweat patches on their clean, pressed shirts. No-one had complained.

Mac, for one, was enjoying every minute. He was very glad to be there. Everything was as it should be, he thought. Even the pipers had sounded better than usual. His eyes were drawn repeatedly to the trestle-table standing almost at the centre of the baked pitch. Draped in a cloth, it flashed a blinding, almost painful white in the sunlight. It was a simple piece of furniture, yet he marvelled at its significance. It means we've won! he told himself again, smiling. Careful not to move too much, Mac soaked up the atmosphere.

To one side of the table, chatting, stood Major-General Harrison and other officers of 23rd Indian Division. To the other stood an honour guard, bayonets fixed, around a British flag and a collection of regimental colours. Twenty yards from the table were two rows of Seaforth Highlanders also with fixed bayonets.

The rest of the Seaforths and 178th Field Regiment, Royal Artillery, were at the north end of the field. Lined up around the sides of the field were other representative units: Mahrattas, Rajputana Rifles, Bengal Sappers and Miners, Punjab Regiment, Gurkhas, Patalia Infantry and Royal Indian Artillery. A Sherman tank, barrel lowered, was stationed at each corner of the stadium, their crews stood beside their machines.

Behind the Seaforths a tiered grandstand was occupied by local dignitaries and their families. On the three other sides, behind low walls, the general public jostled for position on earth banks. Many were cheering and waving homemade British and Malay flags.

Not long now, Mac thought excitedly. He could hardly wait. Five years in uniform! He remembered the words of his friend, Bill Stuart. They had been in Burma, knee-deep in mud in a trench. 'One day, Mac,' Stuart had said, 'it will end. They'll say, "The war's over, men. It's all settled. Time to go home. Run along now." We'll have no idea of the how or why of it. We might be back in India, miles from the nearest Jap and that will be that. But no matter what the brass say, it won't be over for me until I see those bastards bowing and scraping and handing over their bloody swords. I want to see it for myself. They owe us that.' Three days later Mac had helped bury Stuart in a temporary, rain-filled grave at the Shenam Pass.

Mac's thoughts drifted. Images of the suicidal Japanese assaults and the desperate fighting in the muddy darkness rushed back to him in chilling flashes. How could they sacrifice themselves like that, he wondered? Sometimes the British and the Japanese lines had been so close that grenades had been thrown back and forth three or four times before they exploded.... The Japs never surrendered, not even the wounded. His jaw hardened as he remembered Archie Ferguson.

He was brought noisily back to the present by sudden, gleeful cheers from the crowd. A pipe band marching four abreast entered the far right-hand corner of the stadium. Following them, between a platoon of guards front and rear, came twenty-four Japanese officers and about one hundred and fifty other ranks. Heads still and keeping their eyes low, the Japanese came forward. But as they marched, the officers with swords at their sides, Mac saw the white knuckles and quick, nervous glances. He smiled. It was good to see the bastards humiliated!

At the sight of the enemy, Mac felt himself tense. In the centre of the field, the British and British Indian officers moved to form a line behind the table. As one, the Seaforth guard came to attention then stepped forward in a half lunge, rifles at the ready position, their bayonets forming a corridor of steel. The crowd jeered in a mixture of English, Malay, Chinese and the coarse Japanese that they had learned in three years of occupation. *'Baka!'* Fools!—'Scum!'—*'Maketa-yo!'* You lost!—'Bastards!' Rotten eggs and vegetables flew in salvos but fell short of their targets. Sentries moved quickly to restrain several spectators from charging forward with buckets of human waste.

The Japanese officers did their best to ignore the insults and smartly came to attention a few feet from the table. The other ranks lined up quickly to their rear. When the Japanese general saluted, General Harrison followed Mountbatten's orders and waited a full five seconds before it was returned.

Harrison slowly unfolded a sheet of notepaper and stepped up to the microphone. His tone was clipped and formal. '... we are today conducting this ceremony to receive and witness in front of local civilian representatives the formal and unconditional surrender of Japanese military forces in this vicinity to Allied Forces. As Senior Allied officer in this area, I now call upon the Senior Japanese officer present to come forward to sign the document of surrender. In addition, as ordered by the Supreme Allied Commander South-East Asia, he and his officers will also surrender their swords.'

Uniformed interpreters repeated the General's words first in Japanese, then in Malay and Chinese. As Harrison gestured to the Japanese general to approach the table the crowd roared exultantly.

Mac savoured the scene. The Japanese general was a short, rather chubby man and the only Japanese in a full dress uniform. His tunic was dotted with award clasps and ribbons. His face pale, the defeated officer swallowed hard and stepped forward, clearly struggling with emotion. Reaching to his left, he unclipped his sword from its strap then lifted it horizontally in both hands with his arms outstretched. A short white ribbon was laced through the guard. He bowed low to Harrison and laid the sword across the table. Then he picked up a fountain pen, only to hesitate and look up. A British aide stepped up quickly pointing to the spot. Hurriedly the general signed and stepped back in line.

One by one the Japanese offered up their swords until the pile on the table was over a foot high. When the last officer had returned to the ranks, their general saluted again. This time Harrison returned the salute promptly. Then the Japanese were marched out of the stadium.

Mac laughed when he saw the escort lead them much closer to the crowd, well within range of eggs, fruit and worse. That afternoon the Seaforths were stood down. Their celebrations lasted until dawn.

Kandy, Ceylon

Van Zanten and Hurwitz were met at the sprawling, busy RAF Kandy base by a smartly dressed and, as Hurwitz quickly pointed out to Van Zanten, a rather junior British captain named Hinton. To Van Zanten's immense irritation, Hinton felt obliged to liven up the journey by describing Kandy's cultural attractions.

'We'll be passing the Temple of the Tooth,' he told them enthusiastically. 'It's supposed to have one of Buddha's teeth. Mind you, the old boy's molars crop up all over Asia. Must have had a mouth the size of Wembley Stadium!' When neither Van Zanten or Hurwitz responded he sought refuge in the weather.

'The air here is wonderful. Spent a while in Burma a few months back. Damned oppressive, very unpleasant.' Finally, sensing his two passengers' lack of interest, Hinton gave up.

Van Zanten closed his eyes against the glare of the sunlight that flashed through the palm-tree canopy. When the car stopped for the first of two checkpoints, Hinton made another stab at conversation.

'Almost there. The HQ was a hill station before the war. The owner's big in tea. He was at school with Lord Mountbatten and offered it for the duration. Most generous.'

An expanse of high, white stone wall appeared ahead. Sentry boxes manned by tall, bearded and turbaned Sikh guardsmen stood to either side of the wrought ironwork double gates.

Some shops—little more than huts—and stalls were clustered a few yards from the gate. At the approach of the car, vendors and beggars surged to it from either side. The Sikhs blocked them and the car whisked through the gates, then turned sharply behind a tall, clipped privet hedge. A few seconds later they were driving past neatly kept shrubs and lawns that appeared to run on to the horizon. Flamingos and other colourful water birds preened themselves in ponds that dotted the huge expanse of garden.

The road followed a gentle, rising sweep up a hill where a grand, gleaming, white estate house dominated the brow. Set back from it on either side were a number of guest villas. As they drew nearer, Van Zanten noticed incongruous rows of squat, prefabricated huts that presumably provided accommodation and office space. Near them, a large array of tall radio masts emphasised the scale of South-East Asia Command.

In front of the main house several people lounged on deckchairs around a luscious and startlingly green lawn where a game of croquet was in progress. Apart from the fact that most of the people were in uniform, the scene could have been of a summer fête at an English country house.

As their car pulled up two others were pulling away. Van Zanten glanced behind and saw another car a few hundred yards behind them. Their arrival was attracting no interest other than a casual turn of heads. 'No one here to receive us!' Hurwitz muttered in Dutch.

From behind another tall hedge came the sounds of happy, excited voices and the dull thwack of tennis balls. Van Zanten remembered how one British combat veteran had referred scathingly to Mountbatten's HQ as 'Wimbledon' because it was 'all balls and rackets'. He managed a weak smile. No-one could poke fun at the British like themselves.

With an effort he put his mind to work and started to pump the effusive Hinton for information. 'How many are there on the Admiral's staff, Captain?' he asked cordially.

Hinton jumped at his chance to impress. 'Well, people come and go all the time but at the last count, just over seven thousand.'

'That is impressive,' Van Zanten replied.

'Of course, they were mainly here to plan Operation Zipper. Now all that's been cancelled I suppose we shall all be moving on. Pity really. The riding, shooting and parties are marvellous.'

Van Zanten looked around at the couples sitting on the veranda. A number of older officers were strolling arm-in-arm with much younger uniformed women. 'I'm sure they are,' he said with only a slight trace of the cynicism he felt.

'Uh, Operation Zipper?' Hurwitz boomed, disturbing a number of people on the deckchairs. 'What's that?'

'The invasion of Malaya,' Van Zanten said quickly, wanting to silence the loose cannon beside him. He shot Hurwitz a firm look to reinforce the message.

'Oh, of course…' Hurwitz mumbled and then was quiet.

Hinton looked a little quizzically at Van Zanten. 'You're well informed, Sir. The codename has only just been declassified.'

Van Zanten patted his shoulder. 'We're on the same side, Captain.'

Hinton excused himself and the two Dutchmen were shown to an airy if simply furnished bungalow. A cook was already at work preparing their dinner. Hinton had informed them that they were to meet Mountbatten the next morning at eleven o'clock. Before leaving Australia, Van Zanten had requested an immediate meeting with Mountbatten but by now he had realised he was in no condition to open negotiations. Glad for the chance to rest, he bathed and was asleep by nine.

At ten forty-five the next morning, Van Zanten and Hurwitz were ushered into a large reception lounge in the main house. Before the war it had been a ballroom. Now rattan chairs and tables formed island clusters on the lustrous teak floor. Servants in crisp white jackets darted from table to table with trays of refreshments.

Van Zanten scanned the room, noting groups of Westerners, Indians and Asians. He deliberately chose a middle table and sat facing the polished double doors that he presumed led to Mountbatten's inner sanctum. Each time the doors opened conversation in the room died until the next party of diplomats or businessmen were called. Mountbatten was running late. Van Zanten felt like a court petitioner waiting for a royal audience. Hurwitz, as usual, took it personally.

'It's disgraceful that Asiatics get preference!' he snarled in Dutch. 'Those Burmans were in there for almost half-an-hour!'

Van Zanten tried to ignore him. Here they were at the very heart of British operations in Asia. An uncharitable American diplomat had told him once that SEAC really stood for 'Save England's Asian Colonies.' Van Zanten listened. Amid the noise, he made out English, Urdu, Malay, French and Siamese. He sat back, quietly enjoying the sight of the harassed-looking administrators rushing back and forth clutching files and signals. Yet he was also intrigued. He had expected an air of smug satisfaction among the British but it was not the case. Most of those who emerged from their meeting with Mountbatten seemed far from happy.

At eleven-twenty, Hurwitz lowered his fraying, five-day-old copy of *The Times*, looked elaborately at his watch and loudly pronounced the obvious. 'Fah! They're running round like chickens. They'll never get anything done this way. I will tell Mountbatten so myself!' Having made his point to everyone in the room, he returned to his newspaper.

Idly van Zanten wondered if Hurwitz had any idea of the implications of his petulant observation. In contrast, he had been trying to visualise the contents of Mountbatten's mounting in-tray. It was an instructive exercise.

It was another ten minutes before they were finally invited through to see the Supreme Commander. Mountbatten sprang up from behind his desk, his hand extended.

'Dr Van Zanten, welcome to SEAC HQ. I'm dreadfully sorry to have kept you waiting.' He turned quickly to Hurwitz who made to salute but Mountbatten's hand was already proffered. 'Admiral Hurwitz. It's been a long time. How are you? Wonderful to see a fellow sea-dog for a change!'

Hurwitz coughed in pleasure, instantly disarmed. Van Zanten had to admit that the Supreme Commander certainly had charisma.

Mountbatten introduced a short, older man in civilian clothes. 'Gentlemen, this is Major Dening from the Foreign and Colonial Office.'

Van Zanten was on his guard immediately. He knew Dening by reputation. They shook hands.

'It's been an amazing three weeks,' said Mountbatten smiling again. 'God Bless the Yanks for ending the war!'

'Yes,' replied Van Zanten. 'They can certainly keep a secret!' He was watching Mountbatten very closely.

'You're referring to the A-bomb? Indeed—I was only told days before. Astounding!' Mountbatten paused and in that brief moment Van Zanten glimpsed his exhaustion and, he was convinced, the truth. So, he thought, most of the British field commanders had been kept in the dark too. But still, not as long as the Dutch....

They spent a few minutes chatting about the celebrations in Europe and Churchill's defeat in the British general election. When Dening opened a file Mountbatten ended the pleasantries. 'Now, Gentlemen, we hope to have you back in Batavia as soon as possible. But I have one or two problems. Just look at the size of my office.' Mountbatten waved at a large map of Southeast Asia that took up half of a wall. It was dotted with pin-flags and cut-out coloured shapes from Calcutta to Saigon. Instinctively, both the Dutchmen's' eyes flashed to the islands of the East Indies. The area was unmarked.

'This is the extent of my command,' Mountbatten continued. 'As you can see, my main resources are in Malaya and Burma. But the extra men assigned for the invasion of Malaya are either still in India or already on their way back to England. This means I have no troops available for a presence in any strength elsewhere. As for the Indies, well, I fear it will be some time before I can send any troops at all. Developments have caught us all on the hop.'

Van Zanten took the opportunity to draw closer to the map. He did not waste words. 'Just how long is "some time", Admiral? As you can imagine, we are keen to return to the Indies immediately. My administration in Australia is ready as are other units in the Netherlands. All we need are a few ships—'

Mountbatten stopped him with a tired shake of his head and a shrug. 'Food aid and the repatriation of Allied troops and prisoners of war have been given priority. Ships are one thing we haven't got. There is a huge shortage. But I do appreciate your concerns and I have ordered the Japanese to maintain law and order in the Indies until British troops can arrive to take their surrender and then move them out, preferably back to Japan, if not, then to Malaya.'

Van Zanten, who had already seen a copy of Mountbatten's secret signal to the Japanese, said nothing. It was too much for Hurwitz. 'British troops, Admiral? Why not Dutch?'

Mountbatten raised his hands in exaggerated helplessness. 'The Potsdam Agreement permits only American, Russian or British forces to disarm the Japanese and take their surrenders. British units must go to the Indies. We also have POWs there, so naturally we are making efforts to get them medical care as soon as possible. We are going to drop small teams in over the next few days.'

Hurwitz appeared unable to compose a reply. Van Zanten's tone remained even. 'Of course, Admiral. That makes sense—for London,' he added pointedly, looking at Dening.

'Dr Van Zanten,' Dening replied pleasantly, we will be delighted to see a speedy handover to your administration.

'Most certainly,' Mountbatten added quickly. 'Everyone wants to go home.'

'The Indies are my home, Admiral,' replied Van Zanten quietly. 'I was born there.'

For the first time Mountbatten seemed caught off-guard. 'Yes, of course. I understand,' he said nodding vigorously. He glanced at Dening who indicated the wall map. 'The, er, very limited information we have on file from the Netherlands Government and your own Civil Administration suggests that the situation in the Indies is relatively stable,' he stated dryly. 'All the signs are that the Japanese in Java and the other islands are obeying the surrender order despite Marshal Terauchi's initial opposition. Did you know Hirohito's brother was sent to Saigon to convince Terauchi to play along? Anyway, a short delay in the arrival of our forces need not be problematic.'

Mountbatten was looking inquisitively at the two Dutchmen. 'Is there any new intelligence that would suggest the situation is not as we understand it?'

'No Admiral, as you say, we expect a smooth re-establishment of Dutch administration,' Van Zanten said with a confidence he did not feel.

Mountbatten raised an eyebrow. 'I see. But surely the declaration of independence was *something* of a surprise?'

Alarm bells began to ring in Van Zanten's head. He kept his face relaxed but his scornful tone was genuine.

'Just a Japanese plot, Admiral. There is no serious independence movement I can assure—'

'Traitors! Quislings!' Hurwitz thundered.

Van Zanten let him rant.

'Sukarno's a known collaborator,' Hurwitz raged, his face flushed pink. 'We'll soon have him and the others swinging from a yardarm!'

'I see,' Mountbatten replied with obvious disquiet. He turned to Van Zanten. 'I hope you are right, Doctor.'

That night Van Zanten and Hurwitz dined with Mountbatten's staff and some of the other delegations. By the time they returned to their bungalow Van Zanten was in a very good humour indeed and Hurwitz, in contrast, thoroughly perplexed. Van Zanten, however, had had a very productive day. From the depths of depression he was now soaring.

After the meeting with Mountbatten, he and Hurwitz had spent hours in meetings with SEAC staff. They had been able to inspect files on the Indies at their leisure. Entries ended in February 1942 with the Allied surrender. At first Van Zanten was sure the small number of documents was a ruse. But after a while he had become convinced that the files and co-operation were genuine. It had taken all his self-control to contain his growing elation. Apart from information from the Japanese since the surrender about their garrisons' strengths, there was little more than general reports on Java's climate and beaches.

Van Zanten lounged in an armchair and began to laugh. 'You know, Jurgen,' he said, shaking his head, 'it never even occurred to me that the British could be less prepared than we are. They think it's all over!'

'Isn't it?' Hurwitz ventured. 'They will send troops....'

'Until today I thought so, too. But now we are back in the game—but it has become a race.' His tone was suddenly formal. 'A toast!'

'To what?' Hurwitz was encouraged but still confused by Van Zanten's change of mood.

'An English king,' Van Zanten replied.

Hurwitz frowned. 'English?'

'To King Ethelred the Unready,' chuckled Van Zanten. 'May his spirit live on in SEAC!'

Chapter Twelve

A black, Model-A Ford sedan slowed and then stopped with a smoky rattle in the middle of the Red Bridge, the main crossing over the Kali Mas river which ran north-south through the centre of Surabaya. Three men eased themselves out of the car. It had been a long, jarring and thirsty drive from their internment camp near Magelang. They stretched stiffly but happily, glad to be back in their home city after nearly three years. In their good humour they failed to notice the suspicious stares from the steady stream of locals who kept a wide berth from the thin, raggedly dressed white men.

Hans Wijk stared across the bridge towards the imposing, neo-classical building that had been the International Bank. Red-and-white striped bunting hung from lamp posts and railings, and on the large flagpole outside the bank, a six-foot square nationalist flag flapped in the gentle afternoon breeze. Dismayed, he turned to look down towards the Willemskade business district where he had spent most of his working life with the Royal Packet Navigation Company. Many of the windows along the Societeitstraat were smashed, Dutch signs removed or defaced and the once-neat white brickwork daubed with slogans. Wijk's felt a flush of anger.

Beside him, the bald, toothless Oscar Boer, was also taking in the scene. He was a watchmaker by profession. In the camp he had supplemented his rations by turning his skills to repairing appliances. 'For Heaven's sake,' he said pointing. 'Look at that. "Indonesia is Free! Dutch go back to Holland!" How dare they write such things!'

'We don't seem very popular, Dad,' said the third, much younger, man. Leo Wijk was twenty-two and impatient to enjoy his new freedom. 'They're all wearing rebel colours!' he sneered accusingly.

Wijk saw his son was right. Nearly everyone passing them sported a red and white badge or ribbon of some kind.

'Our soldiers will deal with them,' Boer scoffed sharply. 'My shop is on the Kembang Djepoon. Can we go there now?'

Wijk shrugged. 'You can if you like. First I'm going to get a room and have a shower at the Oranje, then see if Hellendoorn's is open for lunch. After that, we'll go and see what's left of your shop.'

A few minutes later, their car turned into a boulevard dissected by a pair of tram lines. Imposing, three- and four-storey Art-Deco buildings with flat roofs, rectangular chimneys, pillared verandas and rectangular buttresses lined either side. The Oranje Hotel was a place of special significance for the Wijks family. Before the war they had gathered there each week for Sunday lunch. Anniversaries, confirmations, christenings and funerals had all been marked at the Oranje. Only four years before, Wijk's eldest son had held his wedding reception in the elegant, teak-panelled banquet hall. He expected Leo to do the same.

Wijk got out of the car, relieved to see the hotel was open and undamaged. A painted sign over the entrance read 'Yamato Hotel'. As he looked higher, his face clouded. Mounted on top of the high chimney stack was a flagpole. Wijk had never seen it without the Dutch tricolour but now the flag of Indonesia had replaced it. He looked quickly along the rooftops of the adjoining buildings. Several others flew the same red and white.

'I'm looking forward to a hot bath,' said Leo.

'And clean towels!' Boer added, raising his finger for emphasis.

They looked expectantly as the hotel doorman, a youth of about fifteen in shorts and short-sleeved shirt complete with red and white ribbon, came running out. When he saw them he drew up sharply. Alarm and confusion played on his face. Then he turned and bolted back inside.

'Disgraceful!' Boer muttered as the three of them strode into the lobby. 'Blom will be furious when he sees his staff wearing those colours.'

'Hello, Abdul,' Wijk said pleasantly in Dutch, recognising the clearly surprised middle-aged man behind the desk. 'Not much has changed here—except that I see you've been promoted.' On the breast pocket of Abdul's white shirt a badge read 'Manager'. Before the invasion he had been the reservations clerk.

'Hello, Mr Wijk.' Abdul replied a little nervously.

'I'd like the Oranje suite for my son and I, and a double room for Mr Boer.'

'Yes...of course. It's called the Raya suite now,' Abdul mumbled. 'How long will you be staying?'

'As long as is necessary.'

'Excuse me, Mr Wijk but how will you be paying?'

Wijk fanned out several high-denomination guilder banknotes. 'With these. I should also think I have some credit left on my account.'

'I am sorry, Wijk-*tuan*,' Abdul said uncomfortably, 'we accept only Japanese rupiahs.'

Wijk's eyes narrowed. 'Enemy money? Somehow I don't think Mr Blom will like that.'

Abdul looked to the floor then at Wijk. 'Mr Blom no longer owns the hotel. It is now the property of the Revolutionary Council of Surabaya.'

Boer stepped forward, outraged. 'This is absolutely—'

Suddenly the young doorman reappeared and began shouting in Javanese at Abdul. 'We should not let any Dutch stay here! Why did you call him *"tuan"*? You are speaking their filthy tongue! Where is your *Merdeka* grit!'

Abdul silenced him curtly. 'A hotel needs guests!' He turned to Wijk who had understood the exchange. 'I will be happy to give you rooms for this evening but payment must be in Japanese rupiahs. I'm sorry.'

'Very well,' Wijk sighed resignedly. 'I have rupiahs.'

Abdul visibly relaxed. 'Oh, good. I will—'

'One thing,' interrupted Wijk. 'I will not sleep under that flag. Take it down now. Mr Blom will want it down as well.'

Abdul's face fell. 'Mr Wijk, please. You should not say such things.'

Wijk turned to his son. 'Leo, rip down that rebel rag!'

Leo grinned at his father. 'With pleasure!' He bolted up the stairs.

The Javanese youth ran out into the road and began yelling and pointing. Soon a small crowd of youths formed. They hurled abuse.

Wijk went out. 'Listen to me,' Wijk said sternly in fluent Javanese, ignoring the shouts. 'The war is over. Everything changed by the Japanese is illegal. People will soon be returning to take back their property, including this hotel!'

Leo let the flag fall. It dropped at Boer's feet. He picked it up and tried to tear it but he was too weak. A youth grabbed at the flag and punched Boer hard in the face, knocking him down. 'Aah! My nose,' moaned Boer. 'The bastard's broken my nose!'

Without thinking, Wijk seized the youth by the arm and slapped him across the face. There was sudden silence.

Defiantly the youth stared back, then he bellowed '*Merdeka!*' and spat in Wijk's face.

Wijk was genuinely stunned. For the first time he looked carefully at the hostile faces and saw the rare *mata-gelap*— the wild-eyed fury—that could send the Javanese running amok. Too late, he realised he had completely misread their mood. Beside him, Boer was suddenly quiet. He, too, was finally sensing danger.

Suddenly the youth who had spat drew a knife. 'Death to the blue eyes!'

Menacingly the group started to encircle the two Dutchmen. More knives were produced. Wijk and Boer began backing away.

'Father, I've—' Leo called, rushing out of the hotel doorway.

'Leo, run!' Wijk shouted as the knives slashed at him. Boer tried to flee, but he was easily held. Both men went down under a wave of blows.

'Bastards!' Stop!' Leo shouted frantically. He pushed his way desperately into the midst of the struggle then he, too, was seized by a dozen hands. Knives rose and fell.

In the hotel Abdul had not moved from behind the front desk. The young doorman entered the lobby, brandishing the blood-splattered flag high like a trophy. He snorted at Abdul, then ran up to the roof.

Hesitantly, Abdul went to the door. Three figures lay in spreading pools of blood, their battered bodies almost unrecognisable. Passers-by stared in silence and walked on. Abdul steeled himself and went out. The Wijks had been kind to him over the years. He would see to them....

As he stood over the corpses he glanced back at the front of the hotel. His lips quivered. The message on the wall had been stamped by blood-soaked hands. 'No Dutch!'

Abdul darted back inside. He would wait till dark when it would be safer. Out in the street, stray dogs started to sniff at the corpses.

The Java Sea

Once they were out in the shipping lanes, the crew and passengers aboard the *Melchior Treub* settled down for the journey. To Meg's relief, the galley seemed well-stocked and the meal of freshly caught fish she took with Jarisha was delicious. Unable to face the heat and dirt of her cabin, she settled for a hammock on the deck, passing the time with her guidebook, committing the map to memory and trying to learn a few words of Malay, though she had doubts about the usefulness of phrases such as 'Here, coolie, take my luggage'. She was looking forward to reaching Java. Already she sensed her assignment was more complicated than her editor had anticipated.

Whenever the Javanese crew and passengers gathered, she heard the word '*Merdeka*'. It was used as a greeting, as a farewell and even punctuated conversations. It didn't take her long to ask what it meant. As someone from a country that had itself been a colony, Meg felt herself sympathising with the Indonesian cause almost instinctively. Yet she knew the young Javanese with their bright, determined faces were caught in a downward spiral of danger. She had seen the same look in young Spanish faces. But their dream had died, and with it tens of thousands of young men just like these. Meg had written bitterly that they had died because democracies had convinced themselves to look the other way. It occurred to her that now those same countries, exhausted by war, might prefer to look away once more.

As she was about to sleep, she noticed a small gathering at the ship's stern. Several passengers and some of the crew were kneeling. A single candle flickered, protected from the breeze by the gunwale. Curious, she moved closer and saw a broken comb, a small mirror and a white flower laid out on the deck. Prayers were said before the items and the candle were placed in an old pail and then lowered gently over the side. For a few seconds she could make out a faint glow bobbing in the ship's wake.

At breakfast she mentioned it to Jarisha. 'Ah,' he replied knowingly, 'It was a ritual offering to the Goddess of the Southern Seas to ensure a safe voyage.'

'But I thought the Javanese are Muslims?'

'Hmm!' He laughed. 'Our religious convictions are sincere, but can be a little confusing. Let me try to explain. Over the millennia, our islands have been home to many faiths. Originally our people were animists who worshipped the spirits of the natural world—mountains, rivers, animals— and so on. Both Hinduism and Buddhism came to Java in the fifth century, and the existing folk beliefs merged easily with the new faiths.'

Jarisha paused to check that he still had Meg's attention. 'Islam—actually Sufist Islam—arrived only in the 1400s. Sufi teaching also contains mystical elements, and these also fused with established beliefs.' He shrugged. 'It may seem strange, but in many inland villages people will pray at a mosque one day and leave offerings for village gods or perform a fertility rite the next. They see nothing odd in this. I suppose we are a strange people! I consider myself a good Muslim, Miss Graham, but I adore the puppets and music of the *wayang*, which are Hindu in origin.'

'So there are still Buddhists and Hindus?' Meg asked, smiling, encouraging him.

'Most definitely. Bali island, for example, is entirely Hindu, and the millions of Chinese are Buddhists. Inland, the old beliefs, called *Kejawan,* still have a powerful hold. Before the war, anthropologists from universities all over the world came to study it. Islam has become the dominant religion in the cities and along the northern coast. Still, we are tolerant of others' beliefs. If you get the chance, you should try to see some festivals.' Jarisha stopped, then chuckled. 'I apologise. I sound like a guidebook!'

Meg laughed with him. 'You're much better than a guidebook. But you haven't mentioned Christianity? Surely the Dutch sent missionaries?'

'Oh, there are some Christians but they are a minority, mainly on the island of Ambon. The Ambonese were loyal to the Dutch during the invasion.' He frowned. 'It will be difficult for them now.'

'And the Goddess, what's her story?' Meg asked lightly, trying to recapture the mood.

It worked; Jarisha's good humour returned. 'Well, there are several versions. My favourite is that she was an unrivalled beauty named Dewi Kadita, a favourite daughter of King Siliwangi and one of his consorts. But the King's wives and other consorts became jealous of her and they cast a spell to make her ugly and repulsive to men. Only her maid remained faithful. Eventually the king banished her from the palace and she wandered, dressed in rags, along the southern coast. She sheltered in a cave, hoping her father would forgive her. But one day, in despair, she threw herself into the ocean, intending to kill herself. Her tearful maid saw her disappear under the waves but then rise up in the surf, safe inside a huge, open clam shell. Her beauty was restored by the Golden Mirror of the Moon and the *kteis*, a sacred comb made of mother of pearl. That day she became Nyai Loro Kidul, the Goddess of the Southern Seas. She wears the finest green silks, emeralds and pearls. No other woman can match the splendour of her *konde*—her hair coil.'

Meg sighed, 'How sad! Did she get her revenge?'

'Most certainly!' Jarisha declared emphatically. 'She sided with a rival kingdom to cause eternal trouble for her father's descendants. Today, her cave is a shrine and girls make pilgrimages to the southern shore to seek her blessings for beauty and guidance in affairs of the heart. But she preys on young men, especially those who dare to wear green, her sacred colour. She appears naked, entices them into the ocean, then causes them to drown. If a man escapes her, she flies into a rage and creates storms. To placate her, fishermen and sailors make offerings like those you saw last night.'

'Oh dear. Nothing like a woman scorned!'

'Indeed not,' he laughed.

There was a shout from the wheelhouse. She listened as the Captain chatted with Jarisha, pointing to his watch and then at the sun. Jarisha explained. 'He thought you'd like to know that shortly we will be crossing the Equator. Let me be the first to welcome you to the Southern hemisphere!'

The morning of the third day was cloudless and fresh. Passengers and crew were delighted to be nearly home. Meg saw Jarisha growing more relieved by the hour. During the voyage he had given her a detailed summary of the events in Java since the Japanese surrender and the declaration of independence. They were sitting together near the prow. Sensing it might be her last opportunity, Meg touched on politics again.

'Why the guns, Doctor? Surely the Dutch will follow Britain's example in leaving India?'

Jarisha looked pensive. 'I think most people would agree that the concept of empire has had its day. Alas, colonies can be highly profitable. To put things simply, the British were stretched. They needed Indian troops in Europe to fight the Nazis. Independence was Mr Nehru's price. The Dutch have owned my country far longer than the British have ruled India. Batavia was seized by the Dutch East India Company in 1619. These islands are beautiful and bountiful. I can understand the Dutch being reluctant to give them up.'

Meg was surprised. 'You don't hate them?'

'Hate them?' His eyes widened. 'Good Heavens, no! I have many Dutch friends. Our oil, rubber and coffee industries are all Dutch creations. Without their irrigation techniques we could not grow sufficient wheat and rice to feed ourselves. And they have built hospitals, railroads, roads and schools. Overall, they have been benevolent conquerors—but conquerors nonetheless.'

Meg nodded in understanding. 'The Japanese conquered the Dutch. Is that why the Javanese didn't resist?'

Jarisha stared at the ocean. She heard the controlled anger.

'At first we welcomed the Japanese. Their propaganda was very good. They promised to help us, even give us independence. But it was a sham. I saw them strip my country bare. Machinery, locomotives and rolling stock went to Malaya or Japan. They only took—oil, rubber and rice— they cared nothing for us. Coffee and tea plantations were left to go wild, and our rice went to their armies in Asia. But we could only just feed ourselves *before* the Japanese came. There was no foreign trade, so people lost their livelihoods. Tens of thousands were sent overseas as slaves for *"Dai Nippon"*...the Great Japan. Speak to those who boarded with you at Singapore. Each saw fifty or more die of starvation, injury or disease!'

Meg caught a glimpse of the passion that drove the man. His voice was becoming softer, almost mournful. 'The Japs demanded a huge rice levy but they couldn't maintain the irrigation systems. Much *sawah*—what we call paddy—was lost. Then last year the rice harvest failed.'

He turned to face her. 'And do you know what was so utterly ridiculous? Even though the Japs had no freighters to ship the rice, they *increased* the levy! Now it lies in warehouses while people are starving.'

He looked away in frustration and, Meg realised, despair.

Jarisha had not finished. 'Last year, one of our militia units rebelled at a place called Kediri. It was a protest by a hundred boys with a few old rifles. But the Japs sent in tanks and elite troops. It was a slaughter! Later they beheaded fifteen of them in public. They were just boys!'

'Now the food shortage has turned people against each other. Smuggling is rampant. Village suspects village of stealing livestock or rice. There is violence and robbery on the streets. People show no respect for the law, village headmen, teachers or priests. Civic officials are intimidated—'

'Can't the Allies give you food and medicines?'

'Who outside Java knows or cares?'

'What about the Dutch?'

Jarisha sounded weary. 'Every day Holland Calling broadcasts about a "new Commonwealth" but in the next breath they promise to hang our leaders! "Holland Warning" it's called now!'

He sighed. 'They think they can put the clock back and carry on as before. I have been fortunate to study at universities in Holland and Great Britain. In contrast, most Javanese have never been more than a few miles from their village. They are not sophisticated but they understand betrayal. The Dutch promised to defend us. Instead, they deserted us, leaving us defenceless against the Japs and their brutal secret police. We've had enough of foreign masters.

For better or worse, Indonesia must now stand on its own feet. We must make our own decisions and face the consequences. If we act quickly, with the authority of a government recognised by the United Nations, we have a chance of success.'

'And if the Dutch won't accept that and try to force their way back?'

'The Japanese did us two great favours. First they showed us the Dutch could be beaten. Second they gave our young men some military training. If we are forced to fight, then we will do so.'

Suddenly Meg felt very afraid for Jarisha. 'I hope it won't come to that.'

'So do I,' he replied quickly. 'Alas a lot depends on the British. They have authority over the Indies. If it had been the Americans, the first Indonesian embassy would be opening now in Washington! But the British and Dutch are close allies. Unfortunately, there is a strong rumour in Singapore that they have agreed to reinstate the Dutch. We shall see.'

Jarisha gestured to a bank of clouds ahead. Beneath it, barely visible in the haze, was a dark mass. He relaxed and pointed. 'Over there is Java. You can start work soon…if we don't hit something on the way in!'

He stood up, his expression serious. 'I ask no favours for Indonesia in your despatches, Miss Graham, only the truth.'

Meg met his gaze. 'I write what I see, Doctor.'

'That might make you unpopular in certain quarters.'

She shrugged. 'I'm used to that.'

'Yes, I'm sure you are,' he said quietly. 'But take care, please. Today life is cheap in Java.'

Jarisha excused himself. Meg spent the best part of an hour engrossed in jotting down notes of their conversation. When she next looked up, the haze had lifted and the island of Java stood before her. She let out a gasp of surprise. The coastline forest shimmered in rich blues and greens. The Goddess's colour, she thought to herself. Inland she could just make out the towers and spires of Djakarta's cathedral and churches. Far beyond the city, the dark angular slopes of Mount Salak rose steeply until they were lost in voluminous white clouds that rolled in off the ocean.

Tandjong Priok harbour, Djakarta (Batavia)

Gently the *Melchior Treub* swung to port to avoid a chain of small islands that appeared to stretch to the looming coastline. Around them the water was startlingly clear. Meg glimpsed shoals of thousands of brightly coloured fish feeding off long expanses of luxuriant coral reef.

She was in awe of the natural beauty before her. The islands ranged in size from just a few yards across to large enough for a group of fishermen's huts. Others boasted more substantial structures set back in shaded clearings with views to secluded, golden beaches. Meg assumed these were the weekend retreats of the wealthy. She did a quick calculation of the real estate value of this mini-Keys that lay virtually within the city limits and was impressed.

Jarisha reappeared and came to stand beside her. Much of his unease had gone. Meg gazed at the islands. 'They're idyllic,' she said softly, lulled by the scenery.

Jarisha, too, was lost to the view. 'So beautiful!'

'What are they called?'

'To the Dutch they are the Agenietens. We call them the Palau Seribu...the Thousand Islands.' He laughed. 'Actually, there are only about a hundred and twenty!'

After a few minutes the ship entered a large bay and Meg caught her first real glimpse of the city's larger buildings.

They stood white and angular, topped with red, brown and blue roof tiles. Above them she could make out the twin, openwork-metal spires of the cathedral. Jarisha's comment about names had started her thinking. 'Doctor, tell me, what about the other places. Where am I reporting from? Is this Djakarta or Batavia?'

Jarisha paused. 'Ah, in fact both were chosen by foreigners: "Djakarta" is a Japanese contraction of the old "Djayakarta". When the British arrive I am sure they will call it Batavia. After all, it's what will be on their maps. I'm sure most people will understand both! It's just a name.'

Meg's tone was cautious. 'Sometimes words can take on a power out of all recognition to their size. People can die for them. We Americans have a few. "All men are created equal...certain unalienable rights...life, liberty and the pursuit of happiness". I know one of yours already, "*Merdeka*". "Djakarta" could become another. You just have to be sure it's worth the effort.'

Jarisha pursed his lips. 'You are right of course. I speak four languages. My first is Dutch. I think in it, write speeches in it, even love letters!' Yet to many it is now the language of the oppressor. The other day I realised that I could not translate some western concepts such as universal suffrage or even democracy in a way that would make sense to many Javanese. Most of the new government are men like me, privileged Javanese or Sumatrans nurtured in a colonial system. Not long ago you could have called us Uncle Toms and been right. In truth, our claim to represent the people of Java is no more valid than anyone else's. That is what the Dutch will say.'

Meg looked at him reprovingly. 'Don't get cold feet, Doctor. It's a big job but someone has to do it. At some point the Indonesians will have to negotiate in Dutch and, perhaps, English. Your country is lucky to have you. If it makes any difference, you've already got my vote.'

Jarisha seemed a little taken aback. He bowed. 'It does. Thank you, Miss Graham.'

She took his hand gently. 'Please call me Meg.'

Jarisha held her gaze as he kissed the back of her hand. 'Thank you, Meg.'

A sudden booming, piercing blast from a Klaxon brought Meg's hands to her ears. Instinctively she ducked. Two more blasts followed the first. When she looked for Jarisha he was leaning over the side, staring astern.

Directly in their wake was a warship. It was bearing down on them fast but not, she thought, quite fast enough. As if to confirm her guess, the Captain leant out of the wheelhouse and signalled to Jarisha not to worry. The ship would not catch them.

Jarisha glanced at Meg, widened his eyes and then let out a large breath in exaggerated but genuine relief. 'The water is too shallow for it here. At least I hope it is,' he said, still unsettled.

Even as he spoke the warship turned sharply and then steamed parallel to the coast. The captain shouted to Jarisha, who interpreted.

'He says it's a British destroyer.'

The *Melchior Treub*'s engines suddenly slowed and Meg thought they had cut out. In fact, they were only slowing to steer through the narrow entrance of the concrete breakwater. The graceful U-shape barrier extended about a mile and a quarter from the shore. Masts and funnels of another ship were visible behind it. As they drew closer, Meg saw the structure had seen better days. Cracks and splits ran along it and in several places large clumps of concrete had fallen away.

Nervous shouts from the crew distracted her. A pipe draped with seaweed was sticking up out of the water. Her stomach tightened as she thought it was a periscope but it was only the mast top of a sunken ship. Forty yards from it she saw another. She understood why the captain was manoeuvring so carefully.

They slid through the narrow gap at a snail's pace. The large steamer she had seen from outside the breakwater sat low in the water with its deck awash. Above the water-line its superstructure was peppered with rust. Meg saw it was called *Montoro*. It was another name from her guidebook. She felt a little uneasy.

She looked at Jarisha. 'Was it bombed?'

'No, scuttled. It came to evacuate women and children. Unfortunately, by the time passengers were assigned to ships the Japanese had invaded. Captains were ordered to block Java's harbours with their ships. It didn't make any difference.'

Ahead of them were the entrances to three long quays. The ship slowed yet again as it nosed carefully into the middle one. Directly in front, beyond the harbour and half-hidden by the dockyard warehouses, stood an imposing building topped with a radio mast. 'Radio Holland' was set out in contrasting brickwork just below the eaves. Some of the letters in the second word had been defaced.

There was little visible activity in the docks. Cranes and other equipment stood idle and rusting. A few fishermen were unloading their catch in baskets. But as the *Melchior Treub* approached its berth, people began streaming on to the quayside carrying banners and flags.

Elated by his successful voyage, the Captain gave a deep hoot on the ship's horn then lent out of the wheelhouse to shout triumphantly. *'Merdeka!'*

His shout was returned enthusiastically from the quay, yet Meg sensed she was already the subject of some inquisitive stares.

Two young militiamen in tattered khaki uniforms pushed their way through the onlookers to the edge of the quay. Meg saw pistols stuck in their belts. On Jarisha's advice she had slipped on her safari jacket with US press corps insignia. Now she was glad she had done so.

People began waving and the *'Merdeka!'* chanting began yet again, this time interspersed with 'Jarisha!'.

He was standing some way from Meg, waving to the crowd. She watched him carefully. 'Just who is he?' she asked herself in amazement, delighted that she might have had an exclusive, two-day interview with a revolutionary leader.

As if reading her mind, Jarisha turned and joined her. 'Forgive me, Meg. I didn't tell you that I have some political influence here. I've enjoyed talking with you these last three days. Now, to my great regret, I must say goodbye. I hope to see you again very soon.'

Meg looked at him warmly as he held out his hand. She took it wondering what might have happened if there had been a third night. 'I should thank you, Doctor. It's been a wonderful voyage. I learned a great deal.'

Suddenly he was sombre. 'We have a word,' he said softly. It is *"Keligsahan"*. The nearest translation I can think of is "trembling". Please be careful, Meg. Java is trembling.' He let go of her hand and left her.

The two militiamen sprinted up the gangway and saluted Jarisha. Meg saw them glance in her direction. When Jarisha answered, the open surprise on their faces was almost amusing. Any worries she might have had disappeared when the Captain pointed at her to the crowd and bellowed, 'American!'

On the quayside several people began clapping and shouting. 'Truman!'—'MacArthur!'—'Liberty!'

A battered, red 1935 Chevrolet Town Sedan turned swiftly on to the quay sounding its horn. Fastened to its bonnet was a small red and white pennant. Two men got out and waved politely to Jarisha. As he moved to leave the ship, he gave a polite bow to Meg for the benefit of the onlookers, then strode down the gangway to be lost quickly in the cheering throng.

Suddenly remembering their duty, the two militiamen rushed back down to the quay and elbowed their way into the crowd in a frantic attempt to escort him.

Meg watched from the ship until the car drove away. She was halfway down the gangway when two porters rushed up to her and started arguing over who would carry her bag.

'Well!' Meg said under her breath. 'Let me just say it's a privilege to represent the US of A!' Then she held up her hands, shrugged helplessly. 'Hotel des Indes, anyone?'

Chapter Thirteen

Semarang

Ota and Nagumo were alone in the bathhouse at the Officers' Club. That morning Kudo had ordered the battalion to prepare for their withdrawal from Semarang to one of their prepared positions inland. All arms and ammunition were to be taken, as well as three months' supply of food.

'I hope,' Kudo had told them, 'that we will be at the new camp for three or four weeks at the most while the British establish their bases. They will then arrange for our disarmament and transport to a holding camp, probably in Malaya. In the meantime I think it is better if we keep out of their way. Unfortunately, our civilians and technicians are being harassed and robbed by Javanese, so any civilians who wish to join us at the camp will be permitted to do so.'

Ota closed his eyes, feeling the heat from the water easing his muscles. Yet unease gnawed at him. It was a week since the surrender but still no British troops had arrived. Semarang certainly did not feel peaceful. Several soldiers had been assaulted by local gangs. In response, Kudo had confined everyone to barracks at night, so Ota had moved out of the guesthouse. Nothing was making any sense! His thoughts drifted to Kate. He had kept his promise. Soon she would be on a ship to Holland and safety. He felt glad for her even though they would never meet again. 'I still can't believe it's over,' he said suddenly, trying to put her out of his mind.

Nagumo was staring up through the vapour at the bamboo ceiling. 'Hmm,' he groaned. '*No-one* can believe it!'

'Captain Seguchi reckons we'll be imprisoned for five years at the least,' Ota ventured, wanting to talk. 'We'll be thirty then. Just as long as we can go back....'

'If there's anything to go back to!' Nagumo scoffed, wiping his face. 'On the radio it said atom bombs destroy everything. No bodies, no bones, no blood. Nothing but dust!' He took a swipe at the water and swore. 'Shit! We still don't know what's really happening!'

Over the last week Ota had never been more thankful that his family were farmers who lived far from targets for the Allied bombs. Others in his unit were not so fortunate. 'Mura's from Hiroshima,' he remarked quietly. 'And Yanase's from Nagasaki. They're both nervous wrecks. Mura's been drunk for three days.'

'Yes, I know,' Nagumo said sitting up, calmer now. 'The Major's got someone watching Mura round the clock just in case.' He wiped the perspiration off his face with a small towel which he then soaked, folded and placed on top of his head before easing his shoulders under the water once again.

Ota's mood was dark. 'I heard two more *kenpei* killed themselves last night. They used a grenade!'

Nagumo shrugged. 'There are rumours that the Allies are going to hang them all anyway. It's those going over to the Indos who worry me. Some from the 203rd—Watanabe and Hayashi, remember them from Toyama?—they've joined the militia units they trained. A handful from the 48th as well. Plus the odd *kenpei*, of course, including Shirai!'

'Shirai, too?'

'Yeah, good riddance I say,' declared Nagumo.

Ota frowned. 'I'd have put money on him doing himself like his lieutenant. He's that type.'

'Well, apparently he's in command of one of the Indo military police units along with a half-dozen of his men. They cleared out their armoury before they left.'

'But it's over!' Ota said exasperatedly.

Nagumo shrugged. 'Not for Shirai! He's desperate for a last crack at those hairy white apes. I wouldn't be surprised if Yanase and Mura are thinking the same thing.'

'It won't change anything.'

'No, but if your family, everyone, had been turned to dust, what would you do? Bend over for the new lord or try to rip off his balls?'

Ota looked at him carefully. 'Is that what we're doing, bending over?'

Nagumo let out a long sigh. 'Our war is not Shirai's or Yanase's war. Not now, anyway. We might be officers but we're still conscripts! I wasn't fighting for the Emperor. I just wanted it over so I could keep my family out of it. You were doing the same.' He paused, lowering his voice. 'To tell you the truth, I'm glad it's finished.'

Ota felt a weight lift off him. 'I thought I was the only one.'

Nagumo sighed. 'Only the madmen wanted to carry on.'

They sat and soaked in silence for a while. Ota began to hum a folk ballad then stopped. 'Well, whatever the reason, I think the Major's right to leave here. The locals are starting to worry me.'

'And me,' agreed Nagumo. 'Let's hope the Tommies come soon so we can be off.'

Ota stretched full length. 'I'll miss this bathhouse, though. Can't we dismantle it and take it with us? Two months is a long time to go without comforts. After all, we'll be in a prison camp soon.'

'Uh huh. I've been thinking the same thing. But don't worry,' grinned Nagumo. 'I've invited Kiriko and her "civilian technicians" to come with us. I'm collecting them from the Sakura tomorrow.'

'Trust you!' Ota grinned. 'What about the girls at the Akebono and Otowa?'

Nagumo grunted in dismay. 'That sly bastard Ueda from the 203rd beat me to them!'

They glanced at each other and for the first time since the surrender they laughed together out loud.

Around noon the next day, as preparations for the battalion's move were almost complete, a black Peugeot 301 arrived at the main gate of the barracks. The car was bedecked with red-and-white nationalist pennants. 'BKR' was daubed in red paint on both sides.

A few minutes later the delegation from the local revolutionary council was allowed into the compound. One was middle-aged, balding and, despite the heat, wore a suit and tie. The other two, dressed in brand new militia uniforms with captains' insignia, were no more than twenty. All three looked intently at the activity outside the armoury and storerooms.

'Good afternoon, gentlemen,' Kudo greeted his visitors in slow but fluent English. 'I am Major Kudo.' Captain Seguchi and Sgt-Major Tazaki stood a few feet away.

The older Javanese stepped forward and bowed. Pinned to his lapel pocket was a small red and white ribbon.

'My name is Orubu, Major,' he said politely. 'I am the new mayor of Semarang. With me are representatives from the *Badan Keamanan Rakjat*—the BKR—the People's Security Force.'

Kudo gave him a small but polite bow.

Orubu looked across the parade ground at the vehicles. 'You are leaving Semarang, Major?'

Kudo kept his voice casual. 'This barracks will be used by British troops. We are relocating.'

Concern flashed in Orubu's eyes. He spoke quickly in Javanese to the two militiamen. They, too, suddenly became tense and spoke among themselves briefly. Orubu turned back to Kudo. 'When will the British arrive?'

'I am sorry, Mr Orubu, all troop movements, even those of the British, are confidential.'

Abruptly Orubu stood to attention. 'On behalf of the Government of Indonesia,' he said officiously, 'I demand that you surrender your arms and ammunition. We guarantee you no harm, Major.'

Kudo's expression did not change. 'I am under direct orders to maintain law and order. Surrender of weapons has been expressly forbidden.'

'Unfortunately, Major, the Allies are not aware of the new situation here.' Orubu's tone was impatient. 'This is now the Republic of Indonesia and the legal government has authority in all negotiations over foreign troops.'

Kudo stared at him impassively. 'Demands are not negotiations. My orders are very explicit, Mr Orubu. I cannot agree.'

Orubu interpreted again for the militia men who glowered. His own irritation showed in his voice. 'Major Kudo, two days ago, Major Koga at the Banjumas Garrison had no hesitation in surrendering his arms to BKR representatives.'

Kudo kept a poker-face. He hoped Orubu was lying. If not, what was Koga doing! 'I am surprised to hear that,' Kudo said with a troubled frown. 'If it is true, Major Koga is in breach of his orders. I intend to obey mine.' He beckoned to one of the nearby privates for his rifle. The soldier presented it with parade-like precision. Kudo showed Orubu the circular, multi-petalled design stamped into the blued metal of the breech.

'Mr Orubu,' he said sternly, 'the chrysanthemum is the personal symbol of His Imperial Majesty. We carry these weapons on his behalf. They are not mine to give up.'

The Javanese glanced at each other in confusion. 'I believe you are playing with us,' Orubu replied derisively. 'No doubt the gallows the Americans are building for *His Imperial Majesty* will also be decorated with a chrysanthemum!'

Kudo's stared back at him frostily.

'We can guarantee your safety Major…,' continued Orubu, 'but only if you co-operate.'

'And if I do not?'

'Our people wish to be free. Emotions are running high. You have two hours to make a decision. Good afternoon, Major.'

The three men returned to their car and left. Kudo turned to Seguchi and Tazaki. 'Double the sentries, then set up heavy machine guns and a mortar battery at each gate. Station observers and runners at the canal bridge. They are not to shoot under any circumstances, even if they come under fire. Is that clear?

Both men saluted smartly. 'Understood, Sir.'

Tjandi Camp III

'They won't listen to me anymore, Lucy,' sighed Jenny Hagen. 'Yesterday I was called a bossy bitch. All I did was ask who was on latrine duty.'

Lucy Santen laughed sarcastically. 'I know what you mean, Jen. I have patients with gastric problems demanding tinned pork.'

They were on the balcony of the infirmary, sharing a cigarette. After two weeks of more and better food, the mood of the women and children in Tjandi had changed from jubilation to mounting frustration over their continuing confinement. Beyond the bamboo fence, life seemed to be returning to normal. Each day, villagers from the neighbouring *kampongs* entered the camp to barter fresh vegetables and fruit for Red Cross food tins and clothing.

Jenny Hagen was taking the brunt of the dissatisfaction. Even on the day of the Japanese surrender, several women had ignored her pleas to stay in the camp and left in search of their husbands and older sons. As the days went on, increasing numbers also upped and left or refused to take their turn at cooking, gardening or cleaning duties.

'Have you seen the vegetable plots recently?' Jenny asked.

'No, but let me guess. A garden of weeds?'

Jenny held her head in hands. 'Hardly anyone is willing to work. They say there's no point because we'll all be leaving in a "couple of days" or "next week". God I hope they're right. But what if they're wrong?'

'Then that will probably be your fault, too!' Lucy quipped. 'I think you should just—oh, look—isn't that Patrice and Erik? They've come back!'

Jenny saw a woman and a small child walking slowly towards one of the huts. They carried rucksacks and looked exhausted. A small crowd was gathering around them. 'I'd better go and see what's happened.'

'I hope her husband's all right,' Lucy replied.

By the time Jenny reached the hut the onlookers had reached nearly fifty. She pushed through to find Patrice sobbing on her former bed. Her five-year-old son, Erik, was standing by his mother. He saw Jenny and spoke. 'Some bad people are living in our house!'

'Who's in your house, Erik?' Jenny asked, bending to look the child in the eye.

Patrice looked up and drew Erik to her. 'Oh, Jenny,' she said sniffing back the tears. 'I went to our house to get it ready for when Johan comes back. There were squatters there, natives. They wouldn't leave.'

There was a flutter of incredulity among those listening.

Jenny frowned. 'But what about the police?'

Patrice began crying again. 'They took the squatters' side. They said that "foreigners" had no property rights!'

There was indignation. 'How dare they!'—'Grasping sods. They have no right to do that!'—'Just wait till our troops get here!'

Jenny gave her a hug. Patrice started sobbing again. 'We walked for two days. I had such a lovely home. All I wanted to do was make it nice again....'

Over the next week other former inmates drifted back to Tjandi with similar stories. A few had been robbed. All over Java, Dutch-owned property had been seized. Around Tjandi hostility and intimidation was growing. Fewer villagers went in to the camp to trade. Food deliveries by the Japanese also became less frequent as they searched ever wider for fresh food. Gradually the atmosphere in the camp changed. Duty rosters were filled without prompting, vegetable plots were tended again and latrines emptied as the women took refuge in a familiar routine.

Bad news had not all been outside the camp. Despite Lucy Santen's repeated warnings about the risks of a sudden, large intake of richer foods, fourteen women had died. She was still attending to eight others in the infirmary with gorging-related complications. Kate's friend, Anna was among them.

Lucy and Kate finished the now much reduced rounds and headed, as usual, on to the balcony while Lucy lit a part-smoked cigarette and inhaled deeply. 'Anna will be fine. Unfortunately most of the others will have stomach trouble for the rest of their lives.' She did not hide her anger. 'You told them, I told them, till I was blue in the face....'

Kate patted her hand. 'Lucy, it's not your fault! You've worked miracles here. We'll always be grateful.'

Lucy gave her a sharp look. 'Kate, whatever you do, don't drop your guard now.'

Kate was startled. 'But the war's over! We'll be going—'

'Listen to me,' Lucy said quickly. 'The war's over but we aren't free or safe. Use your eyes and ears! You've heard those who've come back. It's dangerous! Even the police are hostile. Worst of all, there's no word about our soldiers.' She drew heavily on the last of the cigarette before stubbing it out. 'To be honest, I'm more scared now than before.'

Kate felt a little unnerved. Lucy Santen was probably the toughest, most resourceful person she had ever known. 'You're just tired, Lucy,' she said encouragingly. 'All you need is some rest.'

'Is that your prescription, Doctor?'

Their laughter was cut short by the sound of an aircraft engine. The Mosquito was low enough for them to see the blue RAF roundel on the wings. Kate let out a shriek. 'It's a British plane!'

Below them people were looking up and pointing excitedly. Some began to wave and shout. 'Help us!—Please, help us!—We're here!'

Kate was on her tiptoes waving frantically at the fast-moving craft. Above them the small, sleek, twin-engine plane waggled its wings in a salute which brought a cheer. Kate and Lucy hugged each other.

The aircraft circled lower and Kate could just make out the heads of the two pilots. The watchers cheered as leaflets swirled like confetti in the plane's wake. They scattered all over the camp and beyond the fences. Several fluttered near the balcony. Lucy caught one.

'Oh, let me see it, please, Lucy!' Kate gushed excitedly, hanging on Lucy's shoulder.

Beaming, Lucy began to read aloud. 'From South-East Asia Command. Food and medicines will be dropped by parachute at 1500 hours tomorrow. You are requested to prepare a large white cross in an open area. Stand well clear until all canisters have landed.'

'They're coming!' Kate shrieked. 'At last, they're coming!' They clutched at each other, jumping for joy.

A buzz of excitement gripped the camp. Many had been unable to sleep. Kate and Marja were standing in the parade area where, soon after first light, a huge cross had been made out of white sheets and towels.

'Oh, Kate, I can't wait to see what will come!' Marja said eagerly.

Kate giggled. 'Me too! Our hut was awake most of the night guessing what we are going to get. In the end we settled on pâté, cream cakes, shampoo, underwear and shoes!'

'Is that all?' Marja sniggered.

'Oh, I forgot the silk pyjamas!'

Giggling, they moved to sit on the steps of the nearest hut, shielding their eyes from the sun as they peered above the tree tops for a sign of a plane. By mid-afternoon most of the camp had assembled around the edge of the field.

Anticipation was almost tangible. Small boys were running around the cross, pretending to be aircraft.

After several false alarms they heard it: a throbbing drone slowly increasing in volume. Necks craned to look. One after another, hands rose to point at a black dot to the north.

The C-47 Dakota transport was much bigger and slower than the Mosquito. Kate could see a huge engine on either wing. It came unerringly towards them, descending steadily, then circled twice. Suddenly, it veered off and the watchers murmured in dismay. A few seconds later it was turning again and descending even lower for the final approach.

As it roared past, Kate could see objects tumbling out. Parachutes unfurled to reveal refrigerator-sized, cylindrical canisters hanging beneath them. Tjandi camp erupted in cheers and shouts. The C-47 made a last pass, giving them a farewell waggle of its wings, then gunned its engines for home. By then, all eyes were on the ten parachutes.

The first canister came down at the north end of the camp. Children raced to it, their mothers trailing behind. Slowly the watchers realised that the wind was taking the other canisters well away from the parade area. There was a surge towards the administration buildings as people tried to track the descents.

'Kate, quick!' Marja shouted. 'Or someone else will get your silk pyjamas!'

Movement stopped as the second chute escaped the strong breeze and suddenly dropped very quickly. 'It's going to hit the school!—Oh, the infirmary!'

Helplessly they watched the canister strike the infirmary roof then slide, smashing tiles before it came to rest upright on the balcony. Lucy Santen appeared and waved, hugging the canister. Cheering the crowd sped off as the third, fourth and fifth canisters came down beside the guardhouse. The thin metal casings burst open showering boxes and tins. A mad, noisy scramble developed as women and children dropped to their knees grabbing what they could.

In dismay, Kate pulled Marja back as they saw the other parachutes sail overhead. Two came down just outside the camp entrance but the others drifted out of sight. 'Oh, no!' Kate groaned.

'What's the matter?' Marja shouted urgently, pulling her on. 'Let's get them!'

They joined the small crowd rushing through the gate, then stopped abruptly. One parachute had caught on a palm-tree, the canister hanging by its cords tantalisingly out of reach. The other had landed fifty yards further on. It was already open. Javanese women and children from the nearby *kampong* were helping themselves.

'That's ours!' one of the internees shouted.

'Leave that alone!' Julia Stam yelled. 'Come on, let's stop them!'

Irate, the Tjandi women moved forward. The Javanese stared at them impassively.

Julia strode up to a young woman who had a baby strapped to her back and who held a tin of powdered milk. 'Give me that,' demanded Julia. 'It was sent for us!'

The woman ignored her and bent down again. 'Well, really!' Julia exclaimed, puce with indignation. In fury she snatched at one of the packages. Suddenly the woman lashed out, catching Julia squarely on the temple with a tin. Julia staggered back with a nasty cut. Several of the *kampong* women drew short curved knives from their bodices. Their message was clear.

'Keep calm and move back!' Kate recognised Jenny Hagen's voice.

'Come on,' Jenny shouted as she pushed through to the front. 'Powdered milk isn't worth dying for!'

Cautiously and reluctantly the shocked Tjandi group backed off, two of them helping the injured Julia Stam.

Immediately the *kampong* women went back to their scavenging, picking the canister clean. They left unhurriedly, without looking back, their loot in baskets balanced on their heads, their hips swaying.

As they watched, the camp women seethed. Their mood became uglier when they found they could not release the other canister. 'Thieving bitches!'—'What good is pork to Muslims? I hope they bloody choke!'—'Bolshie coolies! My husband will teach them a thing or two!'

'That's enough!' Jenny Hagen yelled. 'Save your strength! We'll need a ladder and a trolley to take it back into the camp. Better not to open it here. One of the karts will do. Some of you wait here.'

While most of the women followed Jenny back into the camp. Kate, Marja and half-a-dozen others stayed with the canister. Kate wasn't sure what she was supposed to do if the locals returned. They waited nervously for several minutes until a small procession filed back out of the camp gates. It was led by a pedal-kart, now without its seats and pushed by its proud young owner. Other boys carried a short section of ladder. Some of the women had armed themselves with a saucepan or broom. Two boys climbed the tree and soon they were cutting at the nylon cords suspending the canister. The women gazed in anticipation at both the canister and the parachute. The silk was already earmarked for blouses and shorts.

'Ow! My leg!' A girl wailed.

A stone clanged and ricocheted off the canister, grazing another girl's shoulder. 'Ouch!' 'Watch out, natives!'

Thirty yards down the road a line of Javanese youths stood in a half-circle. Some were making obscene gestures. Behind them stood the *kampong* women. The youths began chanting.

'*Merdeka!*'—'Su-kar-no!'

More stones came in a hail and several found their targets. Saucepans became shields as the women fled back to the camp. A small stone caught Kate high on her right shoulder, deadening her arm. She kept running until she was through the camp gate.

Panting and cradling her sore arm, she went back to peer through the fence. Two youths went up the ladder, cut down the canister and quickly freed its chute. Both were wheeled away on the kart.

Kate looked for Marja. She found her uninjured but tearful. 'Oh, Kate you're hurt!' Marja sobbed embracing her. 'How could they rob us like that? It's not fair!'

Kate said nothing. She was thinking of Lucy Santen's warning.

The day's events left the inmates of Tjandi angry, bitter and frightened. In the end, few of the dropped supplies were shared. Only the canister and chute that had landed on the infirmary balcony escaped plunder because Lucy Santen barred the infirmary door.

At sunset no-one had complained when Jenny Hagen ordered the camp gate locked. As darkness fell, the inmates gathered to sit in small groups, suddenly very conscious of how vulnerable they were.

Kate and Jenny were in the infirmary with Lucy Santen, who was re-examining Julia Stam's wound. Lady Teresa van Gaal, a pinched-faced brunette, had arrived a few minutes later to escort Julia back to her room.

'I'm not staying here one day longer!' Julia declared self-righteously for Teresa's benefit. At her insistence, Lucy had tied a full bandage around her head.

'You're quite right, Julia,' Teresa replied. 'We could all be raped and murdered in our beds! Where are the Americans,' she demanded, 'that's what I want to know? Why was it a British plane?'

'It's safer if we stick together and wait in the camp,' Jenny said knowing she was losing the argument.

Teresa was not impressed. 'How dare those natives abuse us...after all we've suffered. They'll regret it!'

Kate heard the venom in Teresa's voice and shivered. She busied herself folding bandages.

'But what,' asked Lucy, 'if the Americans recognise their independence? What happens then?'

'Java is not the Philippines, Doctor,' scoffed Teresa. 'The Indies are Dutch and will remain Dutch. The Javanese couldn't run a fête, never mind a country. I've never heard such rubbish. Sukarno will hang and that will be the end of it, believe me.'

'I'm not so sure anymore,' sighed Lucy. 'It could be time for them to run things for themselves.'

Teresa's stare was withering. 'Well, well! To think we've had a Communist in our midst all this time.'

Lucy rolled her eyes dismissively. 'Oh, for God's sake, Teresa! The world is changing. You know what's planned for the Philippines, Burma and India. Perhaps you don't want to see it.'

'If you want to leave, I'm sure my husband will be able to find you a berth on the first ship back to Holland,' Teresa said disdainfully. 'You won't mind travelling steerage will you?'

'Oh, do stop bickering,' snapped Jenny. 'Things are bad enough as they are. There's nothing to do but wait.'

'Well, my mind is made up,' said Teresa. 'My duty is with my husband in the capital. I should think it obvious that general instructions to remain here do not apply to the Governor's wife and daughter. I am going to pack.'

'I am leaving, too,' Julia asserted self-righteously. 'I've had quite enough of Hotel Tjandi!'

Chapter Fourteen

Bloemstraat, Semarang

There was a subdued, nervous urgency in the offices of the Mitsubishi Trading Company. Half-a-dozen Japanese clerks were hunched over desk drawers and filing cabinets transferring files and ledgers to cardboard boxes. It was a Sunday, the business quarter was deserted, and the emergency removal operation was in full swing.

Akira Sato, the general manager, moved about the room constantly, encouraging his anxious staff to hurry. His instructions from Tokyo were short and clear: destroy all records of shipments of rubber, oil, plant machinery, rolling stock, precious metals and dozens of Rolls-Royce, Mercedes, Bugatti and Alfa Romeo cars to Japan.

They were making very good progress and Sato was beginning to relax. One more hour was all that was needed, perhaps less.

Outside, cars belonging to more of his employees were shuttling the boxes to Mitsubishi's warehouses where they were being incinerated. It would have been quicker if the local staff had been called in to help but Sato had been ordered to keep the plan from them.

A commotion outside made him turn. A group of bare-chested youths burst through the door. They were armed with staves, knives and clubs.

Sato confronted them. 'This is private property,' he said in Javanese. 'There's nothing here to interest you. You must leave at once!'

The youths glowered threateningly. One of them took a quick step forward and clubbed Sato on the temple. He staggered then fell.

When Sato regained consciousness he was sitting, squashed in with many others in a small, dank room. His ears were ringing. When he tried to move his arms he realised they were tied. His throat was parched and it was stifling hot. There was an odour of urine and faeces.

'Sato-san, are you all right?' He recognised the voice of his secretary, Ishihara.

'Yes, I think so. My arms?'

'We are all tied,' said Ishihara quietly. 'We are in Bulu Gaol. There must be two hundred of us. Upstairs there are some Dutch.'

'How long was I out?' Sato asked quickly. 'And who took us?'

Ishihara shrugged. 'Half an hour. The gang call themselves the Student Army. They say that we will be freed if the local garrison surrenders its arms and ammunition.'

Sato's vision cleared and he was able to focus on the barred cell door. A low-wattage bulb illuminated some of the corridor. Opposite his cell was another, equally crammed. 'What happened at the office?'

'We were tied up at knife point and brought here,' Ishihara explained miserably.

'And the files?'

'As we left them.'

'*Baka!*' Fool! The shout came from across the cell. 'Here we are, our lives in danger and all you can think about is the bloody office!'

Sato squinted and recognised Nomura, a junior manager with the Nippon Yusen Shipping Company.

'Be quiet you two. It's bad enough in here already.' Sato knew the voice only too well. It was Kazuo Watanabe, the Vice-Governor of Central Java. Sato despised him because Watanabe had issued an exclusive licence to his brother to open a pawn-broking chain. Weeks later the Japanese had ordered all valuables in Java, including gold, artworks and jewellery to be surrendered through brokerages to fund the war effort. Overnight Watanabe, his brother and a Japanese *kenpei* major called Nakamura had become immensely rich. A year ago, at a party attended by Watanabe, Sato had drunk a little too much and joked about the 'Java Treasure'. For the next month *kenpei* officers had followed him openly every day.

'Out! Out! Quickly!'

Sato felt strong hands haul him up and fling him into the corridor. He crashed into the stocky, balding Watanabe. They were led to a larger, unfurnished room past cells and corridors also full of Japanese civilians. There was more shouting as their captors began arguing among themselves. Sato caught the words 'hostage' and 'guns' from one side and 'thieves' and 'infidels' from the other. With dismay he realised a different gang, armed with rifles and machine guns, was taking over.

More Japanese were crammed into the room. Sato saw two more of his employees, Omura and Nishi among them.

'Silence!'

In the doorway was an older youth, wearing militia uniform trousers and brandishing a pistol. A Japanese army sword hung at his hip. His hair coiled down to his shoulders. 'Black Buffalos are in charge here!' His eyes were wild. 'All others leave now!'

Sato, Ishihara, Nishi and Omura exchanged anxious glances as the group of students that had seized them left looking sullen and dejected. More armed youths took their places. Their leader barked another order. 'Bring in the women!'

A group of six, nervous-looking Javanese women of various ages, filed into the room.

The Black Buffalo leader raised his hands aloft. 'Behold! These are the women of Java! You have robbed them, deceived them, abused them! You are thieves, liars and infidel rapists! Today you will pay for your crimes in the sight of Allah the Merciful!'

Another youth came forward to interpret in simple but clear Japanese. Sato did not need it but most of the others did. He felt their and his own fear.

'Start with him!' The leader pointed at Watanabe.

Sato watched the Vice-Governor quail. The leader looked at the women. Timidly one came forward to stand in front of Watanabe. She held out a sheet of paper. Sato could see it was a receipt for pawned items.

The Buffalo leader spoke without emotion. 'You took from this woman, "in the name of Japan, two gold rings and a solid silver bracelet". They were the only items left to her by her mother. She would like them returned. Now!'

Watanabe gaped. 'I—I don't know where they are! They were sent to Japan....'

The interpreter began to speak but the leader silenced him with a quick wave of his hand. 'Sharia law punishes theft with the loss of a hand. We have a variation, two rings, two hands.'

At his signal the youths holding Watanabe partly untied him then stepped away, pulling his arms out at his sides. The leader drew his sword then raised it over Watanabe's outstretched arm.

Watanabe was quivering. 'No! Please! I'll give her another bracelet—'

The weapon slashed downwards, hacking off his right arm just under the elbow. Watanabe screamed, staring at the blood spraying from the stump. A second, wilder swing took off his left arm almost at the shoulder. Watanabe pitched forward across the stone floor, slipping in his own blood. His cries for help echoed down the corridors.

As he writhed one of the other youths stepped over him and drew a curved dagger quickly across his throat. Sato gagged as Watanabe breath rattled in his throat.

Expressionless, the woman went over to the dying man, bent down and dipped the receipt in his blood then walked out in silence. Horror and disbelief were etched in the faces of the Japanese captives.

Nonchalantly the leader consulted a list. He spoke calmly. 'Hiroshi Ishihara.'

Alarmed, Sato saw his secretary seized. A slight figure pushed through from the back of the women, took off a headscarf and stared at Ishihara. She was about seventeen.

'Reni!' Ishihara gasped. 'Why?'

As he was pulled to the centre of the room Ishihara pleaded in Javanese. 'I have done nothing! She's my wife. I'm a Muslim! Reni, please tell them!'

In mock surprise the leader raised his eyebrows. 'A Muslim? Let's see if you have been cut!'

Ropes were quickly strung over a beam. Two youths upended Ishihara, tying him by his ankles. He was left suspended, head brushing the floor, his arms still tied behind him. He continued to protest loudly that he was innocent. One of the youths drew a bayonet and sliced open Ishihara's trousers and underwear.

Scorn showed on the Buffalo leader's face. 'Hah! You swore you were a Muslim as you took two pure Javanese girls as your wives.' He glowered. 'These women are their mothers. Liar! You are nothing but an infidel defiler of our women!' He raised his sword. 'Now I will circumcise you properly.'

Ishihara was screaming, mixing Javanese and Japanese. 'Reni! *Onegai!* Please! *'Yamete!'* Stop!

Sato closed his eyes....

Tjandi Camp III, Semarang

Teresa van Gaal, her daughter Marianne, Julia Stam and four other members of the 'Bridge Club' headed briskly for the camp gate. Each of them was carrying a small knapsack and a water bottle. About two dozen others had assembled to see them off. Jenny Hagen, Lucy Santen and Kate were among them.

At the gate, Jenny made one last try. 'Please reconsider. It could be very dangerous. I still don't think I should let you leave.'

'Our minds are made up, Jenny,' Teresa replied firmly. 'We accepted your *election* as Camp Representative but your authority has lapsed now that the war is over.'

'Thank you, Teresa,' Jenny said blandly.

'Goodbye, Jenny,' Julia Stam said primly. 'Goodbye, Dr Santen and thank you.' She turned and strode to join Teresa. Two boys pushed open the gate and the group set off determinedly with Julia and Teresa in the lead.

Twenty yards down the road, Julia suddenly spun and fell. Teresa stared at her. In the middle of Julia's forehead was a hole oozing blood. *'Crack!'* The shot echoed around them. There was a second and another woman slumped to the ground. Screaming, the others turned and ran for the camp.

'Close the gate!' Jenny shouted.

Black Sun, Red Moon

Kate darted forward to help. Another shot rang out and a third woman fell. They hauled and slowly the gate swung back, shuddering as it scraped over the prostrate body, then banged shut.

Djatingaleh Barracks, Semarang

Kudo summoned his officers to the Mess. They were in a serious mood and dressed for battle. On the table in front of Kudo was a large-scale street plan of Semarang. They gathered round. Ota found himself looking for the guesthouse and the old school.

Kudo sounded matter of fact. 'I'm not sure yet if the threat from the local militia is real but it looks as if we shall be staying in the barracks a bit longer.'

There was an urgent knock on the door. One of the runners posted in the town entered. 'Major,' the man said panting, 'a few minutes ago we heard shots in Tjandi. It's quiet now.'

Ota felt a stab of anxiety.

'Right,' replied Kudo. 'Send someone to replace you!'

'Yes, Sir!' The soldier rushed out.

Puzzled, Kudo rubbed his chin. 'Tjandi?' He looked questioningly at Captain Seguchi. 'The internees?'

'Could be,' agreed Seguchi. 'They had an air-drop yesterday. Perhaps the locals are after easy pickings?'

Kudo looked back at the street plan. 'Our orders are to maintain law and order. I don't see how we can do that if we are besieged. At the same time, I want to avoid provoking the locals.' He looked up suddenly. 'Ota, you were billeted at Tjandi. You must know the area well. Take your platoon and make the school camp your base. Full kit, two machine guns, extra ammunition and rations for four days.'

'Yes, Major!' Ota replied, glancing at Nagumo as he made for the door.

'Ota, one more thing,' Kudo called him back. 'If the internees show any animosity tell your men to ignore it.'

Tjandi Camp III

Ota was filled with dread as he walked past the three corpses lying in front of the camp gate. There had been no answer from inside to shouts. Behind him, several of his men had rifles trained on the street to their rear. Others were forcing the lock with levers. The gate swung open.

'Let's go!' Ota yelled, leading his men forward. Inside, he stopped abruptly. Facing him stood a row of about thirty tense, fearful-looking women clutching cooking knives, cleavers and sharpened bamboo staves. His men fanned out behind him. Many of the women shrank back.

Ota turned quickly to his men. 'Stand down!'

His men lowered their weapons, staring at the motley group. Ota holstered his pistol. He saw many of them were still afraid of him.

'Good afternoon, ladies,' he said bowing. 'I am Lieutenant Ota. We are here to protect you.'

They stared at him in shock and utter disbelief.

Ota's men were already bringing in the bodies of Julia Stam and the others. Some of the women began to sob. Ota turned away and signalled the troop lorry forward, trying not to think about Kate.

'Excuse me, Lieutenant.'

A woman in the centre of the line had stepped forward and bowed. 'I'm Jenny Hagen. I'm the Camp Representative. We thought you were....'

'I understand. Were there any others killed or injured?'

'No.'

Relief surged through Ota. 'We will mount guards.'

Jenny bowed again and led the women away.

Ota's platoon took over the guardhouse. For an hour Ota concentrated on supervising repairs to the gate, positioning machine guns and organising perimeter patrols. His men were in good humour, amused by their reception committee after his warning about 'animosity'. When he was satisfied he went back to radio to Kudo.

There was a knock on the office door. Kate stood in the doorway holding a tray and tin cups. Her face was flushed. 'Hello, Kenichi,' she said brightly. She was wearing a sleeveless blouse and figure-hugging shorts made out of white parachute silk.

Caught off-guard Ota was lost for words. 'Kate...,' he said eventually, thankful that she was unharmed.

For several seconds they smiled at each other before Kate moved to the desk. 'I thought you and your men might like some coffee. It came in the air-drop.'

He stood up hurriedly, his face reddening. 'Thank you. That's very kind. I—I was worried about you.' Tentatively he reached for her hand.

She took his in both of hers. 'I was scared but I'm fine now.'

'Kate, I—' he was suddenly unsure of himself. 'Everything has changed. I mean we are no longer enemies.'

'I was never your enemy, Kenichi,' she said softly. 'But there was still a war.'

'Yes but I meant—'

One of Ota's platoon strode into the room. The moment was lost. 'I'd better go,' mumbled Kate. 'You must be very busy.' She put one of the tins in front of him. 'Sorry we haven't any real cups.' At the door she paused and bowed hurriedly. 'Thank you for coming to help us.' Then she was gone.

Kate was thumbing through one of the air-dropped copies of *The Illustrated London News*. Read by twenty people already, its pages were frayed and torn. Other occupants of the hut were playing cards, reading, sewing, anything in fact, to try and forget the terrible events of the day. There had been no journey in the straw basket to the cemetery for Julia Stam and the other dead. Instead, they had been buried that afternoon in a corner of the vegetable garden.

Normally, Kate would have been thrilled to have fresh reading matter but she could not concentrate on the articles. All she could think about was Ota. She gave up and lay down but could not sleep.

'Shush! Listen!'—'What's that noise?'

The drumming carried in the night air like an irregular pulse. One by one the neighbouring *kampongs* took up the beat in reply. Whatever it was, Kate realised, it was getting nearer. Conversation petered out. Curious, she decided to go and see for herself.

Once outside she glanced up at the nearest watchtower and felt oddly reassured by the familiar silhouette of the Japanese sentry. She noticed others doing it too. How ironic! *Four weeks ago we cheered to be rid of them. Now we're scared that they might desert us....*

Heavy clouds hid the moon and the stars. It would be quite a squall, she thought. She saw several women, also curious about the noise, heading for the gate. Kate joined them.

Ota stood in shadow, looking down the road towards the town. His men had searched the houses and gardens that afternoon but there had been no trace of the sniper. Even so, he was taking no chances. There were no lights on around the gate. The militia were Japanese-trained after all and standard procedure was to infiltrate a position in darkness....

He was waiting for Suzuki, who had volunteered to scout the nearest *kampong*. There was a short whistle from Ota's right followed by their call sign.

'Red Fuji!'

Moments later the young corporal darted through the gate. Suzuki was a former long-distance running champion. His breathing was relaxed. 'Lieutenant, around two hundred people are coming this way, mostly youths.'

'Weapons?'

'Bamboo spears, swords, machetes, rakes and a few shotguns.'

'Well done.'

Suzuki saluted. Ota addressed the men at the gate. 'No firing unless I shoot or I am hit. Send a sit-rep to Battalion HQ. Get ready!'

By now the drumming was much louder. Ota made out the faint glow from burning torches. He heard Suzuki giving instructions behind him. His eighteen men were split into four groups positioned loosely around the parade area and main school building, with six men at the main gate. He could not defend the entire perimeter if the Javanese called his bluff.

The marchers rounded the bend three hundred yards away. They strode quickly, chanting, roughly ten abreast. 'Death to the Dutch!'—'*Merdeka!*'

They were a hundred yards from the gate when Ota felt the first drops of rain. At fifty yards he gave the command. 'Now!' He closed his eyes as searchlights bathed himself, the gateway and the front rows of the marchers in a sea of white light. The chanting stopped and the youths slowed, shielding their eyes.

Ota walked forward to stand in the middle of the road. A few feet from him, also illuminated, was the machine gun crew.

Again the mob stalled, unnerved by the soldiers' presence. Shouting continued at the rear. *'Merdeka!'—'Allah akbah!'* There was still an air of menace.

Ota could see the indecision on many faces but not all. He strode two paces forward, hands behind his back, away from his sword and pistol. He spoke firmly in rehearsed Javanese.

'All internee camps are under military protection. There is a curfew. Go home!'

Overhead, thunder clapped and in seconds teeming rain began drenching them all. Ota stared, ignoring the pounding drops. He could see only the first few rows of hostile faces.

Curtly he spoke again. 'You are breaking the law. Go home, now!'

The rain was bouncing up off the road. Ota was worried in case the searchlights shorted. He remained in the open, stock still. A few of the front marchers looked about them for support. There was none. Slowly the crowd started to break up. Ota felt chilled but he stood and watched the youths slink away.

As suddenly as it had begun the rain stopped. Bright moonlight lit the camp. Ota turned and ordered the lights switched off and the gate closed. Like him, his men were soaked but they were relieved, and proud of their officer.

Ota glanced at Suzuki. 'Get them into dry clothes in sections. Then some food. Keep the towers manned.'

On his way back to the guardhouse Ota noticed the group of bedraggled women, including Kate, whose drenched silk top and shorts were plastered to her like a transparent skin. There was appreciation in their looks. He acknowledged them with a slight bow and walked on. To his great surprise Jenny Hagen bowed back, then Kate. After some hesitation the others followed suit.

Chapter Fifteen

Tandjong Priok Harbour, Batavia/Djakarta

Landing Craft Infantry (LCI) 217 was designed for short ferrying and not long voyages. It was pitching and rolling in the heavy swell. Along both port and starboard sides men— officers and other ranks—stood shoulder to shoulder, bracing themselves against ropes, as they vomited.

Mac's stomach had emptied hours before and now he was bringing up bile. Beside him, Bob Souness, a six-foot-two Glaswegian, was deathly pale and could hardly hold himself upright. Souness groaned. 'Jesus Christ! We could be on one of the Clyde bridges at Hogmanay! And I hav'nae touched a drop!'

'I've never felt—' Mac's reply died in his throat as a whiff of Souness's rancid breath triggered another spasm. He dropped down to lean against the wet steel plates, hugging his knees to his chest till the cramps slowly subsided. Fucking hell! He wanted to shout. You win a sodding war and as a reward the army have you swimming in your own puke and shit! Opposite him a miserable Stan Nesbit sat huddled and equally pale.

For three weeks Malaya had been a paradise of easy duties, fresh food, relaxation and fraternisation with the locals. The order to leave had come suddenly, late one night. At first, wild rumours circulated that they were going home. Later, the talk was of Japan. Spirits still high, the Seaforths had headed for Port Swettenham singing the old infantry favourite, 'We don't

know where we're going but we're on our way!' Once aboard
the LCI, they were told their destination was the Netherlands
East Indies. Neither Mac nor anyone else had any idea where
that was.

None of them had anticipated four days and nights in a
glorified iron bucket, eating cold sausages and beans out of
tins. They slept where they sat. Pails served as toilets. In turn
they had been roasted by the sun, then soaked by downpours.
The relentless thumping of the large marine diesel engine had
driven them to distraction, except when the bilge pumps failed
and a foul mixture of sea-water, vomit, urine and faeces rose
around them.

Regimental Sergeant-Major Cox was propped against a
gun-mount at the stern of the craft silently cursing the brass-
hat arsehole responsible for their predicament. He glanced
back at the flotilla. He could see two of the three craft that
followed them. Each was pitching like his own, with similar,
wan faces visible along their sides.

A few feet to Cox's right, on his raised seat within the gun
turret, Brigadier King caught the cold anger on Cox's face and
decided to delay the briefing. Not that he blamed his RSM in
the least. King was fighting his own stomach and was equally
furious at their situation. 'Nearly there, RSM,' he said
encouragingly. Cox barely looked at him.

King was glad the end of the journey was at hand. Ahead,
he could see the comforting profile of HMS *Cumberland* on
station just outside the harbour. They would not be completely
alone. Still, he wouldn't know until he landed if he was in
command of a fighting unit or a company of hospital cases.

He thought about his orders again. What the hell were they
heading into? In their present state they couldn't take on girl
guides, never mind Japs. No, not the Japs he reminded
himself, thinking of the last, incredible communication from
HQ. While the rush transfer to Java had been surprise enough,

the sealed instruction that had come just before they embarked was easily the strangest he'd received in five years of war. Once again he read it, even though he already knew the wording by heart.

> *Upon arrival Batavia proceed immediately set up/policing safe zone(s). Japanese NOT to be disarmed until further notice. If situation requires you are authorised to use Japanese to maintain law and order.*

When King had shown him the signal Cox had been left stunned. 'What can it mean, Sir?' he had asked incredulously.

'It means, RSM, that Java is going to be interesting!'

'But us and the Japs together! That's ridic—'

'Unexpected, eh?' King had cut in quickly. 'Keep this to yourself for the time being. It will come as a shock to the men.'

Cox had shaken his head. 'They won't like it, Sir!'

'I don't like it either.'

King's sense of foreboding had grown. Just what, he wondered, awaited them in Java? And what was HQ thinking in using the Japs! What if they refused to co-operate? There were over forty thousand of them on Java. He had three hundred and twenty exhausted men. It did not seem like nearly enough for an invasion! Even so, he thought, anything was better than sitting in this bucket of cess. He looked at the dark strip of land looming ahead, grateful that one torment, at least, would soon be over. His explanation to the battalion about their destination and the Indonesian declaration of independence had been greeted with silent but evident dismay. He had told them patrols from HMS *Cumberland* had reported the city quiet but tense. 'We're here,' he had said, 'simply to look after our POWs and to watch over the Japs.

That's all. However, there are armed groups of nationalists in and around Batavia, so we need to be on our guard.'

Mac felt himself crouching as the steep blue and black roofs of the warehouses and buildings came into view. His heart was pounding. Hundreds of people were lining the wharfs. He knew that beyond the breakwater, *Cumberland* had its guns trained on the city but it did not make him feel any safer. He had seen two of the cruiser's launches join the rear of the flotilla. One carried men in tan-coloured uniforms, the other photographers and newsreel cameramen. Mac paid them little mind.

All too soon he could see the mass of banners and homemade flags, and then the men and women lining the wharf. They stood in an eerie silence, their faces impassive. In Malaya the Seaforths had been cheered. Crowds had waved British, American and even Russian flags. Not here. Then he noticed the placards and slogans painted on the warehouse walls.

> *Atlantic Charter means freedom from Dutch Imperialism—People of Soviet Russia, China, India support Indonesians. Britain?—Hands off Indonesia. Respect our Constitution!—Workers of the world support our fight for freedom!— Monroe said America for the Americans. We say Indonesia for the Indonesians!—Hospitality for anyone who respects our constitution!*

'I've no objection to that,' Souness muttered as he read the slogans aloud. 'Have you, laddie?'

'No, it's fine by me,' Mac replied under his breath.

There was a slight scrape as the LCI slid against the quay. A gangway was pushed out quickly and the first Seaforths shuffled across quickly and gratefully onto the quayside.

Willingly, Mac followed, the feel of land underfoot quickly reviving him and the others. A shore patrol from *Cumberland* formed up alongside them. Still silent the crowd fell back as the British troops moved slowly forward.

Mac found himself facing a short, expressionless Javanese policeman in a peaked cap and uniformed shirt. He wore a flap-holster on his hip. Several more armed police were hemmed in between the crowd and the Seaforths.

A youth jabbed a finger at Mac's cheek yelling, 'Down with Imperialism!' The policeman pulled the youth's arm down.

Mac heard the shrill tooting of a car horn and glimpsed the capped head and shoulders of an officer in naval whites waving a small British flag. 'Make way! Make way there!'

Instantly the policeman in front of Mac began pushing and shouting to people to move aside. Eventually the sullen crowd opened up and the car, a small, battered, black Peugeot, eased through. There was another naval officer at the wheel as well as a partly hidden figure in the back. As soon as the car was inside the Seaforth cordon the policeman returned to his position. Mac realised that the man was simply trying to do his job.

His next surprise was when the rear door of the car was opened by an attractive brunette wearing a safari-style olive jacket and knee-length shorts. A camera hung from her neck. 'Hi, fellahs,' she said to no-one in particular. She looked around and caught Mac's eye. 'Since no-one else will say it, let me. Welcome to Java!'

Mac noticed the US Press flash on her shoulder. Bloody hell! he thought, a woman war correspondent!

'Thanks, Lieutenant Carter,' Meg said to the sailor. 'I couldn't have made it here without you.'

'My pleasure, Miss Graham,' Carter replied. 'I was wondering if you would like to join us on board *Cumberland* for dinner this evening?'

Mac rolled his eyes derisively. Meg saw him.

She gave Carter a gentle brush off. 'Today could be a very long day. Let's see how it turns out.' Before the lieutenant had time to reply she had darted along the quayside, notepad in hand.

Sudden, angry murmurs swept through the crowd and people began pointing. Mac glanced behind him. The launches were moving alongside the wharf. Their passengers were indistinct but fluttering above the second vessel was a Dutch flag. Murmurs became roars.

'*Merdeka!*'—'*Merdeka!*'—'Indonesia!'

Mac turned back to face the crowd. The policeman had moved along and he was facing two pretty young girls and an older man. Reluctantly, Mac pushed them back with his rifle. Behind him he heard the car being turned around and backed up to the wharf. He took another quick look and saw the American woman taking pictures.

Meg could feel the animosity. She didn't think it was a good idea to bring flag-flying Dutch ashore and had said as much to Carter over drinks in her hotel bar the night before.

'Oh, the Javanese are peaceful enough,' Carter had replied lightly.

'With Americans and British,' Meg had countered sceptically. 'But look how they change if you mention the Dutch!'

Carter had shrugged. 'The Dutch officials say they are just a few, noisy collaborators.'

Meg had not been convinced. 'Well they would say that. From what I've seen, it's more than a few. Look around, everyone's wearing red and white!'

'But the Dutch are our allies—'

'Allies against the Japanese. Against the Indonesians as well?'

Carter had suddenly looked uncomfortable. 'Surely, we should help them after all we've been through together?'

'Help them do what exactly?' Meg had pushed.

'Well, get back their property for one thing. There's no law here.'

'Dutch law or Indonesian law?'

Carter had changed the subject and Meg had let the argument drop, hoping that Carter was right. Now, as she looked at the tense situation developing in front of her, all of her doubts returned.

A large Dutch standard was unfurled on the second launch. Oh, boy, she thought, that'll do it! She saw the first launch was full of journalists, press photographers and newsreel cameramen. Meg groaned as they scrambled up the wharf and took positions in front of her.

'Hey, guys,' she called out, 'you're blocking my shot!'

Some turned and looked in dismay at her Press Corps insignia. One shouted angrily in Dutch to a uniformed officer holding a clipboard. 'Major, you promised us an exclusive! What's going on?'

The officer strode up to Meg scowling. 'I'm Major Osten, NICA Information Office,' he said in heavy, Dutch-accented English. 'Reporting is restricted to NICA-accredited journalists. How did you get here?'

Meg had no idea what 'NICA' meant but she was a veteran at the accreditation game. She stood easily, one hand on her hip, the other holding up her papers. 'What's your problem, Major?' Meg asked, feeling perplexed but looking confident. 'I've accreditation with SEAC. This is a SEAC area and, if you didn't know already, reporting restrictions ended weeks ago.'

His bluff called, Osten eyed her disdainfully, then swore under his breath as a bearded, solidly built man in a neat, tan-coloured uniform came up the wharf steps to a barrage of hostile shouts.

'Van Zanten go home!'—'Indonesia Raya!'

Osten rushed back to direct a uniformed newsreel cameraman.

'Asshole,' she said to herself.

'Merdeka!—Merdeka!'

As the chanting throng surged forward, the thin line of soldiers were forced to give ground. An egg struck on Van Zanten's chest and the crowd cheered. More rotten fruit and vegetables followed. British sailors hustled Van Zanten into the back of the car which was also pelted. Then the target switched to the hated Dutch flag and the officials beside it. They had nowhere to hide. In seconds both flag and officials were splattered. Steadily the hail of missiles forced them back to the wharf steps then back into the launches.

In the chaos Meg glanced at the Dutch journalists. Most seemed surprised, even stunned by the attack on their representatives and flag. Only a few were photographing with any conviction. Major Osten's cameraman was not one of them. Van Zanten's car, horn sounding repeatedly, was trying to push its way through the surging crowd. Meg saw there was no chance of success. After nosing forward a few feet it was almost surrounded by demonstrators. Fists and banners were pounding on the roof of the car, matching the steady *'Mer-de-ka'* chant.

Meg heard glass break and guessed the headlights had been smashed. Finally the driver gave up and began to reverse. British soldiers were straining to hold back the demonstrators.

Once the car was back inside the cordon of troops the crowd quietened. Suddenly its windscreen shattered. Meg glanced up behind her. Groups of youths wearing red-and-white bandannas, lined the rooftops. More half bricks and stones rained down dangerously, drumming on the car's sides, roof and bonnet.

After a few seconds the back door opened and Van Zanten dashed for the safety of the wharf steps. Miraculously the stoning stopped. Jeers followed the fleeing Dutchman.

Just as Meg was wondering what would happen next the launch engines burst into life. Van Zanten was leaving. On the wharf the Dutch journalists looked around uneasily. Then they, too, scurried back to their boat. Major Osten was among them. As he ran past Meg he glanced at her and her camera loathingly. Spontaneously the crowd began to sing the nationalist anthem.

Mac had spent the entire episode standing between Souness and Nesbit trying to keep the crowd away from Van Zanten. His arms ached and he was drenched in sweat.

'Oh, the thieving bastards!' Souness was staring at his webbing belt in disbelief. The ammunition pouches had been cut open.

Mac saw his own pouches were also empty and then that his bayonet had also been taken. All along the line, Seaforths began to swear as they realised they, too, had been expertly robbed.

Two hours after Van Zanten's retreat, the Seaforths, guided by some of the HMS *Cumberland* shore party were marching with full kit along the Harbour Road into the city. On both sides the terrain was open, with acres of commercial fish ponds extending to the shore on their right and open scrub to their left. In contrast to the tense soldiers, the sailors were relaxed and seemingly unconcerned about their exposed position. Mac noticed that the few Javanese they met watched them impassively but with no sign of hostility.

Rail tracks ran parallel with the road. Trains passed fairly frequently, blowing whistles to warn the Seaforths to stand clear. Passengers glanced up from newssheets to eye them curiously, as though they were little more than a casual distraction.

A plaintive cry from the middle of the Seaforth column caught the mood. 'Why didn't we take the bloody train?'

The quick reply was predictable. 'Because we're bloody infantry!' Laughter ran through the men, breaking the drudge of the march. At the front, Brigadier King grinned.

'I don't get it, Mac,' said Nesbit uneasily. 'A couple of hours ago they would have brained us with rocks. Now they're just ignoring us.'

One of the marines in the shore party tried to explain. 'That's the funny thing about this shower. One minute they're quiet and happy-go-lucky like, the next they're in a boiling rage. They've nothing against us but the sight of the Dutch drives them bonkers. Blimey, they've battered some of them Dutchies black and blue this last two weeks, killed a few, too, I'll tell you!'

Mac shook his head. 'Why the hell are we here, Nessy?'

'Because we're here, laddie,' Nesbit shrugged. 'Remember when I said the army wouldn't let us off the hook easy? Well, this is—' Nesbit stopped and stared, his face suddenly pale. He let out a shout. 'Japs!'

Mac saw a half-track and two troop lorries heading towards them at speed. Rising-sun emblems were visible. Around him his fellow Seaforths were reaching for their rifles.

King turned to face them, raising his hand to stop the column. 'Easy now, men. The Japanese are co-operating with us.'

RSM Cox bellowed at them. 'Shoulder arms!'

There were some anxious glances and muttering among the Seaforths but the command was obeyed promptly.

Beside Mac the sailor was amused. 'This takes some getting used to, mate,' he said knowingly. 'For the last two weeks, their brass have been driving around town proud as fucking peacocks. You'd think they'd won the bloody war!'

Mac and Nesbit shared a disbelieving look then watched as the Japanese drew up a few yards ahead of them. A Japanese officer, a burly but light-footed man, stepped jumped down from the half-track and walked casually to King and the two captains with him. He looked curiously at the lines of Seaforths.

'That's Major-General Honda,' the marine whispered. 'Only two hours late! Devious bastard if ever there was one. Watch this, though. Jap officers are supposed to salute ours first, whatever their rank. They don't like it one bit!'

After a brief but clear moment of hesitation on Honda's part he saluted. King, apparently unconcerned, returned the salute immediately as did his junior officers. For a short while the two men talked then Honda returned to the half-track. In the lorries, Japanese soldiers sat silent and impassive, rifles braced between their knees, ignoring their former enemy. But as they drove past, Mac noted the darting, suspicious looks from some and the cold animosity from others.

'Now I've seen everything,' declared Nesbit miserably. 'We've just waved cheeri-bloody-o to a bunch of armed Japs who are riding when we're walking!'

'Something isn't right here,' muttered Mac.

The sailor chuckled. 'Welcome to batty Batavia, mates!'

Tjandi, Camp III, Semarang

Ota was crouched behind sandbags by the open camp gate. He was peering anxiously down the street through field glasses, and then back up to the man dangling from the ladder.

The young private had been hit in the shoulder and his leg had caught in the rungs. Now he was groaning as he tried to make himself sway.

'Sano, keep moving!' Ota yelled. He squinted up at the shadows in the bay bedroom window of the large, ransacked house diagonally across the street. Now not even doors, windows or light fittings remained. All the house had left was its commanding view of the approach road to the camp. Ota had put his best marksman, Harada, in there before dawn. He swore under his breath. *'Kuso!'*—Shit! 'Come on, Harada get him!'

Another shot took a chunk out of the bamboo rung a few inches from Sano's head. Sano began a frantic wriggling and let out a shriek. 'Haraadaaa!'

Seconds later Ota heard Harada fire. Silence ensued. Ota could see nothing. Sano, utterly exhausted, was barely moving.

Two hundred yards down the street hunched figures broke from the cover of a garden fence to cross the road. Slung, limp, between two men was a wounded third. Ota grinned and slapped his thigh in satisfaction. He spun round. 'Quick, get Sano down!'

Moments later the lanky, lean-faced Harada appeared at the camp gate. Across his arms he was cradling a Model 98 Arisaka 7.7 mm rifle fitted with a telescopic sight as if it were a baby.

'Well done!' Ota said in congratulation.

Harada saluted. 'I could have got all three, Lieutenant….'

'I know,' said Ota, 'but our orders are clear. Minimum use of force and in self-defence only. Now go and get something to eat. Afterwards try a stint in the school tower. You should be able to keep an eye on things from up there.'

Harada saluted and went over to Sano, who was being tended by a medic. Sano glared at him. *'Osoi ja'nai!'*—You took your damn time!

'*Gomen!*'—Sorry! Harada smiled sheepishly. 'I was taking a leak.'

The rest of the platoon roared with laughter.

At sundown Ota was called back to the gate. Sentries had heard more chanting. Corporal Suzuki handed his field glasses to Ota. 'It looks like mainly women and children, Sir.'

Ota frowned. 'Yes. Let's hope they just want food and that there's no surprises.'

Familiar chants of '*Merdeka!*' and 'Sukarno' grew louder until the ragged procession waving anti-Dutch and anti-Japanese banners halted a few yards from the gate. Two women set a Japanese flag alight.

Ota gave a command. 'Now!'

As the gate swung open six of his men walked out. They were unarmed and carrying sacks of rice. The chants petered out as the soldiers dropped the sacks then stepped clear. For a moment the women hesitated, then they rushed forward, flinging aside their banners and flags. In seconds the sacks were cut open and the delighted women squatted, busily scooping handfuls of rice into their sarongs and headscarves. Ota allowed himself to relax.

Suddenly a woman at the front of the crowd darted forward. 'Help me, Please! *Onegai!*'

A sentry moved out, rifle across his body, to bar her way. Still shouting she flung off her headscarf. Ota saw she was white. 'Help! *Au secours!*'

'Let her in!' Ota commanded.

The sentry stepped smartly aside and the woman sprinted through the gate. She dropped to her knees panting. '*Merde!* I made it! Thank God!'

Ota was coming down from the parapet when he saw Kate shouting to the woman.

'Juliette!' Kate reached her and they embraced. 'I've been so worried about you!'

Juliette burst into tears.

Ota led the distraught Juliette to the guardhouse. She was hungry and clearly exhausted. Corporal Suzuki waited patiently by the door. Ota asked Kate to get her some water.

'Oh, we were so scared!' Juliette sniffed. 'Every night they would stand in front of the Sakura shouting and calling us names. No-one would dare come in. Not even the cooks.'

Startled, Ota realised where he had seen the woman before. While she sipped her drink he interpreted for Suzuki. 'Please, continue, Miss,' he said gravely.

Juliette composed herself. 'The night before last they threw rocks through the windows. Two of the girls were hurt. Kiriko told us she was closing and going with the Japanese soldiers. She said we could all go with her. Everyone was so relieved. There were five internees still there, me and four Dutch. We decided we would go back to our camps. I wanted to leave immediately but the others decided to wait for the morning.' Her shoulders heaved and fresh tears ran down her cheeks. Kate crouched and put an arm around her.

Juliette stared at the floor. 'I found these clothes, then I climbed down a drain pipe and put a basket on my head, like a native. It was dark but suddenly there was a lot of shouting men with burning torches. I wanted to run but I made myself walk. They smashed open the side door. Inside the girls were screaming but I kept walking. When I reached the corner of the alley, I saw Kiriko and the others dragged outside. They were beating them with sticks....'

'You're safe now,' Kate said quietly, gently patting Juliette's shoulder gently. Kate caught his eye.

Ota was lifted by the warmth of her look. 'Please, Miss, what then?'

Juliette swallowed and wiped her eyes with the back of her hand. 'I went down to the next alley then back on to the main road. Javanese soldiers and gangs were everywhere. I saw them take some Japanese from the Hotel Pavillon.'

Ota's expression darkened. 'Do you know where they took them?'

Juliette nodded. 'I heard them say Bulu.'

Ota explained to Suzuki. 'I must inform the Major. Get the radio operator to raise the barracks now!'

Suzuki saluted and left at a run.

Ota turned back to Juliette. 'You have been very brave. Thank you.' He saw Jenny Hagen and Lucy Santen approaching the hut. He looked briefly at Kate and strode out.

Juliette eyed Kate quizzically. 'Wasn't he the one at the Sak—'

'Rest now, Juliette!' Kate interrupted loudly, her face reddening. 'You're very tired!'

Jenny and Lucy rushed in. 'Juliette! It is you!' Lucy hugged her. 'Are you hurt?'

'Just tired—and hungry!' Juliette replied weakly.

All four jumped as more shots were fired at the camp gate.

'Lieutenant!' The shout was from Harada in one of the guard towers. 'Armoured car and infantry approaching from the south!'

Soon Ota could hear the rattle of heavy machine guns beyond the fence. 'That's the Major,' he called to Suzuki.

Harada called down again. 'They're running from the houses, Lieutenant. Many targets!'

Ota stepped up on the ladder and saw *pemuda* fleeing the withering fire from the armoured car.

'Let them go!'

Two minutes later Kudo arrived in a half-track. Nagumo and half his platoon followed him in on the run. Ota saluted

Kudo then turned in surprise at the sound of sporadic applause as small groups of women emerged from the huts. Kudo stared as the clapping spread. Jenny Hagen and several of the others bowed.

Kudo stood up. Unbidden, the women gathered round nervously. Many were still reluctant to risk a direct look at a Japanese soldier.

'Good afternoon,' Kudo said in a slightly laboured English. 'I am Major Kudo. I must try to regain control of the town. Be prepared to leave at short notice. Thank you.' He jumped down and led his officers to the guardhouse.

Bulu Gaol

Sunlight reflecting off the whitewashed walls of the gaol made Ota squint even through the anti-glare filters on his field glasses. For fifteen minutes they had been watching the narrow barred windows and guard turrets that dominated the small square. They were perfect for snipers.

Ota looked at his watch. Nagumo would now be in position at the rear, cutting off any escape via the canal, while Kudo was waiting one street back with the rest of the battalion and a second *kenpei* platoon. It was almost time. A few yards away Captain Wada, the *kenpei* in charge of the assault, blew his whistle.

'Let's go!' Ota yelled. He rushed forward with eight of his men along the base of the exposed wall towards the main gate. Across the square a *kenpei* platoon also charged. There was no firing. Seconds later both squads were beside the heavy wooden gates of the gaol, catching their breath.

One gate was slightly ajar. Pistol raised, Ota carefully pushed it wider. A bolt scraped on the worn stone paving but there was no response, only an eerie silence. Inside, he could see the wall of an inner courtyard and the start of a staircase leading to the parapet. He signalled to Yamanaka, the *kenpei* lieutenant, who darted through the gap. Six of his men followed him.

Ota checked that Suzuki was covering him, then sprinted for the stairwell. The prison seemed deserted. Quickly he sent two men up to the parapet and moved cautiously towards a single door with a small barred window. Yamanaka was already leading his men along the courtyard wall towards the rear gate. Pistol raised, Ota crept up to the door and peered through. He saw several bodies. Gently he tried the door. For a few inches it moved easily then stopped. A blood-stained hand was in the gap at his feet.

Cautiously, Ota squatted and felt for a pulse. He lifted the pale, cold flesh only to find the arm had been severed below the elbow. With a grimace he let go.

Two of his men heaved against the door. It swung open to reveal carnage. Corpses lay piled two, sometimes three deep in a twisted, blood-soaked mass at one side of the courtyard. On the other, hundreds of spent cartridge cases were strewn over the stone flags. A sickly-sweet smell filled the air. Ota moved forward slowly, stepping over the bodies. Clouds of flies rose up off sightless, bulging eyes and bloated, gaping mouths.

A short exchange of shots came from the other side of the prison. Ota and his men sought cover,. Two minutes later there was shout of *'Aka Fuji!'* from a doorway across the courtyard. Ota answered and waited.

Nagumo appeared, pulling a bandanna from over his mouth while taking in the scene in front of him. 'There are twenty-two Dutchmen safe upstairs. The Indos were going to burn them alive. Yesterday they concentrated on us,' he added quietly. There must be at least a hundred more in the cells,' 'These must have been killed last, in a rush. Elsewhere they used spears and swords.'

Ota frowned. 'The shooting?'

Nagumo pointed to the second storey. 'Yamanaka's lot got two just in time to save the Dutch. Both dead.'

Several *kenpei* appeared, leading out the Dutch captives who looked haggard and dirty but relieved. They stared at the corpses as they filed by.

Ota and Suzuki went into the cell-block.

'Take a deep breath,' Nagumo called after them. 'It's a slaughter house....'

The cells were set out in a square on either side of a narrow corridor. Once the stone floor had been grey. Now it was stained with a thick film of dark dried blood.

Ota looked into the first cell then shied away. Behind him Suzuki grimaced. 'Uggh! The bastards!' He pulled out a bandanna and held it over his mouth. Ota did the same. It did not help.

The butchery had been systematic. In each cell it was the same: eight or nine limbless bodies. Bloody hand-prints and *'Merdeka!'* slogans splattered the walls. The two men walked in silence. After the fifth cell, Ota stopped counting the corpses.

On the floor above they found the same gruesome tableau except for two empty cells that had held the Dutchmen. Nearby two *pemuda* lay dead beside a jerry can. Eventually their circuit took them to the dining hall. It was thick with flies. Nagumo was there, squatting beside a figure in a yellow kimono. Ota picked his way through to join him.

'Ahh, Kiriko-chan, I'm so sorry,' Nagumo sighed as he laid a blood-stained shirt over her face. 'I came too late....' He looked up at Ota then indicated another nearby corpse. She lay on her side in a ripped under-kimono, her arms were tied behind her back. One had been dislocated in the struggle.

Grim-faced, Ota drew his sword and bent down to cut Yuki's bonds. He laid her on her back, crossing her arms over her chest. Her fingernails were broken and bloodied and he knew she had put up a fight. He reached for a tunic to cover her and saw the name tag read 'Taniguchi Yuji.' Ota looked around, knowing that Taniguchi's body, disfigured and unidentifiable, was near.

'Strangled,' Nagumo said calmly. 'They didn't cut our women.'

Ota looked up, then followed Nagumo's gaze. In a corner four naked white women lay side-by-side on mattresses from the cells. Their swollen genitals were caked in dried blood. He went closer and saw their ankles had been tied with the cord between left long enough to slip under the mattress, holding their legs apart. They had been repeatedly raped. At the end their breasts had been sliced off and their throats cut. He suppressed a shudder.

Kudo and Captain Wada entered the hall. Ota could feel their rage.

'I must know some of these people,' Wada said solemnly. 'Outside I recognised only Sato-san from Mitsubishi. In the garden we found bodies staked over red ants nests. They were eaten alive!'

Kudo noticed the yellow kimono. He looked questioningly at Nagumo. 'Kiriko?'

Nagumo nodded.

Kudo turned to a *kenpei* private holding a notepad. 'How many?'

'One hundred and eighty-seven, Major.'

Wada bowed to Kudo. 'I will inform HQ.' He strode out.

Kudo stood in a silent fury. A soldier came running. 'Sir, message from Captain Seguchi. He is exchanging fire with a large group of Javanese. They were seen leaving the prison just before we arrived. They outnumber him heavily but appear to be withdrawing. He's requesting instructions.'

Kudo rubbed his chin. 'Tell him he is to pursue and continue to engage. Reinforcements will be coming via the Canal Road. I am declaring martial law. His orders are shoot to kill!'

Djakarta

'*Selamat malam*, Tommy!'

Mac raised a hand casually in answer to the *becak* driver's cheerful 'Good evening' then waved him through the checkpoint and onto the old, narrow drawbridge. The tyres hummed on the worn, ribbed planks then went silent as they hit the flat, pounded earth of the Chinese quarter of the city.

'Want a smoke, Mac?' Nesbit asked him idly.

'No ta, mate,' Mac replied, stifling a yawn.

Nesbit struck a match on one of the thick iron bridge pillars, lit his cigarette and inhaled deeply.

The night was warm and almost still. Every few minutes the sound of gunfire crackled like fireworks in various parts of the city and neighbouring *kampongs*. A slight breeze was blowing along the Kali Besar river but it was not enough to deter the mosquitoes who made the most of the two soldiers. With the breeze came the smell of stale fish from the nearby market. Mac was not sure if it was preferable to the pungent odour coming from the canal. He was quite glad it was dark. The previous watch had reported at least five corpses floating past.

Mac and Nesbit had been on duty for three hours. That afternoon, for the second day running, their platoon had patrolled the maze of alleys and network of soupy canals that made the Chinese quarter look like a teeming, noisy oriental Venice. Friendly greetings and gifts of bite-sized snacks had

soon overcome the language barrier and put the Seaforths at
ease. Relief on the faces of the Chinese had been clear.

'At least they seem pleased to see us, Sir. Just like in
Malaya,' Mac had commented to the young captain leading
the patrol.

His officer had agreed. 'Yes, the Chinese have been getting
it from both sides. First from Japs because of the war in
China. Now the Javans think they're pro-Dutch or black-
market profiteers. Take your pick. Hundreds have been
murdered in the last few weeks.'

Around the old drawbridge it had been quiet with few
people about. Mac was staring at the graceful metal arch
overhead and thinking again about the friendly Malay girls in
Alor Gajah.

Nesbit let out a loud, ripping fart. 'We won't know much
about it if that bastard thing falls on us,' he said idly.

Mac glanced up at the massive, solid-teak counterweight
that sat fifteen feet above their heads. 'Aye, that's been up a
good few years.'

Nesbit was not listening to him. 'I hate this place,' he
muttered. 'We shouldn't even be here.'

'Orders are orders, Nessy,' Mac said shrugging his
shoulders.

His friend looked at him sceptically. 'Oh, for God's sake,
Mac. Wake up! The fucking war's over! This is politics.'

'There are still thousands of Japs here, Stan.'

'Och, the Nip bastards are all packed and itching to go,'
Nesbit said dismissively. 'They'll be sodding well home before
we are! No, Mac lad, no. Think about it. The shooting we hear
every night? That's the bloody Dutchies settling scores with
the Javans or the Javans getting revenge on the Dutchies.
You've seen those arrogant clogheads. They think they can
waltz back in and be lord of the bloody manor again. What
gets me is that for some reason we're helping them!' In disgust

he threw his cigarette into the dark water below. 'I don't know about you but I voted Labour for a ticket home. If the war was all about freedom, what are we doing here? We let them call us up to fight Gerries and Japs, not to help the Dutch keep their empire.' He looked hard at Mac. 'Some Mahrattas arrived today. I bet they and the other Indians are thinking just the same.'

Mac frowned. 'I know what you mean but don't let the brass hear you talk like that or you'll be for it.'

Nesbit was not giving up. 'I'm not the only one saying this. Just wait and see!'

Headlights flashed as a car swept round the bend. Mac and Nesbit were not taking any chances. Two of their comrades had already been injured by stones thrown from passing cars. They readied their rifles and blocked the road.

Mac was caught in the powerful beams from the headlights and had to shield his eyes with one hand. The car stopped abruptly, ten yards from them.

Nesbit was off to one side watching carefully. 'Jap staff car,' he shouted.

Mac went closer, peering at the large saloon. He could see nothing behind the dark windscreen. The only sound was the smooth hum from the powerful engine as it idled. As he moved out of the lights he saw the Japanese pennant over the bonnet. He told himself to relax. His orders were to be civil to the Japanese at all times. How that grated....

Mac went to the driver's window. When nothing happened he knocked. After another pause it lowered. A young Japanese soldier at the wheel shot him a vexed glance.

'*Nan da, aoi-me?*'—What is it, blue eyes? The driver said sharply.

'Just following my orders,' Mac said sternly, understanding the tone if not the words. His animosity surged.

Behind the driver the glass privacy panel was open but the occupant or occupants in the back were shielded by a lace curtain.

'I need to see all passengers,' Mac demanded.

The driver sneered. '*Nani?*'

A voice barked from behind the curtain. '*Shizuka ni shite!*'

Instantly the driver bowed his head to his chest. The curtain flicked aside and Mac found himself looking into a plush, wood-trimmed interior lit by a soft light in the roof. Two middle-aged Japanese officers, each with rows of campaign ribbons across their chests, reclined on the leather bench seat. They were regarding him with casual curiosity.

In the corner of his eye he saw Nesbit coming to attention. Almost too late, Mac remembered his military etiquette. His salute was crisp.

The older of the two Japanese looked almost amused at his discomfort. 'I am General Yamagami. Is there a problem, private?'

Mac's swallowed uneasily. 'There is a curfew, Sir. Only military vehicles are allowed on the roads after eight o'clock.'

Yamagami frowned. 'This is my staff car. It is a military vehicle.'

'Yes, Sir, sorry, Sir. I did not see the pennant.'

More headlights flashed followed by the rattle of a large diesel engine. An open-topped, six-wheeled lorry pulled up a few yards behind the staff car. Mac could see the rows of helmeted Japanese in the back.

Yamagami's expression did not change 'And so is that.' A searchlight mounted on the lorry flooded the scene, blinding Mac and Nesbit.

'*Yanagami-taiji, daijobu deshooka?*'—General Yamagami, is everything all right?

Yamagami quickly wound down his window and raised his hand, signalling his men to stay put.

'May we proceed?' Yamagami asked quietly.

'Yes, General. Sorry to delay you, Sir,' Mac replied crisply.

Both Mac and Nesbit saluted again.

Yamagami returned it promptly. 'Carry on,' he said politely.

The saloon's engine revved as it sped away. Seconds later the searchlight cut and the lorry set off in a lumbering pursuit. As it went past, Mac again noticed the tense stares from the Japanese soldiers.

When the lorry had crossed the drawbridge the two Scotsmen exchanged disbelieving looks.

'Did you hear that smooth bastard sitting there sword and all? "Carry on" he said, just like one of ours!'

Mac stared after the lorry. 'Nessy. We're in a sodding madhouse!'

Chapter Sixteen

Ota's eyes were bloodshot as he peered from the top of a church tower overlooking the imposing blocks of Victorian-style municipal buildings at the heart of Semarang. The fight for the town was proving slow and bloody. In three days the longest spell of sleep he had managed had been four hours.

The Indonesian militia had withdrawn in good order, fighting street by street, house by house as their Japanese instructors had taught them. And they had taught them far too well, thought Ota. So far, Kudo Butai and the Semarang *kenpeitai* had lost nearly forty men dead with dozens wounded.

The *pemuda* had made wild, suicidal charges armed with broken bottles, machetes, knives and clubs. Ota had no idea how many had been killed. Many hundreds lay dead in the streets. Now, though, the last pockets of resistance were crumbling. It was almost over—at least, he corrected himself—it would be if the reports of militia reinforcements coming from the north proved false. He doubted the information. Where could they have come from?

He panned his field glasses to the east, trying to spot the roof of the Army and Navy Club, wondering if it had been damaged. A hot bath would be so good....

Beside him Harada whispered. 'Lieutenant, militia coming up the road to the bridge. At least a company!'

Ota cursed silently and re-focused on the T-junction. Two green lines—worryingly long lines—of troops were visible on either side of the narrow road, making for the bridge over the Kali Semarang, the small river that wound through the town.

Harada moved to slide his rifle out through the stone grill work. Ota stopped him with a raise of his hand. 'Wait, the machine guns will get more of them. Then help keep them pinned down.'

'For a while at least….' Harada said quietly.

Ota counted down as the troops reached the junction. 'Three, two—' The Nambus opened up.

Five Gurkhas were hit in the first hail of bullets. Rai was saved by the corner of the office building and the inexperience of the gunner, who aimed slightly too high. Instinctively he dived through the nearest window. A split-second later John Miller landed half on top of him.

Bullets were churning up the street, drilling into the brickwork and window frames. Chunks of masonry and wood showered down on them.

Miller rested against the side of a desk panting, listening helplessly to the wounded men outside. 'Christ, that was close!' he said breathlessly. Their move up from Semarang harbour had met no opposition. Occasional gunfire from the town centre had put them on their guard but skilfully executed ambush had not been expected.

Rai crawled among the desks to the end window. He took off his slouch hat and raised it gingerly on the end of his tommy gun. Glass shattered and the hat flew ten feet across the room to land on a desk. He retrieved the hat and showed Miller the neat, round hole punched through the crown. He tried the other side of the window. There was no shot.

Carefully he rose to peer across the canal. He looked knowingly at Miller. 'They're well-trained, Major-*sahib*. Maybe some Japs have decided not to surrender,' he added quietly.

Miller sighed. 'Oh, God, that's all we need! I better inform the CO....'

Black Sun, Red Moon: A Novel of Java
reaches its dramatic close in

MERDEKA RISING

The origins of
Black Sun, Red Moon: A Novel of Java and
Merdeka Rising.

Some years ago I was sent a copy of an article published in the London *Daily Telegraph* newspaper entitled 'Old soldier returns surrender sword'. I was intrigued by a reference to 'an extraordinary incident after the surrender, when Japanese troops were re-armed by the British to help them liberate the Java internment camps'. That single sentence fired my curiosity and led me to research and, eventually, to write my story. The newspaper article is reproduced in full on my website (see below). *Black Sun, Red Moon* and *Merdeka Rising* are fiction. The violence, death and valour on Java in 1945-46 is fact.

RM

For more background information, research-related and contemporary photographs, maps and other items please visit:

http://www.rorymarron.com

51233095R00188

Made in the USA
San Bernardino, CA
16 July 2017